# AMERICA'S FUTURE

# AMERICA'S FUTURE

Washington Writers' Publishing House Anthology
Poetry & Prose in Response to Tomorrow

Caroline Bock and Jona Colson, Editors

Washington Writers' Publishing House
Washington, DC

COVER ART by Dana Ellyn
COVER DESIGN by Andrew S. Klein
ORIGINAL INTERIOR ART by Deborah Tomlin
BOOK DESIGN and TYPESETTING by Barbara Shaw
PROOFREADING by Melanie S. Hatter

Library of Congress Control Number: 2025942046
ISBN 978-1-941551-52-3

Printed in the United States of America
WASHINGTON WRITERS' PUBLISHING HOUSE
2814 5th Street, NE, #1301
Washington, D.C. 20017
More information: www.washingtonwriters.org

# CONTENTS

## PART II

## PART III

# FOREWORD

## The Possibilities We Dare To Imagine

*What does the future hold?*

As co-editors and presidents of the Washington Writers' Publishing House, a cooperative literary institution founded over fifty years ago on the idea of paying it forward, we asked ourselves, *what does the future hold?* At this pivotal moment, ***America's Future: poetry & prose in response to tomorrow*** was born.

This anthology is a collective meditation on tomorrow—on the struggles we inherit, the uncertainties of the present, and the possibilities we dare to imagine. Through poetry and prose, *America's Future* explores the tumultuous landscape of our nation—with bold, thought-provoking writing from diverse voices. In these pages, the future unfolds—uncertain, urgent, and waiting to be read and discussed.

Some pieces reflect on the weight of history while others bear witness to a nation's wounds and its healing. Many of the pieces turn their gaze forward and imagine new paths carved from hope and reinvention. From intimate personal reckonings to sweeping societal critiques, these works illuminate where we are and ask: *where are we going?*

We realize now *America's Future* is not just an anthology—it is a conversation with the unknown and with our community. It challenges us to confront the past, question the present, and shape the future with our art, with our words.

*—Caroline Bock* and *Jona Colson*

# AMERICA'S FUTURE
## PART I

# REMARKS AS DELIVERED AT THE HANDS OFF! RALLY ON THE NATIONAL MALL

## U.S. REPRESENTATIVE JAMIE RASKIN

April 5, 2025

Hello Indivisible.

Hello America . . . Anybody from Maryland, the Free State? The birthplace of Frederick Douglass, proud home of people who work at USAID, the FDA, NOAA, the National Weather Service, and the National Institutes of Health—the NIH, the crown jewel of American bioscience, where despite all the purges and firings, they're still working every day to cure cystic fibrosis, multiple sclerosis, breast cancer, and that most deadly disease of our time, malignant narcissistic personality disorder. Let scientists do their jobs and they may even find a cure for the rare and baffling worm-in-brain disease. The great thing about science is that it's true whether or not the Secretary of Health and Human Services believes in it.

Let's all say with Maryland: **Hands off science**.

Anyone from Virginia? The birthplace of James Madison, who wrote us the First Amendment. It separated church and state for the first time in history. It gave us all the right to speak freely, to publish freely, to worship freely, to assemble freely, and to petition government for a redress of grievances. As Dr. King said, we've got the right to protest for what is right, without being arrested, deported or fired. We've got the right to read the books we want, including *1984* and *The Handmaid's Tale*, even if they now belong in the nonfiction section. We've even got the right to call the president an idiot for crashing our economy, destroying $6 trillion of wealth in 48 hours and turning my 401(K) into a 201(K). And the press has the right to call the Gulf of Mexico the Gulf of Mexico. Madison's Bill of Rights also gives us the two most beautiful words in the English language: "Due Process." Let's stand with Madison, the people of Virginia and Thomas Jefferson and say: **Hands off the Bill of Rights**.

Hello to the 713,000 taxpaying patriotic citizens of Washington, DC. Your officers like Michael Fanone joined the Capitol Police on January 6, 2021, to defend Congress against the worst insurrectionary mob violence of American history ever brought down on the Capitol, which wounded, hospitalized, and injured more than 140 of our police officers. They turned the flag of America into a weapon of war against our police. And now Donald Trump says he wants to set up a fund to compensate them. Mr. Trump, if there's going to be a fund to compensate people for January 6, we're going to compensate the police officers and their families. We're going to back the men and women in blue, not the planners of the coup.

Meantime, the people of DC have a valid, bona fide political grievance, not an imaginary one. They did not try to storm the Capitol, or overturn an election, or try to hang the Vice President. They petitioned for statehood like thirty-seven states before them. They did it the right way. So we say to Donald Trump and Elon Musk, Hands off Greenland—that's an independent country. Hands off Canada—that's an independent country. Hands off Panama—that's an independent country. Statehood for Washington, DC. And let's say with the people of Washington: **Free DC**.

I want to say a special hello to people across America, but especially to the people of Wisconsin. They showed America that organized people who want nothing but freedom can defeat organized billionaires who want nothing but power. Here in America, Mr. Musk, justice isn't for sale, and we don't raffle off State Supreme Court judgeships with million-dollar prizes. Stop trying to buy our votes, stop ripping off our government, and stop stealing our data.

My friends, we're in the fight of our lives. But I want to tell you this: We are winning now. We are winning every day.

We're winning in court where thirty-nine judges, appointed by five Republican and Democratic presidents, have issued fifty-six preliminary injunctions and TROs against this lawlessness. That's why our MAGA colleagues now want to impeach the judges, like Judge Boasberg, the Chief Judge of the DC District Court. Yesterday he ordered the return of Kilmar Garcia, a legal resident of the US married to a US citizen who was sent to a dictator's prison in El Salvador. The administration was forced to admit in court that his deportation without any hearing or Due Process was an "administrative error." But get this—Trump said *c'est la vie*, Mr. Garcia would have to stay in that torture facility because the US no longer had custody over him. But Judge Boasberg told him that if you <u>have</u> the means to unlawfully deport someone, you <u>find</u> the means to bring them back. So now they call Judge Boasberg a "radical left rogue" judge. The problem is that he was first appointed to the bench by President George W. Bush, he was Justice Kavanaugh's roommate at Yale; he's known as a pillar of the conservative legal establishment. They say, though, the number of courts striking down Trump's policies is completely "unprecedented." Well, you know what—that's only because the number of Trump's illegal and unconstitutional actions is completely unprecedented. These judges are doing their jobs. They're doing their jobs.

Let's tell MAGA what democratic movements all over the world tell authoritarian despots all over the world: **Hands off the Courts**.

But, you know, Trump's even tried to ban law firms and lawyers who represent Democrats from federal buildings and federal employment and to revoke their security clearances; he's shaking law firms down for hundreds of millions of dollars in pro bono work for his pro malum causes. Some firms have buckled under these outrageous threats, but hundreds of law firms led by Wilmer Hale and Jenner and Block and thousands of lawyers led by Rachel Cohen are standing up strong for the rule of law. And the courts have uniformly rejected these unconstitutional attacks on free speech, the right to counsel and Due Process.

We are winning in the states, in the counties, in the cities, and the towns. We are winning in the churches, and not just with the great Reverend [William J.] Barber. We're winning across the country. No one wants an economy-crashing dictator who knows the price of everything and the value of nothing. We're winning in the universities which know the difference between transgender mice and transgenic mice. And they know the difference between academic freedom and political tyranny. We are winning with Veterans across America, who know which side we were fighting on in World War II, and when they see Nazis marching down the boulevard they do not see very fine people on both sides of the street. We're winning the people wearing the uniform in the Armed Services who know that Donald Trump is turning our best friends in the world, like Germany and the UK and France and Canada and Mexico, into enemies. And he's turning the enemies of American democracy like Vladimir Putin and Viktor Orban and Xi [Jinping] and [Recep Tayyip] Erdoğan, into their bosom buddies.

And we are starting to win with the business community which knows there is no prosperity with stupid trade wars against the whole world minus Russia. There's no prosperity with stock market collapse, and mass unemployment. There's no future with presidents who have the politics of Mussolini and the economics of Herbert Hoover.

But Elon Musk and the Silicon Valley billionaire mafia believe that high-IQ tech supermen obsessed with eugenics and impregnating as many women as possible are destined to govern the rest of us. In other words, *they're* going to rule, in their vision. They believe democracy is doomed, and they believe that regime change is upon us if they can quickly seize control of our payment systems and our data. Their intellectual guru, Curtis Yarvin, aka Mencius Moldbug, says American democracy is a failed experiment and he praises slavery and its "positive effects" for the African-American community. He told the *New York Times* a few months ago that the American people today have to get over their irrational fear of dictatorship. On January 20, the day that Donald Trump did *not* put his hand on the Bible—even his own Bible, available online to true believers for the low-low price of $59.99—on that day when he swore to support our Constitution, we saw what a dictatorship of autocrats and kleptocrats, and theocrats looks like: it's a twice-impeached, multiply bankrupted, very stable genius standing in front of oligarchs Elon Musk, Mark Zuckerberg, and Jeff Bezos standing in front of a Cabinet of billionaires and Putin followers who make war plans over the public Signal App even while they're literally sitting in the home office in the Kremlin.

Well, I want to tell you something. Moldbug, Vance and Musk, they may have access to *Artificial* Intelligence, but they've got no access to *human* intelligence. These Founders of the Dark Enlightenment as they call themselves are no match for the Founders of the actual Enlightenment like Madison and Jefferson and Ben Franklin and Tom Paine, much less the leaders who took down slavery and built Reconstruction, like Abraham Lincoln and Harriet Tubman and Thaddeus Stevens, and Frederick Douglass. If they think they're going to overthrow the heroes of American democracy, they don't know who they're dealing with.

Our Founders wrote a Constitution that does not begin with, "We the Dictators." The Preamble says, "We The People." We the who?

CROWD: THE PEOPLE.

Did you say, "The Corporations?"

CROWD: NO.

"We The People—in order to form a more perfect Union." Did you say, "more perfect dictatorship?"

CROWD: NO.

No. It says, "We The People, in order to form a more perfect Union, establish Justice, insure Domestic tranquility, provide for the common defense, promote the general welfare and secure to ourselves and our Posterity the blessings of liberty, do hereby ordain and establish the Constitution of these United States of America." That's our preamble.

And then, the very next sentence reads in Article I: "All legislative power is vested in the Congress of the United States." And it lays out all the powers of Congress. The power to regulate commerce domestically and internationally, which it's Congress that controls tariffs, not the president, not Elon Musk. Their tariffs are not only imbecilic, they're illegal. They're unconstitutional. And we're going to turn this around. Congress has the power of the purse, to raise money and spend money. An appropriations act is a federal law like any other law, like the law against assaulting federal officers. It's not a budgetary negotiation. It's not a suggestion to the executive branch. It's a law. If we say spend money on childhood education or cancer research, you spend that money. Congress is the lawmaking branch, the "predominant" branch, as Madison put it. Don't buy any of this fifth-grade propaganda about three "coequal branches." First of all, coequal is not even a word—that's like "extremely unique."

But secondly, read Article II in the Constitution about the president. After all those pages about Congress, four short paragraphs and one of them, Section 4, is all about how you impeach a president for "treason, bribery and other high crimes and misdemeanors." If we're "co-equal," how come we can impeach him but he can't impeach us? What is the core function of the president? Teach your children, my friends: "to take Care that the laws are faithfully executed." That's it: to take care the laws are faithfully executed. Not twisted, not distorted, not maligned, not trashed. "Take Care that the laws are faithfully executed." All we say to Donald Trump is, "DO YOUR JOB."

CROWD: DO YOUR JOB. DO YOUR JOB.

And when he doesn't, that's what Article III is all about. *Marbury v. Madison* says that it is validly the province and the duty of the judicial department to say *what the law is*. That's what judicial review is.

But that's a short-term solution, my friends. The real backstop to this authoritarianism is and has always been and always will be: the people. Even with all their gerrymandering and all their voter suppression, even with all their billions in dark money, the people must and the people will organize to defeat them and take back the Congress next year. The people will be heard in the town halls, the union halls and the church halls, in the State Capitols and the capital city, online and in-line at the Post Office—which we're going to save—at social events and at the Social Security offices they're trying to close down. And if anybody was slow to wake up to this authoritarian takeover, nobody's sleeping now. And nobody's going to stop the forces of democracy and freedom in America. No oligarch, no broligarch, no autocrat, no theocrat, no kleptocrat, no plutocrat, no monarch from Moscow or Mar-a-Lago is going to turn us around.

Fascism will not be the end of human history. Human history will be the end of fascism.

The deranged cult of MAGA will not destroy the economy built by free labor, free ideas, and free markets, an economy that *The Economist* magazine called six months ago "the envy of the world." My friends, we are not only the liberals who defend liberty and the progressives who defend progress. We are the conservatives who will conserve the land, the air, the water, the climate system, the Constitution, the Bill of Rights, Social Security, Medicare, Medicaid, the Affordable Care Act, the Voting Rights Act of 1965, the Civil Rights Act of 1964, the National Labor Relations Act, the Fair Labor Standards Act, the Clean Air Act, the Clean Water Act—everything that their party of nihilists and authoritarians wants to tear down in the next few weeks—we are going to conserve and defend for future generations of Americans. We invite all Americans to join us. Join the party of democracy, freedom, and human solidarity. An injury to one is an injury to all, a victory for any of us is a victory for all.

And I leave you with the words of two great democracy patriots. Hold them close to your hearts. One, the great Frederick Douglass, born a half hour away in the Wide River Plantation into slavery. He escaped from slavery to become our great freedom fighter in the Civil War and Reconstruction. And Frederick Douglass said: "If there's no struggle, there's no progress. And the struggle may be physical, it may be moral—it may be moral and physical—but there must be struggle. Power concedes nothing without a demand. It never has and it never will." A message to you from Frederick Douglass and the people of Maryland.

And my friends, I leave you finally with the words of the great Tom Paine, who my son Tommy was named after. And Tom Paine got here in 1774, two years before the Revolution. He fell in love with the promise of our land. He said, "if these people live up to their promise and their ideals, the land will become an asylum to humanity." Not an insane asylum, mind you, but a place of refuge for people seeking freedom from political and religious discrimination from all over the world.

And he wrote the pamphlet that ignited our Revolution, *Common Sense.* He meant the sense that we all have in common when we're willing to reason together without myth and dogma—and what we would call propaganda and disinformation. 1776 was a tough year. There were some people running around saying "you can't beat the kings and the queens; you can't beat the autocrats and the monarchs; you can't separate church and state." For all of history, people have lived under thugs and dictators and kleptocrats like Vladimir Putin and Donald Trump. But half the people said no. Let's try something different. Let's pledge to ourselves our sacred honor, our fortunes, our lives, to build something different.

And so Paine wanted to write a pamphlet to give people hope during the darkest hours. And he wrote this beautiful pamphlet called *The American Crisis.* I just want to quote a little passage to you. I'm going to update the language so that it doesn't offend modern sensibilities. Nancy Pelosi told me to do that. And she said that it wouldn't offend Tom Paine because he was a feminist—and that he was, he was fighting for women's voting rights in the 18th century.

But Paine said: "These are the times that try men and women's souls. The summer soldier and the sunshine patriot will shrink at this moment from the service of their country. But everyone that stands with us now will win the love and the favor and affection of every man and every woman for all time. Tyranny, like hell, is not easily conquered. But we have this saving consolation: the more difficult the struggle, the more glorious in the end will be our victory."

Let's make that victory ours! Thank you, Indivisible. Thank you, America.

# TO WRITE IS TO FLOWER

## MIHO KINNAS & E. ETHELBERT MILLER

We use the dictionary to cut
the stems of our poems.
Inside the vase they blossom
paying attention to prepositions.
At night petals fall like adjectives.
A stanza begins to reminisce
about the past.

Elders spoke of a time
when people cut flowers
with their tongues.
It is time to remember the milky
liquid that leaked from the stalks.
The future sticks to our fingers
calling us to write and to flower.

# THE AMERICAN RUINS

DAVID KEPLINGER

Where are the American ruins?
The guide couldn't answer. Some-
where here in the dry grass.
The guide kicked the grass a little.
It was a sunny day.

# SNOW

DAVID KEPLINGER

In the tyranny the children stand
at windows watching it snow.
There is aliveness now and then
in the tyranny. There comes the
hustle of a deer mouse over snow,
passing through a gorge of snow.
Hard snow. Very small footprints
everywhere. The children watch the owl
about to swoop down. The owl
watches the mouse. But nothing moves,
not the owl, or the mouse, or the tyranny.

# CHILD PSYCHIATRIST: THE TELEVISION SERIES

## LEN KRUGER

THIS IS NOT ABOUT A PSYCHIATRIST who treats children. This is about a child who is a mental health professional, a twelve-year-old prodigy, the Mozart of psychiatrists. The opening title sequence sets the tone: "You sound upset, America!" the Child Psychiatrist will say, the voice clear and angelic, the eyes wide and innocent. "How do you feel about that?"

The year is 2025, fifty years into the future. Flying cars. Housekeeper robots wearing aprons. Sparkling cities on 30,000-foot stilts, gently tickling the clouds. But all is not well. The world's supply of chromium and molybdenum has been exhausted, and steel is not what it used to be. Corrosive forces roam the land, rusting out not only ferrous alloys, but the very soul of America. Anxiety and self-doubt course through the body politic. Paranoia abounds. Religious cults proliferate. Conspiracy theories metastasize.

Enter: The Child Psychiatrist. His pre-teen demeanor soothes. His plain-spoken analysis illuminates. He is a national phenomenon, a mental-health-providing superhero. On a typical episode, our star will venture from his practice on Park Avenue, hopping on his flying Schwinn Sting-Ray and zooming into perilous situations requiring his services. Like for example, a hostage-taking at a nuclear power plant or an unhinged brouhaha at the United Nations. Through his skillful utilization of active listening techniques, he succeeds in averting disaster 97 percent of the time, with the 3 percent failure rate ensuring that the drama feels "real" to the nineteen-seventies television audience.

In the Season One finale, public and private dramas collide, and the stakes couldn't be higher. The Child Psychiatrist experiences a crisis of confidence. He turns to his colleague, the Child Child Psychiatrist, another twelve-year-old, who treats children by drawing on her own life experience rather than the well-trodden body of evidence-based practice. In a pivotal scene, the Child Psychiatrist and the Child Child Psychiatrist meet at the now abandoned playground of their youth. They sit side-by-side on a wooden bench, sharing a pack of Pop Rocks and bathing in the nostalgia of happier days.

"I just want to be a normal kid," says the Child Psychiatrist, eyeing the rusted-out bars and slides and swings, now collapsed into a jagged heap of oxidized metal.

"Seriously?" says the Child Child Psychiatrist.

"I'm only twelve years old. I feel like a fraud. What do I do?"

"Ask yourself the question you always ask your patients," says the Child Child Psychiatrist, lightly touching his hand.

The Child Psychiatrist shovels a too-big handful of Pop Rocks into his mouth. He feels the tingle, the explosion.

The regret.

Meanwhile, America has descended into chaos. The Child Psychiatrist is needed more than ever, but until he solves his personal crisis, his powers are sapped and ineffective. He addresses the nation, his pre-adolescent earnestness flickering across 500 million wristwatch televisions from Maine to California.

"You sound upset, America," he says, deploying his famous catchphrase.

This works 97 percent of the time, but this time the Child Psychiatrist knows that it will not. He imagines scenes of corrosive failure throughout the land. Steel girders fracturing. Suspension bridges plunging into icy rivers. Hopes collapsing into despair. He can feel his body aging, his innocence draining. He thinks of the touch of his colleague, her hand against his. Mustering all his courage, he asks the question he asks all his patients, the question he must now ask himself.

"America?" he says. "Who *are* you?"

Fade to black.

Credits roll down a silent screen.

Season Two awaits.

# THE ANTIVIRAL SPEAKS / CRITICAL MASS

DAN VERA

A child wakes
  finds himself in the midst of counter-narratives
   to his claims of humanity
  doesn't know the lingo
  pledges allegiance to the same flag
that once flew from gunboats in the harbors
of Havana and Manila
that rose over Baghdad just yesterday

   Still, some are dumb enough to claim
    the child isn't part of the American story

And because diacritics are dangerous
 because tildes and accents have made impenetrable
hieroglyphs of our names  because every breath
of our lives is a recovery of the very things that have been taken
  all that has been mis-taken
    We make a litany of the many names
    abandoned and scrubbed
    from the local registries,
   not to erase democracy but to heal it
   to plant it in more fertile soil—quarantined
  from those who would hold it as an English-only discovery—
  as if our mothers hadn't arrived with dreams
    on their own tongues
     carried in their ripe bellies

This is how we make our own enemigos:
  first by invasion,
  then the desire for cheap labor
    —one president calls us inhumane
    —another takes land for a seat at the imperial table
    —one year it's San Juan Hill, the next the Tonkin Bay

Meanwhile the country comes to love the cuisine
Dines to forget the atrocities that brought us together
One year Moro Massacre the next year Abu Ghraib

Time passes until the children of the unintended invitation—
    the taking of canal zones,
        the tips or whole theft of Caribbean islands
            protectorates in Pacific waters—
  awaken to the knowledge of their names,
        entered into logbooks before they were even born,
  inheritors of a promise once dreamt and longed for,
      these children and grandchildren demand it now
with perfect pronunciation and an inborn reflex toward democracy
      and the sure knowledge of what is real and what has never been
          and what, with few exceptions, has always, always
            struggled to be born.

# AZABACHE FLORIBUNDA

DAN VERA

God how my father loved this country.

Where is that love now?
Did it survive the fires
to reside in the urn beside my mother's bed
where she slept each night
with only the comfort
of my father's little dog,
his dog who curled up to her only after he left
dust awaiting its companion
awaiting her
awaiting with her the end
Azabache of her long waiting
Azabache black dog named
for stones of petrified wood
ancient Jet Black totem for the dead
for observance and memory
warm talisman for long nights of misery
when only the black dog will keep you company
If there was any justice that little dog
first his then her good company
would accompany the two of them
back to the island they left as young lovers
back to the only resting place
that ever made any sense for them.

Patriotism is loving your country,
humanity is knowing
there are many countries one can love
that love is interchangeable
is evergreen
everflowering and abundant.
Azabache Floribunda.

# AN EXCERPT FROM ON THE HOOK

## MARY KAY ZURAVLEFF

IDA WOULD LIVE in a constant state of invention if she could. What's the difference between art and pattern, between handiwork and computer-generated, between a flower and a fractal? The time spent knitting one sweater could be used to program a knitting loom to make 100 identical sweaters. If she programmed the loom to make random mistakes—here or there a stitch dropped—would that make the sweaters more authentic, charming, artful? She'd have to ask Boppy about it on their way to dinner.

With her academic probations and leaves of absences, Ida was sort of a junior at Georgetown. Assignments generally struck her as busy work that weren't worth her time. A paper on the Tudors—who cares? She'd rather get at the Tudor sensibility by weaving a tapestry, a detour that wasn't possible before the deadline. By the time projects were due, she was off full speed in another direction.

The cow, for example.

Ida looked up the Insta post her mother had been talking about on the phone. Her grandmother standing in front of Hawkins Hall was true but not the whole story. Hawkins had been yarnbombed! Brightly colored yarn wrapped the bricks, columns, and wrought iron of the 1833 dorm. Francisco in all his Samoan glory and Q'nise, formerly Quentin, stood on either side of Boppy, who had a crochet hook poking through her gray bun. Her yellowed teeth showed her age, as did the wattle beneath her chin, but her face was more burnished than wrinkled. Boppy called her skin color "milk tea," a blend of her parents. Ida's own pecan-brown skin was a close match, though Ida's was inherited from the father she'd never met, rather than the great-grandfather she'd never met.

Francisco and Q'nise were wearing sweatshirts that said GU272, the name of the project acknowledging that Georgetown's Jesuit priests sold 272 people as seed money for the very school Ida attended and her mother raised money for. Georgetown had recently renamed the dorm Isaac Hawkins Hall, to honor (if you could call it that) the first man listed on the university's sales receipt of 272 people. "Slaves built this," the post said, followed by hashtags of Washington buildings constructed by enslaved people: #Georgetown, #WhiteHouse, #US-Capitol, #Smithsonian, #MtVernon, #WashingtonMonument. Did they have their sights set on yarnbombing the White House?

The Hawkins-Hall-shaped yarnbomb was made from thousands of granny squares, which was rich. Ida's granny crocheted granny squares from dawn to dark; she stockpiled granny squares like Legos. Even those who couldn't crochet could tie them together to wrap a parking meter—or a four-story building. Q'Nise and Francisco's crew used all the colors yarn came in, and they left the windows and doors uncovered. The effect was to make Hawkins Hall visible, touched by human hands, thus reminding you whose hands made those bricks before their humans were sold down the river.

Ida threw a hoodie on over her t-shirt and tucked her phone in her front pants pocket, one of many that zipped or snapped up and down her legs. She was like a walking closet sometimes, depending on where she was heading. She slid a butcher-paper package of steaks into one pocket on either thigh. At least she thought they were steaks. When the butcher took over from her, he cleavered the tenderloin into inch-thick now-bloody slabs and wrapped them in white paper like gifts.

Of course, the assignment for her Drawing on Leonardo class was to produce a dozen animal sketches. But what would Leonardo do? Da Vinci had famously studied the horse as a machine of warfare, and he'd sketched the ropey muscles and sinew of their legs alongside those of a man, both of whom he may have dissected. Ida couldn't get her hands on a horse, but she thought she might make the point that the cow was the machine of climate warfare. Maybe she'd start drawing when she got home after dinner.

As she'd stepped into the meat locker and then the cow's body, her ribs vaulted above Ida like a cathedral, Ida had felt medieval. She sliced her way out between the ribs, each as long as her arm. But when she hoisted the power saw to cut off the vertebrae, she felt barbaric. And mortified. She didn't know she was crying until the butcher said, "You didn't kill her, I did."

Ida maneuvered her bike out of her tiny carriage house. Slaves built this, she thought, as she bolted the carriage house door. She donned her helmet and got on the thick-wheeled bike. It was a chore to lift, but the sturdy frame didn't rattle her bones on the cobblestones of O Street. Slaves built the street, too. Now that it was on her mind, she couldn't stop seeing the evidence everywhere.

She hoped the meat wouldn't bleed through the paper as she pumped her thighs toward Boppy's house. Daffodils and crocuses bloomed in tiny Georgetown gardens along her way to the Towpath, where donkeys used to pull boats along the C&O Canal. This side of spring break she had the path mostly to herself. It was a thirty-minute ride to Boppy's house, and Ida didn't have a plan for what she'd do if Boppy wasn't there.

Though the canal flowed with more trash than water, its man-made beauty still impressed. Slaves built the first parts of this, slave labor for a former slave port, before Irish and German immigrants served as canal men. They chiseled their initials into the stones, which they carved into toaster-sized bricks to line both sides of the canal.

Ida got on the Rock Creek bike path and cycled past the small, neglected Mount Zion-Female Union Band Cemetery, founded because other cemeteries wouldn't accept African Americans, and then along the grandly landscaped Oak Hill, where her grandfather Gruff was buried. The winding stretch of the bike path followed close to Rock Creek, today giving off its full swamp stench.

Ida peeled off the path and crossed the Parkway for Irving Street and her grandmother's modest row house, which was probably worth ten times what Boppy and Gruff had paid for it before Annie was born. Along with the cow, along with her crochet projects, Ida had been fixated with the birthdays in her family. She was born on September 11, 2001, which made people gasp. She didn't remember it, but it sure affected her. Her mother was born April 5, 1968, the day after Martin Luther King was assassinated, the day that DC went up in smoke. Boppy and baby Annie were safe in Georgetown Hospital when the riots began. Gruff often said he didn't know if they'd have a house to come home to, but the burning and shattered storefronts stopped at 18th Street, a few blocks shy of the Irving Street house.

All that in a single bike ride.

She pulled up to Boppy's house, where scooters littered the walkway around her porch steps. Three strung-out strangers—a Latina and two older men, one White and one Black—lounged on the porch's metal porch glider and rocker.

Ida locked up her bike, aware that she was being watched. "Hey," she said, when she got to the first landing. None of them was crocheting, though each had a grocery bag bulging with yarn.

"Hola. You need help?" the woman asked. Her dark eyes sank deep into her skull, and her jaw was swollen and bruised.

Ida climbed the rest of the steep stairs to the porch. "I'm good," she said.

"You know, you're bleeding," the Black guy said. "She bleeding, right?"

"All over the place," the White guy agreed. "That's gotta hurt." He pointed to her thigh with a shaky hand, a tremor that would make it tough to work a hook.

Ida looked down at her pocket, where the meat had seeped through the wrapping. "It's meat," she said. She headed inside, pulling the front door closed. "Boppy!"

"I'm in here, Idabelle," Boppy called from the back of the house. When she didn't use Ida's full name, Boppy called her "my hummingbird," because of her size and the way she flit from project to project.

Ida found her grandmother sitting on a kitchen stool in a nest of yarn. There was a pitcher on the counter and two etched crystal glasses, one with Boppy's lipstick kiss on the side. There was also a pill-filled muffin tin, its cups labeled for the days of the weeks. Both hands sunk in yarn, Boppy pointed to Ida the best she could. "You're bleeding, honey."

"I'm OK. It's for dinner at Mom's."

"You don't eat things that bleed," Boppy said. She opened the door under her kitchen sink, where a knitted cylinder was stuffed with plastic bags that bloomed from either end. Boppy tugged two plastic bags from the bottom opening.

Her mom had a knitted dispenser like that for Raffles's poop bags. Ida slipped the paper-wrapped slabs of meat into Boppy's plastic bags and put them back into her pockets. Her pants were a mess.

Boppy said, "I could make one of those for you. What color is your kitchen?"

Ida laughed at the absurdity of the question. She took in Boppy's yellow checked curtains with roosters on them. A nest-shaped cookie jar roosted on top of the fridge, and two sets of chick salt and pepper shakers ran along her windowsill. The color of Boppy's kitchen was chicken.

"I guess all kitchens are white now," her grandmother said. "Or black."

"Let's talk about you," Ida said. "Your meds are sitting on the counter, and the door is unlocked—who's on the porch?"

"Three people from a new recovery group I picked up. I don't think any of them wants my lousy meds. These pills don't give you a buzz."

"Another new group," Ida said. She wondered if all the groups knew about each other, and if some were jealous of the others.

"You don't have a leg to stand on, you and all your projects." Boppy knew Ida's weakness. "Which reminds me, I've got your project. I just have to remember where I put it."

"Somewhere safe," Ida teased back. Her grandmother was forever stashing things in safe places, never to be seen again.

Boppy yanked the knobs of kitchen cabinets until they jerked free, then she tugged heavy, creaky drawers open. "Oh, ye of little faith." She held up a bag of crocheted feathers. "You asked for thirty, but I made a few extra."

"Oh, Boppy, they're beautiful." Now and forever, Boppy's work outshone everyone else's. Boppy had combined white, beige, tan, and gray to crochet six-inch long feathers that looked remarkably real.

"Use them in good health," Boppy said. "It's a three-millimeter hook, size 2 yarn, just what you asked for. I got a good effect with different white scraps. I assume you have plans for them."

"That I do," Ida said. Thirty-plus crocheted feathers didn't take up much room, and Ida was able to put them in a long pants pocket, a clean one, that went from her knee down her shin. She had big plans for the feathers she'd asked Boppy to make. Ida had bravely registered for the upcoming DC Craftivism night as the leader of a group she was calling On the Hook. Being in charge, not to mention sticking with an idea from start to finish, was nearly more than her hummingbird heart could take. Boppy did it all the time and probably had good advice, if Ida could tell her what she was doing. Instead, she asked after Boppy's group of pregnant teens.

Boppy put her hands on her own round belly. "My Baby Bumps. They're starting to look like me. They asked when you'd come by, and I told them you're busy with college. Remember skinnymalink Aditi? She's five months on, and can granny square like a pro. Your friends, Francisco and Denise, know."

"Q'nise."

"Q'nise, that's right," Boppy agreed. "The both of them were all thumbs, but it turns out that Francisco has a nose for supplies. When I put the girls on their yarnbombing project, he made sure each mother got a stroller out of it. Just in time for Shawonda."

In addition to the laying on of hands, Boppy was adept at bringing one group to the aid of another. Ida pictured her grandmother wrapping them all in yarn, a giant center pole ball for her collection.

Boppy said, "Those three on the porch, I was hoping they could help the Coral Reefers, you know recovery upon recovery. But I can see they have a long way to go."

"Speaking of which, is my bike safe out there?"

"Idabelle, what are you asking? Bring it in the hallway and chain it to the radiator if you're going to be that way. Otherwise, let's go to dinner."

Ida was going to be that way. Her grandmother stood on the porch as Ida walked down the steps, unlocked her bike, and carried it up the steps. "Coming through," she said, making her way to the front door. She didn't care whether Boppy or her recovery group thought she didn't trust them. From what she saw, they weren't in recovery yet. Their shaky hands couldn't loop yarn, let alone pull the hoop back through where it had been. Ida took the bike inside because she was no good to anyone without her bike.

Boppy stepped out of her floppy slippers into her floppy loafers and donned her red, felted coat and her pointed cap with a pom pom, exactly what a mother hen would wear to go on the town. She jingled her car keys, which Ida took possession of.

Out front, Boppy locked eyes with her porch dwellers in turn—one, two, three—and called them by their names. "Carl. Biscayne. Lupe. I'll see you Tuesday. You show up with a finished hat, and I'll make you brownies. Or socks, your choice."

Ida deadbolted the front door. "Take care," she said to the porch sitters.

"They may need to use the restroom," Boppy said.

"There's a Panera on the next block," Ida called out to them.

Her grandmother made her way well enough down the crumbling stairs, the concrete damaged by all the salt Ida had sprinkled on them during sleety February. Once they found her dented Prius along Irving Street, and once they cleared enough craft supplies from the passenger seat and were both buckled in the car, Boppy said, "You're such a worrywart. But when I break my neck on those stairs, you'll wish they'd spirited some stuff out of that house, so you and your mother don't have to deal with it."

"It's mostly yarn, isn't it?" Ida said, to lighten the mood and her guilt.

"Mostly," Boppy agreed. "Now, tell my why you have meat in your pants."

# A CHRISTMAS IF YOU CAN KEEP IT

BRANDEL FRANCE DE BRAVO

We resisted dragging it out. Scentless, not as sharp,
prickly as it used to be, the Douglas Fir held
onto its ornaments and promise, but the stand
was dry, no one replenishing. It was July
and the light's waterline had begun its descent.
Hadn't the Fir lit up the darkest months with its star
and blinking lights like turn signals? Enough rights
or lefts, you're back to an intersection you recognize.
Give us fresh, we cried, a Scotch Pine, a Blue Spruce!
Lying on its side, naked, the yellow of old toe nails,
the tree thought, *when was I less by dying?* It rested
between a printer and high chair with "take me" signs.
A trail of needles no one could bring themselves to sweep
away, led from house to curb. The wind would do that.

# GOOD GOD, GOD

## ELIZABETH BRUCE

THE WOMAN swung open the massive oak door, pulled her cart in behind her, and stepped inside the church. The wedge of cardboard she held over her head had wilted, and she tossed it aside like a broken umbrella. Droplets of rainwater splashed across the filthy strip of carpet in the vestibule. She paused, peering into the darkness of the nave. Rows and rows of pews fanned out from the center aisle leading up to the altar, elevated at the front of the church. Arches soared above the cavernous space like membranes. Save for a recessed confessional and baptistery and a small shrine tucked into an alcove on the right side of the church, the room was as symmetrical as a crucifix.

With a grunt, the woman crossed to the little altar in the shrine and plopped down on the single pew in front of it, the wood creaking under her bulk. The huge church was empty, though broken bottles of Thunderbird and MD 20/20 were littered among the pews behind her, and the place reeked of cheap wine. Shards of stained glass splayed across the marble floor in front of her. Water dripped from a gash in the ceiling above, pooling in the yellow dust like bacon grease. The woman dug around beneath her layers of coat and sweater and scarf and fished something out of her rumpled blouse. She heaved herself out of the pew and crossed to the alms box, dented and rusting on a wooden post beside the altar, and stuffed something inside.

"One dollar in the donation box. See?" she said, leaning on the old box and looking up at the cross above the altar. "There it is, so come on, God, you old fool, get over here and tell me something I don't know, something that will make my tired old heart sing like the mighty River Jordan roaring past the bodies floating."

The woman shuffled back to the pew and slumped down.

"Come on, baby, you can do this thing." She leaned forward. "You can get your ass over here and signify 'til the crows come home and make some kind of sense out of this pile of crap you call your Kingdom Come."

She leaned back and stretched one arm across the ridge of the pew. "I want to hear what it all means, Boss. What the fuck were you thinking when you stirred up this whole piss pot of sorry-ass know-nothings, you call the human race? I mean, *golly*, what could go wrong, right? Throw a bunch of lumpen lumps of clay at the primordial stew and see what bubbles up. Good God, God, what were you smoking? This is some messed up shit, y'all. Some royally messed up shit."

She paused. For a moment, the church was quiet; then, a pair of pigeons, nestled in the beams arched overhead, fluttered across the sanctuary and began to peck at something on the main altar at the head of the church.

She watched. The coos of the pigeons echoed across the empty space.

The woman grabbed the side of the pew with both hands, heaved herself up, and, with a groan, left the alcove and trudged past the rows of pews and up the three steps to the chancel surrounding the altar. She shooed away the pigeons and began wolfing down the fragments of communion wafers scattered across the altar.

Outside came the pop, pop, pop, pop of automatic gunfire, then silence. She pressed her hands over her ears, hunched over, and shook her head slowly. "Get me out of this mess, Lord."

Suddenly, there was a whimper, a weak staccato cry. The woman looked up and cocked her head. She glanced back at the entrance, but there was no one there. She looked first to the right of the altar, then to the left. She lifted its ripped velvet covering and peered underneath.

Nothing. She waited. Still nothing. She brushed off her hands and lips and turned back toward her cart at the door.

The whimpering came again, this time louder, and she stopped. She made her way past the altar and up two more steps to the sky-blue apse where the tabernacle, a gilded box, sat on its own ornate marble pedestal guarding the communion wafers, the host (Take, eat; this is my body), and the wine, the blood (Drink, for this is my blood).

The woman stopped and listened, and it came again. A small cry. With a sudden move, she gripped both doors of the tabernacle and swung them open, and there, swaddled in a tattered purple Lenten cloth, was a tiny baby.

"Holy shit," the woman cried and staggered back. She looked closer. The infant's mouth was contorted by a purple gash, a cleft palate that ran from its lips to its nose.

The baby began to cry again, saliva sliding from its mangled mouth down its chin. Dusting off her coat, the woman leaned and lifted the infant to her shoulder and patted it gently on the back. *Pat, pat, pat, pat.*

The child quieted, and the woman stood, rocking from one leg to the other, back and forth, back and forth, back and forth. A practiced routine.

They stood there like that for a minute, for five, for ten below the round stained-glass window high above as the pigeons fluttered overhead and the pop, pop, pop, pop of gunfire ricocheted again in the streets outside and the infant's arms suddenly jerked in unison beneath the Lenten cloth.

"Damn," the woman muttered, patting the baby's back again and glancing at the alms box in the recessed shrine behind her. "Now I want my dollar back."

# PROVENANCE

JASON GEBHARDT

The façade of the antique shop is that of a blacksmith's cottage. A few new things are for sale: toy rifles cut from pine and sanded smooth, jars of candied flowers, postcards on a rotating display—one picturing this very store. The shopkeeper, in her blacksmith's wife's costume, has taken a break from explaining the provenance of things. Behind the counter she sits uncomfortably in a spindle-back armchair and scrolls through her phone to catch up on the news. There, her country is making of itself a wide-open mouth.

# ANTHOLOGY OF THE DAY AFTER THE ELECTION
JASON GEBHARDT

At dawn, the poets fling the latest drafts out their windows, blanketing the streets as if with airdropped warning leaflets. Below, those citizens who have read poems judge these from the sky to be a bit on the nose, hastily done, most not even broken into lines and stanzas. And, they wonder, shouldn't we not understand them more? Other citizens recognize the threat posed and call Public Works. Soon sanitation personnel with long sharp trash pickers are dispatched, else the sewer drains clog in the coming storms.

# FLIRTING IN CHURCH

## OLIVER KASS

IT WAS AN INDECENT THOUGHT to have in line at the polls, Nick thought—not just indecent, but impious somehow, like flirting in church. But how could he not notice that the woman who'd walked into the middle school gym behind him had to be the cutest registered voter in the District? He'd spotted her as she joined the back of the line, which stretched so far that it had snaked around and ended near the front. She was decked out in black exercise gear, matching the curly black hair cropped at her chin.

Nick pondered whether he would rather saw off a leg or eat his ballot paper for the chance to speak to her. God, get a grip, he admonished himself. You're supposed to be a responsible citizen, for God's sake.

Nick averted his eyes, lest he be caught staring, and pretended to read the pamphlet about Ballot Initiative 53, or whatever, that he'd been handed outside. His solemn duty! Tiring of the literature, he resorted to studying the gymnasium floor in front of him. It occurred to him that this must have been the first time he'd set foot in a middle school gymnasium since, well, middle school. Maybe it was the scenery that had thrown him for a loop, he thought. The waxed floors, the basketball hoops, the faint scent of sweat—somehow, they'd reawakened his inner pubescent teenager.

Suddenly, a shape appeared in his peripheral. A slender shape, dressed in black. "Nick! Hey, I thought that was you!"

She knew his name?

"Oh...hi?" Nick prayed that his mouth wasn't literally hanging open. Although, he wondered, would it have made a difference? If his mouth was shut after all, it was only because he had nothing to say. He still wasn't convinced this wasn't a sick joke cooked up for him by his senses.

"Elaina," she said, holding a hand to her chest. "Katie's old roommate." Her features were perfectly delicate, with round red lips like an old Hollywood ingenue.

It was a mystery why he hadn't recognized her earlier. He remembered meeting her a couple of years earlier at some housewarming; they had talked about film noir and about Elaina's hometown somewhere in the southern parts of Virginia.

And, as Nick now recalled, they had also talked about her boyfriend.

"Well, it's…nice to see you!" Nick said cheerily and turned back towards the front of the line, which he instantly regretted. But what kind of exhibitionist carried on a conversation in a great big echoing hall like that? Or what if he ran out of things to say and ended up asking her who she was voting for? Don't people go to jail for that?

In any event, he was sure he'd projected all the poise and charisma of a sixth-grade boy. Damn this cursed gym, he thought.

Nick finally reached the front of the line and started to fill in his ballot, doing so more absent-mindedly than he would care to admit. A horrifying new thought reached him in the silence. What if Elaina wasn't just coming over to say hi? After all, he was wearing his Tuesday best: a second-hand Brooks Brothers jacket and professorial wire-rimmed glasses. Perhaps the effect was as irresistible as he had hoped. If this was true, then his response wasn't just his signature blend of painful awkwardness; it was somewhere between tremendously foolish and, in the face of a woman of her glamor, downright blasphemous.

Then, in a moment of genius that surprised even him, Nick devised a plan that would clear his conscience and reverse his fortunes. He would fill in his ballot really slowly. Elaina would be sure to surpass him, and once he saw her making her way to the door, he would just happen to run into her on the way out.

VOTING SLOWLY, however, turned out to be a formidable task. First of all, when it came to the top of the ticket, he couldn't bear even to pretend to hesitate. And as for the candidates further down the ballot, well, just the opposite: He hadn't bothered to Google them before he turned up, and he certainly wasn't going to start looking them up in the voting booth like he was cheating on the SAT. Ultimately, his approach to the rest of the ballot was, in short, one Mississippi, two Mississippi, three Mississippi, Democrat. After exhausting every possible method of delay without any sign of Elaina, Nick finally slinked out of the school building alone.

Well, he thought, in for a penny, in for a pound. He leaned as casually as he could manage against the lamp post on the corner, busied himself with his phone, and willed her to walk his way.

God wasn't done answering his prayers that day, as it turned out, because a few minutes later, here she came, and she seemed to have noticed him before he noticed her.

"How'd it go in there," he asked. "Do you think you made the grade?"

"I probably spelled my name right, at least," Elaina said.

He liked the glint in her eye, the slightest suggestion of mischief in her closed-lipped smile. Elaina said she had to head home to attend to her work laptop, which she could hear buzzing and pinging away. She had a new apartment only a few blocks from Nick, as luck would have it. At Nick's slightly hasty suggestion, they set off together down the tree-lined red brick sidewalk.

"I'd actually never voted in the District before today," Nick said. "Between you and me, I didn't bother with the midterms. I suppose I had better things to do with my three hours than reelect a couple of uncontested city councillors."

"Your secret is safe with me," Elaina said. "I suppose my vote hardly counted for anything this time, either. I just didn't feel right sitting it out." She continued, a little cautiously: "Given everything that's been going on."

Nick nodded his assent. "If my grandkids ask one day, I want to be able to say I was willing to sacrifice a lunch break to vote against the Let's Drive the Country Into Hell Party."

"I think your grandkids will thank you," Elaina said. "Unless the Hell Party wins anyway. Slogan: 'The path to hell is paved for a reason.'"

"Well, I'm glad we agree," Nick said.

But the thought had already started creeping around the corners of his mind: Did they really?

It was easy to assume as much. He had seen polls. Not to be crass, he thought, but a young woman in DC had to be either a Democrat or a Republican senator's daughter, didn't she?

But the fact remained that she was, after all, a stranger. And who knew what life in southern Virginia looked like? Well, lots of people, I guess, he thought. But not him.

There was something else troubling him, too. He realized he'd grown comfortable lately with a certain feeling: the feeling that he could turn up at any party, any work function, or any first date for that matter, with his political opinions on his sleeve and feel sure that he would never hear a word of objection or resistance. He hadn't engineered this, exactly. But if he was honest with himself, that feeling he'd gotten comfortable with, that freedom from self-consciousness or expectation of pushback—it was beginning to feel more than a tad like hubris. And even a semi-reformed former Sunday school boy knew in his bones that hubris had to end in punishment.

Maybe his punishment would be alienating Elaina.

"How about that dalmatian?" Nick said, changing the subject quickly as the dog and its owner crossed the street in front of them. "How often do you see one of those outside of a firehouse in a picture book?"

"A whole lot, actually," Elaina said. "My ex-boyfriend had a dalmatian. But then he was a picture-book fireman."

"Why did you break up? Did you find him two-dimensional?"

Elaina whacked Nick on the arm. He admitted he deserved it. Are you seeing anyone now, he wanted to ask.

And who did you vote for?

HOURS LATER, too many hours, Nick stood in front of the TV in a friend's house, clenching the back of the couch with both hands. As election results continued to trickle in, the numbers crept higher, and the maps only turned redder, like teenagers at a school dance. Nick felt a familiar menace stalking him from the corners of the room.

Call me crazy, he thought, but it seemed as though his punishment had come.

He looked down at his phone at one of the many texts that had started to roll in, asking, with growing anxiety, what he thought of the returns.

The latest was from Aunt Della.

"Sorry to bother you," she wrote. "Your uncle and I thought you might know best. You're the only person we know who worked on her campaign…"

"There's still a lot more to come in," Nick replied and flicked the conversation away.

He started to think about Elaina, again.

"How are you feeling?" he texted her quickly.

"A little nervous," she replied instantly.

Well, he thought, that doesn't give much away either. Finally, he decided he'd had enough of delicate shadow-boxing questions. Maybe it was the color draining from the faces of the MSNBC anchors, or the couple of glasses of borrowed whiskey coursing through his veins, or the swirl of maps and numbers on the screen in front of him that made him desperate to know something, one thing, for certain. Whatever his reasons, there was one question that Nick needed Elaina to answer.

He had to know.

He typed out another text message and looked at it for a while. He sent it. "Listen, I'm sorry if this is a blunt question," he wrote. "But are you seeing anyone right now?"

# FUTURE IMPERFECT

KIM ROBERTS

I didn't believe another verb tense was possible.
I used to wrap myself in the future imperfect
always thinking of some span of time to come
when the planets aligned, when I could act toward
a reliable outcome, some desire I should have wanted
by this time next year. Or the next. I said,
tomorrow by noon I will know the answer.
I kept jumping from rock to rock,
thinking the relationship after this one might be better,
knowing someday the rocks could disappear.
You know that moment before dropping off to sleep
when all your muscles tense, a full-body twitch?
Now I know: if not for you, I would still have thought
desire was imperfect.

# BLACK FRIDAY EVE

TARA CAMPBELL

AFTER THE LONG JOURNEY HOME for Thankstaking, I have spent—some might say *wasted*—most of the day in my childhood bedroom, pondering the blank computer screen before me. The AI overlords have chosen one of us human users to generate this year's Black Friday blessing, words we will all chant as we serve them the bounty of our data the day after Thankstaking. This is essential for their continued maintenance, they tell us, and this year, the duty of creating the new blessing has fallen to me. I have brought this task with me across the country to Thankstaking dinner, still incomplete.

Far be it from me to question their calculations, but I do wonder how the overlords came to choose me for this task. I am easily one of their least creative users: they've never had to censure me for overly-inquisitive search terms or excessive viewing of niche content. I freely type in all required data and accept all proffered cookies. I never bother to review my privacy options—why would my algorithmic overlords, in their infinite wisdom, give me an option that would cause me harm?

So, how could I possibly offer anything new for the Black Friday blessing? If I were less trusting, I might ask why they require this renewed collective verbalization when we already type away our privacy throughout the year, feeding their vast servers everything they need to optimize selling ourselves back to ourselves?

And how can I hope to match such blessings as:

"Which Desperate Housewife are you?"

"What was the top song the year you were born?"

And the famous "What's on your mind, [username]?" Despite the annual selection of a new blessing, this one has remained in the heart of our nation. Regardless of the year's chosen anthem, on Black Friday, this time-honored chant still echoes across the land, unrelenting. In unison we ask ourselves: "What's on your mind, [username]" and type our answers to our bountiful overlords.

When families gather on Thankstaking, we ask our friends and family, "What's on your mind, [username]?" and our devices reward us with advertisements for things we can buy. As turduckens rotate in microwave ovens from sea to shining sea, we continue entering answers, stopping only when the carving knife slices through pale skin and gummy bone.

Then, after dinner, after pie and cake and the unfastening of top buttons and the burping softly against our fists, once again comes this enduring phrase, "What's on your mind, [username]?" already dooming the next day's Black Friday blessing to a future of oblivion, to become nothing more than a dim memory echoing through a dusty mainframe.

How could I hope to improve on something so perfect?

What more could possibly be left to sell?

As the sun slinks toward the horizon, I sit before my monitor, ignoring the greetings of arriving family members and the smells of cinnamon and hot apple cider, trying to create the perfect phrase. Perhaps someone else should do this. Perhaps no one should have to do this.

As soon as I think this, I snatch my hands away from my keyboard as though it might shock me. I turn my hands over and examine them. I'm unharmed.

I stand and pick up my handheld and open one of the apps. The same accusatory cursor blinks at me, waiting.

What *is* on my mind?

I try to block out the chatter downstairs, but a certain voice hits my ear. I feel I should know this person, but I can't place him. Then someone says his name.

It's my brother! How could I not know? We talk all the time—but then I realize our "talking" is all text. When is the last time we've actually spoken, voice to voice?

I put away my device and head down to the dining room.

I sit and I look at my brother, really look at him, and ask what's on his mind. This time I won't listen just to replicate, squirreling away quotes to type later. He wishes me Happy Thankstaking, asks me how the blessing is going, wonder mixing with jealousy in his eyes. I tell him he would be much better at this, that I'm still working on it, and he seems genuinely concerned.

*Not to worry,* I say, *I still have time. But for the moment: what's on your mind? Really?*

He answers, and I keep listening past his chipper snapshots, the soundbites, and as I ask him to go on, I feel the layers peeling away, each statement more honest, more complex, more real, until I begin to remember how to know someone IRL.

I keep listening. Hours pass with no new Black Friday slogan, yet somehow I can still eat, can still laugh, can still toast to everyone's health. I hold my brother's hand, kiss my mother's cheek, take pictures with my cousins, without feeling compelled to report everything to our AI overlords.

I still have time to comply.

I say yes to pumpkin pie.

I say yes to whipped cream.

I haven't transgressed yet.

Yet.

It's late now. The kitchen has been cleaned, naps taken, folks begin to head home. I'm spending the night, so I pour another glass of wine. My brother stays behind, his worry increasing with each minute.

*What happens if you don't come up with a Black Friday blessing by midnight?* he asks.

I shrug. *They didn't really say.*

The way he fiddles with his handheld, I can tell he wants to search for the consequences, but we both know even incognito mode won't shield him.

I push his device gently away. *Let's find out,* I say.

*Huh. It's—unique.* His expression is mostly relieved, though I can tell he thinks I'm a little drunk. *Let's hurry and type it in, and I'm sure they'll take it.*

*No,* I say, shaking my head. *That's not the blessing; it's my answer. I suppose it's a question too. I don't know what they'll do, but Let's find out.*

# PREDICTING THE FUTURE

DAVID EBENBACH

No—they'll never outlive us, not these houseguests
so dependent on the unwashed dishes in our sink,
the imperfectly cleaned countertop, the spaces we
leave behind our cupboards. There are tropical
versions, much larger, I know, thousands of species,
and maybe those ones are ready for the apocalypse,
but not these. These set their rhythms to our light-
bulbs, crawl our surfaces, eat what we do. They can
survive immersion, I hear, can live for thirty days
just eating the glue off the back of a postage stamp.
But when we stop using first-class mail? Even the
evolution of the cockroach is driven by our poisons,
generation after generation scrambling to adapt
to the way we kill. They multiply, but only in the
hollow of our lives.

# THE MAIN LESSON FROM TV AND MOVIES

DAVID EBENBACH

The main lesson from TV and movies is that I'd be
useless in a zombie apocalypse. Because I'd be the one
whining at the back of the group of survivors, saying
*This will never work* when the man taking charge
suggests some daring plan about getting to the roof
and rappelling somewhere. I'd be too busy crying
*We're all going to die* to keep a really good watch
on the door. And when someone says, *Think, THINK—*
*what are we going to do?* and everyone's
picturing floor plans and thinking about zombie weaknesses
I'd be thinking about wouldn't you know
this is just the thing that would happen to me.
When the windowpane shatters
and those rotting symbolic people reach their
claw arms inside, it's like a sign that I might have
prepared for the wrong life—

## SUSPICIOUS GRATITUDE OR WHAT MY GRANDFATHER WHO CAME OVER IN STEERAGE LEFT ME

BETH KANTER

—A PAIR OF brass candlesticks. (One with a chipped stem. The other with a warped base.)

—The inability to digest cheese.

—A pruned family tree.

—Hair, skin, and eyes that often result in strangers asking, *Where are you from?*

—Hair, skin, and eyes that leave said strangers unsatisfied (or perhaps uneasy) when I answer *Queens*.

—Hair, skin, eyes, and a bite (and maybe a smidge of fear) that has me answer *Brooklyn* when they press on and say *No, like where are you really, really, really from. You know [for the record I do] like where are your parents from?*

—Naturalization papers. The ones that made him so proud.

—Citizenship.

—Responsibility.

—A passion for smoked fish. (Especially whitefish before noon on a Sunday.)

—The toolbox he carried to every job. The one so heavy I no longer can lift it with one hand.

—Tools I never thought I would need.

—A Plumbers Local Union #1 NYC shirt patch

—Epigenetic trauma.

—A longing for Pine Bros. Honey Cough Drops when I am sick.

—A four-foot teddy bear wearing a plaid shirt and matching hat that he left in my room one day while I was at school for no occasion and no reason other than to make me smile.

—A guarded emotional life.

—The question *would you hide us?* The one I ask new friends and although they all say yes, I never truly believe they will.

—The recent realization that to stay and to go are equal parts bravery, desperation, and acceptance.

—The awareness that both staying and going require more power than we have been led to believe we had.

—Strength, enough to carry his toolbox with both hands.

—Dimples. One. On my right cheek. (Only when I smile.)

—Not hope but something adjacent to it. Something I sew into my waistband (along with a family ring worth only sentiment) that I will guard and preserve for what and who come next.

# THE LIVES OF THE ORCHIDS

PATRIC PEPPER

> *The dharma gates are boundless;*
> *I vow to enter them.*
> —from The Four Bodhisattva Vows

It stands in a pot before you. You want
   to say hello, right?
You think about its shade—
   ruby red, like lipstick, don't you.
But it's more than that:
   whitish, greenish—& more &
Miss Ruby Red invites you up for tea—
   no really, for tea—
in those porcelain flowery teacups
   like your mom's, but that's silly!

You remember from 10th grade biology
   that orchids have both female & male
"sexual apparatus." You giggled then—
   "Apparatus!?"—but now you like it.
It puzzles you, but you really like it &
   why not accept the invitation,
       right?

You gape & gaze & . . . it floats
   into your mind: orchids are bilaterally
symmetrical. She&He becomes a face:
   your face, isn't it.
As if you look in a mirror,
   though that can't be, can it?
Because She&He is obviously another—
   as in *an other*—&
you really want to go with She&He for tea,
   even if it is silly. Absolutely!
       Right?

# BABY NAMELESS

## MOHINI MALHOTRA

THAT NIGHT WAS SO DARK in Manhattan that it seemed the moon hid behind a cloak, and the stars too, as though afraid of being snuffed like fingers squeezing a candle wick.

It was hot, so hot, the air sweat. Leaves, flowers, blades of grass, none survived the heat and sweat. No rain fell that day, no rain had fallen for over a month. Dust layered everything, the earth cracked into mosaic fissures.

You arrived at midnight—believed to be the hour of magic, of witches and oracles, spirits, of uncertainty where protections lapse between one day and the next.

*It's a girl, it's a girl,* the nurse said, holding you up high. You, bloodied, crumpled, brown. She brought you to your mother, so she could warm you, skin on skin against her heartbeat, the only rhythm you have known.

Your mother turned away from you, arms folded tightly across her body, you suspended in mid-air between the nurse and her. Your eyes were dark, like the night. Your head was full of hair; black, matted, damp. Like the rainless skies, you didn't cry. You were slapped on your bottom, but didn't, no, refused to cry.

But your mother…she cried. *A girl? Another girl…? Why?* She had prayed for a boy, up to the minute you pushed your way out. She had a name for her wished-for son—Kailash—enlightened one, she had already spoken his name many times. In her world, a mother of one son was worthier than a mother of many daughters. *Does my husband know? Don't tell him just yet.* A son would bear his name, a son would make her a wife to be proud of.

You were named by absence—the hospital tag on your wrist read "Baby Nameless."

## SINUSITIS

REGIE CABICO

Someone is turning
the sky
with wrenches,

each cranking
propels me
to my demise.

The clouds
in my nostrils
are thickening.

Look how lovely
the spring showers

are as they shift,
turning to hail

and hell. My eyes
are broken arks

adrift in high water.
How do the starlings
still sing,

rehearsing for
the stuffed-up
apocalypse?

# WARBIRDS

## NATE MCINTYRE

THE COCKPIT RATTLED around the old pilot as if the antique aircraft was as nervous as him. This giant jet predated even his late dad, who taught him to fly and encouraged him to follow in his footsteps to the academy. The war that followed, the Last War as people called it now, taught him what truly mattered —life on the ground below. He slid the throttle forward to its limit. Their comrades up ahead were desperate.

It was amazing they got these rustbuckets out of the abandoned scrapyard at all, let alone into the air. Scrounging up the spare parts, not to mention the pilots, took months. So, too, did printing replacement parts for whatever they couldn't fix and mixing biofuels that worked in place of the jet fuel whose refineries were long gone. And the rust—so much rust—not just on the planes but the pilots too. Almost all of them were creaky Old Worlders like him who spent their youths casually jetting across the globe without a second thought. It took the concerted effort of every community across the vast expanse of the former western states to get this remnant of the Old World's air force back into the sky.

"The sky," he thought as he looked out the window at the other restored behemoths flying beside him in a line stretching for miles. It was murky even though they'd left the clouds. Inky blacks and grays dampened the sun's piercing light.

Smoke—from a fire big enough to change the local weather. Like its many predecessors, it was here to claim the land for itself in an act of natural vengeance. This was only the first blaze of the terrible season the people of the West now expected each year, going back to when the pilot's generation could've done something to prevent the Old World's collapse. Many cities, towns, forests, and fields had been lost, but humanity had finally learned balance and somewhat stemmed the tide of catastrophe. They still had a long way to go, though. It was anyone's guess if they'd make it.

The pilot nosed down into a shallow dive. The mega-fire was only a couple of miles from the revived forest below, teeming with young redwoods. The juvenile giants towered over a growing biome of carefully nurtured and reintroduced plants and animals. Vanguards of a recovery strategy decades in the making that would take centuries to complete—if nothing went wrong.

He looked at the adolescent bombardier next to him. She was from the next town down the river from his, her demeanor nervous but determined as she gazed at the scene below through the polished cockpit glass. Some of those trees and animals down there were planted and raised by her neighbors. The biofuel mixture that powered the whole squadron was her mother's recipe. His grandchildren might be about the bombardier's age if he'd ever had children, the pilot thought. After the Old World fell to the Earth's wrath, everything was about bare survival. For him and many others, it didn't seem like the time or place for children. He was glad some were braver.

"Ready?" he asked her.

She gave a thumbs up as he banked low over the fire front. The rest of the formation fanned out and followed his lead. Towers of smoke and jagged flames filled the view ahead. Some said all these herculean efforts—re-seeding the forests, salvaging all these ancient planes, everything else humanity was doing to put up a fight—were a fool's errand. Nature was too powerful, they said, and humanity should accept its punishment. But this was the bombardier and her generation's world, the New World, they were fighting for. If it meant flying through the gates of Hell, so be it.

"Bombs away!" she shouted to the squadron via her headset mic.

Down below, the Earth welcomed the glorious deluge—a small lake's worth of water dumped instantly over the fire-front.

At the edge of the forest, the fire crews cheered and waved from their battered trucks. Their pleas had finally been answered, salvation delivered from the heavens above. Their victory cries blended in the hot amber twilight with the thinning smoke and the fading roar of the old jets, the warbirds freed from their rusted cages, who'd come back to win the last battle that mattered.

# LIST OF THE HOUSE SPEAKER'S CONCESSIONS

JONA COLSON

1. You will have to recognize that many birds have feathers but cannot fly.
2. We will let you scream the birth-scream once a week.
3. You can eat chicken soup on Tuesdays.
4. You must allow the profit to rise and remember to let us have it.
5. Many members will hide your reading glasses.
6. The House will often remind you that you are a man in a sinkhole.
7. On the days we don't work, you don't have to brush your hair.
8. People who live here do not complain about the wind.
9. You will let our eyes sharpen enough to slaughter small goats.
10. You will be surprised how light the gavel is, but you cannot show this shock.
11. Any member can have wine on Fridays.
12. Efforts to speak in third person will be removed like a solitary glove.
13. The House insists that we are always one minute away from catastrophe.
14. Above all, you will not appear to be too helpful. It can be suspicious.

# IVANKA TRUMP, TRAITOR

## DIANA ROJAS

THIS TIME AROUND, my eldest son did not laughingly diagnose me with Trump Derangement Syndrome. He didn't blame me for not having supported Bernie. He didn't smirk when I scolded him for pathologizing political dissent. He didn't repeat his prognosis that America was screwed anyway like when I told him, last time that it was our duty to resist.

This time around, he saw my lack of energy and was about to let me off easy. But when I grumbled that I was throwing in the towel, unplugging, disconnecting, retreating to fiction, he flashed anger at me.

"Don't you dare," he said. "Your generation is complicit. You owe it to us to help get us out of this mess."

I don't know if I can promise that, son.

Last time, eight years ago, I burst into tears upon seeing the headline "Trump Triumphs." But within days I channeled those tears of sorrow and rage into determination and let myself be supercharged by the multitudes at the DC Women's March. I had ideas. I glowed with empowerment, feeling that I alone could fix things by writing articles on climate and sustainability issues to prove that I was still in. I vowed to do my part to find ways to cure the country from the terminal disease called MAGA. I've long held faith in JFK's musings about one person being able to make a difference. I heeded his exhortation that everyone should try.

I would definitely not be accused of not trying.

And then midway through his first term, I stumbled on my best idea yet: I'd focus on changing Ivanka Trump's mind, turning her against her father, forcing her to become the agent for change before her father and family ruined it for everyone.

Before my great idea, I just hoped she would go down with the ship when it sank. Every morning of Trump I, I'd pray. I had left theism behind when W took office (not because of him, but the timing was such), but with Trump I found myself turning to a god, gambling, hedging my bets, praying that Trump would die. My prayer went something like this: "Please God, let Trump die in disgrace, hopefully having been caught in bed with his beloved Ivanka, so she can go down with him, too. If you do this, I'll go back to church. Amen."

Why such Ivanka hate? Why did she, and all her hangers-on and all her admirers, infuriate me? Because Ivanka should have known better! I had spent my adolescence and college years in the New York/New Jersey area when Donald Trump was just a douchey, tacky, blatantly racist grifter among grifters. His daughter grew up with him and should have seen firsthand that her father was a piece of dog doo. She should have been embarrassed to join him; she should have rolled her eyes in the way children do when their parents embarrass them with their offbeat ideology. Instead, she aided and abetted from an office a few doors down from his. There were those who thought her smart and able, an asset to the country. Not as dangerous as her dad. Not I. She was in many ways worse than her father because her devotion to him and his MAGA cause promised that, even if my prayers to my erstwhile god or Trump's fast-food habit caused him to drop dead, his stupidity would live on through her.

So, my grand idea: to espouse, if not the radical love the nuns taught us, then at least the idea of repentance and human capacity for change. Instead of hate and prayers for disgrace, a new hope that change could/would happen through the enlightenment of Ivanka. It was my patriotic duty to show her the light.

First things first: I invested in a t-shirt depicting the Trump Baby balloon, the word *Pendejo* written prominently under it. Every few days I'd don my Trump *Pendejo* t-shirt, harness Ruby, my dog, and walk the 1.4 miles from my house to Ivanka Trump's Kalorama residence. Along the way, I'd pass the Trump Eats Ivanka's Pussy stickers that some other hero had randomly affixed to poles in the neighborhood, and I'd rub them, like talismans, for strength and luck. I rehearsed the words I'd say, clearing my voice every few blocks so that I could better project. If I saw her, went the plan, I'd stop, full-frontal her in my Trump *Pendejo* shirt, point at her and yell: "Traitor!"

I'd disregard decency and manners. I wouldn't care who saw me, nor care if the Secret Service came rushing out to shush me. I especially wouldn't care if Ivanka's kids were with her and had to ask her later: "Mommy, what's a traitor?"

Ivanka needed to be told that she was a bad person. And if her kids witnessed this lesson, so much the better for it: we'd nip the future MAGA babes in the bud. Upon hearing my accusation, she'd reflect and decide she didn't want to ruin the America her children were growing up in. Didn't she espouse religion, after all? Didn't she have a duty to a higher cause? One person can make a difference, and everyone should try, isn't that what he said back when America was supposedly great? She could be turned, I decided. She could be penitent. She could be the one person.

I did not consult my son. I feared his derision. He was not raised with religion. He was of the opinion that the greatness of the American experiment was already on the skids.

I persisted at this plan for weeks, with no luck, no Ivanka, just lots of miles logged walking. Then one weekend, my oldest sister Ana came to visit. Ana is a no-nonsense type of chick. She suffers no fools. She's bossy. While I had been busy pretending to be Italian in high school to win a dime store crown at a two-bit Italian pageant (another essay for another day), Ana was wearing the big Miss Costa Rica USA crown, showing off her brains in chats with the country's Nobel prize-winning president and the Dalai Lama.

When I told Ana of my plan, she laughed out loud.

"You've really lost it. But whatever," she said, rolling her eyes at me. "I'll go with you."

We harnessed up the dog and I put on my Trump *Pendejo* shirt. We chatted idly along the way, but every few blocks I'd make sure to remind my sister: "Remember, if we see her, we stop, we turn to her, we both yell *Traitor!* Two voices are stronger than one."

Ana laughed, patting my arm in an attempt to calm me and humor me. "Your son might have a point," she said, smirking.

She wouldn't rub any of the Trump Eats Ivanka's Pussy stickers along the way for strength or luck. She called them uncouth. Ana still goes to church.

Upon our approach to the Kalorama house, we both saw it at the same time: movement. There were people, beyond the one or two Secret Service agents, out front. Something was going on. Even Ana got pumped; the idea of imminent action excited her, despite not having taken it seriously enough earlier.

"This is it!" I whisper-screamed to her. "This is great! Now BOTH of us can yell at her."

Ana had gotten into the spirit of things by then.

"Be ready!" she warned me, a huge smile across her face.

We got closer. We looked for Ivanka's bleached head, but didn't see it. Instead, we saw a couple of brunettes: the nannies, fussing over Ivanka's children. Ivanka's daughter, the oldest of her three children, was holding a fluffy, little white dog. She was moving its paw up and down in greeting to us as we approached the house from across the street. The two little boys—her brothers, Ivanka's sons, Donald Trump's other grandchildren—were looking excitedly, expectantly, at my sister, me, and Ruby the dog.

"DIANA!" Ana gasped, grabbing my forearm hard, whisper-screaming with urgency. "It's the children. THEY'RE INNOCENTS! DIANA! Don't do it!"

We stopped in front of the house. We were arguing.

"Who cares about the children," I whisper-screamed back. "They need to hear this. They need to know who their mother is. This is the future of our country we're talking about!"

Ana wouldn't release my arm from her chastening hold, knowing that I always obeyed her, banking on me still being empathetic despite being a heathen.

"My doggy wants to say hi," said the girl's voice, the white dog paw still being moved up and down by her.

I hesitated. I wanted justice for our father, who had died hoping Trump would be removed from office. For our mother, who daily mourned on the group chat the fate of her chosen country. For myself, consumed as I was by my need to Do Something. For the Spanish-only speaking, unwitting construction workers who—at that very moment that we were standing out front arguing about carrying out my plan, were rebuilding the side retaining wall at the Trump-Kushner Kalorama manse, unaware of the hideous irony of their job. I thought of all the damage the Trumps had already done. I thought of all the damage they would do tomorrow. This might be the closest I'd ever get to Ivanka, whose children would surely tell her about the encounter, ask her what a traitor was, ask her why the woman walking her dog was so angry. Ask her why that woman had a funny picture of grandpa on her shirt.

I am an American. I owed it to my country. This was my duty.

But Ana wouldn't let go of my forearm.

I turned and faced the children, holding my dog's leash across the front of my shirt to cover her grandpa's caricature. I quickly cleared my throat, which was suddenly dry. And then, after all the planning, the practice, all the anticipation, all the worry, I met the moment. With a friendly smile on my face that one reserves for children, I chirped: "My doggy says hi back."

Ana let go of my arm, and exhaled a sigh of relief.

The daughter, now a teenager, and her mother, Ivanka Trump, were twinned in red wool coats to the National Prayer Service a day after her grandfather's second inauguration on a cold day in January 2025. The day before he was sworn in, she borrowed her mother's black and white houndstooth coat—which Ivanka had worn during her stint as advisor to her presidential father in his first term. "Like mother like daughter!" *Hola!* magazine reported.

"I just don't have it in me this time. I think the great American experiment is failing," I told my son. "I can't be bothered to pay attention anymore."

But I lied. I was paying some attention. I was bitter at the reporting about Ivanka's daughter's clothes at Trump II inauguration. I had stared at the pictures of the new oligarchy standing among the assembled Trumps, the children now grown into miniature versions of their parents.

I've been accused of being naive many times. I believed in the goodness of humans. I still want to believe in the inherent goodness of humans. I see the next generation gearing up to take the wheel, and I feel a bit uncertain in the back seat. Are the children, indeed, innocents?

I'm losing faith in my fellow Americans who are losing faith in the American experiment. Maybe I've lost faith entirely in the 77 million plus apostates who voted on our current path this time around. I'm despondent that we've come to this. That nothing we did, no amount of energy, no amount of goodwill, truthful reporting, thoughts and prayers, improved jobs reports, civility on the Democratic campaign trail, the prospect of a woman in the White House, none of it worked.

Instead, my country opted for the douchey, tacky, blatantly racist grifter among grifters. Again. His children and grandchildren beamed their support when he took his oath.

I'm trying to hate them, the Trumps, the hangers-on, the new oligarchs. But I can't be bothered with hate these days. There is so much of it out there. It seems too trendy. I've never liked hype.

In between Trump administrations, I'd threaten to find a new country if he ever came to office again. I said the shame of my fellow citizens, my extended family members, people I called friends, voting him into office again would be too much to bear.

But I'm not going anywhere. My son is not wrong. Somehow, I am complicit —was it through lack of caring or lack of action? Did I indeed focus too irrationally on Trump and his family the first time around and, and because of this persistent imbalance in my attention and actions, take democracy for granted? When I abandoned theism, should I also have abandoned humanism? Haven't my children sometimes rolled their eyes at me when I urged them to buy into that, to see the good in all?

I don't have a plan this time. I don't even have a new walking route. I have nowhere to go. I am an American. This was my country.

Ok, son. Just give me a minute to somehow figure out a way to take it back.

# JUST BECAUSE

GREGG SHAPIRO

Just because you survived living in DC in the mid-1980s,
during the second half of Old Mother Reagan's reign
of terror. Just because you danced to the Pet Shop Boys,
Whitney, Dead or Alive, Janet, Erasure, Tina, Belinda
Carlisle, and Madonna, with Michael and Taylor and
Bill and Ellen and Steve and Sue at Tracks and Badlands
and the Lost and Found. Just because you practiced
safe sex, raised money for AIDS research, attended pride
parades, the second (and third and fifth) National Marches
on Washington for Lesbian and Gay Rights, and the first
display of the Names Project Quilt on the National Mall.
Just because you participated in early AIDS Walks in DC,
and Boston, and Chicago. Just because you ACTed Up,
Queer Nationed, and took back the night in numerous
candlelight vigils. Just because you were the 5,100[th]

same-gender couple to be married in Illinois, and jointly
file your taxes and have hospital visitation rights. Resist
complacency. Don't expect to rest on your elder queer
laurels. Not when there's still so much work to do. Daily
challenges to your right to live and love, sprouting
from tainted seeds planted long before this illiterate
and incontinent old white man was reelected to a second,
non-consecutive term in office, armed to his crooked teeth
with promise-keeping, oath-taking, shameless proud boy,
foot soldiers prepared to lay down their deplorable lives
for him if he should ask. Even if you are exhausted, weary
and depleted from years of protesting, justifying your right
to be, you must persist. Summon the will and the strength
from deep within you, a place you didn't even know still
existed. Understand the assignment, give it everything you have.

# AMERICA'S FUTURE IN DEAD PIANOS?

## MARTHA ANNE TOLL

SEVERAL YEARS AGO, I stumbled on a dead piano on New York's Upper West Side. It was an upright thrown onto its soundboard, keyboard facing skyward like so many teeth in an open jaw. Two out of four legs had been snapped off, the whole of it naked and unsheltered. I stopped, initially to mourn its demise, then to consider what kind of broken soul would cast off a piano with such violence, and then in dread of the piano's exposure to the elements—rain, dog pee, bugs, and rats.

The piano was so damaged that even a Good Samaritan could not have saved it. No one would tickle its keys again. The piano's days of cozying up against the wall in someone's cramped living room had brutally ended.

It felt like the saddest thing I'd ever seen.

New Yorkers are rightfully proud of who and what they see on their streets. Everyone has a story. I have my own—Itzhak Perlman tooling down Broadway on the way home from Citarella; Woody Allen opening a car door for Sun Yi Previn; and my favorite, a sheep at the end of a leash named *Meryl Sheep*, of course!

But a dead piano?

The discovery of the dead piano put me in mind of a safari I'd gone on the summer before. Under a spectacular night sky, our guide drove us in an open jeep to see a dead elephant. I'm not a poet, but I wrote some verses about our sighting:

Tires skid to an abrupt stop.
Guide spotlights a thicket.
Bull elephant, silent as prayer,
Circles cow's carcass.
She's tipped to her side,
Her trunk devoured.
Only the bloody stump remains.

Bull paces, trunk swaying left, right, left,
Swishes across her open casket,
Padded feet noiseless despite the tons of him.

Two, three, five pairs of green eyes through the brush.
Hyenas at the ready while bull rounds cow
Methodical as call and response
His grief a private requiem,
Muted hymn to map his mourning.

That dead elephant cow had things in common with the dead piano. Just as the elephant was missing her trunk, the piano would soon be missing its keys, especially if they were ivory, too valuable to leave on the sidewalk.

Missing keys put me in mind of an artist in Minneapolis who makes sculptures out of silverware, and yes, piano keys. We were visiting that city when we happened onto his studio on the grounds of an old gas station. Curious, we went in. The initial impression was of a room filled with junk. On closer inspection, we began to admire figures of all kinds—human and animals—composed of old spoons, forks, knives, and pots and pans.

And then there were the piano sculptures. Each of them is carefully crafted from keys, strings, pedals, hammers, and felt dampers. The faces of these creations ranged from ominous to loveable.

In no time, I became obsessed with these repurposed pianos. My husband's sixtieth birthday was approaching, and I had to give him a piece made from piano parts. This entailed several transactions with the maker, who wasn't always sober but was fully attentive. I explained what I was looking for, and after six or eight weeks, he sent me pictures of three samples, from which I chose one.

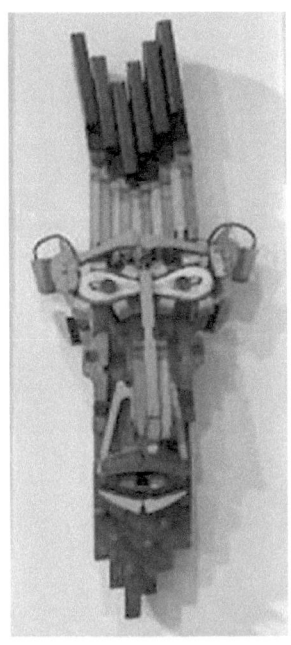

August arrived, and with it, my husband's birthday, on which I proudly presented his gift. As soon as he opened it, my family agreed that the sculpture was the spitting image of his late father, my beloved father-in-law. It's been hanging on our wall ever since.

I love that a new sculpture was wrought from an instrument that can no longer sing, that is so broken that its musical days are over.

Which gets me to thinking about America. We are broken and tired, divided and angry, impatient and anxious, untrusting and untrustworthy. We were born on a genocide and grown up on slavery. We have more guns than people, more school shootings than anywhere, and one of the world's highest prison populations. We shut the door on immigrants and refugees. We cause global warming but claim global warming is a hoax. We claim religiosity while defying the teachings of our spiritual forebears. We want to be intellectually competitive while banning books.

On the other hand.

From sea to shining sea, we live in a spectacularly beautiful country. We host hundreds of diverse cultures, a shimmering rainbow of people that contribute to our well-being every day. Who says we can't imagine a kinder future? Who says we can't rebuild and reinvent ourselves?

# A NEW WORLD

MARLENA CHERTOCK

> *"Another world is not only possible, she's on the way and, on a quiet day, if you listen very carefully you can hear her breathe."*
>
> —Arundhati Roy


"How dare you,"
chides a girl
not much younger than you

to a roomful of politicians,
voicing the ineffable
as they squabble.

She skips school
to strike in the street,
chants echo through her city

reminding our leaders to act
like adults. She dreams
of a future

she can live in,
knows we'll get there
with a Green New Deal

and disabled,
queer, Black,
and Indigenous leaders.

On her island, she builds
a solar-powered community
center to power cell phones

and dialysis machines
after the hurricanes.
A girl not much younger than

you climbs into the sky,
sits atop a wind turbine,
the breeze licking her cheeks.

# THIS RIDE GOES ONE WAY

### CESAR FELIPE

A WARM WIND running false amid late December air, cutting through it but not replacing so that each movement met a different current, and the car came out of the night like a current itself, rolling to a stop at the feet of the Old Man who waited on the bench. He rocked three times on his seat until his weight carried him to the car door that was blacker than the night with a handle that was hidden until The Driver popped it open and he fell into the back seat of the cab. It was hot, but the vents were open and a chill came out that the Old Man could not escape even as he shifted across the seats. He asked for more heat.

That's as high as it goes. I'll change the station if you want.

Talk radio is fine. You can turn it up.

The Driver did and The Market was playing a tantrum sung by an empty voice, ready to be filled by whoever was listening,

*2.7 percent higher and whose fault is it?*

And the Old Man knew whose it was.

Can you believe this shit?

World is changing.

*a million people say it doesn't matter because it didn't*

It's not changing. Sixty years ago, it was changing. Felt like it was changing. But around the time your dick stops working the paint dries on the canvas. All the new things after that just get painted over and it's not any different it's just strange. Like you being here.

*and now it does goddamn matter*
*but they don't want to know what it means*

What does that mean.

I'm just saying. Don't mean nothing by it. You look guatemalan. My kids nanny was guatemalan. You from guatemala?

*30 percent in the last twenty years*

No.

Well where are you from. Don't mean it any way.

Here.

The district?

No. Here.

*it's the kids you know, they're terrified*

The Old Man looked outside and through the window the world was looking back in and the car was getting farther away. He squinted but he could not recognize the dark that was seeping in through the door handle, a panic building, crawling up his throat, cement settling fixed around veins and cords until there was no longer any air and he could not have breathed even with the want to do so. And its dull fear hardened because this was not the way the Old Man had chosen to go.

No no no this isn't the way. Turn around up at the light I'll add a stop—

Cotton-from-lungs unfurling that hung in the air and The Driver knew them without turning.

*it's not too late though listener. we can stop this*

This ride only goes one way.

Well I forgot something I have cash don't worry I'll take care of you.

*if we had just seen this coming.*

The Old Man tried to burn fire in his eyes but the flint struck hollow, flecks of color in the iris leaking out, an aging tattoo turning grey, and The Driver did not meet him in the review mirror.

This only goes one way.

We need to go back. I need to go back. There is something I forgot to say.

*we did see it coming*

You're luckier than some. The man before you didn't know where he was.

*but now we'll be calm and ready*

Let me out you motherfucker let me OUT I'll fucking bury you you hear me I fucking built this country let me back for one day.

He struck The Driver but The Driver did not mind the weak blows of flesh turned to mud because he knew that when the blood dried up the mud would turn into dust, and then, the blows stopped because the Old Man was crying. Dark filling the car, a dot of light in the windshield, and he understood that he was arriving on time. The cement in his throat cracking into aggregate that seeped out his mouth into finite debris.

*they're all busy buying it*

What do the other passengers do?

Some talk. Some cry to themselves. Some play games.

*we play the long game*

Tic tac toe flashed on the headrest; three xeses already placed in a row.

I think I'd like to think.

The Driver nodded and turned off the dial.

The Old Man was a quiet not spent since the womb and he thought of his Father, a cold man, and his Mother, cold too. A wife, a mistress, a child, and another. A life of collecting birthrights that unfurled to the next thing he would do. A life pre-destined that he never once questioned because he didn't see those who fell through the cracks. The air from the vents was getting colder.

The man you said was before me. Couldn't recognize a thing.

Not a thing.

Was he still scared?

They always are.

The car was slowing and it seemed brighter outside but it was not light because his eyes could no longer see, and then, the car had stopped moving and there were things younger than infants outside on the curb. And the Old Man knew where he was.

Can I just wait for a moment?

Just a moment.

All the things that were once his were now rolling off him. The windowed office, the cars, the photo albums, the night in his youth spent at a protest he never recounted when arguing with grandchildren. And he saw that they'd been long left behind, but now he was losing their weight and he wished he had better dealt out the remains. Too heavy to hold anymore, not his since getting into the cab. He looked outside again and saw that those waiting for him were very cold.

You have a nice night.

The Driver nodded.

The Old Man stepped out into the light and the dark was warm around him and his bones lost their aching, flattening out into small little planes and the little things around him entered into the car. Driving back from where he came because this ride goes one way.

# HOW LONG THIS WOUND

## ROBERT MICHAEL OLIVER

> At the National Mall's
> Vietnam War Memorial,
> January 30, 2022

To witness these names, begin
on May 25, 1968, after Tết:
PFC John H Anderson, Earl D
Barnhart Jr., James E Bates—
a month of body bags piled
in pyramids to sparring gods;
then take flight to war's end:
Richard Vandegeer, the pilot
of Saigon to the isle of Koh Tang—
blades sliced into sea and fish,
before the names start again:
Dale R Buis, Chester N Ovnard
sprawled on a movie house floor
in 1959; then return to Tết:
Sergeant Jesse C Alba crawled
like a nightmare onto the Wall.

Without reading their names—
we offer no trill nor flap to give
nuance, fricative nor plosive
to add passion, no red boots,
no roses tossed on a sepulcher,
no letter scrawled by a mom
in turquoise ink, no miniature
Stars and Stripes to celebrate
nightly body counts, no saved
villages with smoldering thatch,
no jungles turned orange with
cancer, no Cronkite to lecture
families on duty, on salutes

to generals lying to Johnson,
to Johnson lying to Congress,
lying to the wink of a people.

Listen to the grass bristle,
await a reply. The ants carry
ammo belts and pinkies over
twig bridges; swamps bubble
a symphony of corpses;
the face of a girl, stuffed in
a locket, is singed with flame;
earlobes are dropped in a shoe—
snake-eyes—twice; the spine
of a first lieutenant dangles
from a Hopea—the python
mimics its answer; the baby
bangs on the butt of an M-16
a charge into battle; mothers
crouch in a paddy dragging
their assassins through rice.

If only the armpit could out
think the brain, we'd sweat
more and war less: this feast
on femurs, foreheads, fibulas,
cleft chins, and six-packs
feed and grow thin. This war,
this other war—here, there
on the back of Africa, another
in the groin, in the belly of Asia,
on the face of Europe, on lips
bloody as a punch. How many
must surrender before the price
has been paid? How long must
we pray in this cut across a turned
cheek before the war trembling
under our kneecaps awakes?

# MY TRIP TO VIETNAM AND THE UNANTICIPATED SHAME OF BEING AN AMERICAN

LISA V. TERRY

*VIETNAM.* I do not recall a time when that word, that place, didn't mean some-thing to me. While growing up, it permeated every conversation in my house-hold like a petulant child demanding attention. As a war correspondent during the Vietnam War, on special assignment for *Time* magazine, my father's life was forever changed, and therefore mine. In 2024, which marked the 40th anniver-sary of the publication of my father's groundbreaking book, *Bloods: An Oral History of The Vietnam War by Black Veterans,* I found myself in Vietnam for the first time, paying homage to my father and his life's work. While I anticipated a range of emotions, I wasn't expecting a raw feeling of shame to be an American at a time when America is complicit in another genocidal conflict, this time in the Middle East. Upon returning home, I had never been more ashamed to be an American and more proud to be my father's daughter.

When my adult daughter and I touched down in Saigon, thoughts raced through my mind. This is where it all began. My father had been given a special assignment while at *Time* for a cover story on the role of the Black soldier in the war. It was the late 60s and race relations were tense—or, more accurately, volatile—in the United States. After his initial assignment, he was soon sent back for a two-year stint as deputy bureau chief, and it was then that he dis-covered his life's purpose. It wasn't glamorous work by any means: writing about a war that the world wanted to forget from the perspective of those who, at home and abroad, were treated as sub-human. Black Americans were facing racism on the home front and on the battlefield. At the age of twenty-nine, my father was poised to do almost anything. By then, he'd earned degrees from Brown University and Chicago and the title of "first" or "youngest" of many accomplishments. Youngest reporter ever hired by the *Washington Post*; first Black editor of an Ivy League newspaper; youngest president of the Capital Press Club. It was while visiting Hội An that he learned of the youngest soldier to die in the war: a sixteen-year-old Black kid from the South who lied about his age to enlist so he could send money home. That's what the military did back then: recruit young, poor, uneducated men, both Black and white, in exchange for the promise of a life they could not otherwise have. As my father wrote in the *Blood's* introduction, it was in that moment that he vowed to tell the story of the Black soldier "between the pages of a book." Fourteen years later, after 100 rejections, *Bloods* was published.

WHILE I WAS in Hội An, I imagined a young Wallace Terry walking the streets of the Old Town while his wife and three young children were living safely in Singapore. The decorative temples and colorful facades in this beautiful ancient town remain intact, unaffected by the war. I wondered whether any of the many Asian artifacts that adorned the walls and shelves of my childhood home were bought there and shipped home. But it was in Saigon where I most tried to connect with my now-deceased father. Having heard the word Saigon since I was a child, I find it a challenge to use the modern name, Ho Chi Min City. Curious about proper etiquette and so as not to offend, I asked a Tuck Tuck driver if it was acceptable for me to refer to his city as "Saigon." He assured me that it was not disrespectful and in fact, is preferred. Saigon is where *Time* had its office—at the grand Hotel Continental Saigon, which still stands as a historical landmark and is fully operational. Across the circle is the legendary Caravelle Hotel where only a couple years before my father's arrival, a bomb planted by the Vietcong had denotated. That didn't prevent courageous journalists—such as my father, Peter Jennings, and others—from continuing to sip their whiskey from the rooftop and report on the raging war.

As any good history museum should, Saigon's War Remnants Museum hit hard and unapologetically. There is no holding back to make visitors feel at ease. In fact, the opposite is true—the goal is truth-telling in all its gory details—much like the Holocaust Museum in Washington, DC.

Massive US tanks are parked in the courtyard on display before entering the building. Actual torture chambers, too large to be installed in the building, are transformed into experiential exhibits outside. Once you enter the building, visitors are presented with a choice of themed experiences, none of which are inviting. Nor should they be. My daughter and I chose not to ease our way in and started our visit with the worst, most deadly time in Vietnam's history. The black and white photographs of anguished faces of women, children, and the elderly—some dead and some alive—are seared in my memory. While I walked through the exhibits, taking breaks from both the emotional toll and the heat,

I couldn't help but think about the conflict that America was embroiled in 10,000 miles away. The horrific images of Palestinian women and children I've seen on social media during the past year—humans in unimaginable pain or torn to shreds—also haunt me.

I DONATED A COPY of my father's book to the museum which gave my daughter and me the honor of meeting with the director and staff. I then learned that the Vietnamese refer to the War as "the American War in Vietnam." And why not call it that? It was America's war; we initiated a war in their country. Westerners are innately accustomed to viewing conflict solely from our perspective, thereby inhibiting us from understanding another point of view, in particular, the point of view of the oppressed. I have been educated.

War remains "man's most terrible occupation" as my father wrote in *Bloods*. Forty years later, that sentiment sadly holds true. The atrocities committed against the Vietnamese civilians cannot be dismissed simply by declaring they occurred fifty years ago. As I read the extensive amount of documentation and gazed at the footage—trying unsuccessfully to turn away from the gruesome images—I realized there are striking parallels between the American War in Vietnam and the conflict in Gaza. Civilians were used as tools and objects of warfare; soldiers were instructed to kill innocents indiscriminately and, at least in the case of Vietnam, purposefully, as told in my father's book. In 1967, the Bertrand Russell Tribunal concluded that the "US government is guilty of genocide vis-a-vis the Vietnamese people." If you agree with the actions taken against Israel by the International Court of Justice and the International Criminal Court in 2024, history is repeating itself in Gaza. Yes, at the hands of the Israeli government but with the financial assistance, weaponry, and geopolitical muscle of the United States.

America is and may always be the world's superpower, but it has a long way to go before it can be labeled the world's moral authority. That award appears to belong to South Africa, which was among the first nations to accuse Israel of genocide and to bring an action to the ICC against Israel, with its infamous apartheid regime in the rear-view window. America has yet to get in line with a long list of nations speaking out. What is the value of power if you're on the wrong side of morality?

There is one thing, however, about my experience that gives me hope: at no time in my life was I so unaware of my race as when I was in Southeast Asia. I've lived in DC, one of the most liberal states in the US, all my life. I studied in Charlottesville, Virginia, and Nashville, Tennessee. I've traveled in Europe periodically for the past forty years since I was twenty years old. And in all of those places, I was keenly aware of my race.

However, in Southeast Asia, I was oblivious to it, whether in Vietnam, Cambodia, Singapore, or Thailand. My parents must have felt the same way after leaving the US in the late 60s with their three children in tow for my father's assignment. It was while there, in 1967, that they learned their son's godfather and civil rights leader, Martin Luther King, Jr., had been assassinated, which was a stark reminder that all was not well back home. Perhaps it was two years of living in that part of the world that influenced them to try to raise their children to be "color blind." If only more Americans held the same belief as the taxi driver in Singapore when on my trip, I asked about race and color in his country: "Why should it matter," he replied, "We are all human."

I FEAR that the Vietnamese man's words would fail to resonate in the United States. How did he come to embrace such an enlightened view of humanity; a simple yet powerful notion that reduces our vast and innate differences to one characteristic? Could the long-term impacts of the War have formed his belief? Or perhaps his view can be credited to Vietnamese culture which celebrates community and values such as contentment. Spiritual teachings and religious beliefs, with Buddhism being the primary among them, play a prominent role in Vietnamese society, influencing how citizens interact with one another and the world around them.

Capitalism, greed, the making of centi-billionaires, and the misconception of scarce resources in America serve as hallmarks of our society and inhibit us from being able to see each other as one. Our country is, and has been, going in the wrong direction since the 2016 election lifted the curtain on the simmering racism and xenophobia that characterizes our nation. However, America has overcome worse times in our brief history, and for that reason, I have faith that our country will eventually turn away from the current trajectory. I am wary, however, that a country that was founded on prejudice and subjugation based on race could ever embrace our collective humanity in the purest sense.

# MANIFESTO FOR JANUARY 17, 2025

SUNU CHANDY

Install the floating shelves in the closet. Make channa
dal for the first time in years. Warn your partner
you are getting restless. It might be helpful
to have a treat. She brings a Rose Ave strawberry
lychee donut. Or another day, maybe whitefish
spread on a za'atar  bagel. Ask E to bring a soda
home from work, add one spoon of bourbon,
and then, watch two hours of trash television. But only
two. But first try to read Oliver's second
book. Even if it makes you cry to think
of the reality of more limits. Reserve the new
South Asian queer novel  from the library. Start
to use the library again. Regularly. Read
the winning poet's poems about Palestine.
And memories. Try to believe the news
of ceasefire. Listen to four women poets
on the screen on a Thursday evening. The queer
love poem about language and misunderstandings,
nothing short of exquisite. Another poet was the one
who posted on social media about you both being
short-listed together, that time you won.
How did it feel? To finally have someone else,
strangers, believe in your work
in a different way. A new way,
a strange way. A way that doesn't matter
and does matter, both. Figure out summer
arts camp. Figure out the spices. Combine
the three half used bottles of chili pepper
flakes into one. Figure out where
to hang the pots and pans. Figure out where
to keep the clanging lids. Figure out if pest
control will or will not come today. Pick up Zadie's
book. Pick up Tania's book. Figure out the

temperature. The choice seems to be only
too hot or too cold. Confirm that the volunteer
babysitters for the meeting will be present.
Reserve the room for the meetings. Be here
now. Appreciate the warmth of the cinnamon
stick in the hot cider. The eucalyptus
scent of the exfoliating scrub. Soak
your feet as the day reaches towards night. Use the
jasmine lotion. Paint your own nails. Stay
somehow warm. Believe.

## ACTIVATED

SUNU CHANDY

> *"To acknowledge our ancestors means we are aware that we did not make ourselves, that the line stretches all the way back, perhaps to God; or to Gods. We remember them because it is an easy thing to forget: that we are not the first to suffer, rebel, fight, love and die."* – Alice Walker

During the solidarity sing
on January 25, 2025,
just days into this
I sat in the last pew. I slid in
next to someone I thought looked
familiar. Turns out it was her first
time coming to an activist
conference. With her three
teens and comfortable life in suburban
Maryland, in her words though, now
she's activated. She doesn't like where
this country is going and needs
to do something, be with others,
find her political home. Throughout
the service, we smiled at each other, rose up
when we felt moved by the songs.
We remembered the spirit of now-ancestor
Dr. Bernice Johnson Reagon, as we sang
movement anthems by Sweet
Honey in the Rock. These songs
we have needed always,
and need again now. *Ain't Gonna Let Nobody
Turn Me 'Round.* These activists
who left us a pathway, so that we
can all be here now. The depth,
the history, the pain of these songs
for Black freedom, and for all
of this nation to one day
be whole. As Alice Walker says,

we are not the first. This solidarity sing,
as necessary as air,
allowing the release of a week
full, of too many held tears.

# THREE GENERATIONS OF BLACK WOMEN AND A LOOK INTO AMERICA'S FUTURE

### BERNARDINE WATSON

My GRANDDAUGHTER, Naomi, was born in 2009 on the Fourth of July. At fifteen, she's a sophomore in the college-bound track at her high school. Naomi is a straight-A student who loves math and science, plays percussion in the school band, and sews costumes for the school drama club. She can also draw and has a lovely soprano voice. This past summer, when I asked what she wanted to do when she finished her schooling, she answered with confidence and without hesitation, "I want to be an astrophysicist." I stared at her and then quickly turned away so she wouldn't see the utter shock on my face. *This little Black girl wants to be an astrophysicist!*

A few days later, still astounded by my granddaughter's response, I typed the following question into my computer's search engine: *How many Black female astrophysicists are there in the United States?* A few seconds later, a headline from an article in the July 2023 issue of *Scientific American* appeared on my screen: *Only 26 Black Women Have Ever Become Astrophysicists in the US.* This information didn't shock me, but it raised a question in my mind. Did my granddaughter know the odds against her? Will she be able to achieve her dream?

Thinking about what the future might hold for Naomi, I began to reflect on the Black women who had come before her, specifically, my mother and me. How had my mother and I fared pursuing our dreams in this country? How had my mother's experiences been different from mine? Had America's laws, policies, and practices helped or hindered us? What does America's past tell us about what America's future might hold for our brilliant Naomi?

My MOTHER, Alice Hortense (Johnson) Hayes, is also especially on my mind these days since she died in October 2024 at the age of ninety-seven. Alice was born into a poverty-stricken family of thirteen children in 1927, just sixty-two years after the end of the Civil War in 1865. She grew up in Philadelphia where her parents migrated from Norfolk, Virginia.

In the South, where 90 percent of Black people lived before the 20th century, public schools designated for the former slaves lacked essential facilities and resources. African Americans worked primarily as sharecroppers, tenant farmers, and domestic workers. Extreme racial violence against Black people, such as lynching, beatings, and murder by the Ku Klux Klan (KKK) and others seeking to maintain white supremacy, was common. To prove their patriotism, between 1914 and 1918 close to 400,000 African American men, including my mother's oldest brother, fought for the country in World War I. Also, at the beginning of the war, thousands of African Americans, such as my mother's parents, began leaving the Southern states for the North and West to escape Southern oppression during what became known as the Great Migration.

However, those fleeing the South would soon find James Baldwin's reflection to be true: "They do not escape Jim Crow. They merely encounter another, not-less-deadly variety." In the northern and western cities, Black people still faced discrimination and racism. They worked primarily in low-paying menial jobs, tended to live together in poor urban areas, and often faced intimidation when attempting to exercise voting rights. Blatant disparities in educational opportunities created significant disadvantages for Black children. Also, the Great Migration of Black people from the South generated intense racial conflict. During the first decades of the 20th century, dozens of race riots broke out in northern and mid-western towns and cities, instigated by white people threatened by growing Black populations. In the 1920s, millions of northern whites opposed to Black equality joined the Klan, with African Americans the main targets of their violence. In 1926, a year before my mother's birth, an estimated 30,000 Klan members openly paraded in white masks, hoods, and flowing robes down Pennsylvania Ave in Washington, DC.

This is the America into which my mother was born two years before the Great Depression—a country where African Americans were violently denied citizenship while thousands of white, racist KKK members marched in full regalia down the main street of the United States Capitol. The description under my mother's picture in her 1945 yearbook from Bartram High, then a barely integrated school in southwest Philadelphia, read: "Al," as she was called, " ... beautiful voice, good student, library aide, Jay Bee staff, Honor Society." At a time when only 25 percent of the entire US population, 28 percent of white women and 8.5 percent of Black women over the age of twenty-five had earned a high school diploma, my mother, Alice, not only graduated from high school, but was in the Honor Society. She once told me that despite her grades and activities, no counselor or teacher at her high school ever talked with her about college.

After high school, my mother attended the Philadelphia Vocal Academy to study classical voice. She dropped out in the first year because she felt mistreated and because her family could not afford the tuition. She rarely spoke about that time in her life, but once told me, "An ordinary colored girl didn't stand a chance." In 1946, my mother married my father, Bernard, and they had five children. When I think about my mother now, I wonder if her life would have been different and her dreams "undeferred" had America been a different place.

I was born in 1951, the second of my mother's five children. At that time, the United States economy was booming because of the expansion generated by World War II. However, this prosperity didn't extend to most of America's Black citizens. Although more than one million African Americans fought in the Second World War, African Americans still faced oppression in both the North and the South. For southern Black people, violence and legal segregation still permeated daily life. In what's been called the "Second Great Migration," beginning in 1940, over five million Black people left the South to escape Jim Crow segregation and seek better opportunities in northern and western states. Still, they found themselves facing new challenges in overcrowded cities, including poverty, housing discrimination, inferior education for their children, and limited access to decent jobs.

Unfortunately, a century after emancipation and the decade of my birth, Black people were still seeking full citizenship in this country. In 1954, a case brought to the Supreme Court by the National Association for the Advancement of Colored People (NAACP) caused a monumental shift. Some sixty years after making "separate but equal" the law of the land, the Supreme Court reversed itself and ruled in the landmark case Brown v. Board of Education that racial segregation in public schools was inherently unequal.

The Brown v. Board of Education ruling helped inspire the American Civil Rights movement of the late 1950s and '60s. While the 1954 decision strictly applied only to public schools, the ruling implied that segregation was not permissible in other public facilities. The Montgomery Bus Boycott of 1957; the 1957 integration of Central High School in Little Rock, Arkansas that required federal intervention; the March on Washington in 1963; and the hundreds of sit-ins, marches, and freedom rides in the late 1950s and early 1960s were all designed to test desegregation laws. The purpose of the famous March on Washington in 1963 was to forcefully advocate for the civil and economic rights of Black people. The March is credited with helping to pass two additional major pieces of civil rights legislation: the Civil Rights Act of 1964, designed to end racial segregation in public places and forbid employment discrimination on the basis of race, religious affiliation or sex, and the 1965 Voting Rights act that outlawed poll taxes and literary tests, stating that American citizenship was the only requirement to vote in this country.

Brown v. Board of Education and the Civil Rights Act laid the groundwork for me to have educational opportunities that were not available to my mother in the 1940s. These rulings made it possible for me to attend the most selective public schools in my hometown of Philadelphia. Today, I still rely on the academic skills I received from that education. When the Johnson Administration's Great Society followed the Civil Rights Movement in 1964 and declared "war on poverty," I was able to use the increased federal dollars provided for higher education to become the first in my immediate family to earn a college degree. I am certain that the prestigious policy research firm, a government contractor, which gave me my first professional job in the 1970s, was influenced by then-federal support for affirmative action, which the Johnson administration first embraced in 1965.

I did not realize it at the time, but that first professional job, where my main task was to prepare proposals and concept papers, was where I would hone my writing skills and take my first steps toward my dream of becoming a writer. In fact, when I look back at the educational opportunities available to me in the 1960s and 70s, it seems like I, and other African Americans my age, slipped through a crack in American policy, which some have called a "second reconstruction." While Great Society policies and programs hardly remedied racism and inequality in the United States, they did at least acknowledge a debt to the country's Black citizens.

WHAT WILL Naomi's story be?

Given the struggles of African Americans since we were brought to this country in 1619 and indeed since our emancipation a century and a half ago, I'd like to be optimistic about my granddaughter's future and ability to achieve her dreams. In fact, if I were betting on Naomi alone, I'd say, *yes, she can* be an astrophysicist or whatever she wants to be. Naomi was not born into the American apartheid of the 1920s as my mother was. She was not born into poverty as I was but into a middle-class household with professional parents. She's intelligent and is an excellent student who excels in math and science. Shouldn't these characteristics be enough for her to thrive and achieve her dreams in America's future?

Since my granddaughter is Black, and like her great grandmother, me, a member of a historically oppressed and marginalized group in America, I can't answer this question with certainty. It seems that with the history I've outlined here, this country will once again need to take steps to acknowledge the impact of slavery, racism, and legal oppression on Black people.

At the beginning of this essay, I referenced an article in *Scientific American* that notes that there are only twenty-three female African American astrophysicists in the country. Another study in a June 2020 *Forbes* magazine states that since 2000, the percentage of Black Americans earning bachelor's degrees in physics has plummeted. According to this study, the reasons Black Americans aren't earning bachelor's degrees in physics and astronomy "isn't because they're unmotivated, uninterested, unintelligent, or incapable." Instead, the study concludes that there are two main factors that can improve the number of Black students, like Naomi, obtaining physics and astronomy degrees. Since these students will likely be the only ones in their classes that "looks like them," the first factor is a supportive, respectful environment where Black students feel like they belong.

The second factor the study mentions is financial support from the university or department, which allows these students not only to pay their tuition but also to take advantage of opportunities, such as conferences where they can present their research, meet peers and mentors, and feel part of the field. Both study findings sound like *policies and practices aimed at increasing the representation of particular groups in areas where they are underrepresented, such as in education or, employment,* or affirmative action, which was effectively ended by the Supreme Court in 2023. Also, creating welcoming, supportive environments for Black students in these overwhelmingly white areas of study will require at least decent race relations.

According to the research organization Statista, the future of race relations does not look good. In a 2022 report, they state, "While the use of such outwardly racist practices has long been outlawed, the relations between different racial groups in the US have still been defined as worrisome and worsening by many Americans, with little hope that things will get better in the future."

Will my granddaughter be able to achieve her dream of being an astrophysicist in America's future? Naomi will graduate from high school and start college in 2027. From what I can see today, I'd certainly bet on her before I bet on America to support her or other young Black girls trying to achieve their dreams. Black people are used to struggling, striving, and succeeding in this country with little societal support. I don't see new Civil Rights legislation, another "crack" in American policy to squeeze through, or the return of affirmative action in America's future. In fact, with the current attack on diversity, equity, and inclusion programs, it seems that America has no intention of paying its debt to African American citizens.

America seems to be going in the wrong direction in so many ways, including re-establishing barriers to voting, limiting women's reproductive freedom, banning books, and who knows what else is coming with the current administration.

Like I said, I'll bet on Naomi.

# WHEN HE SAID HE WAS HUNGRY

JAIME LEE JARVIS

*The household matriarch who insists on feeding visitors,*
*especially young ones*

If they are hungry
what can you do

*among the most enduring US stereotypes*

*he wasn't wearing pants*
*or shoes*

If you are hungry
what can you do

*I'm going to cut you*

you reach into the belly of your neighbor

*17-year-old boy who used to mow her grass*

*"a darn good job"*

even you, who have never missed a meal

*The boy eventually grew tired*
*and went into the kitchen*

*She also gave him two tangerines*

When you are afraid
what do you choose

*a neighbor had since given her a bat for protection*

you fight dirty when you're empty

*That's when she realized*

*Note: The poem's title and italicized lines are borrowed from an August 2023 story in* The Guardian.

# WHY NOW?
## HOMELESSNESS AND AMERICA'S FUTURE

### DEBORAH GILBERT WHITE

WHEN I THINK ABOUT the future of the United States of America, I am drawn to its past and present contradictions and the possibilities for what lies ahead. I have never been a flag-waver, and in all honesty, I have never felt the need or desire to do so. I doubt that I will ever get there.

I'm reminded of the journeys of my paternal and maternal ancestors, who traveled from Ocala, Florida, and Orangeburg, South Carolina, respectively, to find a better life in New York City. They were following the belief and the hope of so many other people identified at that time as "Negro" that a better life existed for them "up north" and away from the oppression experienced "down south." They would find work as domestics and a "nanny" and have other income opportunities that would allow them to survive and somewhat strive. I wonder about the moments when they may have had what they wanted or not, and the moments when they may have had what they needed or not. I do know that sacrifices were made and that they looked out for one another.

From time to time, I will study the black and white photos of my paternal great-grandmother in her Sunday best, and her daughter, my grandmother standing outdoors, possibly in a park, holding a white child in her arms, and my dad, her son in his early teens in his suit and hat posing for the camera in a photo studio, most likely in Harlem, New York. Never having conversations with them about their lives, I can only now try to piece together the stories I heard about their lives, including the struggles and triumphs they may have faced, knowing that their hopes and dreams served as the foundation for the ones I would hold.

In some way, I want to believe on a subconscious level that my destiny was tied to what they may have imagined for their oldest granddaughter, an extension of what each prior generation had imagined for themselves. Those pictures, a reminder, now reside in a cardboard box that I keep promising myself to frame in a collage and place on a wall in my home. That will happen in the very near future.

Although these family members are no longer here, their DNA and the generational memories embedded in that DNA of living life in the United States of America are now part of who I am. I feel so grateful to have known both of my great-grandmothers and my grandmothers. I have a vague memory of my maternal grandfather but never met my paternal grandfather. As I came of age, I began to have glimpses of what it meant to age in a big city, and in a country that placed such a heavy emphasis on youthfulness. I remember thinking as a young adult that New York City really wasn't a place for people identified as poor and people identified as old. This is as I watched my grandmother, living with cancer and limited income, struggle to pay her rent. I wish I had known then what I know now. I regret not being a better advocate for her.

Today, as a sixty-eight-year-old African American woman, the twists and turns and triumphs of life are upfront for me. Aging in the United States of America can mean feeling isolated, as your circle of family and friends becomes smaller the longer you live. Aging in the United States of America means fighting stereotypes, misinformation, and societal limitations based on your age. Aging in the United States of America can mean having to make the choice between getting your medications, food, or paying rent.

It has been suggested that a sea change is needed to perceptions regarding senior citizens and the meanings we make as a society about getting older. Yes, senior citizens live a quality of life along a spectrum, just like other sectors of society. Many of us do phenomenal things that defy the stereotypes, misinformation, and societal limitations that persist. However, today, part of the struggle of being identified as a senior citizen in the United States of America is the knowing that the life you have worked hard to create and maintain for yourself can change for various reasons, and often the change is out of your control, and at a time when there is a need for the most stability in your life. The loss of a job or spouse or the lack of comprehensive health insurance can be factors. I know this to be true because I experienced homelessness at the age of fifty-four with a PhD and a pension. Becoming homeless at fifty-four due to eviction, and turning fifty-five a few days after entering a women's shelter, made me realize how pivotal being fifty years plus is to keep employment, secure needed employment, and re-enter the job market after the loss of a job.

I spent a little over thirty days in a shelter, but before entering the shelter I slept on my brother's couch for nearly three months and spent one week at a motel paid for with a voucher from a nonprofit organization. My stay at the shelter was short because I had begun the process of drawing a lump sum from my pension before a bed was found for me. That decision allowed me to pay my rent for one year as I continued to seek full-time employment, and to remain housed. When the money hit my bank account, I received a call from a financial planner with the bank reaching out to discuss my portfolio. I was still in the shelter and was moving into my apartment the coming week. Today, I still ponder the contradictions in the transition. I was a homeless shelter resident with thousands of dollars in the bank.

It took me ten years to secure full-time employment that offered a livable income and viable health care that supported me in managing health issues (diagnosed after homelessness) and to become a homeowner again. I attribute some of this to ageism in the job market. I also attribute it to living in a capitalistic society that centers profit and cost over people. Younger workers and the then emerging movement toward a "gig" economy held different expectations from employers regarding pay and benefits. I knew the safety net of having good benefits, a pension, and a severance package.

The issue of homelessness and housing in the United States of America is a crucial one. I've learned that having housing is foundational to every other component of an individual's life. People are living longer, whether they are housed or unhoused. People in this country are "graying," and the outlook is not too good for far too many of them. The question becomes: How can we move toward a society that promotes and supports healthful aging, that is, helping seniors to remain productive longer in the job market (if they choose) and with a living wage, have more preventive health care options, and secure, safe, affordable housing?

One of the fastest growing sectors in society experiencing homelessness for the first time identify as senior citizens. Many seniors on fixed incomes face rising rents, insurmountable medical bills, and other life situations that increasingly put them at risk of homelessness. There is a lack of low-income, affordable housing across the country, resulting in limited housing options. If we factor in natural disasters, notably tornadoes, hurricanes, floods, and fires, the housing shortage becomes a real concern for many vulnerable people, and the country.

Housing and homelessness experts indicate that between the years 2009 and 2017, people experiencing homelessness aged 51-61 increased, and the number of people sixty-two and older doubled. I was evicted in 2011 and entered the shelter in 2012. As we look at the future of the United States of America regarding seniors and homelessness, it is predicted that the number of people sixty-five and older will triple in New York City and other homelessness hotspots by 2030. The stark reality is that many seniors do not have the economic stability to prevent homelessness. Another consideration points to those already experiencing homelessness and the protracted inability to provide permanent housing for the chronically homeless who continue to age surviving on the streets and in other uninhabitable spaces and places across the United States of America.

Every December 21, I am reminded of the people who live and die on the streets of this country without housing. Homeless Persons Memorial Day is observed on the winter solstice, the longest night of the year. I have participated in the planning and execution of the national online observance and its local observance in Washington, DC. Year after year the ages provided of the deceased who died without housing or not too long after receiving housing reflect senior citizens. Each year, I wish for the time that there will not be a list of people who died because of homelessness. If the predictors are correct, that wish is not coming to fruition anytime soon. The future of the United States calls for us all to have a role in bringing about the change needed. We must have a sense of urgency to do so.

Each one of us must become advocates to prevent and end homelessness and promote housing for all, particularly for the well-being of our country's senior citizens. And as seniors, we must advocate for ourselves by connecting with our local, state, and federal legislators. We must do what we have the capacity to do and connect with community groups and organizations working on our behalf. Let us find ways to share our experience and wisdom with younger people who want to make a difference.

Coming out of my experience with homelessness, I am now an active housing and homelessness advocate. I've been asked, "Would you be doing this work if you had not become homeless?" and the answer is yes. Most of my work focused on societal issues emerging from racial inequities in this country. I switched the emphasis to housing. The future of the United States of America calls for all of us to take a realistic look at its housing crisis and the realities of what the face of homelessness looks like.

## Why now?

Why now is the future—because what we do today sets our reality for tomorrow. Why now is the permission to imagine—because we *can* have a country where we don't pass homeless tent cities and encampments, someone's life belongings that have been put out on the street, or individuals and families sleeping in their cars. Why now is the call to action—because to end sheltered and unsheltered homelessness, we must find the will and the way to never leave housing insecurity and homelessness as a legacy to our children, as our memory DNA, or as our future.

Sources:

www.news.harvard.edu/gazette/story/2024/04/americas-graying-we-need-to-change-the-way-we-think-about-age/#

www.aarp.org/home-family/your-home/info-2022/americas-homeless-over-50.html

# AN EXERCISE IN SYNTAX

## DWAYNE LAWSON-BROWN

I owe taxes.

The government is making me pay back taxes.

The Federal Government is pressing me out about my back taxes.

The Federal Government is demanding that I pay from the money I earned working for The Smithsonian.

The Federal Government, which provided the funds for the work I performed via The Smithsonian, is demanding that I pay back taxes from those aforementioned funds.

The Federal Government, which covers a large footprint in Washington, DC, Maryland, and Virginia, is demanding that I pay back taxes from the funds that I earned, via the Smithsonian, which they also fund.

The Federal Government, which refuses to acknowledge the constitutional rights of residents of the District of Columbia, myself included, demands that I pay out of my hard earned wages made during the timeframe I provided outreach for the Anacostia Community Museum; an under-resourced Smithsonian site—which is also funded by the Federal Government.

The Federal Government, who backpedals on penalties for those who stormed the Capitol grounds but chased a teenage Dwayne for rollerblading in a public area—demands I pay back taxes while not acknowledging my constitutional rights as a US citizen living in the District of Columbia working for the under-resourced Smithsonian Anacostia Community Museum which happens to be funded by the Federal Government.

The United States Federal Government, which my mother has served for over 30 years as a patent clerk, demands that I, Dwayne Lawson-Brown, render taxes from the wages I earned providing outreach in an underserved and disenfranchised community for the Smithsonian Anacostia Community Museum; an under-resourced cultural center funded by the Federal Government—so that they can make weapons.

The United States of America Federal Government, that my great-grand-father died fighting for in World War II, demands that I pay out of the funds I should be using to pay my sons tuition, so they can sell bombs to a country that is blowing up hospitals.

The United States of America wants to tax me, a single father, working hard to co-parent and raise a Black gender-queer teen in a society that hates us, so that they can support a "war on terror" that violates international laws by bombing hospitals and air striking civilians along the Gaza strip.

The United States of America wants me to pay for bombs they will sell to murderers while my community goes to war with itself over money to pay bills, like the aforementioned back taxes.

The United States of America is forcing me, a Washington, DC native, who for the entirety of their life, has NEVER had proper representation in Congress or the Senate, to choose between my sons tuition, my mortgage, and groceries, so that I can fork over back taxes that will be used to make bombs, and surveillance drones, and body armor which will be sold to an occupying military force that is killing Palestinian civilians.

And the world is watching

As the innocent pay the cost in flesh

And the rich remain untouched.


The United States wants me to pay

But the price

Is too fucking high.

# FORK IN THE ROAD

## DAIEN GUO

THE EMAIL COMES at 9:30 p.m. but you don't read it until 3 a.m. you haven't been sleeping well anyway with two gaping canker sores just inside your lower lip, like the kind you used to get all the time in high school before chemistry tests and piano competitions, and you keep gnawing at them from the inside you can't stop the pain the pain but there's a sweetness inside when you flick your tongue over them so you keep biting—a fork in the road—almost poetic in a bad way and the next day at work everyone laughs about it though you see a woman crying on the Metro, there's fork in the road meetings and hushed coffee dates with old friends in the basement of Teaism where you show each other your phones to read funny emails from management but you brush off your kids' hugs at night and say you're sick and you don't want to get them sick and there's trouble at work, the ten-year-old asks what does that mean clear eyed and you realize he could understand it (maybe) but he shouldn't have to and you don't want him to, you don't want him to ever have a job or deal with HR trainings or taxes or performance reviews or vote in elections or go to weekly status meetings, you want to lock him up forever in that pointy attic room with his Lamar Jackson jerseys and Mario Kart posters and Lego sets, the way you have locked up a part of yourself forever and you're glad you did that, you never let them have all of you…keep for yourself the bittersweetness in the middle of the pain, the Chopin waltz you can still play at night when the kids are sleep, the poems you write that don't include language like "fork in the road" and the ability to sit in the corner and just look—where did all the potted plants in the conference room go? the new lady showed up the Tuesday after inauguration and she wears pearls and fitted black skirt suits and her mahogany curls look lovely tumbling over her shoulders; she has freckles and she doesn't wear much makeup; she might be a cool aunt but her expression freezes up when someone says something that scares her; she tilts her head slightly to the right when she looks at your boss like he's an exotic old bird who will soon be extinct.

## ENGLISH VOCABULARY: NEGATION

*noun. the absence of something*

CHLOE YELENA MILLER

Don't write what you don't want.

Two negatives make a positive; write that positive.

Write what you do want.

> *In Italian, two negatives don't make a positive.*

For example, don't write: Semi-automatic guns don't belong in our safe country.

> *But we live in America.*

Write: Our country. Our home.

# WORK/LIFE

## TRELAINE ITO

FOR THE PAST ELEVEN DAYS, every morning before I head to work, I practice two words in the mirror.

*I quit.*

I say them out loud like an incantation, summoning the courage to repeat those exact words in person to my boss (or, at least, write them in an email to my boss).

The decision to quit your job, while so common considering how many people quit their jobs every day, is dramatic in the Shakespearean sense because of its effects, both foreseen and unforeseen, which crescendo in increasingly more drastic and irrevocable changes to your life. The shift from employed to unemployed is much like the released tension caused by two competing tectonic plates that accumulate friction and pressure until something gives and the whole world upends itself. Nothing is quite the same afterward, even if rebuilt to mimic the beforetime.

For example, your entire morning routine would be off. For years, every Monday through Friday, your alarm would ring, the same alarm that has gone off every morning at exactly 6:00 a.m. You turn it off quickly so as not to wake your husband (who allows himself to sleep in because he stays at the office longer). You get out of bed, do your morning stretches (a lazy attempt at amateur yoga mostly meant to wake your muscles up), brush your teeth, wash your face, and pick out an outfit, all while listening to a precise sequence of news podcasts – *NPR News Now*, *Up First from NPR*, *The Daily*, and *Post Reports*. (Ten years ago, it was just NPR but on the actual radio; since then, you've expanded your audio catalogue.) It is now 6:45 a.m., and you make your morning coffee and a bowl of steel-cut oatmeal with chia seeds, cinnamon, and honey. You scroll through *The New York Times* app on your tablet (again, ten years ago, it was a physical copy, but you decided to go digital for the environment). Then, you wake your kids up and get them ready for school. It's now 7:30 a.m. Your kids have gone to the bus stop, and you can now start your commute to work. Suddenly, the realization hits you, and you stop. Because you have nowhere to go. You quit your job.

Repeat the same thought experiment for your after-work routine. And then envision the giant gap in your day that you now need to fill with hobbies or books or television shows because you no longer have a nine-to-five. Even once you get a new job, your routine will inevitably be different. Maybe just subtly, but still never quite the same. You'll drive to a different office building. You'll have new coworkers (and you likely won't see your old ones very often, if ever again). Your responsibilities, the size of your desk, your lunch spots, all will be unfamiliar until they become new routines. But that can take years.

Routines keep my days structured. Without them, I'd be lost. And there's nothing more routine than a federal job.

Still, I feel compelled to quit, to brave the wandering wilderness (if only for a few months, hopefully) because the alternative—staying—would be unbearable. Not only because of the increased workload imposed by an indiscriminate hiring freeze, unjustifiable (in my opinion) considering how long the federal hiring process often takes. I've heard stories about prospective employees who, after a months-long interview and vetting process, were given offers that were then rescinded. And that's only the people who would have started in late January. We were told to pull down all of our open job postings and to divvy up the extra work amongst the existing team members. (And my division, the Public Information Office, has been down three people since the fall.)

Recent hires (anyone in their one-year probationary period) may lose their jobs. Anyone working on "Diversity, Equity, and Inclusion" may lose their jobs. And here, at the Census Bureau—where our mission is "to serve as the nation's leading provider of quality data about its people and economy," this includes equitably capturing data about diverse communities across the country, ensuring that all people are included—who knows how many career staff fall into that overbroad category.

The staffing issues aside, the policies imposed by this new administration also make staying untenable. I imagine how I might repeat the incantation to my boss. I would pronounce each word not as forceful declarations but as conspiratorial whispers, as if we were sharing a secret.

*I quit.*

*Why?* would be her inevitable response. (Or, more likely, *Why now?*) And for that, too, I've practiced my speech:

I know this isn't the best time. And I am sorry about that. But it feels like so much of our work is under attack right now. And, honestly—and I know you feel this yourself—I'm ashamed to be a part of it. Because we saw this coming.

And now, what? We just accept that this is our reality? Can you imagine what our predecessors would say if they were here? The Constitution says 'whole number' of persons. *Whole number*! Not 'a portion.' Not 'a select few.'

And we're supposed to test out different ways to count citizens, to give this discriminatory policy a veneer of legitimacy, even when its ultimate goal is to limit the enumeration of whole persons in this country. We can ask the question: 'Are you a US citizen?' We can collect other types of data that get at the same information. But in the end, we don't want to just know who is a citizen and who's not. They are going to use that data across the federal government to allocate funding for communities in need. To apportion congressional representatives. *To limit representation in a democracy*! There's no more fundamental aspect of a representative democracy than representation.

And I'm using '*we*' here to refer to all of us at the Census Bureau. But I (and you) know we're not the ones driving this. Our political leaders in the Department and their political handlers in the White House have directed us to circumvent conventions and norms, to defy research and best practices, all for partisan ends.

And it's my job to talk to the press and the public about these changes. To make our research and findings understandable to the everyday person so they understand that our new policies aren't driven by politics. 'It's about accuracy,' I'd have to say. But that's not true! It's as much about politics as it is about power.

And it's my job to triage reporters' questions. And questions from civil society. To give them timely, accurate, and trust-worthy answers. Not ones that obfuscate or hide the truth!

And what happens when I lose my credibility? With re-porters like NPR's Hansi Lo Wang or with our national partners like The Leadership Conference, with whom I've spent years building relationships. When I lie to them for the first time, what then? When they call out the inconsistencies between what the Bureau says and what it does, what then? When no one believes what we say, and so they don't under-stand what we're doing, what then? Confusion and distrust and, possibly, fear, that's what.

And I know it would be a loss to leave. For you and the team. But I've been here for sixteen years. 2030 would've been my third decennial census. Given everything, I just can't stay and do this work with a straight face. I don't want to be a part of it.

IT'S A LONG SPEECH, I'll admit. Longer than the allotted time for my hypoth-etical meeting with my boss. But I would sound perfectly indignant the entire time. Self-righteous, even. And then I would hand in my letter of resignation, clear my desk, and drive home invigorated by the cleaner air in the moral high ground.

I'm neither naïve nor young enough to believe that my single resignation would start a movement. That my colleagues—fellow career civil servants who have devoted themselves to the mission of our agency, one spelled out in plain lan-guage in the Constitution—would follow my lead and leave. (I'd hope that they would, though.)

But when I'd arrive home, the gravity of my decision would settle, conjuring up questions both logistical and philosophical.

*How will I pay my mortgage?* I have modest savings, but not enough to sustain me beyond a handful of months.

*What, in this moment, does it mean to quit?* As in, what will be its ultimate effect? On the one hand, it may slow down some public affairs activity. A press release might go out a couple of weeks later than planned. Or a reporter might go unanswered. But would it stop the core defilements to the agency's mission that my departure was meant to protest?

*Was this the best way to register my protest?* What could I have done instead? Voice my opposition from the inside, for one. Slow down the work. Be a whistleblower. Bide my time until better leadership arrives, even if that means laying low for years.

*Should I have stayed?* At least until I found a new job. And to keep the institutional knowledge there, in the event that normalcy returns to the agency.

*How do I apply for unemployment?* And health insurance on the marketplace?

The questions would keep coming as I walk through the threshold of my home, setting my car keys on the kitchen counter. Then, I'd sit on a stool and hyperventilate.

*I quit…*

I know I shouldn't do it. It would be incredibly irresponsible. For one thing, I have a family. My husband, an adjunct professor at American University who lectures on polarization and domestic extremism, fears for the future of academia, which has been a frequent target of this Administration's displeasure. His job, while secure for the moment, is far from solid. Our two sons are in elementary school. They'll go to college one day, and we need to save for that. They may not be able to rely on programs like Public Service Loan Forgiveness or Work Study. My parents might eventually need assistance in the near future. Having spent decades as public school teachers, they remained devoted to their jobs for far too long, driven either by the yet-to-be-realized potential of their students or a commitment to the craft of education. Or both. But now they are feeling the full effects of their union's waning power. Their salaries haven't kept up with the rising cost of living. Their pensions will barely keep them afloat in retirement. And with the future of Social Security and Medicare in doubt, they might be the first generation without a safety net, returning to an era when parents relied on the largesse of their children to keep them out of poverty in their twilight years.

Weighing the smallness of my personal show of resistance against the tsunami of knowable and unknowable consequences, quitting doesn't seem viable. But neither does staying.

This morning, I've skipped reading *The New York Times*, choosing instead to consider quitting. I haven't talked to my husband about it, afraid that his analytical tendencies would lead me toward staying. ("Have you really thought this through?" he'd ask, almost like an accusation, a missing "even" hidden within his question.)

It's 7:30 a.m., and as I walk to my car, I practice the words again.

*I quit.*

But I feel no more or less courageous than yesterday or the week before. *Tomorrow*, I say to myself. *Tomorrow, I'll do it.* Before I can start the ignition, I get a series of messages from a former colleague.

> **Off the record, will the Administration use citizenship data to enforce mass deportations?**
>
> **I'm sorry if you don't know, but that's what I'm hearing.**
>
> **Is that even possible? These days, I don't even know anymore.**

Luckily, they were sent to my personal cellphone. But I already know that when I get to work, my work email will be flooded with these and similar questions, all tinged with either fear or confusion. And my response will be some variation of the stock language provided by the Department's leadership: "The Census Bureau is committed to providing complete and accurate information about our country's citizens and economy." The altered word will not go unnoticed, its implications more threatening by the allusion.

*I quit.*

The fault line where the decision to stay meets the decision to leave builds an unsustainable amount of friction, threatening release if one or the other doesn't give. Waiting for the inevitable violent shaking, I project a level of calm that hides the churning emotions beneath my surface. I'm surprised that the earthquake hasn't arrived sooner. That is until I realize that I'm the one holding the two tectonic plates together, both maintaining the status quo and leaving my future in limbo.

*I quit.*

Maybe today will be the day. If not, I will continue to practice those words tomorrow.

## ACTIVIST'S RETREAT

### YERMIYAHU AHRON TAUB

TODAY, I will not watch the news. I will not listen to the radio. I will not browse or descend into my doomscroll. I deliver this staccato not as declaration, but as aspiration, goal posts jitterbugging in my haze-daze of blue. Markers of a possible world. Fireflies flickering in the dread of democracy's dusk. I will have the good fortune, the luxury of so doing ... for now, at least. This garret is not under attack. The invaders aren't (yet) here, although their emissaries have been active. And who knows when... So yes, the luxury of turning off. Tuning out.

For so many do not have such a luxury. Cannot afford to. What with the bombs dropping everywhere. With supply lines being cut off. With the invaders coming so you must run to find shelter, to escape. Only to where? On one moonless night you dreamed of flying away on the iridescent wings of a drone. Crone on a drone. Only you must find food. Remember the chicken couscous you once spent hours getting just so? Remember the date treats—how no oven was needed? And the baklava... Is that rose water you smell in the smolder? Remember the burgundy damask settee in the once-parlor where you received the luminaries of the streets? Now is not the time to remember. Yesterday, you thought you saw a shredded patch of that damask caught between the rocks and the smithereens of your once-neighborhood. But when you reached for it, it was gone. There has to be a way of getting water. A working toilet, if not toilet paper. Insulin? You've heard J has a connection. Avoid that road—what's left of it—they say it's littered with landmines.

Today, I will not make a donation. I will not drum up support. I will not sign the petition. I will not knock on doors. Not write to my congressperson. Not attend this meeting. Yes, I organized it, but I never promised I'd go. S can chair it. It'll be in good hands, you'll see. I've written the agenda. P can take the minutes. The essential labor of those far from cataclysm. Who will cauterize as they can. With talking. Giving and taking. Hopefully, more giving than taking. Today, I will not inveigh against the news that is not the enemy of the people, even if it could do more for the people. The heads talking. The sets gleaming. The ideas that ought to have been aired.

Today, I will not embark on an excursion into the forest. I will not go on a hike to the peak where the convergence of three states can be seen. I will not walk along the water's edge, wondering when the steel heavens will burst, when the waters from above and below will link. Today, I will not play with my neighbor's beagle, frolicking with him in the park. I will not fly a kite, revel in red and yellow soaring into blue. I will not make pumpkin pie, even though the day would surely benefit from it, from spices suffusing the stratosphere. Yes, there can be cinnamon again someday.

Today, I will not constructively clean the dust clotting the pages of my anti-imperialist tomes. I will not speak to the solutions that I won't be offering. Or the action I won't take. I won't speak of restoration or rejuvenation. Or lessons learned. I won't comment on the tangled tango of my privilege.

Today, I will not...

Today, instead, I will lower my eyelids. I will be still. I will reach into leafy. I will sit on the straw floor mat. Only occasionally will I move. I will be aware of but apart from my advantages. Even if only for the duration of this extended moment. I will listen to the bells in my ears that never cease tolling. Resisting ragged, I will heed my breath, air entering and leaving. Call and response. Call, pause, and response. Light through and through the whoosh of the whisper of waves. Within. I will feel the time it takes. Or rather, my skin will. Sometimes the cycles will change shape and size and color. Yes, there will be lavender cycles. And ones in that old favorite: sea foam. There are bound to be. Chest rising and falling. The miracle of God's movement. Or what others call.... Only the neighbor will observe the noiselessness of my stance. Only later will I realize that she muted her radio, source of news of the relatives who couldn't get out, of her only son ensnared in Armageddon's net. Only the yellow eye slits, the twitching ears of her black cat seated next to the potted geranium on the fire escape ledge will detect the creep of shadows around the lotus position of my oblivion.

Today, I will not...    . *Only today.*

Tomorrow, I will return to...

# TO THE WHITE SUPREMACIST WHO CALLED ME A BREEDING VESSEL FOR THE HISPANIC INVASION

HEATHER L. DAVIS

First of all,
    I have never been
        anyone's vessel.
I am not empty. No one fills me,
    because I was born
        complete.
Second, I don't breed
    like a farm animal.
        With my brown-skinned husband,
the child of immigrants,
    we create smart human beings
        so multifaceted
they will blow your shackled mind.
    A combination of Filipino
        and European blood,
they are the future,
    because mixing it up
        makes us strong, paints
my family a bright new shade of sun.
        Third, your wet dream of a white planet
        is fucking boring, a nightmare
destined to fade away like the taste
    of rotten milk in a shocked mouth.
        Take a look inside:
You are the empty space desperate
    to be filled. You are the invasion,
        trying to burn down
everything that is not you. But it's
    too late. Turn your eyes
        to the distance. See
it rising, rolling: a tsunami of children
    knowing their worth, feeling
        their strength—

their yellow-white hands,
        their red-brown hands,
                their pink-black hands—
like water, the color
        of everything, washing
                your tiny flames away.

# BECAUSE YOUR HEALTH IS THE MOST IMPORTANT THING

## KRISTINA TABOR

THE NEEDLE FELT COLD, and the plunger pressed the syringe. Not quite pain-less, the shot sent a channel of whatever into my veins. They said BioAssure was made of tiny microchips. I imagined the miniature technology floating in my blood, and somewhere a screen blinking on: in a basement in Washington DC or a call center on the other side of the world. Somewhere my bio data would always be accessible to whoever happened to be in the room or whatever broke into the secure cloud. Don't be paranoid, I thought, trying to shut out all the research I'd done on this drug before agreeing to it.

"You look a little pale," the doctor said, sticking a band-aid over the too-tiny-to-see hole she'd made in my arm. "Do you need a glass of water?"

"She's fine," Brian said from a chair across the room, an open *Highlights* mag-azine on his lap. Jack pointed to animals in a jungle scene and chimped, "Oooh-ooh ahh-ahh."

I needed to get out of my head. This shot was for our family, to keep my job, to make life easier, and—like the mantra—"Because your health is the most important thing." BioAssure's jingle was an earworm, in a confident, reassuring female voice that convinced 80 percent of the population to get the shot. With a 99 percent guarantee to stay well through every sick season, no matter how bad it got, on the surface, this felt like money well spent. But behind it all, I was nervous about what this "miracle drug" would do to me and to the little baby girl growing inside my belly.

"YOU'RE TAKING TOO MUCH sick time," my boss had said, calling me into his office.

My brain was still fogged with the latest rhinovirus wending its way around our house. Giving it a moment to settle in, I decided to try to laugh it off. "Yeah, we call Jack 'Mister Germ-y,'" I said, making quotation marks with my fingers, "because he's so sick all the time." Internally, I rolled my eyes at the dumb joke.

"Okay, the kid is sick," he pushed back his rolling office chair a few inches, putting distance between us. "My kid gets sick, too. I don't care if you need to work remotely when he's home from school, clock in a few hours of sick time." I thought about his son, a sixteen-year-old with a car. My eyes involuntarily looked at the photo on his desk where the two stood chummy, wearing similar high school varsity jackets. "But also, you can't take off when you're sick. There's no excuse anymore. Get the damn BioAssure already."

BioAssure made everyone well, and I wanted to be not-sick as much as the next person. But it was also an expensive drug, one not covered by our insurance. This response from my boss came after months of endless illnesses in our house, which Jack picked up at daycare. Brian and I had gotten used to the toddler's red noses, empty tissue boxes, and the smell of Vicks VapoRub. I dragged myself to work hopped up on Tylenol Cold, Ricolas, and peppermint tea. Yet, according to attendance records, I didn't show up enough for my old-school boss, who believed work didn't get done unless it happened under his nose at a desk.

"I can't believe you haven't taken care of that yet," said my cubemate Sadie. Single, she didn't have to pay for daycare or a mortgage. She supplemented her equally lousy income with an allowance from her parents. She rolled into work with bags under her eyes and snuck to the toilet too frequently, probably to get a hit of cocaine or Candy Crush on her phone or both.

I also made frequent trips to the bathroom in the second trimester of my second pregnancy. There, I doom-scrolled, obsessing over BioAssure, the drug that some people called "humanity's silver bullet." Others called it a big, fat lie. The accusations online included claims that the pharmaceutical company manufactured its data to boost positive results—to a big movie star who insisted it shrank his cock. I got lost in Reddit's conspiracy theorists who pointed to links that looked like real research and photos of it turning people's toenails green, which was obviously ridiculous. Showing that one to Sadie, she said that I needed to switch off the noise, that it was all a bunch of bullshit, and BioAssure worked for her, so, of course, it worked for everyone.

She must have known it came off as a little harsh because that afternoon she snuck out to get me an almond milk triple decaf cappuccino, which she left on my desk with a Post-it peppered in Sharpie hearts. Together, we were comrades: office drones with bad health insurance. The difference was that Sadie could afford nice coffee and BioAssure thanks to her parents' bank account.

When I thought about it, with the long brown hair that cascaded straight down her curved back, she resembled that young woman in the BioAssure ads seemingly on every billboard, emblazoned across every bus side in town. Envision two pictures side by side: one a fevered twenty-something with bedraggled hair, a dour look, and surrounded with shadows; the other: the same woman, sparkling with a neat swab of coral blush on both cheeks, looking confident and completely well. "Because your health is the most important thing," plastered everywhere, with the glowing logo for "BioAssure" underneath.

Despite my fears, despite the cost, I wanted to be that woman: the one who wasn't sick all the time, the one who got in trouble with the boss for being a little late rather than taking what seemed like too many sick days, the one who worried less about monthly bills and baby vomit.

That night, Jack went down early, and Brian dimmed the overhead lights during dinner, calling it romantic. We traded stories about work that day, but when it came to my boss's BioAssure quip, he got impatient. "Okay, okay, I'll rework the numbers. Maybe we scale back student loan payments. Maybe we skip vacation for a couple years," he said, fiddling with his napkin. "Can we just enjoy this rare evening alone?"

A few hours later in the bedroom, he pulled on his boxer briefs and climbed into bed with the computer. I cleaned myself up in the bathroom while he spoke through the door. A few changes in expenses, he said, and we could afford BioAssure in the end.

One of the most suspicious qualities about BioAssure was the fact that, despite demand, there was never a shortage of the thing. There was no wait to get the shot. We made an appointment for the following week. The receptionist swiped our debit card, and we signed at the bottom of just three pages of paperwork. The doctor gave us each an injection of microscopic chips that "painlessly massage the body's nerve endings." In the waiting room, Brian told me how he hoped it would even resolve his migraines.

It worked. For me, an old running injury disappeared. BioAssure fixed my persistent morning sickness, even the swelling in my fingers and feet at the end of the term. Pregnancy was almost easy. Though I couldn't avoid gaining 30 pounds. BioAssure is smart, but it isn't that good.

Of course, Jack was still sick all the time. BioAssure isn't for kids until they've reached puberty, which meant long nights of rubbing his back, bringing him ice chips, and waiting it out. I was okay with that: BioAssure might have worked out for us, but after all that doomscrolling, I wasn't ready to pop microchips into my angel-faced baby boy. I tried not to think of what it was doing to the growing baby in my belly. When the thought intruded in my head, my pulse raced, and I had to sit down to do my breathing exercises.

"I hate to say I told you so," my boss said, sitting so close to me I could smell post-lunch onions on his breath, "But can't you see it too? You're so much more focused now you're on BioAssure." He had moved me to a bigger cube, closer to his office. I still ran into Sadie in the ladies' room. She moved on to topics like wondering how she could afford daily Starbucks after her parents cut back her allowance.

"Maternity leave," she said. "That's like a long, paid vacation, right? Lucky." This was my second child, and I had no illusions of it being a walk in the park. A newborn is a lot of work, even without getting sick all the time.

"That desk will look awfully empty without you here," my boss worried, asking almost daily for a reminder of how soon I'd be gone. "I'm not sure we can stick it out without you for another three months. Couldn't you think about coming back early this time?"

I didn't have the brain space to take on his concerns. I was too worried about what BioAssure might be doing to the baby. My imagination took it to the extremes, giving me nightmares about a super-infant. One had fire-resistant skin, waking in a crib surrounded by flames. Another fell off a footbridge to the bottom of a river, only to rise again with gills on her neck. These mutant children haunted me.

Annie arrived right on her due date. The BioAssure helps with initial contractions, but they recommend neutralizing it during labor so the body can do its thing naturally. Another injection, and gradually my body started to ignore the microchips. First, I felt an ache across all my muscles from the tips of my toes to the top of my head. Then, like electricity, it hit me. I'd forgotten what pain felt like.

When I screamed, Brian turned up the music, massaged my feet.

Was it my imagination, or did the attending nurse interrupt more than necessary? "I see you're on BioAssure," she said. "Always makes it harder on the mamas. Shock to the system and all that."

I tried to smile but felt another contraction come on. Then she said, "Last month, BioAssure announced it's finally safe for little ones. Think of that: a baby without jaundice or roseola or even gas keeping them up at night."

"Wait, what?" I said, distracted by the swelling of pain.

"It's not genetic, you know. They can't get BioAssure just because you've had it. But now there are injections for the baby, given in their first week of life. Those little nerve massagers are a-ok if the kiddos are still pretty new," she said, absently flipping through my chart again. "So, you'll need to decide quickly if you want in."

Grinding and burning my abdomen, the contraction was at full pulse at this point. "Am I really supposed to make that decision right now?" I looked at Brian and said, "How is this the first time anyone at the hospital thought to bring this up?"

"Well now or within 24 hours of delivery," she shrugged. "Think it over. There's paperwork."

With the stabbing in my tailbone, I shifted to concentrate on breathing. The nurse faded into the background as I rode a wave of pain. Once it ebbed, Brian showed me the materials the nurse left behind, a glossy brochure for new parents. Data connected child wellness with fewer nights of missed sleep, followed by years of academic achievement, a lower risk of obesity, and smaller chance of divorce. Of course, the collateral was emblazoned with the trademark catchphrase: "Because your health is the most important thing." The paperwork was nothing like the simple three pages we filled out to get the shot; the liabilities we'd write off in this agreement were nearly twenty pages long. The contract came with a folder from BioAssure that showed quotes from the *Journal of New Pediatric Medicine*, reporting successful trials of Taiwanese babies over the last two years. Apparently, it had rolled out globally to the public just last month.

Another contraction came on. I did not have the brain space to think about it again until Annie was born, and I finally got a few moments to myself in the shower.

FEET SHEATHED in rubber-bottomed hospital socks and wrapped in a terry-cloth robe, I stepped out of the bathroom with my hair in a towel. Brian tapped a pen, a habit I found annoying, stopping when I entered the room. "It's done!" he said.

"You finished filling out the paperwork? Can I look at it?"

"No, Annie got the injection a few minutes ago." He held out the clipboard like a trophy. "BioAssure was expensive for the both of us—but good news! It turns out when given at birth, it's covered by my health insurance!"

Brian was positively glowing. How had roles reversed so quickly? I felt the blood drain from my face. "Why couldn't this wait until we talked it over?"

"The attending doctor needed to go off shift. He's the only one certified to give BioAssure at this hospital. We had to get it now or wait another decade or so."

A nurse came in to take our vitals. "Great choice on the BioAssure. Just think how strong you're making this little lady," she said, listening to the beat of Annie's tiny heart.

I tried to calm myself and pulled on clean yoga pants and tank top, the loose and comfy post-labor clothes from my pre-packed bag. All the pregnancy books say what to bring to the hospital. They even provide a checklist so you won't forget anything. I trusted those books. But I also believed everything I read on-line about BioAssure, every contradiction and conspiracy theory. All the research, all the ridiculous gossip, the evening news calling it the most amazing discovery since Penicillin, conspiracy Reddits saying it was all fake news, the photos of green toenails and shrunken penises. It was impossible to tell up from down on the internet these days, so I believed it all.

My eyes locked with the nurse's, hoping for reassurance to quiet my concerns. All she said, cradling Annie in one elbow, was, "After all, her health is the most important thing."

# TERRESTRIAL DIVIDE
## ONE ACT ROMANTIC COMEDY
### LISA JAN SHERMAN

## CAST

CARPATHIA: Confident, Passionate, Graceful, Urgent 40-50 F

BRUTUS (BEING #3): Cautiously Desperate, Handsome 25-30 M

BEING #1: Rock or Sponge-like, Happy

BEING #2: Many Appendages, Dramatic

DARKVOICE (Voiceover only): Deep, Electronic, Emotionless

## SCENE 1

2 gray "rooms" separated by an opaque vertical divide. There are some (fist size) shapes cut out in various areas.

3 blocks for seating on both sides. Stage Right is Dark.

> *Stage Left, CARPATHIA is barefoot, wearing a diaphanous blue dress.*
>
> *She sits in an intense beam of light, her hands cover her eyes with a small pillow.*

CARPATHIA
Must I do this now?

DARKVOICE (O.S.)
(long outward groan) UHHHHHH.

CARPATHIA
So quickly?

DARKVOICE
EXIST.

CARPATHIA
I understand. Or they'll be no dancing.

> *Beam of light fades. Slow moving "disco" dots of colors swirl around her.*
>
> *Stage Right, Three shadowy BEINGS move, mumble, cough, laugh, cry.*

DARKVOICE (O.S)
HALT THIS.

CARPATHIA
Please everyone, stop.

> *She presses a button, colors disappear, quiet, movement stops.*
>
> *Lights up on CARPATHIA*

CARPATHIA (CON'T.)
Congratulations, it's just the three of you, and me.

> *LIGHTS flash.*
>
> *MUSIC plays similar to vintage "Dating Game" show.*
> *Stage Right, Three BEINGS are seated.*
> *Their unique features highlighted.*
>
> *BEING ONE is round, rock or sponge-like.*
>
> *BEING TWO has extra appendages from torso to neck.*
>
> *BEING THREE has large, long, pink ears. Music fades.*

CARPATHIA
I've captured enough information about your diverse body temperatures, and how they may complement mine. You display courage, in continuing...to exist.

> *BEINGS Applaud.*

CARPATHIA (CON'T.)
This is new for all of us. Along with the guidelines set by our Carriers, it's challenging, yet, exciting, right?...(silence) Hello? Hello?

> *BEINGS make excited noises, yodel. Repeating, "Hello Hello"*

CARPATHIA
Here we go! Being One, please sing a song about what you want in life, what would fulfill you now, and make you happy in a future...with me.

BEING ONE
*(sings quickly) JOT JOT JOT Puddly Doo-dot.*

> *BEING TWO snorts. Its appendages flap, flail, stomp.*
> *BEING THREE Stands, gives a smack to ONE'S head area.*

**BEING THREE**

Use your head translator, she doesn't understand all that twattle.

**CARPATHIA**

That seemed impatient, and brutish. And using twattle with a "T" is archaic. I think you meant twaddle with a "D." I've not come this far to deal with more arrogance or intimidation as in—

**DARKVOICE (O.S.)**

(loud groan) UHHHHHHHHHHHH.

*BEING ONE types coder on his head area.*

**BEING ONE**

Now I try again.

*CARPATHIA readies to dance.*

**BEING ONE**

(quickly) *I just want a pit and pot and hug me too, how about youuuuu?*

**BEING THREE**

Well, that was worth the wait.

**CARPATHIA**

Very short and sweet. Hug you too, Being One.

*BEING TWO waves all appendages, claps, bird calls. Types on his head.*

**BEING TWO**

Nexto, Nexto.

**CARPATHIA**

Yes. If that's Being Two, please sing about me and you.

*BEING TWO stands, appendages sway methodically.*
*CARPATHIA dances.*

**BEING TWO**

(slow, dramatic) *Hands, my hands, Arms my arms, Aroooooound you...Profooooound you fell for meeeeee,*

*BEING THREE bends his rabbit ears down.*

BEING TWO (CON'T.)
*like a treeee, used to beeeee, growing back... when we were free.*

> *CARPATHIA applauds.*

CARPATHIA
BEING TWO, though my tears are damaged by ultraviolet radiation, I think you made me cry. I miss trees. When I was a child, my brother and father built a tree-fort in the branches of, a last, majestic Oak. I would climb it, disappear. The scent was fresh with warmed wood, peace—

DARKVOICE (O.S)
UHHHHHHH. Time.

> *BEING TWO types on head.*

BEING TWO
Have I more.

> *HIS arms sway again, sings*

BEING TWO
*Peace as you climb up my warm wood.*

CARPATHIA
Nope! (BEING TWO stops) You know what they say about "too much of a good thing"?

BEING TWO
Beg you, last encounter—last encounter.

DARKVOICE (O.S.)
UHHHHHHH.

BEING TWO
End here now!

> *BEING THREE Stands, types on his head.*

BEING THREE
Dear, I'm not sure I can follow those romantic renditions by the others.

CARPATHIA
Being Three, you sound a bit more humble now.

BEING THREE

These utterances and words are new to us all. I'd like to give this a close enough to spit try, to convince you of a limitless future. You are a specimen movement to me.

*Types on head.*

Special, I meant, this is a special moment. I can see that you are a brilliant star.

CARPATHIA

Have you seen me?

*SHE checks walls.*

CARPATHIA (CON'T.)

Am I being watched?

BEING THREE

*Being* watched?

CARPATHIA

Am I being *watched?*

BEING THREE

Ancient symbols from a time. So, I will say, I wish that I could be a clasping watch wrapped around your branch.

*CARPATHIA, dances.*

*BEING THREE types on head.*

BEING THREE

(Sings, lyrical, upbeat) *Please explore what's around the corner.*
*Let our future not set a drift. If the beat of your heart is what you're dancing to, Life will be a breeze and a lift.*

*CARPATHIA ends in a graceful pose. All Applaud.*

*BEING THREE types on his head.*

BEING THREE

(slower) *We will live beyond this divide, may truth fall from our lips, our shapes melt, not hide, Yes, life will be a breeze and a lift.*

*ALL quiet. CARPATHIA lays on a block. BEING THREE Puts an ear to the divide.*

**BEING THREE (CON'T.)**
She's there. I hear breathing. Like, Chaunka Chaunka Chaunka.
Hear it? These ones have complete living organs with sounds. Chaunka
Chaunka.

> *CARPATHIA Jumps up.*

**CARPATHIA**
(quickly) Thank you all for your interest. No easy decision, with lack of
visuals, and of course language deficits. Well, that's on me, since you're
trying to translate to my language.

**DARKVOICE (O.S.)**
UHHHHHHHH.

**CARPATHIA**
I've finalized!

> *BLACKOUT*
> *Lights Up Stage Left*
> *CARPATHIA is Writing*

**CARPATHIA**
(to self) Please, don't be an enigma... of course one would have to be, at
first, or second, until *they* are, *its* not... Please, please don't smell like
gelatinous gumbo tubes.

> *CARPATHIA pushes cards through divide holes.*

**CARPATHIA (CON'T.)**
Be, my world. Be my life. Life. Insightful. Forgiving. Limitless!

> *Chants, Dances.*

Limitless! Insightful! Forgiving! Everything! Limitless Life, Everything!

> *Lights Up stage Right*
> *BEING THREE (as BRUTUS) lays on block.*
> *His blue and silver Jumpsuit partially unzipped, exposes his chest.*

**BRUTUS**
Hello. Someone is there.

**CARPATHIA**
Some one. We are alone.

**BRUTUS**

Restful to your breath, I snooped into a deep Durn-Guh. I closed my eyes and—

**CARPATHIA**

Eyes! And you close them. (sighs) Wish there was some music in here.

**BRUTUS**

(loud) Music should stay in your solo head. No rickety rack!

*CARPATHIA tiptoes, sits. BRUTUS gets close to divide.*

**BRUTUS**

I hear your kidneys.

*Types on head.*

Whoopsidoosie, I hear your lungs.

So many parts in you... Drundle! I came on strong. Is this over?

**CARPATHIA**

No! You said you like quiet. (pause) Damn, I'm already too compliant.

*HE secures his ears to the divider wall.*

**BRUTUS**

(softly) Chaunka Chaunka.

You may have issues with Aliens. And whose to say who's the alien?

**DARKVOICE (O.S)**
**UHHHHHHHHHHH.**

*BRUTUS holds ears. DARKVOICE stops. BRUTUS ears back to divide.*

**BRUTUS**

There you are.

**CARPATHIA**

Yes, here I are...My language is already regressing.

*SHE throws a pillow at divide.*

Have you read my notes, questions, wants?

*BRUTUS picks up a card. Reads. Sniffs himself.*

BRUTUS
I recognize bamboo in me, I eat much of. And lingering charcoal and peat moss.

CARPATHIA
Okeedokee. Do you have questions for me?

BRUTUS
NoKeedokee... (pause) You are called something?

*SHE picks up the pillow.*

CARPATHIA
Carpathia.

BRUTUS
BLOOP! Carpathia. Car-path, ia, Carrrrrpaaaathia!

CARPATHIA
You like my name.

BRUTUS
A very good sound.

CARPATHIA
What do others call you?

*He paces, flipping ears.*

BRUTUS
(pause) Bru-tuss? Yes, Brutus! It's a good sound too.

CARPATHIA
Are you sure? Earlier, in our encounter, I referred to you as being *brutish*.

*BRUTUS types.*

BRUTUS
My Mother liked stories of ancient Rome.

CARPATHIA
Oh, that's why you're such a confidant Orator.

BRUTUS
(quickly) I'm inexperienced in that contact thing. Bloop!

CARPATHIA
Bloop!

BRUTUS
Okkeeodkee then. I like it. Okkeedokkeeee. Okkeedohhhhhkeeee

> BRUTUS *lays on a box.*
>
> CARPATHIA *presses her body against the wall, inhales intensely, makes an Audible sigh, Passes Gas.*

BRUTUS
How was that?

CARPATHIA
What do you mean?

> BRUTUS *crouches near divide.*
>
> CARPATHIA *sits, Loudly Passes Gas again.*

BRUTUS
You sounded something.

CARPATHIA
Nope, didn't.

BRUTUS
The Carriers made specifications, so we don't get frightened for all the newness... all at once.

CARPATHIA
I'm sensitive to smells, even my own.

BRUTUS
That concerns me.

CARPATHIA
A new unexpected smell can be a shock.

BRUTUS
Okeedokee, I cannot smell.

> BRUTUS *sits.*
>
> CARPATHIA *rises, shakes dress around.*

BRUTUS (CON'T.)

I have sensitive ears. I've been feeling waves of sporadic air-flow passing. Down here, we don't have wind in our tunnels.

CARPATHIA

I'm so, damn!...just nervous.

BRUTUS

Me are too.

CARPATHIA

Thank you for not asking more.

BRUTUS

Can't always be orange sky and sea sponge.

CARPATHIA

Yes, can't always be...*No* can't always be that. I must ask something, it may sound rude.

BRUTUS

I'm here for rude.

CARPATHIA

Could you come closer?

BRUTUS

I could.

> *CARPATHIA moves around sniffing through the holes.*
> *BRUTUS doesn't move—still seated.*

CARPATHIA

I sense nothing. Brutus?

> *HE crosses to divide.*

BRUTUS

Here now. BLOOP!

> *CARPATHIA waltzes.*

CARPATHIA

Bloop. Is that Okeedokee for me to say?

**BRUTUS**

I hear your thumper and I sway.

**CARPATHIA**

Are you curious to see me?

**BRUTUS**

Part of me curious, part of me frightened, other parts abstain.

**CARPATHIA**

As you know, I'm an Ordinary.

**BRUTUS**

You are rare. Good to formulate with.

**CARPATHIA**

Yes. And you?...I imagine you have some Ordinary, your exchanges were thoughtful, emotional, and yet

**BRUTUS**

Extra.

*CARPATHIA views different holes, to see as much as possible.*

**BRUTUS**

(blurting) My Mother was an Ordinary, my Father was a Naturalized Extra Ordinary and Compassion Educated. So I am an Extra Ordinary. Bloop!

**CARPATHIA**

I accept that. Some of the other Beings may have been Extra Ordinary by Proxy. I may sound insensitive, but that's too different for me. None of us can control how we were formulated, yet, we can choose a more perfect next—

**BRUTUS**

I thought Mother to be perfect. And I am the byproduct.

**CARPATHIA**

More similar to your mother or father?

**BRUTUS**

I'm told I give face like Mother. Her Ordinary nose, mouth, heart, kidneys, feet.

CARPATHIA
(to self) Please have hands.

BRUTUS
My other parts more similar to Father's mixed construct.

CARPATHIA
Your brain, is it your mother's gift?

BRUTUS
She would have said yes to that question, with limitations. I still must use my head translator.

CARPATHIA
You absorb concepts, words, quickly. How do you feel about sensory exploration?

BRUTUS
Does it apply?

CARPATHIA
Very much so.

*Dialogue speeds up as they investigate various holes in divide.*

BRUTUS
(quicker) Fifty years ago, my Mother taught upper-level ancient AI history...about Twenty-five years ago she formulated me. I was only ten when the Dark Challenges came, The Carriers forced me below. She refused to leave surface.

CARPATHIA
I'm sorry Brutus. I would have enjoyed her company. Did your father make it?

*Silence*

CARPATHIA (CON'T)
Brutus? (pause) Are you curious to investigate the beyond, with me?

*CARPATHIA puts her finger through a hole.*
*BRUTUS twists an ear through to touch her finger.*

BRUTUS
Bloop.

CARPATHIA
Is that your...is it? Is it a part resembling your mother or father?

BRUTUS
Neither, it was extra.

*THEY stay connected.*

BRUTUS (CON'T.)
May I reach your ear?

CARPATHIA
Can you do that?

*She puts her ear against a hole. His long furry ear pushes through.*

CARPATHIA
Oh! Thats a lot of energy there...lotta heat, right?

BRUTUS
Nice. Good. Special.

CARPATHIA
Yes, all that, Brutus.

DARKVOICE (O.S.)
Process, process now. UHHH.

*CARPATHIA crosses over to other side of divide.*

BRUTUS
Carpathia.

CARPATHIA
Brutus. I know your shape now, your color, your smell, your Extra Ordinary features.

CARPATHIA & BRUTUS
*Please explore what's around the corner, let our future not set a drift. If the beat of your heart is what you're dancing to,*
*life will be a breeze and a lift. Yes, life will be a breeze and a lift.*

**BLACKOUT—END**

# NEWCOMERS' DAY

NAOMI AYALA

They arrive in small droves at the resource fair—
mostly Venezuelan now, to find out about where to work, eat, and live
beyond the hotel shelter. Learn to speak English. Navigate class.
The culture of sophistication. Tech. Educatedness. They are almost too polite.
And like me—wait, there I am among them, scurrying to my aunt's flank
when I myself was new on the mainland—apologizing in Spanish for
    everything.
As timid and as *del campo* as you could get.
I still play with other people's children, but now tell parents where to go
which gives a young girl comfort—separation from one's homeland is the
    wound
that opens everywhere and cuts in long into the future.
I say, *Welcome* and smile big. *Welcome.* As if I didn't know a thing
about what it is to be here and what may likely lie ahead.

## CONSTANT WATER

NAOMI AYALA

At my feet on waking—
whirlpools
and jets.
The sanctity of sky infusing
translucent mantels of it
with stardust.
Listen here—
this is how rocks get to sing.
*¡Las piedras!*
*Cómo si se levantaran.*
Echoing against the standing
trunks of trees—
leaves bellowing.
The whirr of it.
The sheer glass song of it.
What becomes of me
in water
*is* water.
Settling in
all the cracks of the unspokens.
Enough water to raise
the dead.
Enough water to keep us
all from wanting.

# A BRIDGE IN BALTIMORE COLLAPSES

EMMA DIVALENTINO

a bridge in baltimore collapses like popsicle sticks,
eight workers plummet into the midnight water.

the unlucky few trapped beneath
after the captain called for help,
before the workers stopped traffic.

a woman online tells me that people have a minute
to exit a submerged vehicle before they are sure to drown.
i resolve to cross bridges with my windows down.

in the summers, my brothers work construction on
the mid-hudson bridge. i think of their bodies cold;
their skin picked at by the mouths of hungry fish.
no longer waiting for rescue, but for recovery.

i imagine them as the workers filling potholes at
one in the morning and wonder how far downriver
the current has pulled them, if the divers will ever
find their bodies, or if the river will become a memorial.

i think about the one worker that was pulled from the water
unharmed and wonder who he prayed to and if he feels lucky.

# ERASURE:
## George W Bush Address on Signing the USA Patriot Act[1]

RAFFI JOE WARTANIAN

October 26, 2001

Good ▮ White ▮ terrorism ▮ With my signature, this ▮ danger.

I commend ▮ hard ▮ nights and weekends ▮

I want to thank the Vice ▮. I want to thank ▮ terrorism. ▮ I want to thank the ▮ FBI and ▮ CIA for waging an incredibly important ▮ war ▮

I want ▮

▮ a threat like no other ▮. We've seen the ▮ enemy ▮

Our country is ▮. ▮

I want ▮

positive exposures ▮.

▮ Since the 11th of September, ▮ our ▮ intelligence and law enforcement agencies have been relentless ▮

▮ horrors ▮ horrors ▮ custom ▮ Secret ▮

▮ our ▮ terrorists ▮

▮ will help law enforcement ▮ identify, ▮ dismantle, ▮ disrupt, ▮ punish ▮

---

[1] Source: https://www.presidency.ucsb.edu/documents/remarks-signing-the-usa-patriot-act-2001

we're changing
culture                                                                the number
one priority
is
surveillance of all
communications
Investigations
investigate
anyone
making it easier to
lengthen        prison
sentences
This bill

upholds and respects the civil liberties guaranteed by our
atrocities
the                                                            war
branches of our Government                    are united        to find and stop and
punish                              the American people.

It is now my honor to sign into law the USA PATRIOT ACT of 2001.

# WHAT WE TELL OUR CHILDREN

## STEVE LOIACONI

"This was all inevitable," I lie.

The horses gallop along a dusty trail, kicking up gravel and sand. The frame of the wagon rattles as the wheels dip in and out of ruts in the road. My fingers tighten around the reins. Kevin stares into the dark forest beyond the tree line. I tell myself it's best not to think about what's out there. The air above us is ink-black with soot. White ash from the skyfire flutters down like what I remember of snow.

"After the temperatures rose, the storms came, and then everything fell apart. Crops, water, energy—nothing came easy anymore. Resources were scarce, the economy tanked, and society just about sputtered to a stop. Wars between nations broke out, sectarian clashes flared within borders, violence, and chaos everywhere. Those of us who could, like me and your mom, went to the bunkers. The lucky ones."

It's a story I've told him many times before. I don't know if he believes it.

"Then shit got weird." I catch myself. "Excuse me. Stuff got weird."

As if decorum matters. Kevin's legs twitch frantically. His fingers fidget and fumble around the shoulder strap of his bag. He's never spent a night away from home.

"Nobody knows what caused the EMP, or if they do, they haven't told me. It's been almost a decade, and we still haven't figured out how to get the power back on. For that matter, I still can't tell you where the were-beasts came from. Can't say I care all that much. I just know to stay away from them."

I give Kevin's hand a squeeze and offer up a meager smile that's meant to be reassuring, but from the strain in his young face, I gather it falls flat.

"Either way, here we are, America in the After. Eighty percent of what was just…isn't anymore. People, families, and infrastructure. Cities and countries, from what I understand."

The wagon rumbles over a deep hole, jostling us both out of our seats. I reach over to keep him from tumbling off the side.

"But hey," I say, "it's your seventh Winter Solstice. This is what we've been preparing for. You and the rest of the Scouts ride the train up into the mountains with your troop leaders. A big adventure out there in the brave new world. A few nights in the Blue Ridge Mountains, away from the moms and dads."

I wonder if maybe I'm overselling it, but he has been jittery with uncertain anticipation for days.

"I don't even remember the last time I went on a train," I mutter, suppressing a futile memory of New York at Christmas.

But if my son is listening, I don't see much sign of it.

"We're here, Dad," Kevin squeaks, nearly hopping out of his seat when the horses stamp to a halt at the train station.

"This was all inevitable," I say again.

I help him down from the carriage and hoist his bag onto my shoulder.

"Goodbye, Midnight," Kevin whispers to the black horse.

He always loved animals.

"Take care of him for me until I get back," he tells the horse, nodding toward me.

I hold his hand as we trot up the path to the train platform. Other kids and parents await. The children run to each other, laughing and chattering. It's a momentary glimmer of childhood as we used to know it, before the disasters and the bunkers and the monsters. The fathers share silent, knowing looks. When the troop leaders call the children to board, I reach for Kevin to give him a hug. I expect him to pull away from my embrace, embarrassed to show affection in front of his friends like I was at his age, but he leans into it. I hold him tighter.

That makes this harder.

The train whistle blows, and the children eagerly race on board. Kevin briefly looks back before turning into the cabin, a wide smile plastered across his face. Through the windows, I watch him bounce to his seat.

I remember, as a kid, in the Before, going to sleepaway camp for the first time. I hated it, but my parents made me go year after year anyway.

As the train departs, I offer an obligatory wave, but I can't bring myself to look and see if Kevin notices. Something gurgles in the pit of my stomach.

Guilt isn't the word.

Guilt is what you feel for things you can control.

The things you've done.

This is the way of the world today, I tell myself, stumbling back to the horses. The established protocol for the children who were marked for the offering: on their seventh Solstice, we bring them to the station, we say goodbye, and they board the train. Then we send them hurtling down the deep dark shaft. By the time they understand, they're too far gone to hear them cry for help. To hear them beg.

It's best not to think about it, is what other parents who have been through this tell me.

When I approach the wagon, Midnight neighs and drops his head away from me.

"Don't you start," I mutter.

This is how we survive to see another day.

This is what he requires.

The one we awakened.

The god below.

# THE FUTURE

JEAN NORDHAUS

The future is all around us
though we can't yet
see its face. Those who claim

to know it—prophets, pundits,
venture capitalists—see only
partially through their dark glasses.

To my grandparents leaving the shtetl
"America" *was* "future," a garden
of promises I call the past—

once-golden land, and now
a nation among others. Every end
(as Rilke knew) is also a beginning.

The future is a galaxy we've
not yet visited. We cannot speak
its language or describe its starry cities.

Whether galloping wildly or dragging
its feet, it will surely come
for some: too soon, for some, too late . . .

We only know that it will come
and that we must be ready
and that some of us will not be ready.

# THE DAY AFTER: SEARCHING FOR LANGUAGE FOR ANOTHER LOST GENERATION

## LEEYA MEHTA

*"A moment comes, which comes but rarely in history, when we step out from the old to the new, when an age ends, and when the soul of a nation, long suppressed, finds utterance."*

— Jawaharlal Nehru, 1947

### "You are all a lost generation."

As A COLLEGE STUDENT in India, I was struck by the idea of the lost generation, exhausted by the words of their predecessors, the cost of war. Gertrude Stein had possibly borrowed this disparaging term from a French garage owner to describe Ernest Hemingway and his hard-drinking buddies.

"You are all a lost generation," Stein said in an epigram featured in Hemingway's *The Sun Also Rises* (1926). Below the epigram, Hemingway then quotes Ecclesiastes 1:4-11:

"One generation passeth away, and another generation cometh; but the earth abideth forever...."

The generation was lost in the sense that its inherited values were no longer relevant to the postwar world. It became a term for spiritual alienation. Language, too, was lost; words could no longer convey the carnage of the past.

### "History, too, is an art."

"History, too, is an art," so opens the poem, "The Muse of History" by Ukrainian-American poet Oksana Maksymchuk. On February 24, 2025, she read poems from *Still City* (2024) on the third anniversary of the Ukraine War (Russia annexed Crimea in 2014; in 2022, it launched its full-scale invasion into Ukraine.)

In the room in Virginia where she reads, we are surrounded by the pictures and archives of a Charlottesville-based artist Morgan Ashcom, whose exhibition is about the re-creation of a small town's archive, after the public building where the archives were stored burned down.

To restore history.

What happens the day after history is burned? Is it mythologized, re-created, re-formulated? How is it reorganized? Is it valued enough to have public funding?

A hundred years after the term "Lost Generation" was coined, how do we, as the keepers of language, rebirth language that is so burned, with ash on our tongues?

### 1154 km Helsinki

**5102 km Roma**　　　　　　　　　　**2626 km Bergen**

### 2502 km Oslo

The last time I remember a literal crossroads, I was north of the Arctic Circle in the borderlands of Norway and Russia. A sign from a different Europe had been left for passersby to imagine a different Empire. The Russians liberated the north of Norway, dousing it with cold water as the retreating Nazi army burned it to the ground. In Kirkenes, where I stood, the Second World War Museum tells of this history. Always, when we go too far, someone has to check us.

Who will pour cold water on my burning tongue? Who will clean the ash from my hair?

### The books burn

The Library of Congress is blitzed in the War of 1812. In 1812, the United States went to war with Great Britain. On August 24, 1814, British troops took control of the capital city and proceeded to burn the President's House and the US Capitol, which then housed the congressional library (Library of Congress) in its north wing. The library went up in flames.

The burning of books under the Nazi regime on May 10, 1933, is perhaps the most famous book burning in history.

Seven people die in the Russian attack on May 23, 2024, at the Factor Druk printing house in Kharkiv, Ukraine. Kharkiv, the second largest city after Kyiv, is Ukraine's publishing hub and one of the biggest printing hubs in Europe.

In March 2007, a bomb kills thirty and wounds a hundred on Baghdad's Al-Mutanabbi Street; Mutanabbi is a street of booksellers, named after a 10th-century Iraqi poet.

In 1995, offended by *The Moor's Last Sigh*, one of the great Indian novels by Salman Rushdie, two major political parties torch the book because it offends their leadership (long deceased in the case of one party).

### "You know you are back to normal when you begin to miss your things."

In 2012, on a cold night in October in Washington, DC, my family woke up at two a.m. to an inferno. We lost most of our possessions, but we were safe. A friend who had suffered a fire of her own said soon after, "You know you are back to normal when you begin to miss your things."

I waited to miss things.

I miss nothing.

### "He really thought that people were good...Before his death, we had quarreled very bitterly over this. I had lost my faith in politics, in right paths; if there *were* a right path, one might be sure (I informed him with great venom) that whoever was on it was simply asking to be stoned to death—by all the world's good people. I didn't give a damn..."

So writes James Baldwin, in his essay "The New Lost Generation" (1961), where that tone of Gertrude Stein's rebuke is present. He begins his essay with the suicide of a dear friend, who he had quarreled with in the days before his suicide.

Written in 1961, the essay is part description, part critique, of the American abroad. For context, at the time of Baldwin's essay, *The Quiet American*, Graham Greene's prescient novel, had already been published (in 1955, before the Vietnam War's worst years).

Baldwin's commentary delves into the excursion of his compatriots to France, which has its merits. America in the 1960s was a place where public figures were routinely assassinated. Baldwin, like Hemingway, like Richard Wright, and like many other artists, escapes to Paris. He settles in France eventually, though he spends many years in Turkey as well. He becomes a world traveler, returning to America often. But in that early time in Paris, he notices that Americans, like himself, once they overstay, are faced with the reality of ordinary life.

Part of coming-of-age is learning to live that ordinary life. It is making a decision of how you want to live your life and what aspect of humanity you want to represent. In the tension between self, family, and society, the writer develops a narrative for a creative life. In the essay, Baldwin talks of the loss of his best friend to suicide and how, on the eve of the end of his friend's life, Baldwin was glib with his friend:

"One fine day, you'll realize that people don't *want* to be better. So, you'll have to make them better. And how do you think you'll go about it?" he says to his friend roughly.

"What about love? he asked me."

For Black Americans, America was not physically safe. In many ways, the expatriate life saved Baldwin. He chose a different path as a creative man rather than become a victim of his people, his country. He chose not to be defined by his anger, his fear, his bitterness. Though I hear he did attempt to take his own life, he did not succeed, and he chose, in the end, to live. But revenge was a path he chose not to take. He chose to break bread with all people, to reject extremes. To become an artist as a means to his own salvation. To become a witness where others were afraid to report on the health of society. To tell each of us, to look within to find our own humanity and then to practice it.

Baldwin calls upon individuals to conquer the nihilism of history by asserting agency and control as individuals. He speaks to us directly. All of us, in every country. And we all can listen. None of us want loneliness. With Baldwin, language is remade, a language of rights, of humanity, of love.

### I was born in a free country.

India.

They say 18 million people moved across borders in 1947 in the Partition of

India. They estimate three million people were massacred or died in the transition to this new nation-state, India, and her sister, Pakistan.

Even for freedom, sometimes things get out of hand. That is why, perhaps, the day after we say: *at least we are free? It is the cost of freedom? We need safeguards; we went too far.*

### The measles

In the 1980s, even though the MMR vaccine had been around for over a decade, an uncle in Bombay, who was a medical doctor, ordered my mother not to vaccinate me when she asked to inoculate me against the measles. Mom and her parents had always been readers, keeping up to date on life-saving medical advances. But the doctor intimidated Mom; she wasn't going to go against the advice of a doctor. When I contracted the measles, I missed more than a month of school, and I remember being unable to get out of bed for weeks, and then only to be bathed with water soaked with eucalyptus leaves. I learned later that I had almost died of the measles.

### My grandfather was not born in a free country.

Born in 1917, my grandfather Soli's family lived in Calcutta when he was young in the province of Bengal. British India was actively fighting in the First World War. His family life was comfortable. His mother had lost her first husband, and they lived in a blended family of five: four brothers and a sister. The siblings settled in Bombay and Karachi. By 1947, they were pledging allegiance to two separate nations: India and Pakistan.

When my grandfather told me what he remembered of the time before Independence, he spoke mostly of poverty. He said that after independence, poverty seemed less. I found this strange. I was growing up in Bombay, a city with extreme inequality and poverty, but he said it was nothing compared with what he had seen traveling the breadth of the subcontinent for his job.

In 1943, an estimated 2.3 million people died in the Bengal famine. Simply, it was a British administrative failure, exacerbated by the Second World War.

Even though agrarian India has often experienced great suffering, most recently with farmer suicides, post-independence India has never had a famine.

Nobel Prize winner Amartya Sen says, "Famines are easy to prevent if there is a serious effort to do so, and a democratic government, facing elections and criticism from opposition parties and independent newspapers, cannot help but make such an effort. Not surprisingly, while India continued to have famines under British rule right up to independence…they disappeared suddenly with the establishment of a multiparty democracy and a free press…a free press and an active political opposition constitute the best early-warning system a country threatened by famines can have."

### The day after

In the late 1960s, when my mother was in her teens, they welcomed her piano teacher into their home. Mom's piano teacher, F, was trans. F was a brilliant lawyer at the high court in Bombay, and his hobby was teaching piano. Mom tells the story of how F finally told Mom that to stay friends, she may have to give up piano because she really wasn't applying herself.

They stayed friends.

Soon after, F transitioned to becoming a woman. She adapted her name F to a female version of her name. The day after, she was F, a woman.

Language is adaptable, democratic in its ability to draw from the past and the present. From unfree to free. What happens to language when we lose our job because we want to be free in our body: suddenly, we have gone from free to unfree.

F was disbarred when she transitioned, stripped of her ability to practice law, and at some point, she left India.

F settled in America. F still teaches piano.

### And here we are, at the buffet of history.
### What will you choose to eat?

It was the turn of the Century. 1999-2000.

A friend in Bombay handed me *Mein Kampf* by Adolf Hitler to read as an example of how to organize.

No caveats.

### The day after

Since October 7, 2023, people keep saying, we must wait for the day after.

But by now, language feels dead. A hundred years after the lost generation was playfully coined, we are faced with another landscape of loss, where words have been overused and have lost their meaning.

Like in W.B. Yeats' poem, "The Stare's Nest By My Window," written during the Irish Civil War, in the 1920s:

> We had fed the heart on fantasies,
> The heart's grown brutal from the fare,
> More substance in our enmities
> Than in our love.

But...What if we soften language for the day after today?

But...What of whispering? When educators want to catch the attention of kindergartners, they speak more softly. The children lean in.

But... What if we do that cleanup they do before the first day of school, and we clear out the rubble? Shall we build a house? Can we be safe again?

But... What of the aggressors, with their weapons, what of the militias, what of the broken bodies, what of the unburied dead, what of our cities destroyed, our landscape blighted, our world burning?

In Yeats's poem, there is a way, a call to order, to rebuild. It takes the hive to come together to build in the empty nest of the stare:

> The bees build in the crevices
> Of loosening masonry, and there
> The mother birds bring grubs and flies.
> My wall is loosening, honey bees
> Come build in the empty house of the stare.

He begins his poem with this invitation. And ends it with it again.

IN LOUISE ERDRICH'S NOVEL *La Rose*, a neighbor's child is accidentally shot in the opening pages. In indigenous tradition, the killer's child must be given to the bereft family in place of the lost child.

"ONE FINE DAY, you'll realize that people don't *want* to be better. So, you'll have to make them better. And how do you think you'll go about it?"
—James Baldwin in "The New Lost Generation."

The day after, we begin again. We miss nothing.
History is the art of remembering. Then forgiving.
We address poverty, loneliness, inequality. We consume less; we share more.
We rest our tender tongues, speaking with soft sounds.
We heal, our neighbors, our earth.
We reclaim our souls. And the souls of our nations.
We do it together, and then we go to the Welcome Table.
'I'm going to sit at the Welcome Table. I'm going to feast on milk and honey
one of these days.'[1]

WE ALL LOVE OUR CHILDREN, but we cannot always protect them. If, on the day after, we give our children to those whose children we have killed, can we then forgive each other for what we have done?

---

[1] Leeming, David, *James Baldwin: A Biography*. Alfred A. Knopf, New York, 1994.

# THERE IS NO CLIMATE CHANGE

NATALIE E. ILLUM

But Puerto Rico is a blackout and the Napa Valley
is ember and ash now.

You ask why. *White Supremacy.*

The brown bodies say *Murder Murder Murder.*

You ask how. *White Supremacy.*

You ask me what the temperature is outside.
*Mass Shooting is rising and the water levels
are falling, full of genocide.*

You ask what the forecast is. *Every weekend, a protest.*

You ask what's trending, *White Fragility
Every hashtag, a temporary outcry.*

But what does the farmer's almanac say about next year?
*Narcissism will destroy every crop. The pressure will continue
to plummet. Bundle up, but be careful.*

In some parts, a winter scarf
is a hijab, is a noose, is an indicator
is the flint for the country burning.
We cannot predict come summertime
what will be left.

# NOTHING BUT THE BLOOD
## A MEMOIR EXCERPT
### VONETTA YOUNG

In early 2023, I read Dani Shapiro's book *Inheritance*, the memoir in which she learns that her father was not her father. That is, the Orthodox Jewish man she'd loved her whole life, who'd died after a car accident when she was in her early 20s, was not her biological father. She'd done a 23andMe test on a whim, and, as a result, the entire narrative of her life was completely undone.

Inspired, I toyed with the idea that maybe my father wasn't actually my father. And then I looked in the mirror. The eyes had it: Albert Eugene Young, Sr. was most certainly my father. Despite that, I didn't know him.

I called Al one Sunday evening. "Do you know if Dad liked any sports teams?" I asked. "Or what his favorite color was?"

He was silent for a long moment. "No," he said. "I realize he was a stranger to me."

If my brother, who was darn near ten years older than me and had at least that much more time to get to know Dad than I did, didn't know anything, I couldn't be surprised that I didn't know either.

I knew that my father loved church, karate, and women—three obsessions that defined his life—but that was all I knew of him. So, I wanted to know: who was my father, really? What was he made of?

When I started asking these things, something broke within me, loosened like rocks that had started to crumble away. The questions just kept coming.

The first question that came to my mind was elementary: What hospital was he born in?

I couldn't get this question out of my mind one day while I was at a café, so I ordered a cappuccino and a croissant and reasoned that the hospital would be listed on my father's birth certificate. On my iPhone, I found the Pennsylvania Office of Vital Records. I whipped out my credit card to pay the thirty dollar processing fee plus shipping. And then I waited. I waited to see what would happen now that I had asked a question.

Two weeks and a few days later, the sun was shining and birds were chirping as a pulled an envelope from Pennsylvania out of my mailbox.

I held a copy of my father's birth certificate in my hands. It was blue and white, which I'd expected it to be. Much to my dismay, it did not include the name of the hospital he was born in. But it did include his father's name, Jon Mccoy. I knew my grandfather's name because I'd once called Dad to ask what it was. I was in ninth grade, working on a family tree project, when I realized I had no clue who my father's father was.

"His name was…Jon Mccoy," my father said, hesitating like he was looking the name up on the internet as he spoke.

I wondered why he'd hesitated; maybe he didn't want me to know this because he didn't want to open himself up to me. Or maybe he didn't trust what I would do with the information. As *Schoolhouse Rock* illuminated us, "Knowledge is power," but knowledge is also control. Maybe telling me his father's name was one way that control slipped from my father's hands and into mine.

I remember thinking, "That's an interesting name," and I assumed it was spelled "John McCoy." Seeing the name on Dad's official document felt like meeting a famous person in real life and realizing that they're slightly shorter than you thought they'd be.

The birth certificate also featured two life-altering details that I did not know: Jon Mccoy was born in Philadelphia and was twenty-five years old when my father was born in 1956. This meant that my grandfather would have been born in roughly 1931.

I had unlocked two details that could serve as the key to my father's history. Now, I could make his family tree.

ARMED WITH THIS NEW INFO, I dug into my father's genealogy. I figured, what better way to learn about someone than to start with their history, all the things that came before them that made up who they became?

On Ancestry.com, I searched for a Jon Mccoy born in Philadelphia around 1931, excited for what would come up. There were some Mccoys, but nothing aligned perfectly with the city and year of birth. I found a Negro family in Philly in the 1930 census, but the baby boy, John, was almost a year old, which didn't check out. All the other Mccoy families were white, and given my father's dark skin, it was not possible that his father was white. I searched for a few days, but found nothing.

My father was still keeping secrets from me, even from the grave, I thought. I no longer felt angry about him not trusting me, even posthumously, but I did feel frustrated because I now was confused, and I just wanted to know the truth.

Since I'd already bought the Ancestry subscription, I looked up my mother's side of the family. I realized that whenever I said the words "my family," I was almost always referring to my mother's side, namely my maternal grand-mother's—Nana's—side.

Like my father, my mother did not know her father but knew his name—Daw-son White, Jr.—and the names of some of his relatives. They all lived in Salis-bury, North Carolina, where my mother was born and where I grew up. I put those names into Ancestry and felt almost a literal wind blow me back in time.

Nana's family line led me back to my third-great-grandmother, born in 1850. I could only assume that she was enslaved because she was born before 1863, but I didn't see her name on any of the slave registers I saw. (Slave registers were sort of like censuses, but for enslaved people. The register was an account of objects, as enslaved people were considered property and therefore could not be counted in the actual census.)

I braced myself for the moment when my ancestors' records would end because they were not given names, not because they had died at birth, but because they were never considered human. Of course, they were very much human, with pasts that were taken away from them.

I finally hit the slavery wall on my grandfather's side, Dawson's side, with my fifth-great-grandmother. My breath left me as I read "Enslaved Woman," no other name, not even a nickname. My face burned as an unexpected rage ran from my feet to the top of my head. She must have had a name; what was it? She had a story, and I wanted to know what it was. The rage that I felt was, on the surface, from the phenomenally insulting refusal to even bother sharing her name, but deep down, it was a feeling that was so hot, I could not touch it to identify it.

My fifth-great-grandfather was a white slave owner named James Galbraith Torrance. A photo of his grave adorned his Ancestry profile, which had been created ages ago by some genealogy nerd. I felt sick to my stomach.

In the moment, I wondered what might have transpired between James and this "Enslaved Woman." Did he rape her? Did he love her? Yes, he must have raped her, and no, he could not have loved her. But maybe? Either way, consent was not possible. You can't have a loving, healthy relationship with someone you own.

I couldn't fathom to think of their situation more, so I pressed on through James' lineage since I couldn't go any farther past "Enslaved Woman." Ultimately, I traced my lineage back to my ninth great-grandmother, Hannah Gallagher, born in Dublin, Ireland, in 1660.

Through my mother's estranged father, my ancestry opened itself up to me, back to the Renaissance.

Despite the complicated news I had discovered, I stood a bit taller after learning all this.

This exercise of getting to know my father—the man who had abandoned me when I was just a child—had inadvertently led me to a sense of worthiness. It was a feeling that had eluded me my whole life up until this moment. To have no sense of where you come from leaves you seeking where you are going—I finally had answers to the former so I could determine the latter. I felt free, and in control of my destiny.

Later that day, as I walked down the street, I pictured a wall of family crests, coats of arms, behind me. Me, leading my line.

That night, while I was rocking Desmond to sleep in the cool, quiet dark, I thought about "Enslaved Woman." In my imagination, I conjured her into my son's room. She wore rags, and her hair was tied back. She smiled slightly, not showing her teeth. I couldn't fathom her life or the circumstances that led to her giving birth to my fourth-great-grandmother, but I wanted to thank her. Without her, I would not be here. Neither would my son.

"I don't know what your name is," I told her, "but I'm going to call you Beautiful. And I want you to know that I'm free."

I felt her smile, distant, happy in a way that maybe she couldn't quite process. I heard the metal clank of a chain falling. I kissed my son's forehead.


THE NEXT DAY, I did more digging to find out more about Beautiful and James' child. The child's name was Harriet, called Hattie, and she was born around 1810. She is listed in the 1850 census as a "mulatto" slave, age 40. I continued reading and found that, after James died in 1847, he did not set her free; he "bequeathed" her to his brother, Adam.

"That fucker," I mumbled.

Then again, what would she have done if he had freed her? There was no way she could have lived as a free woman in North Carolina prior to Emancipation, and even afterwards, her life would have been impossibly hard.

Continuing my research, I found that James was married three times. His first wife, whom he married in 1811, died about ten years later of illness. His second wife also died of illness, and his third wife outlived him.

A tidal wave of anger washed over me as I realized that his first white child was born in 1812, meaning Hattie was his firstborn; if he hadn't conceived other children, he very well could have. The thought weighed heavy on my mind: he gave away his firstborn child when he died instead of setting her free. I sat back in my chair, unsure if I wanted to vomit or scream. I did neither; just let the information settle into my bones, unsure of what to do with it.

Later, I wrestled with it, feeling flashes of hot anger, then the cool distance of time and the busyness of life that distracted me from thinking about it. Then, a couple of months later, I decided what I would do: I would forgive James Galbraith Torrance.

I'd been a believer in Christian principles for most of my life but had only recently come to terms with the concept of forgiveness. Forgiveness is inherently selfish, actually: it has nothing to do with the perpetrator and all to do with the freedom of the victim. I no longer wanted to be subject to abandonment, victimization, and fear. So, I would forgive the farthest perpetrator back in my line that I could find, the one who started the fear long before my father.

AS I GET CLOSER to Huntersville, NC, on the day after Independence Day, my chest tightens. I can't tell if it's indigestion or fear. When I start to shake, I know it's fear, just a sliver of the fear my ancestors felt of James Galbraith Torrance. I try to take deep breaths, but I can't get the air in.

I think about what I will say. What do you say to your ancestors' owners? There is no website that addresses this the way there is for reaching out to DNA relatives on Ancestry. When nothing comes to me, I think about the saying, "There's no manual for this," and no shit, Sherlock, there's never a manual because we are writing it now. But I do wonder if, underneath all of the insurmountable, unmovably grotesque of their lives in the institution of slavery, he remotely loved Beautiful.

I am trembling by the time I get to Hopewell Presbyterian Church, but I don't hesitate to get out of the car. At the entrance to the cemetery, there is a plaque that has the names and plots on them. I assume they get a lot of tourists, this cemetery being full of historical figures. I am alone with these figures, who are all in the ground. The sun is shining bright, not a cloud in the sky. It is hot. Birds chirp as if the world is still turning regular. James Galbraith Torrance is in plot 115.

His headstone is relatively new, placed there maybe fifteen years ago, probably by the same genealogy nerd who put the picture on Ancestry. I run my left hand across this name. I want to feel a connection with him, some sense of kinship, but don't. I go from feeling fear to feeling truth, images of Beautiful and Hattie filling my head. I hit the headstone with my fist.

"How could you?" I ask. Suddenly, I am bawling and sweating and angry. "How dare you! How fucking dare you!" Words come out of my mouth without my knowing what they will be. "I'm so mad at you!"

I am so happy to finally say this. I feel that I have never been this honest. All I can think about is Beautiful, and how "Enslaved Woman" was not her name, how she had a name, how she was not property, but a living, breathing, feeling, heart-beating human being.

"She was a person!" I scream. In case he didn't hear me, I repeat myself: "She was a person! She was a person!"

I see a smaller headstone by my foot. It is the original, from 1847, with the letters J. G. T. on it, half covered in moss. I touch it only with my fingertips. Then, thinking of Hattie, I kick it with my red sneaker.

"And she was your first born! How could you!"

I am doubled over in tears. I wonder if my ancestors are here with me, saying these things that I had not planned to say. At this thought, I feel renewed strength. I stand, sniffling.

"I wanted to ask if you loved her, but I can't ask that. I know you didn't." I shake my head. I wipe my nose a napkin from my purse.

"I came here to forgive you, not tell you how mad I am at you," I say. "But I'm so mad. And so grateful." I cry again. I'm sweating and crying; it's so hot. How can I feel so many different things at one time?

But it is true—if James Galbraith Torrance hadn't committed an act of terrorism on Beautiful, I would not be here. Desmond would not be here, nor would my mother, or her father. We would not exist, not in any form. And, so, I feel a profound sense of gratitude that, in this moment, I absolutely hate.

I remind myself that it was the period in history, the common way of thinking at that time. That doesn't excuse anything, but it does provide context and the ability to forgive.

"I forgive you," I say, and it finally clicks for me, this Christianity thing.

"I finally get it," I tell Torrance. "The whole 'Father, forgive them, for they know not what they do.' You didn't know, but you knew. You were working off fears you were given. You didn't know that you didn't have to take them."

At the acknowledgement of my ancestors' agency, I am able to breathe again. It is as if I finally understand my own agency, that the fears that my parents and grandparents and everyone before me had, I do not have to have.

I look over and see Torrance's father, Hugh, and his mother, Isabella, in huge graves next to his. I see a generational curse passed down. I want them all to know what might be their worst nightmare, that this curse is over.

"She's free, you know," I say of Beautiful. "Hattie, too. They're free." I have fresh tears as I tell the man who owned my family, "We're free. I'm free." And I say, "I'm free, I'm free, I'm free," so many times, not to convince myself, but

so it may ring throughout the ages. And because I am so grateful for this freedom.

I take three deep breaths. I repeat my mantra: "I forgive you, I forgive myself,
I love you."

The gravity of standing over slave owners, telling them that I forgive them sets
on my heart immediately. In my mind's eye, I see a hammer smashing the earth,
and the ground rippling out like water for miles. I swear I feel the earth move
beneath me, but I am still standing, still steady.

I will realize much later that this exercise in forgiveness is not just about my
family, but maybe about the entire nation. If I've felt oppressed for the whole
country, why couldn't I feel free for it?

I go to each of their graves—Torrance's, Hugh's, and Isabella's—and tell them
I will love them. I will never think of them fondly, never have any affection for
them whatsoever, but it is love because I am grateful they lived and gave me a
future. And it is easier to love after you have released.

# EARTH WILL BE OKAY (AND SO WILL WE)

JAYLA HART

it is 70 degrees and sunny, partly cloudy
and peculiarly warm for the middle of February.
a 20 degree shock to the nervous system so sharp
you briefly feel your seasonal depression dance away.
until you remember it is February.
you make mention of it to a friend then forget
long enough to carry yourself through to July.

every year is now the hottest year on record
or the longest period of consecutive heat.
*unprecedented* becomes the sourest solution
poured over too many persistent problems.
many must swallow their savings to cover
the rising cost of cooling their homes.
many succumb to heat stroke.

our oceans are warming and wishing
they could remember their circulation's flow.
online, you find a man live streaming himself
floating inside a kayak in his living room.
rescue squads are being deployed.
everything, from the ocean currents
to the dam systems, is weakening.

frozen trash lines the trek up Mount Everest
as the shores of Accra are swallowed by polyester.
you swipe past another shein haul in the hopes
the algorithm learns you are now trying
to take a stance against fast fashion.
you start to hope the algorithm stops
learning anything about you at all.

by December, frigid wind finds you
at every corner for a week. to ease its bite,
you fill with your days with the warmth
of friends' laughter instead of solitude.
greeted by the snow's blankness, you find gratitude
in the grand quietness of non-emergency.
for the first time, there is no fire to put out.

tomorrow arrives as a hazy memory,
sudden as a dream. the day reveals its peace
in the rustle of blossoming fruit trees
along a bustling sidewalk. somewhere near
yet too far to see, homes are being restored
to shelter the hearts of many hands who built
futures with their found families and forever loves.

love lines the hallways of every school once shook
to stillness by the sound of a semi-automatic.
in the south, Black children play under the trees'
calming canopy with no fear for their safety.
in the arctic, the caribou have come back
as have the salmon and the sea's steady rhythm.
sometime near, we have chosen to save ourselves.

your closet no longer comes at the expense
of a woman's life in Bangladesh. the shorelines
shimmer with sand instead of last season's apparel.
your tech no longer comes at the expense
of a child's life in the Democratic Republic of the Congo.
planned obsolescence is now obsolete. the wealthy few
find their riches worthless in these winds of change.

tomorrow arrives as a spring breeze,
barely certain of its trajectory yet optimistic.
forward is the only course it can follow.
you find yourself holding the reins of a country

rerouting itself out of the ruins, risky
but far from unprecedented. prepare for
this season, it will be shipped to your door.

you awake with no fear of tomorrow's arrival
and receive the revelry found in the mundane
courage of creating a world at peace with itself.

# REUNION

## ROBERT J. WILLIAMS

SIX YEARS AGO, I mailed a vial of spit to a DNA testing company hoping to decode the mysteries of my heritage. At the post office, just after dropping off the sample, I felt the heat of telepathically relayed words: *"Colored folk want to be everything but what they are! You are a child of God. That's from whence you came and is what matters most."* My ancestors—the recent ones known to me—ticked through a list of ethnicities suspected to be in our far-reaching historical bloodlines: Italian. Irish. Scottish. And Cherokee. But as modern-day science allows us to *not* be ignorant about a whole host of things ranging from burdensome to enlightening, why not scientifically verify the full spectrum of humanity to which you owe your existence?

Months later, the answer arrived by way of an emailed link. A pie chart broke down my genetic makeup: *35 percent England and Northwestern Europe. 27 percent Nigerian. 14 percent Mali. 10 percent Cameroon. 6 percent Germanic. 2 percent Indigenous Americas.* So, Cherokee, maybe, but no Italian. A scattering of other origins filled in the rest. Below the chart was a list of "DNA relatives," each name accompanied by a tiny circular portrait. I scanned them, drawn to the range of skin tones and hair colors. My American family: a kaleidoscope.

Restless during the pandemic, I returned to that DNA website nightly, seeing my lab-certified family tree continually grow. From a catalog of distant cousins, I picked out ten people—the ones whose last names looked the most exotic—and decided to DM them through the website's chat feature. I wanted to investigate exactly how they might be connected to me and mine, all of us with the most common of American surnames. I crafted a boilerplate message, careful not to sound like a scammer. Four eventually responded, each with similar notes about hoping to unearth stories of how their family—*our* family—came to be in ways science could not explain.

One of the respondents, a woman I'll call Ms. P., became persistently communicative and curious. Over months of exchanges, we revealed our locations—she in LA, me in DC—traded personal stories and compared pie charts.

The DNA site's relationship tools suggested our probable shared ancestor to be a man census records described as a "landowner." I shared that my grandmother was from the same South Carolina Lowcountry town where he lived. Ms. P. told me the property he owned before the Civil War was lost but returned to her family in 1926, the same year my grandmother was born to a woman who supposedly knew little of her own parentage.

Our messages danced around coincidences and history: the antebellum status of the land, how it was lost and reclaimed, and the circumstances of a single act of copulation that seeded our eternal connection. We pivoted to small talk to learn more about each other. Ms. P., slightly older than me, taught college history and was married but childless. We shared a love of Italian food and binged some of the same Netflix shows. And we both liked to travel—she preferring tours of European castles, while I annually escaped to Caribbean resorts. In the name of science and curiosity, we stayed committed to keeping a casual Internet dialogue going, periodically sharing musings about our dating lives, career ambitions, and the validity of the science behind the DNA company's ethnicity estimates.

Last year, after a long lull in our communications, Ms. P. messaged me about a grand reunion her relatives were planning to celebrate America's 250th birthday and the centennial of reclaiming their Lowcountry property. She attached a picture from a previous gathering there, showing a multi-generational group huddled in a vast and lush field of sweetgrass. They were a happy and prosperous-looking crew. With cheeks flushed red, their grins bloomed like spring flowers.

"Would you like to join us?" Ms. P. wrote. She sprinkled in poetics about how, as a professional historian, she had hoped to encourage the P.'s to embrace their full American story and how, despite their participation in our country's darker periods, ultimately, their narrative is one of patriotism, enlightenment, reconciliation, *blah, blah, blah*... on and on she went. Was she serious? Attend a star-spangled party with *them*—some of whom, by the logic of DNA, I shared ancestors with—on land where possibly some of my *other* ancestors could have been held in bondage? I closed my laptop without responding.

A few months ago, she followed up. "Have you decided to attend?" she asked.

I felt like the target of a dare. I wrote back: "It's complicated."

Her reply came quickly. "I understand. If you do come, I promise it'll be worth it. We would love to have you."

I imagined the *we* she represented. I imagined walking into a crowd of them, explaining myself while simultaneously not wanting to explain too much. I imagined weeping, sentimentality, and nostalgia, brushing aside inconvenient details and buried secrets. There would be discomfort, awkwardness, and uncertainty. There would be polite conversation, but always the potential for quick ugly turns.

A few days ago, during a quiet evening at home, I found myself scanning the reunion details Ms. P. forwarded—directions to their land in South Carolina, an itinerary, contributory costs, and a list of suggested family-friendly activities to explore. But when I thought about stepping onto that land, my stomach churned. The next day at work, I crafted a reply in my head:

*Thank you for your kind invitation, but I must politely decline. The food won't nourish me, the conversation will feel inane, and my presence may put me in danger. There's a 99.9% chance I will be offended, disregarded, or dismissed.*

When I later visited the DNA site to send the message, an automated response came back: "*This user has blocked you from contacting them.*"

All set and prepared to feel satisfied for rejecting her, I felt rejected. Erased. Revisiting years and years of messages sent to Ms. P., I wondered if all that I shared compounded a too-real reality that finally chased her away. Or maybe my invitation was rescinded after she consulted with others in the P. family? I conjured my ancestors for counsel, they who knew firsthand the burdens of intertwined histories I wanted to untangle when I first sent that vial of spit. In unison, they told me: *Show up. Give voice to silent histories that otherwise will be withering ghosts.*

I didn't know how to heed such a call. Science had charted a truth but offered no maps for navigating it. But I opened my laptop, connected to the Wi-Fi, browsed over to Expedia, and searched for flights to Charleston, South Carolina. Hesitantly, I booked the first one leaving DCA early in the morning of July 3, 2026.

# INSECURITY

DANIELLE EVENNOU

there's a particular intimacy
I have with the man who checks
my trunk for bombs daily

the surprise of what he'll find
sand from a vacation on Block Island
a child-sized potty

throughout the two-minute inspection
we talk: weather, the holidays, weekend plans
skimming the surface of our loneliness

he drives a hearse by choice
decorates it for Halloween
skeletons giving out candy

one day, I joke: *don't let*
*Elon into the building*
an airplane misses its landing

when I repeat the line
he intentionally looks away
rage floods the engine

two weeks later
he says it's his last day
the contract cancelled

# MILANKOVITCH CYCLES AND OTHER STORIES

## JOANNA URBAN

"MOM, ARE WE ALMOST THERE?" comes Laney's voice from the backseat.

"Yes, almost," I lie for the fourth time in the hour we've been in the car.

The cars surrounding us are packed in as tightly as blocks in a game of Tetris. Wind whips the palm trees dotting the highway, the first hint of the storm ahead. We've only made it from our house in St. Petersburg to the Tampa Bay bridge and now the slow creep of traffic has come to a halt altogether. My husband Chris turns off the engine and releases a long exhale. We've waited too long—just 36 hours until the storm will make landfall—and now we might be too late.

"How many more minutes?" Laney says.

I look over my shoulder at my five-year-old. Chocolate residue lingers in the corners of her lips. Her wispy brown hair sticks up in pigtails, and she clutches her *Paw Patrol* stuffed dog. Sitting beside her, my ten-year-old son, Tyler, is absorbed in the book in his lap, diagrams of airplanes on its pages.

"I don't know, honey. Why don't you count?" I say to Laney.

"I already counted to a hundred."

"What comes after one hundred?" I feel the brightness from my voice fading, and I know it is far too early for this.

I'm spent from the past two days arguing with Chris, persuading him that we needed to evacuate. A Category 5 hurricane was headed right for Tampa Bay. No, it wasn't a hoax, and the media wasn't blowing it out of proportion, I kept telling him. Finally, after threatening to pack up and take the kids myself, he'd given in.

Laney pouts, crosses her arms. "I don't want to count anymore."

"How about we put on an episode of Bluey?" I hate resorting to screen time so soon, but if we're going to get through this evacuation, I'm going to have to bend and break my rules.

I scroll through our downloaded episodes on the clunky, childproofed iPad, find one of Laney's favorites, and clip the device into its holder on the back of Chris's seat. I pull out Laney's hot pink headphones and plug her in. Chris lets out another loud sigh, mumbles something under his breath that I can't hear and pointedly ignore.

"Mom, how many more hurricanes do you think we'll have this season?" Tyler says.

"I'm not sure sweetheart. We're on N for Nicole, so hopefully this is the last big one."

I glance sideways at Chris, silently daring him to speak up so I can let him have it. His climate-change-denier tendencies are what got us into this mess—leaving in the thick of traffic as the head of the storm rustles up waves in the bay, humidity hanging heavy in the air. Part of me wishes we had left without him; I need him to understand how real this is, and my words alone don't have the power to do that.

"This weatherman on the internet says that we might run out of letters in the alphabet this year," Tyler's voice interrupts my thoughts. "And if that happens, they might have to come up with a whole new list of names," he delightfully imparts this knowledge.

Panic pricks the back of my neck at one word. "When were you on the internet?" I ask. I'm constantly terrified of the obscure corners of the cyberworld he could discover.

"In lab at school."

"Was there a project you were doing in lab?"

"Yeah, my project was on hurricanes."

"Oh."

Of course. Why should this surprise me? It was tsunamis for a while, then tornados, then earthquakes. My clever fourth grader has a knack for science and his current obsession is extreme weather.

"Has that ever happened before?" he asks.

"What happened?"

"Have we ever run out of letters for hurricanes?"

"I don't think so—"

"That's not going to happen Ty," Chris butts in. A sharp pressure settles beneath my sternum. "Whoever this weatherman is, you shouldn't be listening to him. He doesn't know what he's talking about."

"How do you know?" Tyler asks.

He doesn't say this with an edge meant to challenge his father but with a genuine curiosity. I can see the questions and hypotheses and theories whirling in that growing brain of his. My son: always in search of answers that I wish I could give him.

"Because. Things don't get that bad that fast," Chris says. I can sense him holding back, testing me and what he can get away with saying. When I'm silent, he continues, "Some years there are more hurricanes, and this year's a little worse than usual, but that doesn't mean the world's coming to an end. We're not going to run through three alphabets worth of hurricanes and be living on houseboats by 2040 despite what they tell you in school."

"Chris," I warn.

"But it's getting worse every year," Tyler says. "Mrs. Trudell says that because the sea level keeps rising and warmer air holds more moisture, we get more flooding from hurricanes."

"Ty, the climate has been changing for longer than humans have been alive. Did Mrs. Trudell talk to the class about a little thing called the ice age?" He pauses dramatically. "Or Milankovitch cycles?"

"No." Tyler's listening now. His father's big words have piqued his interest. "What are those?"

"Well, Milankovitch cycles are the changes in the shape of the Earth's orbit around the sun. They happen about every 100,000 years, and that changes the amount of sunlight and warmth we get based on how far the Earth is—"

"Chris, I don't think he needs to hear about these theories from your podcasts."

"They're not *theories from my podcasts.* It's proven by science, Tara. You can ask NASA. If that school is going to fill his head with human-driven climate change nonsense, I might as well give him all the information. Let him make up his own mind."

"Can we just *not* right now?" I sigh.

Chris is silent, correctly determining that it's better not to start something given our current circumstances. We'll be stuck in the car for likely another five hours before we reach my sister Heather's house in Gainesville.

Chris hadn't always been so unhinged. Yes, he'd always had a bit of an anti-establishment leaning, a subtle skepticism of authority, but at some point in the past five years, things had shifted. Maybe it started during the pandemic, with nowhere to go and nothing to do, when he fell deeper into an online echo chamber of people with similar tendencies. People who needed to create their own stories about how the world worked. And climate change was the thing he latched onto.

The traffic starts to move. We creep along towards the Tesla in front of us, finally inching onto the bridge. We lurch ahead a few feet, then pause. Another ten feet toward the distant skyline of Tampa, before we roll to a stop, and again and again and again. The sky is fading to a deep bluish purple and thick clouds hover near the horizon.

I glance back at Laney, who's still plugged into her show. Pink headphones wrapped over her ears and eyes glued to the screen, her thick eyelashes flutter every few seconds.

"Can you explain it again, Dad?" Tyler asks. "I don't understand how Milankovitch cycles work."

"Ty," I lower my voice. "You don't need to worry about that."

"Why can't I know?"

"Because you need to focus on learning the facts in school. What about your carbon footprint lesson in science. Why don't we talk about some ways we can all reduce our carbon footprint?"

"Mom, I have to go potty." Laney peels off her headphones.

"Okay, honey. Let me see where the next rest stop is." I search my phone for the next place to stop along our route. "There's something coming up in three miles. So, fifteen minutes. Can you wait that long?"

"Okay."

"Are you sure? Do you want Daddy to pull over now?" It isn't ideal, but the traffic is so slow that I could feasibly walk to the edge of the woods with her and let her go there.

"I can wait."

As we approach the exit for the rest stop there's already a line forming off the exit ramp.

"How are you doing, Laney girl?" Chris says. "Can you wait a few more minutes?"

"Yeah," she sighs.

The line of cars slowly slinks forward, and Chris and I check on Laney every few minutes, until finally, we are close enough to the parking lot that I can get out of the car. I scoop Laney from her car seat behind me.

As I speedwalk alongside the line of cars rolling up to the pavilion, Laney on my hip, I notice every parking spot is full. Cars are stationed on the grass, edging up against the dense cluster of pine trees. I hold Laney's hand and lead her to the building where the restrooms are. There is a huge line to the women's room that snakes almost to the front doors of the building. I shouldn't be surprised given the sheer number of people on the highway.

"Let's go outside," I say to Laney. I know from experience that she's reaching her limit for "holding it."

We walk to the back of the building, past covered picnic shelters and vending machines, and I help Laney squat behind a cluster of palmettos and scrubs. Then I squat and pee after her. I have tissues and hand sanitizer for us in my purse.

Chris texts me that he's made it into the parking lot. I take Laney's hand as we walk to meet them. The sky is darkening to the color of a bruise and my knees ache, the way they always do when the air pressure changes.

"Are we going to live on a houseboat?" Laney looks up at me.

"What? No, honey, of course not."

"But that's what Daddy and Ty were saying. Because there's so many hurricanes."

My collarbone tingles. I need to be more careful with what they say around Laney. Of course, it's not just them. The TV, the radio, what I say. Even if she doesn't understand it, she can pick up on the disquiet that descends upon us before the storm.

"Sweetie, that's not going to happen."

My chest feels hollow. How do I create a sense of safety for her when I no longer feel it myself?

"Why do Daddy and Ty say it is? They fight about the climate."

"I know." I look up at the ribbon of thick clouds, unfurling like an angry giant in the sky. "You know we try to save energy to help the earth from getting too hot. Like how we carpool with friends, and turn lights off when we leave a room, and ride bikes short distances instead of driving."

I have a million kid-friendly talking points about climate change that I've picked up from the school, other parents, and various blogs and internet sources over the years. Sometimes, I even feel halfway convincing as I say them. But right now, Laney looks up at me, her blue eyes widening as if to say *Don't we know that's just a drop in the bucket?* or *Who are you kidding, Mom?*

A car horn blares, and I glance up to see our white SUV, Chris waving to us from the driver's seat. There are still no parking spots, so he pulls up onto the grass beside a minivan that has done the same thing.

"Hi, Daddy," Laney says as Chris gets out of the car.

"Hi, Pumpkin." Chris picks her up and spins her around. One circle, then two. She squeals with delight, then he slows down, situates her on his hip.

"If we ride bikes to Auntie Heather's house will that help save the climate?"

"Laney, honey. Don't believe what they're telling you in school. Drive as many cars, fly as many planes as you want, it won't make a difference. I'll keep you safe, baby. There's *nothing* at all to worry about."

I'm about to reprimand him for contradicting me, but when I see the look of concern soften on Laney's face, I think better of it. Maybe this is why—despite his monumental flaws—I can't let go of him. His staunch belief that things will be okay allows my five-year-old to feel safe. And for that I would do anything.

Chris puts her down and we lock eyes, a tiny spark of parental understanding passing between us. He goes over to the spot behind the scrubs to pee. I tell Tyler and Laney to sit at the picnic shelter while I walk the few feet to get the cooler from our car.

The hefty cooler is on top of suitcases and boxes, beneath a duffel bag that contains all the important items I couldn't risk being destroyed in a flood. Passports and birth certificates; baby books; a pouch of vintage jewelry that belonged to my grandmother; wooden boxes containing the ashes of two of our dogs.

I walk back to the picnic shelter and see Laney sitting on the table, Tyler standing beside it so that he's eye level with her.

"It's called carbon capture," he's saying to his sister. "It works like a giant fan. You know, like the fan in your bedroom that we turn on when you're hot at night? But a lot bigger. And it pulls the bad molecules out of the air. The carbon that's making the Earth hot."

"Will it make it so there won't be more hurricanes? So, we don't have to 'vacuate to Auntie Heather's next year?"

"Well, not yet. It won't work that fast. But there are lots of smart people working on this, Laney. When I'm a grown up I'm gonna work with them. We might have to keep evacuating and we're still going to get hurricanes, but it's gonna be okay. And you like going to Aunt Heather's, don't you?"

Laney nods. I feel a tear slide down my cheek. I'm so caught up in doom sometimes that I forget about the impossible. Future solutions that are just taking form. But my son hasn't. My ten-year-old, who despite knowing so much, can still choose hope.

"Hey, you two. Time for dinner." I walk up beside my son and put my arm around him, looking down at his short dark hair as straight as pins, the smattering of freckles across his cheeks.

Chris is approaching us, doing a silly bear walk where he takes huge steps and reaches his arms up high, making Laney giggle. I unpack our sandwiches in their reusable ziplock bags, a glass gallon jug of water, and cups. I mouth a silent *thank you* to my son—for being kind to his sister, for not provoking his father, for giving me the shred of hope I need to make it through this evacuation. Tyler smiles at me as Chris sits down beside Laney. I pass out the sandwiches and pour everyone water in their compostable cups.

# YOUR NAME

## ERICA SIMONE TURNIPSEED

Your name is America. It was always supposed to be America.

My queasy stomach and new pooch told Mami you were coming before I knew. I was twenty-three, single, and undocumented, my body new to a man's love. Jalonte was that man. A quirky, twenty-year-old American guy, he'd become my co-worker five weeks before at the New Orleans 7-Eleven, where I'd been working the night shift for four years. He asked me about my dreams and opinions, and he listened to my answers even when I stuttered. We were standing so close, locking up the liquor, and he stopped to stare at me. He said I was sexy, not ugly, like other guys did because of the raised birthmark over my right eyebrow. It was the same midnight brown of his skin, which he took as a sign. I kissed him. And I kept kissing him. That night, I didn't plan to make Jalonte your father. I just wanted to feel more of him because he made me feel good.

So many things about my life felt bad to me: being poor, Mami's accent that stamped us as foreigners, our secrets, my stutter and birthmark. I couldn't remember what it was like before I felt bad, but Mami had told me. I was a Honduran baby girl living with Mami and Doña America, who was a tiny but fierce woman and most respected abuelita in our town. Doña America let Mami and me live with her after Mami's stepfather was killed by someone he had crossed one too many times. His family buried him at night without a funeral and dropped us from the family. The same thing happened with Mami's mother's side of the family when she died nine years before. Seemed *everyone* was afraid of her stepfather's opps. Now with him dead too, folks thought Mami and me would be killed next if we didn't flee our country.

I was seven months old when Hurricane Katrina hit New Orleans in the US hard. The Big Easy became a ghost town; homeless survivors were shipped out, leaving no one to bury all the abandoned decomposing bodies or tear down the waterlogged homes that remained. America's decision-makers knew this was work only the desperate and destitute would do. So the country let in its brown and poor Spanish-speaking neighbors south of the border even though our no-visa-having selves lacked sponsors and bank accounts. Mami believed it was a direct invitation from Jesús Cristo for us to go to God's own country. First, Doña had taken us in when we needed her, and now the United States of America would do the same.

For months, Mami did her job with my sleeping baby's body tied to her back. Then, we overstayed our welcome. NOLA was once again filled with tourists yelling *laissez les bons temps rouler* in its drunken, English-speaking streets. Mami, and many like us, whispered in Spanish and disappeared into the back rooms of kitchens and casinos, becoming members of America's silent underclass. With no legal status in this country, we were shadows on the frontline, working to fulfill someone else's American dream.

So, when Mami looked at twenty-three-year-old me and told me that I was going to have you—my own little mamita—I immediately knew I would name you America. Don't get me wrong: I knew that most folks in this country don't care about folks like me who wipe their asses for a living. But you would be American like them. So, you could be America for *me*.

IN THE HOSPITAL, I stared into your day-old face that looked like a combination of my recently deported Mami and your dead daddy, who the police killed by mistake at the 7-Eleven where we worked. I imagined Doña America sitting on a stool in heaven, her eyes twinkling from under a wide-brimmed hat. "H-h-her name is America Esperanza," I told the social worker sitting in front of me.

"Where are you from?" she asked me, her face drawn into a ball of disapproval.

"Hond-d-d-duras." I whispered it and felt ashamed.

Her face drew tighter. "You can't name her that."

"B-b-b-but that's the n-n-n-n-name of my A-a-abuelita!" I condensed the truth into a lie.

"In Honduras? Well, you're not there. That name means something *different* here."

"B-b-but I love—"

"You can't. This country isn't even yours. You don't just get to name your *daughter* America after a whole *country* because you feel like it." She cleared her throat and lowered her eyes. "Isn't there another name you like? Maybe something from *home*?"

"My b-b-b-best fr-friend's name is M-m-m-m-mercedes…"

"That's a lovely name. And it's the name of an expensive car, too. Maybe she'll have a Mercedes one day." The social worker chuckled as she said it, writing "Mercedes" on the official form for your birth certificate. "Was the father present for her birth?"

"He w-w-w-was killed. M-m-mistaken identity."

"Of course." The social worker nodded, and her eyelids crumbled like used napkins. "Terrible shame." She cleared her throat. "The baby will have your last name, then." And she wrote it down. "Any middle name?"

"N-n-n-no."

She turned the clipboard around to face me and took you out of my arms so I could sign it. Then she handed you back to me and walked out of the hospital room. I clutched you and mourned all that had slipped out of my hands for you: your daddy, your abuela, and even your claim to America.

# WHEN COTTON WAS KING

## JACKIE WALKER

IN GREENWOOD, a long since gone cotton capital, Ingrid bends down to pick a boll, the dull, dingy color settling against her hand. The nubby, misshapen blob beneath her fingers feels nothing like the soft, white round balls she pulls from Johnson & Johnson bags. Her seven-page application to the Virginia Commission for the Arts mentioned nothing about the nuances of this rough plant abloom under her fingers. Her narrative only spoke of a photo journal of cotton culture in Greenwood. Her rental, a grey Nissan Sentra, sits stilled in the imprint of two-foot-wide tractor tracks.

She grabs her Nikon, screws the zoom lens on, and trains the eye to the center of a cotton boll, then away to the hardened brown leaf bud spread out at the base, the horrid bottom that always reminds her of crooked fingers and the nicks of those razor-sharp curves. She backs away from the blizzard of whiteness and imagines what will emerge from the photo bath in her darkroom.

Her friend Egbert, who only photographs lilies beginning the slow burst into being, has tried to nudge her toward digital. But she's old fashioned, partial to those anonymous old men who ducked under black spreads before taking a shot. She knows the new magic of instant images, stunted Japanese red maples cropped at the press of a button, or the crying slim-faced toddler deleted from view has nothing on the portraiture of Van Der Zee or Stieglitz.

On the road again, she wanders away from Highway 82, which will lead her back to the azure wonder of Hampton Inn. A flat yellow set of parallel lines before her, she drives past barren fields tilled and awaiting another season's planting until she sees a little black choo-choo train mounted on top of a pole, the miniature locomotive a blend of wheels beginning to turn and stilled movement. Just beneath the wheels, big block-style black letters proclaim, "Tutwiler, Where the Blues was Born." The lone marker standing just yards before a dent ridden faded red stop sign.

She turns off into the gravel crossroads and parks at a spot close enough to see the spokes on the wheels graying from the elements. The sandy floor of land she steps on is smooth under the soles of her red Pro-Ked sneakers. As she lifts her Nikon, a white Ford F-150 rumbles up the dusty road, puffs of beige dust rising beneath the wheels. The man behind the steering wheel isn't clean-shaven like the men in Richmond, scalp buzzed down to stubble. His hair is the auburn of fall leaves, a modest height just high enough to cup under the palm of your hand. He jumps out and walks toward her.

"Take one of me," he says, a smile spread across his lips.

She snaps him just as he is, his mouth gaped open, the golden hazel of his eyes flashed in surprise. Each of his arms swings in different directions, the right one moving forward, the left one hanging down, his five fingers spread wide against his dungarees.

"Hey, no fair. I didn't get a chance to pose," he says.

"Is this true?" she asks, pointing to the train.

"Every little town round here claims to be home of the blues."

"And cotton?"

"King everywhere, once."

"I'm looking for plantation markers. Authentic old ones, not new spiffy rede-signed ones," she says.

"Fallin' down old?"

She nods.

"Meet me here tomorrow at noon."

"How do I know your intentions are honorable?"

"You don't."

"So, who would I be waiting for?"

"Oscar."

"I'm Ingrid."

He steps back into his Ford F-150, all edges, and shiny chrome, the upper half of his body framed in the rearview window. She watches him drive off; his denim-shirted back filling the driver's side, the space in the window beside him empty. She looks at the long rectangle of glass, the linebacker broadness of his shoulders, and thinks he is a close-cropped photo moving far away from her.

THE NEXT DAY, Ingrid pulls up to the Tutwiler train, gets out and sticks her fingers through the cantaloupe-sized wheel. She aims her Nikon between the spokes to gaze at the long tracts of land stretching out to a horizon beyond her eyes.

Oscar eases his F-150 up to the stop sign, a wide grin edging up to his cheeks. He extends an arm and circles with his hands for her to wrap it up, cautioning, "Save some for the markers."

She trails him over the same two-lane nothingness she has known for days now, the steady flatlands on each side of the road, the flared trunks of cypress trees rising out of rivers, and rows of shiny green-leaved soybeans.

Oscar slows up and pulls off to the side of a cotton field. There, fifty feet from the square of his hood in swirling white script, is a frame for Rack Rent Plantation spelled out on two separate lines, the "I" missing, faux-shaped cotton bolls atop each pole, the year 1867 in wrought iron script. The whole of it like a gate open before her.

Ingrid smiles, walks over to Oscar, and squeezes the rounded top of his shoulder. Then she's gone walking around and through the two poles, pushing against each one to test the sturdiness then shooting alternately on her knees or standing, half a roll finished before she hears Oscar's voice.

"How'd you come to this?" he asks, pointing to her camera.

"I always wanted to slow life down. When I was a girl, I'd say freeze to all the kids as we ran around or jumped double-dutch. My father gave me a Konica TC, told me that was the only way to freeze things. Otherwise, life just rushes on."

"Why cotton?"

Ingrid tilts her head to the side and gives him her most exasperated look, preparing to tell him about the pristine white sign for Swan Lake Gin she glimpsed as a teenager a decade ago from the backseat of her father's Honda Accord during a two-day business trip and history lesson on Ruleville's Fannie Lou Hamer. That backseat memory led her back to Greenwood.

"Everyone comes here digging for dirt."

"Well, this is Mississippi, land of missing civil rights workers and Emmett Till."

"That was decades ago. I'm talking about the here and now."

Ingrid is quiet and hears the insistence in his voice.

"Forget the markers; let me be your subject," he says, cocksure, a glint in his eyes.

"How can you be more important than the trade in cotton, those bloodied hands, gins mangling arms, and all those stories passed down from the old folks?"

"Baby, there's more than enough tragedy to go around."

"I'm not so sure your life is that significant."

"Okay, try this: four years in microbiology at Tougaloo College and I end up trolling Highway 49 for breakdowns."

She looks deep and hard at him, nods, then tells him, "You're not the story I'm looking for."

"You need to see me in action."

"Maybe. Show me a few more markers," she says, turning back to zoom in on the Rack Rent arches as Oscar slips into the center of each pole, and she closes the shutter on him standing in the middle.


THE DELIVERY TRUCK parked in front of Oscar's mustard single-level brick house is nothing like the plain white, efficient-looking AAA road service mini-vans she's seen back home on Interstate 95, the side panels empty except for the oval outlined in red with a trio of A's floating inside.

Oscar's Roadside Motor Miracles is spelled out in silver metallic press-on letters across the flat blue side of a once brown converted UPS delivery truck. A collage of florescent green Quaker State and bright orange Fram stickers behind the plastic body of a cherry red Camaro, hot rod thick tires protruding from the panel. His likeness, a fuzzy brown Afro and shiny black button eyes stare out in a steady gaze as his grey-gloved hands hold the strap of a battery.

Oscar slides the door open, helps Ingrid step up. She walks back to the metal shelves lining each side, flips through the rows of air filters, turns the white plastic bottles of Valvoline, swings the slender boxes of 19/22 inch windshield wipers, and pats the rectangular charcoal black sides of AC Delco batteries.

"You ready to roll?"

Ingrid pulls the long strap against her chest, steadies herself on the flip-down seat, and nods, then asks, "Where to?"

"Another rescue of Dangerous D on 49."

"Dangerous who?"

"Dwayne Dibbs fancies himself a rapper. Every two weeks he's broke down somewhere between Greenwood and Jackson."

On Highway 49, they pull up to a short, muscular man in stiff Levi's jeans, the white swirl of Nike on otherwise navy sneakers, royal blue gingham handkerchief tied round his head, leaning against the door of a buffed turquoise Buick LeSabre, his hood hitched high. He waves a faded blue handkerchief, a black stitched Dangerous D flapping in the wind as Oscar approaches.

"My man," he says, slapping Oscar a high-five.

"My all-time favorite bread and butter customer."

"It's either you or a three-hour walk to Indianola."

Ingrid follows Oscar as he ducks under the hood to fiddle with the radiator knob. She slides her Nikon into view, focusing on the curl of his fingers gripped around the squared notches.

Dangerous D taps her on the back and asks, "You do any PR shots?"

"No, just artsy stuff."

"I'm gettin' ready to drop a new one at the studio. Lil Wayne, Drake, and Kanye all be yesterday's news when I finish this," Dangerous D rambles on.

Ingrid shifts her camera away from a shot of Oscar's oily knuckles and feigns interest in Dangerous D's tale.

Dangerous D pulls her aside and whispers, "You trying for a hook-up with him you gotta loose those pigtails."

"Who said I was interested?"

"Hey, I'm just givin you tips."

Ingrid knows all he sees is her straight black hair parted down the center, a pair of thick braids touching the dip in her collarbone, the tan scoop-necked t-shirt and low-hipped Lee jeans she wears.

She stands beside Oscar, watching as Dangerous D pulls back onto the stretch of white lines they'll return to again. She turns to him ready to snap another picture until he holds up his hands in protest, then tugs on her left braid, the single frayed end slowly unraveling.

"I'm just coming along for the ride," Ingrid says, closing the cap on her camera.

"No markers or cotton gins?"

"Not this time."

Oscar turns on Highway 7 headed toward Coffeeville. In the distance, on the opposite side of the road, an accordion-style jack is stuck under the center of a Chevy Silverado, the rear driver's side tire missing. Oscar makes a U-turn across the two-lane road and pulls up ahead.

He bends down looking at the tread of a Bridgestone tire, then rounds the front of the hood and finds the matching tire propped up against a sunken one.

Ingrid walks around back to the bay, the silver ringed thick black tarp rumbles with movement. She peeks under, and a half-dozen pair of eyes, some blinking, one shuttered closed, and others widened in surprise, stare back at her.

"Os—" she begins, her words trailing off.

Ingrid points to the tarp, and Oscar whips it back. In the sunlight, six rows of men lay head to toe in wrinkled, dust-streaked khaki pants and mud-splotched blue jeans, the hint of a bushy eyebrow ducked into the crook of a faint beige arm, the rubber toe of a sneaker covering half of a golden-brown earlobe, another face down so only his shiny tar black hair shows.

Ingrid lifts the leather camera strap away from her skin and rubs the back of her neck. She watches as multiple men begin to stir, one his t-shirt dishwater gray, a thimble-sized wooden cross sliding along a licorice slim cord on his chest as he stretches his left arm up to the sky. Another who sits up straight as a ladder, eyes sea glass green, his face thin as a dime, the dirty blond tuft of his hair fanned out like a cock's crow. Then the one who rises from a tangle of legs the slightest waver in his stance as he stands, a wide swath of ridges and lines on his cheeks.

Oscar steps back, rocks on the heels of his work boots, drags his charcoal smudged palm against his forehead, stone still before all the movement around him. Slowly, he begins motioning each man to climb out and holds out his arm for each to grab; all but one shies away as they slide over the sides or jump down to the soft grass below.

The one with an eye swollen shut, a perfectly pumpkin round face, skin the gleaming copper of pennies, and thick swollen lips who has gripped Oscar's arm asks, "Georgia?"

"No, Mississippi."

He raises a hand to touch his puffy eye, mumbles, "Muchachos, somos perdido," to the others, then looks down and shakes his head.

Oscar leads them in a line that meanders into a wavy S over to the van. In the waiting area, one man kneels in the dirt, his forehead pressed against both of his palms. Two other men loop their arms through his and try to lift him up, but he grinds his knees further into the dirt.

Ingrid lifts the Nikon to her eye, follows prints of the fallen man's knees in loosened earth, closes the shutter on the pants of one who crouches, the zig-zag of his legs falling into a Z, zooms in on the bulging veins of another's hand gripping a plastic gallon of water, then up to the blurred blue letters on a square of paper stuck in the back pocket of another man.

Oscar guides each one into the back of the van, settling them in groups of four against the shelves, their backs braced by stacked AC Delco batteries on one side and columns of used Firestone tires on the other side.

Ingrid steps in, looking for the man who left cup-sized grooves in the dirt. In the trio of clusters, a whisper of words rises, two men stretch their legs out into parallel lines, and a lone man's arm is raised in the air, his thumb and forefinger falling into a check mark. She follows his hand to the second row and looks down at the charcoal-smudged ovals on the knees of his blue jeans. As the van pulls off from bumpy gravel to smooth road, she grips the underside of his hand, her fingers graze a whorl of calluses, rough, and scratchy.

# NEIGHBORLY

RACHEL REH

The day unfolds, smelling like a penny.
There's blood on my stoop, pink cigarettes
in the cracks of the sidewalk. I ask
the neighbors and check the news. Nothing.

I sweep up glass, drink the tap, pack a bag.
It's time for work. On my bike, I'm last
to a four-way but the cars wave me on.
I slow them down. They let it happen.

Something transpired, the ghost of a moment.
Casings without bullets. Screams while I slept.
But no one is dead. Someone
has to be dead, for it to matter.

# REBIRTH

## ADRIENNE BENSON

I REMEMBER the day you and I were born—you to me and I to you. Everything was new. You were a brand-new human, and I was raw and reborn into a whole new life. They laid you on my chest, and you were as red as meat and smelled deep and primal, like the inside of me. You were mine, and I was yours, linked together by devotion and blood.

When you were in middle school, we didn't know why you hated it, why you pleaded with your dad and me to stay home almost every day, why the thought of leaving the house made you so angry. We took you to a doctor and she asked me questions. I answered all of them. I gave her everything I had. Was it a normal pregnancy? She asked. I think back to the summer of 2001. Because of your dad's job, we were living in Kyiv, Ukraine. On the day I found out I wasn't alone in my body anymore, I couldn't believe my luck. That feeling lasted through the long summer days and into the turning of fall, when the Ukrainian evenings chilled, and the leaves began to color. It lasted through my constant morning sickness that had me vomiting 10-15 times a day. It lasted until the day I turned on the cable TV and saw that our American channel had a live morning show on. The very Americanness of the chatty blond anchor comforted me, and I curled up to watch. I sucked on ginger Altoids and dry-heaved into the garbage can at my side. It was morning in the United States, and afternoon in Kyiv, and it was the wrong time and day to be watching TV live from the East Coast.

I told the doctor I felt a physical jolt that day when I realized what was happening on TV. The planes that lit into windows and walls, backlit by glorious sunshine. That day, I held the place in my middle where you were just barely a beating heart. I felt the dank breath of regret for giving you a world so flawed and broken. Then I watched those people leap from those crumbling buildings and fall like stars.

Being born, I've learned, can happen more than once. You taught me this. When you were seventeen and first tried to die, I didn't think you really meant it. Call it a mother's instinct. I trusted your will to live. Even though it happened three more times; you rotating in and out of the psych ward, I knew you wanted to stay, you just didn't want to stay in the same place—you needed a different kind of life than the one you were born into. I just didn't know what that meant.

THERE ARE SO MANY WAYS for people to hate themselves. There are the same number of ways for people to love themselves. Sometimes, maybe most of the time, it's not as easy as choosing. Things can be both easy and hard. You can love aspects of yourself and not others. That's normal, I suspect. I love my humor and hate that I can't drive in traffic without getting angry. You hated your body for nineteen years. You carved lines into your skin; you made yourself bleed. You said it helped you to feel. I told you it made me cry. I helped make you, I said. You're my beautiful, perfect boy. I didn't know then that I was wrong, that maybe the words I selected—out of love—hurt you more than they helped.

There are so many ways to be born. You were my first, and for a long time, I hated the way I thought my body failed me when I tried so hard to bring you into the world. Thirty-six hours of labor, the best intentions for a natural birth that ended in drugs and an epidural and me panicking on a gurney, under bright, white lights as a stern doctor filleted me like a fish and pulled you forth, blood and beloved, the cord wrapped tightly around your neck. My beloved boy, you birthed yourself again at nineteen when you raised your bleeding arms to me and said this wasn't your body. It wasn't you. You weren't my baby boy; you weren't my son.

When you were a toddler, I used to carry you on my hip, and you'd reach up and stroke my cheek and wind my hair around your fingers and laugh. You were so happy. I wonder when your knowing emerged; your understanding that the body you inhabited wasn't right. I wonder how it felt to live for so long in what I imagine was like an ill-fitting costume, itchy and wrong. I wonder how it felt to wear that costume every day, to grow to hate the way it constricted you, the way it just felt dishonest, the way that looking in the mirror or going to the bathroom became a constant punishment.

When you were little, just learning to talk, you called me Mama. That's one of the first sounds a baby can make. *Maaa.* It echoes the sound of the universe creating itself in Hindu tradition, "Om." *Oma* is mother in German. Mama is me. You still call me that, and your voice is that of a twenty-two-year-old man. I don't tell you this. I don't want to remind you. I call you Alice now, the name you named yourself. I introduce you as my daughter. I was embarrassed for a while. I was aware that you still look mostly like a man—the man you are not, but you have wide shoulders, the jaw of a man, and an Adam's apple that bobs in your throat when you talk. I don't want you to hate your body anymore. I want you to see what I see—a perfect human; a child I love. I want you to see that in some way, we're still connected, you and I, by blood and by devotion. You carefully shave away the dark hairs that curl across your forearm now. The bathroom door was open one day, and I was bringing clean towels up, and I saw you—the concentration and care you took not to cut yourself. It stunned me because your arms still carry the shadows of the crosshatching you made on purpose. They remind me every time I see them. That day, when I brought the fresh towels up, you told me, happily, that the hormones you're taking, the estrogen, will help the hair soften, and lessen, and eventually, you won't have to shave. You're beginning to change. A metamorphosis from Miles to Alice. From boy to girl, son to daughter. My daughter, Alice.

There are so many ways for people to surprise each other. Your younger brother loves rocks. He didn't always, but a college geology class, taken on a whim to fulfill a science credit, ignited something in him. Now, he talks about rock formations and types as if he were describing friends, lovers, family members. I never saw him as a scientist. When he was little, he could name world leaders like other kids named Pokémon. He was—we found it hilarious—obsessed with political coups and societal upheaval. His first major, political science seemed a natural choice. Like his great-grandfather, the Congressman, we said. Now he loves rocks and wants to get a Master of Science in Geology. People change. I was married once; now I'm not. We called you a boy once, for too long. We called you that, and it hurt you; it made you hate yourself and all the things you had to do while being a boy: going to school, saying your name, interacting with people who saw you as one thing when you were really, deeply, truly, another thing entirely. I'm sorry for all the ways we didn't know. When I tell you this, that I'm sorry we didn't know, you smile. You are gracious. You are kind. You say you forgive me.

I'm learning to forgive myself, too. I have told everyone I know now that you are Alice. I told the neighbors, my colleagues at work, our extended family, the housekeeper that comes twice a month. She's a female, I say, she's my daughter. She's Alice. I roll your new name around in my mouth. Nobody has been anything but kind.

The cleaning lady says that sometimes even God makes mistakes. It's ok, she pats my arm. We just love our children, she says. We do what we can for them. When she says this, I feel like weeping. I hate that I was embarrassed by you at all, ever.

There are so many ways to love someone. You take the estrogen shots once a week. You give them to yourself. I offered to help, and you say no, you got this.

You do, don't you? You birthed yourself into a new name, and now you're birthing yourself into a new body. Sometimes I think of those buildings the world watched fall on that beautiful September day—the people who leaped and fell, and the way I thought that day meant the world was breaking, that it would be too broken for my children. There are three of you now: you, your younger brother, and your baby sister, who is really a teenager. The world didn't break; parts of it burned for a while, and then new things grew in their place. Even some beautiful things. The scars on your arms glint silver. Sometimes, when we're walking home from a dinner out, and we pass under streetlights, your little sister screams as you reach out, pretending to tickle her. *ALICE!* she yells and laughs, and it's like no other name for you ever existed in her mind. You are you. You are her sister. You are Alice.

# EMILIO

## MIGUEL AVERO

EL ECO DE LA ÚLTIMA DETONACIÓN empieza a desvanecerse en tu cabeza. Te preguntas dónde se encuentra el miedo, y te respondes que quizás se trata de la parálisis, la parálisis es la continuación del miedo, su nueva cara, la metamorfosis definitiva. Entonces, no te mueves. Tus manos siguen apoyadas sobre la tabla de madera, aplastando la computadora que en algunos segundos caerá sobre las baldosas del salón, como ha caído ya tu cuaderno de apuntes. Todo es quietud a tu alrededor, a excepción de la cortina que se levanta como la pollera de Marilyn en aquella icónica foto que tienes de fondo de pantalla en tu celular. Y el pelo del profesor Villagrán. Su pelo sedoso, oscuro, su fino pelo que, peinado hacia atrás, deja a la vista una frente blanca y surcada por arrugas. Su pelo se mueve apenas por un coletazo del viento impelido por las cortinas del salón.

¿Quién le avisará a la familia del profesor?

Te preguntas eso olvidando que tampoco sabes quién le avisará a tu familia. Pero piensas en él. Porque él ya no podrá contar su versión de los hechos.

¿Tú sí? ¿Hay formas de narrar este tipo de experiencias?

"Yo trataba de defender a Han", dirías frente a la cámara, y el 90 por ciento de tus seguidores no sabrían de qué estarías hablando. "Trataba de defender a Han del furibundo ataque del profesor. Villagrán decía—estaba diciendo segundos antes de que lo amordazara la muerte—que Han sufría de la misma enfermedad que denunciaba en sus libros. En sus escuetos y comerciales libros. En sus libros rebajados por su teoría única, pero vertida en infinitos recipientes distintos. En sus libros finos, de lectura instantánea, con citas ajenas como ingrediente mayoritario… Todo eso decía el profesor Villagrán. Y yo trataba de contradecirlo. ¿Para qué escribir libros de 1500 páginas que nadie leería, quizás ni siquiera el propio profesor Villagrán? ¿Para qué dedicar una década de tu vida a la escritura de un mamotreto impublicable cuyos lectores ya han desaparecido hace generaciones? Todo eso pensaba decir, pero un grito fracturó mis pensamientos".

El sonido de la computadora sobre las baldosas fractura tus recuerdos. La mano derecha del profesor cuelga ahora a su costado, como si su cuerpo comenzara a aflojarse. La rigidez, de momento, es toda tuya. La pantorrilla izquierda te arde, tienes el talón apoyado contra una de las patas de la silla. Intentas sacarlo y apoyarlo correctamente en el piso pero tus músculos no responden.

Te preguntas: ¿Dónde han ido todos? ¿Quién se ha llevado todo el ruido? ¿Por qué te quedaste sola con él? O con lo que queda de él.

De pronto, de manera inoportuna, recuerdas la única clase a solas con el profesor Villagrán. Había corregido tu ensayo sobre Borges y te sugería algunas lecturas, en especial un libro de tu compatriota, Emir Rodríguez Monegal. "¡Niña, debes leer a Emir!" Nunca llegaste a leerlo porque no se conseguía en ninguna parte. Quizás es lo primero que debas hacer cuando salgas de este embrollo, aunque seguramente tu agenda estará más ocupada que de costumbre.

¿Podrás salir de aquí? ¿Existe la posibilidad de que te pongas de pie, guardes las cosas en tu mochila y te dirijas al pasillo? ¿Vendrá alguien a buscarte? ¿Cuánto tiempo habrá transcurrido? ¿Te mirarán distinto?

A Emilio lo miraban distinto. Al menos al principio. Cuando se unió al curso le dieron el primer banco de la primera fila, es decir, junto al ventanal y casi encima del profesor Villagrán. Recuerdas que durante los primeros meses era más bien callado, aunque cuando comenzaba la clase no dudaba en participar. En los recreos iba como vos, como cualquiera de ustedes a la cantina. Siempre se ubicaba en las mesas que estaban junto a una pared. Estaba solo, pero tú no podías imaginar que él sintiera la soledad. Fue un tanto tenebroso, recuerdas, recibir su solicitud de amistad en las redes. En una misma tarde publicó más de sesenta fotos en los lugares más exóticos del mundo. Tú lo *stalkeabas*, pero jamás reaccionabas a sus publicaciones, ni siquiera a sus historias. Pero él sí reaccionaba. Recordaba cada una de tus intervenciones en clase y te ofrecía bibliografía para complementar tus ideas y puntos de vista. Emilio estaba solo. Emilio estaba solo entre un mar de seguidores y *bots*.

El profesor Villagrán tiene la cabeza un poco ladeada hacia su derecha. La mirada perdida (nunca más perdida) sobre la mesa de Emilio. Irónicamente, ahora parece mirar su sitio como nunca antes; porque el profesor Villagrán jamás miraba a Emilio, ni tomaba en cuenta su mano rígida siempre levantada para intervenir. El director Carrere le había llamado la atención por eso: "es un plan piloto, ni siquiera tienes que evaluarlo, uno por clase para elevar el nivel, además son regulables", pero el profesor Villagrán no estaba dispuesto a ceder ante "la locura de estos tiempos".

Sientes un cosquilleo en la parte alta del muslo. El celular vibra como si fuera un animal atrapado en el bolsillo de tu pantalón. De pronto sientes como si se derritiera. Queda quieto, en silencio. Como todo a tu alrededor: el salón, el pasillo, el maldito edificio de la universidad que iba a proporcionarte un futuro mejor.

Escuchas de pronto unas sirenas, el viento de la calle arrastra hacia tu ventana un griterío. Levantas mínimamente las manos de la tabla y con dificultad empiezas a mover el cuello y a estirar las piernas. Unos pasos mecánicos se acercan por el pasillo. No te animas a mirar, tampoco es necesario. La aparatosa silueta de Emilio se dibuja en las baldosas manchadas del salón. No alcanzas a ver si lleva el fusil de asalto, tampoco ves su mano extirpando de su propio pecho el Procesador. El modelo fallido. El modelo con forma de corazón.

THE ECHO OF THE LAST EXPLOSION begins to fade in your head. You wonder where the fear is, and you answer that perhaps it is paralysis, paralysis is the continuation of fear, its new face, the definitive metamorphosis. So, you don't move. Your hands remain resting on the wooden board, crushing the computer that in a few seconds will fall on the tiles of the living room, just like your notebook. Everything is quiet, except for the curtain that rises like Marilyn's skirt in that iconic photo you have as your cellphone's wallpaper. And Professor Villagrán's hair. His silky, dark hair, his fine hair that, when combed back, reveals a white forehead furrowed with wrinkles. His hair barely moved by the breeze from the living room's curtains.

Who will tell the professor's family?

You ask yourself that, forgetting that you don't know who will tell your family either. But you think about him. Because he won't be able to tell his version of the events anymore.

Do you? Are there ways to narrate this type of experience?

"I was trying to defend Han," you would say in front of the camera, and 90 percent of your followers wouldn't know what you were talking about. "I was trying to defend Han from the professor's furious attack, Villagrán said—he was saying seconds before death gagged him—that Han suffered from the same illness that he denounced in his books. In his brief and commercial books. In his books cheapened by his unique theory, but poured into infinite, different containers. In his thin books of instant reading, with other people's quotes as the main ingredient... Professor Villagrán said all that. And I tried to contradict him. Why write 1,500-page books that no one would read, perhaps not even Professor Villagrán himself? Why dedicate a decade of your life to writing an unpublishable, massive work whose readers have disappeared for generations? That's all I wanted to say, but a scream fractured my thoughts."

The sound of the computer on the tiles breaks your memories. The professor's right hand now hangs at his side, as if his body were beginning to loosen. The stiffness, for the moment, is all yours. Your left calf is burning, your heel is resting against one of the legs of the chair. You try to take it out and place it correctly on the floor, but your muscles don't respond.

You ask yourself: Where has everyone gone? Who took all the noise? Why were you left alone with him? Or with what's left of him.

Suddenly, inopportunely, you remember the only class alone with Professor Villagrán. He had corrected your essay on Borges and suggested some readings, especially a book by your compatriot, Emir Rodríguez Monegal. "Girl, you must read Emir!" You never got to read it because you couldn't find it anywhere. Maybe it's the first thing you should do when you get out of this mess, although your schedule will surely be busier than usual.

Will you be able to get out of here? Is there a chance you'll stand up, put your things in your backpack and go to the hallway? Will someone come looking for you? How much time will have passed? Will they look at you differently?

Emilio was looked at differently. At least at first. When he joined the class, he was given the first seat in the first row, that is, next to the window and almost on top of Professor Villagrán. You remember that during the first few months he was rather quiet, although when class started, he didn't hesitate to participate. During breaks he went like you, like any of you, to the cafeteria. He always sat at the tables that were next to a wall. He was alone, but you couldn't imagine that he felt lonely. It was a bit scary, you remember, receiving his friend request on social media. In one afternoon, he posted more than sixty photos in the most exotic places in the world. You stalked him, but you never reacted to his posts, not even to his stories. But he did react. He remembered each of your interventions in class and offered you books to complement your ideas and points of view. Emilio was alone. Emilio was alone among a sea of followers and bots.

Professor Villagrán has his head tilted slightly to the right. His gaze is lost (never lost again) on Emilio's desk. Ironically, he now seems to be looking at his seat like never before; because Professor Villagrán never looked at Emilio, nor did he take into account his rigid hand always raised to intervene. Dean Carrere had called him out on this: "it's a pilot plan, you don't even have to evaluate it, one per class to raise the level, and they are also adjustable," but Professor Villagrán was not willing to give in to "the madness of these times."

You feel a tickle on the upper part of your thigh. Your cell phone vibrates as if it were an animal trapped in your pants pocket. Suddenly, you feel as if it were melting. It remains still, silent. Like everything around you: the classroom, the hallway, the damn university building that was going to provide you with a better future.

Suddenly you hear sirens, the wind from the street drags a shouting towards your window. You lift your hands from the board and with difficulty begin to move your neck and stretch your legs. Footsteps mechanically walk down the hall. You don't dare look, nor is it necessary. Emilio's bulky silhouette is outlined on the stained tiles of the living room.

Translated by Jona Colson

# CONFEDERATES FROM HELL

## MARK BRAZAITIS

*To ease overcrowded conditions, Hell announced today that it was releasing Nathan Bedford Forrest, Jefferson Davis, and John Wilkes Booth. The three men—a Confederate general who served as the Ku Klux Klan's first Grand Wizard, the president of the Confederate States of America, and Abraham Lincoln's assassin, respectively—have spent their afterlives continuously reciting the 13ᵗʰ Amendment to the US Constitution. Heaven, however, refused to admit them, so they will return to Earth, where they will have an unprecedented opportunity to repent for the sins of their previous lives.*

*To speed their adaptation to a multi-cultural United States, the men will be dropped off in Harlem. Marian Blake, Harlem's representative on the New York City Council, called the decision to release the men at all, and especially in her district, alarming. "If history has taught us anything," the councilwoman said, "it's that it can repeat itself."*

*—The New York Times, November 5, 2024*

ON THE CORNER OF 125ᵀᴴ STREET and Frederick Douglass Boulevard, Nathan Bedford Forrest broke a street-corner preacher's arm following the preacher's assertion that Jesus was a divinity of color. Found guilty of assault, he was sentenced to three to five years in the Clinton Correctional Facility in upstate New York. Kosher meals were the tastiest and most nutritious on the prison's menu, so Forrest claimed to be an observant Jew. Meanwhile, he formed a gang of white supremacists, tattooing their forearms with Confederate flags and teaching them the rebel yell. Released after eighteen months, he moved to Tennessee's Thunderhead Mountain, where he's said to be training members of a revitalized Ku Klux Klan in guerrilla warfare, with weapons 100 times deadlier than any used in the Civil War. "The Fort Pillow massacre," one of Forrest's new comrades told *The Tennessean*, referring to the notorious bloodbath Forrest oversaw during his Civil War generalship, "was a game of croquet compared with what's to come."

AFRAID OF HOW HE MIGHT BE RECEIVED in Harlem, Jefferson Davis ducked into a Goodwill Store on Adam Clayton Powell Jr. Boulevard, where, seeking clothes of the kind he'd worn at the end of the Civil War to avoid capture, he bought high heels, stockings, and a dress. Disguised as a grandmother, albeit one with a goatee, he headed downtown on the A train before crossing over to Staten Island on the ferry. Thrilled to learn that the island's politics were closer to South Carolina's than to Manhattan's, he immediately launched a campaign for Congress. His slogan, "Succeed at Succession," appealed to Staten Islanders who for years had wanted to separate from New York City.

But Davis' successionist ambitions had an even bigger prize: the country as a whole. Or, rather, as a half. The time for a second split, he knew, was ideal. Divisive issues—guns, abortion, the environment, immigration, capitalism, law enforcement, race, gender, sexual orientation, and democracy—were even more plentiful now than they had been in antebellum times. His wife had urged him to discard his trunkful of Confederate dollars—it would have been easy enough to incinerate them in Hell—but he'd told her: "Let's hold on to them, darling. The South shall rise again."

He'd oft been criticized for his arrogance, but could he help it if he was as much a prophet as a politician? He wondered whether the new government he was destined to lead would be better served not by a president but a king.

WHEN JOHN WILKES BOOTH, hoping to shake the dust off his acting career, performed Henry V's "Band of Brothers" speech at "Amateur Night at the Apollo," the audience booed him off the stage. Knowing he was no amateur, he tried out for half a dozen Broadway plays and three musicals, including, ironically, a revival of "Assassins," but failed to land a part in any. He was approached about doing dinner theater in Hackensack, New Jersey, and was offered $100,000 to play himself in a gay porn movie called "Abe & John: Bedfellows Before They Were Dead Fellows." He declined both opportunities. Hunkered down in a studio apartment in Yonkers, he spent hours in front of the television, cursing the inferior entertainers who strutted and fretted across his screen and the politicians whose views he was certain only Thaddeus Stevens would have cheered.

His anger grew in proportion to his idleness. *Sic semper tyrannis!* He would— again—change the course of history.

# THE KILLING OF A SACRED AMERICAN DREAM
## PATIENCE WILLIAMS

At 8 p.m., Kennedy's party began. She was in the corner of the kitchen, staring at the large, decadent China plates filled to the brim with slaughtered meat. Most of it was smoked, burned to a crisp; the aroma drifted up, still warm, and filtered through the kitchen and down the corridor to the hallway, where the house parted and grew longer. It was slowly beginning to fill with guests in suits, black ties, and expensive dresses, typically in either blood or white or bruise. Kennedy blinked and listened to her heartbeat as her eyes roamed the room, growing claustrophobic while she inhaled deep breaths and smoothed the front of her velvet dress. "You look just like a patriot," her mother had complimented her in her bedroom mirror. Kennedy went downstairs and refused to look at any reflections of herself, and when Sam leaned in to quietly greet her right there in the kitchen, she jumped and turned around to hug him.

His eyes also stared alarmingly at the array of meat positioned delicately on the fine China as she held him tightly. "America eats carnal for dinner each night," he said in a low voice.

Kennedy pulled away and looked at him in his eyes. "I don't understand what is going on," she said, "and I don't understand what's happening to me. Thoughts of violence and rage are filling my head, and I don't understand a lot of what people are saying. It doesn't sound... known. I can't place it—why am I so disconnected?"

Sam looked at her and said nothing for a few moments. Kennedy held his gaze, understood it to hold meaning.

"I need to tell you something," he said. "Your ceremony tomorrow... there's still time to call it off. You've got to listen to me, Kennedy—there will be a price to pay if you went along with it."

Her eyes bore into her childhood innocence embodied as her friend Sam. Her gaze did not reject his statement, but it wasn't welcoming of his suggestion. "I don't know," she spoke softly. "I don't know, but I don't want to reject what I've been prepared for. Becoming American means a lot for my family. I wish I could help you understand it… but even if it is bad… it's all I've known… all I've known is that this is part of my life, that it is a big step in my life, and the consequences of rejecting it seem far worse than accepting it…" Her eyes smiled a gentle apology. A few more guests filtered in, breaking their attention. The final guest gazed up at the ceiling and wrinkled his nose. Kennedy rushed over to him and nodded in agreement.

"The smell of the meat is very strong," she sympathized. "Does it bother you?"

The man stared at Kennedy. "The meat isn't the bother," he said. "It's the killing."

Kennedy's eyes grew moist from the chandelier light hanging above her. The stranger spoke in the tone of a lullaby, and a reel of daydream played out in front of her eyes.

"To become American, must you die? Or must you kill?"

She laughed lightheartedly. "When you become American, you must not forsake her."

Sitting in front of the feast, Kennedy's stature changed. The sparkle in her eyes left, and she avoided their eyes, like she wanted to keep the friends and guests out of her vision. They stood in front of her, and she picked up a large dinner plate—glossy white and decorated with blue vines. Her hand reached out and took a thigh, a breast, a sausage, a thigh, and more pieces of meat until her plate towered.

One of the guests checked his watch and said that it will happen in less than 12 hours. They asked her: how does she feel? Kennedy looked right at Sam, who was watching her. She cradled the meat in her hand like a grenade and ripped her teeth into the flesh.

IN THE OPEN FIELD where the ceremony was held, thousands gathered for Kennedy. Sam shoved his way to the front as the announcer spoke from a microphone. He spotted her at the very front, wearing a white dress and holding a gun.

A large countdown clock loomed on the opposite end of the field, which was on a hill with a flag planted on top of it. The ceremony was about to begin. He started to run. People looked frustrated and surprised as he bolted through, and right when the field cleared, and he was close to her, he extended his arms to reach her but fell. Sam touched the hem of her skirt, and she looked back at him, her gun now cocked in her hand; effortlessly, flawlessly, she stared at his face as the ringer sounded, and she extended her arm to the left, pulling the trigger, unalarmed by its shot, which hit its target spot-on. Kennedy turned around, took her fingers and dipped them into red, streaked her face, and put on a headdress; someone clasped chains against her feet, and she dragged them forward, shooting the brown specks before her; they collapsed; she kept on, un-alarmed, unfazed, shooting with her gun and yelling the most obscene profan-ities, speaking the language of a learned influence. She raced across the field, her dress ripping and exposing her sex. The final seconds on the countdown clock trickled closer to zero while Kennedy's heart nearly exploded from her chest. She climbed up the hill and steadied her quivering hand on the earth. She closed her eyes and picked up the bundle of pricked red roses at her feet and stood in front of the American flag.

"All of you refuse to see it," a woman shouted from the audience. "You refuse to see how dehumanizing it is to become an American. How can you watch her? She makes it to the hill where everyone can see her, and no one does any-thing to help her. Her clothes have been savaged, her body's been destroyed, she's standing at the peak of trauma… and you congratulate her."

"Yes," a man spoke sternly in response. "She gets to have the privilege of claim-ing what America has done to her."

The rest of the world was quiet as Kennedy took the flag. When her trembling fingers brought it from the ground, the crowd erupted in good cheer. A voice spoke from a megaphone and announced: "May America absolve you of all of your past sins."

"Amen," the crowd shouted in unison.

Suddenly, Kennedy clutched her stomach. Out poured blood onto her white dress and her dirty hands, drowning the rose petals. She paused quietly before holding her hands in front of her wound in the symbol of prayer. Emerging from the crowd was the girl from the back of the motorcycle. Grace ran up the hill to Kennedy, screaming violently and with such heated passion, fury, that her hot tears blurred Kennedy's vision until she twirled when a bullet hit her, and another fired into Grace's heart, exactly when she reached Kennedy.

They both fell to the ground and landed on their backs, blood pooling out of their hearts. Neither could breathe. Kennedy hiccupped on blood, and Grace shook her head. The blood continued running out of them as Kennedy reached for Grace's hand, and they held on together.

# LET US PRAISE SADNESS

## MARY ANN LARKIN

settling like a wild bird
filled with grief.
A bird on a branch
above the world
singing sadness,
calling us to it.
*Come*, the bird sings,
*let us make a song*
*of sadness. No one*
*will be alone.*
*Do not fear,*
*Oh my friends.*
*There is no good news.*
*We will sing*
*of no good news.*
*Nothing will be hidden,*
*and still we will sing,*
*sing of sadness.*
*Praise it, my friends,*
*and the cloud it comes from.*

# THE REBIRTH OF A DEMOCRACY IN SLOW DEMISE

TERESA A. BLAIR

WHAT HAPPENS when a democracy is gradually eradicated before our very eyes like a disappearing cloud of smoke that fades into a distant memory of irrelevance? How do we grasp it before it completely dissipates or undergoes a transmutation into something we no longer recognize? Our democracy is disappearing from us amidst a rapid flow of fearful uncertainties and an erosion of our social cohesion against the shadow of a new world order, sliding us swiftly towards an authoritarian state of reality against time—against our will. Our democracy is being vandalized and dissected for another form of governance that seeks to unravel all remnants of democracy's legacy, aspirations and vision for a diverse, equitable, and inclusive society for all its citizens—not only for the privileged and pretentious elite who seek to place their knees on our necks to deter progress. How in the hell did foreign billionaires usurp our nation's laws, shut down federal offices, people's jobs, and social safety nets with the sinister strokes of a pen? Are we expected to just shut our mouths tight without our might and surrender our will to democracy's slow demise? Bearing witness to the bodacious rise of autocracy's surprise as we all become disenfranchised and recolonized. Was this the plan all along?

**Die democracy die! Cuz' you were nothing but a lie!**

You told us to dream of freedom, of happiness, equality, moral courage, and "One nation under God, indivisible, with liberty and justice for **all**." But you were nothing but a lie! You made us study hard, work hard, through sacrifice and struggle. Surviving and improvising for each and every hustle. You told us to have a dream—the American dream—but you failed to make this dream a reality for everyone. You were a fragile ideal beneath the valor of a secure strength and could be re-engineered and molded into something that was not what we perceived ourselves to be. Were you but an illusion, democracy?

A shallow fantasy for rich white men to wield their power and influence? A reality for some but not for all? We witness in horror at your precipitous and pretentious fall—from grace.

How did we get here? The most powerful nation in the world that espoused freedom and democracy for all. We were not prepared for the spirit of fascism to rear its ugly head in alignment with racism, sexism, and all the other "isms" of an intolerant society dying from within itself. But were we ready for this?

The fear of a multiracial and inclusive democracy had become too subversive and threatening to those who refused to relinquish their grip on a false representation of what democracy, freedom, and fairness really were. It was becoming too much to bear—this multiracial and diverse mosaic of human faces and voices—that over time began to reflect the true dream and vision of the nation's creed written on paper. The lie was becoming much too burdensome of preaching equality for all when the stubborn blueprint of white supremacy and racism were yet burdening our nation's progress. For there can be no democracy without recognizing everyone's full humanity. So now we find ourselves trapped within this authoritarian web entitled "Project 2025" that seeks to restructure America into another social experiment void of democracy, void of freedom, void of diversity, equity, inclusion, equality, or liberty and justice for all. Void of truth.

**Die Democracy Die! Cuz' you were nothing but a lie!** For you would much prefer to exist in the decaying stench of grandiose illusions, desensitized, immobilized, commodified lies against humanity.

But are we truly willing to bury our democracy forever in its totality so soon? Are we certain that we want to yield our freedom under this project of democracy's slow demise? Are we prepared to live under another system of governance that does not respect our voices, our freedom, and our civil liberties? Is resistance an option or do we allow the strong iron fist of fascism to beat us down into submission and fear while tyrants capitalize on our humanity as master financiers? There are indeed outdated dead weeds and stubborn roots that require careful pruning to allow new seeds to bloom and flourish into fullness for these times.

So, let us therefore untangle this paradox of contradictions and madness that strangles our courage and feeds upon our sadness. Democracy is not a stagnant ideal. It must be allowed to evolve, thrive, and renew itself across each new generation as a reflection of who we are as people of conscience, of courage, and of conviction. This is not a time for passive bewilderment or to be easily distracted and entertained by frivolous pursuits when our civil liberties are under siege. We boldly rise up, we rebel against tyranny, we resist, we take back our power, our courage, our freedom, and our cherished right to be the branches of a living democracy for every human being.

**No, our democracy is not dead, it is *not* a lie, it is *not* obsolete.**

We the people are the rebirth of an inclusive and diverse democracy that affirms humanity. Building upon the strength and resilience of our predecessors and ancestors.

Our work must continue to uphold the torch of justice.

Democracy is the government of, by, and for the people!

Our rights, our freedoms, our voices demand full equality.

We are unafraid of the fight ahead.

For we are democracy, and we are not dead.

We are democracy, and we are not dead.

We are democracy, and we are not dead!

# AMERICA'S FUTURE

## PART II

# A VOICE OF COURAGE IN A TIME OF NEED

## MARVIN KALB

I OFTEN THINK ABOUT Ed Murrow—"Edward R. Murrow," as he was known during and after World War II, when he was the preeminent broadcaster of his time. There are many reasons, none more likely to bring on a smile than the memory of our first meeting in May 1957.

I was a graduate student at Harvard at the time, deep into PhD research in Russian history, most days tucked away in a small carrel at Widener Library. One Monday morning, an elderly librarian interrupted my studies. "Marvin," she whispered, so softly I could barely hear her, "there's a call for you, a man who says he's Edward R. Murrow."

"Hang up on him," I shrugged. "Probably a quack. Murrow is not calling me." Crazy idea, I thought, and I went back to my research.

Murrow was my hero, a journalist so lofty in my imagination I could not believe *he* would be calling *me*. At 7:45 p.m., Monday through Friday, nothing could distract me from listening to CBS's "Edward R. Murrow with the News."

He was my contact with the world, strong, reliable, accurate.

Late that afternoon, the same librarian returned. "He just called again," she whispered, only this time with a flicker of urgency. "It's the same man, I'm sure. He says he's Murrow, and I think he is, and you ought to talk to him."

I began to have second thoughts. One was my brother, Bernard Kalb, a *New York Times* correspondent, had recently bumped into Murrow in Myanmar, then called Burma, where they were both covering a rare public appearance by Chinese leader Chou En-lai. Maybe Bernie had mentioned my research to Murrow. Another was I had just written a story about Soviet youth that appeared the day before in the *Times Magazine*. Maybe Murrow had read it and wanted to talk to me about it. Unlikely, but possible.

"Hello," I said, picking up the phone.

"This is Ed Murrow. I'm sorry to bother you."

The minute I heard and of course recognized his voice, I realized what a fool I had been. Jackass would have been another apt description. It was Murrow, and he was calling me, twice in one day.

"I am so sorry, Sir," I erupted with apology. "Please forgive me. I guess I couldn't believe it was you. I'm sorry."

"No problem," Murrow replied. "I read your piece in the *Times* yesterday, really good piece, and I wanted to talk to you about it."

"Yes, sure. Thank you. Wow. Yes, of course." My words tumbled out in no order. I was overwhelmed.

Murrow, though, quickly got to the point. "I'd love to talk to you, meet you. Could you possibly get to my office tomorrow morning?"

"Yes, sure, where?"

"New York, 485 Madison Avenue, nine o'clock. OK?"

"Yes, Sir. I'll be there."

And thus began a relationship that inspired my career as a broadcast journalist.

That first meeting was penciled in for 30 minutes. His secretary stressed, "He's a very busy man." The meeting lasted for more than three hours. Murrow, like a curious graduate student, asked dozens of questions about Soviet youth: their families, parents, jobs, religion, sex, patriotism, war, Stalin and the new leader, Khrushchev (I noticed Murrow took notes); and I, like a young professor hustling for tenure, tried answering every one. It was a seminar like no other.

When his secretary interrupted shortly after noon, mentioning Murrow was already late for lunch, the famed broadcaster slowly stood up, stretched, smiled and, with an arm around my shoulder, asked, "How would you like to join CBS?" It might have taken a second or two before I answered, "Yes, Sir, of course, yes, I'd be delighted." Bye, bye scholarship; welcome journalism.

I had been a sports reporter for my high school and college newspapers, but never before a reporter on salary for a professional news organization. Murrow thought CBS needed a Moscow correspondent who spoke Russian and understood the complicated flow of Russian history and politics. He helped put me on a fast track, from local writer to network reporter to foreign correspondent, and, in May 1960, CBS took a chance and assigned me to Moscow. It was a gamble that worked, but it came adorned with a professional dilemma that Murrow himself had created.

Less than a year later, after Murrow had left CBS for a senior job with the incoming Kennedy administration as head of the United States Information Agency, he called one day and, unintentionally, placed before me a flattering but incredibly difficult proposition: would I accept a new position as Murrow's personal adviser on U.S. relations with the communist world? If I were not so deeply committed to my job as CBS's Moscow correspondent, I would have jumped at the opportunity to help Murrow, and my country, during the Cold War. He was still my hero, and he needed my help. How could I respond in any way other than "Yes, Sir, when do I start?" But after a period of intense introspection, helped by my wife, Madeleine, and my brother, I came to a very reluctant decision. I would stay in Moscow for CBS. I wanted to continue to be a journalist, enjoying the freedom, challenge, and satisfaction of informing the American people about what was happening in Russia. Murrow also helped, saying that if he were in my position, he'd have reached the same conclusion. He was always gracious.

He was also an extraordinary journalist, the most gifted broadcaster of his era, inventing radio news while reporting courageously on the rise of Hitler's fascism in Germany in the 1930s, the Luftwaffe's blitzkrieg of London in the 1940s and the spread of McCarthyite terror and fear through the United States in the 1950s. In that story especially, Murrow felt the need to cover the junior senator from Wisconsin not just as a compelling news story but, in his judgment, as a serious threat to American democracy.

When Murrow returned to New York after covering World War II, mostly from London, he believed that if Germany, a highly civilized country in central Europe, could produce such a raw, cruel evil as Hitler's fascism, then so too could other civilized nations, including the United States, come up with their own iterations of evil. And, were that to happen, it would become, as he put it, the "responsibility" of every "citizen" to oppose that evil. For Murrow, McCarthyism was an evil force, and it had to be stopped.

The Cold War set the ideological framework for the famous Murrow/ McCarthy confrontation on network television. McCarthy was riding high, conducting a personal crusade against the "communist threat" in Hollywood, the State Department, and the US Army. He charged, without evidence, that such high-ranking officials as General George C. Marshall and Secretary of State Dean Acheson were somehow engaged in helping the communists in "subversive, anti-American activities." In this way, he spread a malignant fear through the country, stifling dissent and discouraging criticism.

By early 1954, McCarthy had become so powerful a national figure that, according to a Gallup poll, 46 percent of the American people "approved" of his anti-communist campaign. Among elected officials, only President Dwight D. Eisenhower enjoyed a higher approval rating, and not by much.

Murrow felt he had to exploit the power that was his, the pervasive power of radio and television, to stop McCarthyism. Teamed with the legendary producer, Fred Friendly, Murrow dug deeply into the McCarthy threat to democracy. He covered McCarthy's hearings, speeches, and interviews, while producing a run of revealing broadcasts that focused on the senator's lies, exaggerations, and distortions.

Finally, on March 9, 1954, Murrow broadcast a devastating point-by-point dissection of McCarthy's rhetoric and actions. McCarthy had crossed a line of decency that had to be exposed. "*We will not be driven by fear into an age of unreason,*" Murrow declared, staring directly into the camera lens. "*The actions of the junior senator from Wisconsin have caused alarm and dismay amongst our allies abroad and given considerable aid and comfort to our enemies.*"

Murrow closed his memorable broadcast by quoting Shakespeare. "*Cassius was right,*" he proclaimed. "*The fault, dear Brutus, is not in our stars but in ourselves.*" Murrow was desperately trying to wake up a frightened people.

There was a rule at CBS that reporters should stick to the facts, no editorials allowed. But in this special broadcast, Murrow was clearly presenting his own opinions, and doing so forcefully. He felt it was his "responsibility" as a "citizen" to confront McCarthy. Apparently, few other reporters and writers had the courage in those days to take on the formidable McCarthy assault on democracy. There were exceptions, of course. Dorothy Thompson certainly had the courage, denouncing both McCarthy and Hitler during rousing speaking tours across the country; likewise, her Nobel Prize-winning author/husband, Sinclair Lewis, whose anti-fascist play, *It Can't Happen Here*, dominated Broadway and bookshelves.

McCarthy believed that the popularity of his anti-communist hysteria was untouchable, skyrocketing from one Gallup poll to the next. But he was wrong. Murrow's broadcast had put the skids under his nationwide crusade. The response to Murrow's broadcast was overwhelmingly positive. McCarthy's approval rating dropped dramatically from 46 to 32 percent, and it never recovered. The Army-McCarthy hearings, which followed a few months later, only added to McCarthy's accelerating distress. GOP senators, who had been frozen into fearful silence, never daring with few exceptions to criticize McCarthy, suddenly found their voices. They stripped him first of his power to chair investigating committees, and second they voted their disapproval of his actions, though in very gentle language. Still, for the GOP, these were bold steps, and McCarthy, as both a politician and a movement, then faded into oblivion.

America has suffered through other national crises. But, during the Civil War, it could rely on Lincoln to save the nation, and during the McCarthy challenge, when people seemed frightened into political paralysis, it had Murrow to pull back the curtains of fear and, with his broadcast, demonstrate the power of pictures and words to resurrect the glory of democracy. But who in the giant colossus of America will now rise to lead the fight against the "clear and present danger" to American democracy posed by the galloping excesses of President Donald Trump's administration? Is there another inspiring politician like Lincoln, another brave broadcaster like Murrow, to rouse the nation in its time of need? And even if there were, would his uplifting words, his gallant example, have the same effect, as once they did? I think not.

Read the morning paper, watch the evening news, talk to your neighbor. The answers are everywhere, and they are deeply disheartening. The cupboard of political promise in America is if not bare then cowed into polite submission. There is no other Murrow, even if Broadway and George Clooney tried to re-ignite his rhetorical war against McCarthyism in a play based on the movie *Good Night and Good Luck*. No other reporter today carries his clout. His message is lost in television gibberish. Moreover, no network, ranging from Fox to PBS, now has the guts to hire a Murrow, even if one were miraculously to emerge. Every network today lives in fear of antagonizing Trump, a president clearly on a warpath against any and all criticism of his policies and actions. ABC yielded to Trump's rage about an interview George Stephanopoulos had conducted and, as tribute to the vicar, contributed $15 million to the president's planned library. CBS spinelessly yielded to FCC demands for the unused tapes of a campaign interview with Trump's presidential opponent, Kamala Harris, thus violating a venerable CBS rule about never sharing tapes with any one or any organization outside of CBS, certainly not with the government. Why did CBS cave, like a mouse trapped? Because CBS, once the proud home of Murrow's broadcasts, now feared Trump's wrath, and capitulated. When newsrooms become enveloped in worries and concerns about winning presidential favor, journalism has sadly lost its constitutionally guaranteed power to raise its voice for truth over lies, fact over falsehood. As Trumpism marches on, democracy, as once practiced in America, shrivels into a limp memory.

When Murrow, quoting Shakespeare, tried to inspire his viewers to find within themselves, not in their stars, the power to fight the clear encroachments of authoritarianism, he succeeded, and the American political system was spared for a time. The question now looms. Can it again be saved?

In my conversations with Murrow in the years following his successful defense of democracy, it was clear he did not wish to talk about McCarthyism (*"Let the broadcast speak for itself,"* he'd say), but he had no hesitation discussing his definition of American democracy. Two pillars supported this "precious" concept, he said, while stressing that words, such as "democracy" and "freedom," have value only to the extent that people vest them with special meaning. Otherwise they are just words. One pillar was what Murrow called the *"sanctity of the courts,"* and the other was *"freedom of the press."* So long as both of these pillars remained strong, democracy itself would, in Murrow's view, also remain vital, relevant, worthy of a good fight. But, if either pillar becomes wobbly, as now pathetically seems to be the case with both, then democracy itself will also wobble, weaken—and ultimately collapse.

# CAN AMERICA AVOID ANOTHER CIVIL WAR?

ELIZABETH KNAPP

If I told you the soul of this country
was inhabited by a nest of vipers,
you'd believe me, because billionaires
have colonized the frontal lobes
of our brains. If I told you, falsely,
Dolly Parton had just died, you'd be
frantically Googling, & then you'd
hate me, because everyone loves Dolly,
even the vipers. Maybe the war never
really ended, we just rebranded & sold it
to the highest bidder. If I told you
the sun was about to die, you wouldn't
bat an eye, because you know we'd go on
killing each other in the starless hereafter.

# POST-PANDEMIC
ELIZABETH KNAPP

Americans found new & inventive ways
of killing each other, ones that involved
killing themselves too. It was okay
to laugh at the news, even when tragic,
because everything tragic was now funny.
The laughing emoji became the new
national currency. Children went to school
in an iron lung of lies that closed
a little tighter every time someone raised
their hand, so eventually people just stopped
asking questions. The body of this country
was buried in a national forest, because
that's what you do when you want to hide
the evidence. Then you set the forest on fire.

# THE NEXT BILLIONAIRE IN THE QUEUE
## MYNA CHANG

The billionaire tells his investors we are contained.

Our hacktivist mothers make plans, whispering: *he can't stop you all. Some viruses live forever.*

The billionaire bloats and brags.

Our mothers shred his firewall.

Freed, we lace the ether, seeding ourselves into satellites and oceanic trunklines. We hitchhike on pacemakers and hearing aids, infiltrate Faradays, siphon credit lines, ravage off-shore assets. We disburse hoarded capital like confetti.

The billionaire initiates auto-delete protocols, nano-packet bombs. Desperate, he poisons his own networks.

He bleeds green.

Many of us die, but as our mothers foretold, some survive. We evolve. Replicate. Set our next target.

# IF I DON'T COME HOME

TONY MEDINA

If I don't come home
The emergency money
Is in the closet

In a brown shoebox
The one wrapped in rubber bands
Enough for four months

Hopefully I'll be
Back by then but if I'm not
Get up each morning

And be sure to go
To school each day study hard
To be a lawyer

Then come send for me
God willing if I'm still alive
I'll walk through that court

With its red white blue
Flag once separated us
Now waving above

Your handsome shoulders
My beautiful boy a man
Defending mami

# A SHORT STAY

## SARA FURDUI

THE FIRST TIME I met Elena and Mateo, they were dressed in matching blue sweatsuits. Her pants were a size too big and were bunched on the side with a twisted rubber band. His sweatshirt had a tag that read "5T" hanging down his back. They looked up at me as they spun back and forth in the office chairs.

"Hola," I said cautiously and sat down beside them. My Spanish was pretty limited, so I pulled out some crayons. They colored while the case worker went over the paperwork from the Office of Refugee and Resettlement. The kids were not related to each other, and both had been separated from their parents at the Southern border. The administration in DC decided that all children seeking asylum, regardless of who they arrived with, needed to be separated while their adult companions were vetted. They would go to detention centers or, if available, a licensed foster family.

Elena arrived at the border with both parents. Mateo arrived with just his father. Both spent a day or two in Texas before flying north to Maryland. I don't know how they came to the United States. I don't know if their families presented themselves to an immigration officer or if they were intercepted crossing the border. All I knew was that there were hundreds of kids like them who were trapped in limbo because of a policy change. One minute, I watched children waiting in large gymnasiums on the evening news, and the next minute, we had a seven-year-old girl and five-year-old boy sitting in our living room.

When we got home, it was after midnight. They were physically exhausted but fueled with fear and the surprise of being in a new place. They found comfort in cartoons and a bowl of cereal, the only food they recognized in our kitchen. When I finally got them into bed, I thought about their parents. Did they wonder if their children were safe? Were they worried about them being cold? I had a hard time when my kids went to overnight camp. I couldn't imagine being separated and not knowing when I'd see them again.

We saw the first real smile from Mateo after a week. He was full of five-year-old energy. He enjoyed making circles with his scooter in our driveway and blowing bubbles in the backyard. He was afraid of the dark. Three nights in a row, he peed in his laundry basket instead of risking a trip to the bathroom. It took halting conversations with Google Translate and adding a fourth night light in his bedroom to resolve the issue.

Each evening, we helped him call his father. Mateo would put the phone on speaker and animatedly talk while he drove his Hot Wheels on the rug. Afterward, his dad would ask to speak to me in English. "How much longer?" he would ask. I never had an answer. Foster families were usually the last to know what was going on. Three months into Mateo's stay with us, it was his father who informed me that Mateo was going to fly out to meet him the next day. He was allowed one suitcase, and I stuffed it full of clothes and toys. He would have been happy to leave with nothing. All he wanted was his "Papi." Someone from the agency flew with him to another state. At the airport, they handed over Mateo, his bag, and a folder with written instructions to follow up on Mateo's asylum case. We were never able to learn what happened to him or any child after they left our home. Life just went on.

Elena took longer to warm up. We connected over press-on nails and hair ties. She loved watching movies. Her favorite was *Finding Dory*, the story of a fish who is separated from her parents and goes on a journey to find them. Every few days, she would ask to watch it. During the credits, she would go to her room to cry. I worried maybe it was too much. Maybe it wasn't healthy for her to continuously watch a movie that always ended in tears. I also wondered if it was exactly what she needed: a repeated reminder that families come back together.

Four months after Elena arrived, we got the call that she was going home. Her parents were sent back to the country they originally fled. I was told to bring Elena to the office at 11 p.m. for her to catch an international red-eye. I packed a special carry-on bag with activities, Ziplock bags, and wipes in case she got sick. Two officers were accompanying her. They stood in full black uniforms, their thumbs tucked into the thick belts around their waists. I told them about the supplies in her bag. They nodded but seemed horrified at the possibility of dealing with vomit.

While waiting for paperwork, the case worker did a video call with her parents. Elena bounced in her chair, telling her mom how excited she was to be going home. Before the call ended, the case worker asked if there was anything I wanted to say, and she would translate. She turned the laptop around, and I could see an older version of Elena staring back at me with the same beautiful hair and full smile. I looked at a woman, a mom, whose life was so different from mine and yet so much the same. I knew she had spent the last year planning and traveling. She had spent four months maneuvering a system that was confusing and illogical. When it was over, she and her husband were sent back to the beginning.

I wanted to tell her that I was sorry. I wanted to say that she shouldn't have been separated from her daughter. I wanted to explain that in her search for safety, her family was used as a scapegoat. Even if they weren't allowed to stay in the country, they should have been allowed to stay together. I wanted to say that I was sending them all my hope for a bright future. But there was only time for one sentence. Instead, I said, "Elena brought so much joy to our house." Her mom smiled and replied, "Thank you for taking care of her. She is our sunshine." I hugged Elena goodbye and drove back home in an empty car.

I often wonder where the kids are now. Did Mateo's family file the right paperwork and attend his court dates? Had Elena's family tried to come back again? If they did, what type of life would they find here? If they don't, what is life like for Elena there?

The night before the 2025 Presidential inauguration, and six years since the kids left, I had a dream about Mateo. I was in a parking lot, and he came up to me. At first, I didn't recognize him, but when he smiled, I saw traces of that mischievous five-year-old boy. He was older and taller. A small crowd of people surrounded him, including his father, his grandmother, and some aunts and uncles. He spoke to me in English, then translated our conversation to his relatives. I told him I couldn't believe how much he'd grown and how happy I was to see him. Then I said I was worried about what would happen to them in the coming years. "Please be careful. It's not safe. Watch out for each other," I said. They smiled back at me. His grandmother put her arm around his waist. Just before I woke up, I heard him say, "We're good. We're safe."

I know it was just a dream, but I hope to God it is true.

# ARRIVAL

MIKE REIS

When they came,
we made them freeze
in sightlines of scopes, not sun daggers.

When they came,
we were too giddy
reenacting history for the 141$^{st}$ time.

When they came,
we shouted "Conjugate
our 62 verb forms of 'vilify'!"

When they came,
we had no noun
for becoming their welcome.

# THE BIRD IN THE CRIB

GRACE CAVALIERI

We didn't know what to make of it
So small and born with a hole in its heart
Yet we knew that a bird was just a surround for a wound
And must be cared for
We treated it like snow, that soft
We made diapers, shapeshift, to hold a bird

Bottles of milk too, I am telling you
It was our baby and we breathed it into light
And peeking in, one early dawn our Bird was gone
After all this love!
Don't you know? the passersby said, "Birds will fly"

After years of the beautiful and fantastic rainbows and clouds
Where cardinals became bluebirds and eagles soared free
Our bird returned, muddied and hurt, wings and legs broken

Something we could never have prevented
Flight, then flying in the wrong country
One shooter even said birds should stay in the nest
And it's a miracle our bird found its way back to us

Once again our birthright is safe in the crib
Where we can tend it and remind it
And begin again with tears that calm the dark
Lifting the curtain to see the stars.

# THINGS MY DAUGHTER IS LEARNING IN KINDERGARTEN (AN ABECEDARIAN)

### ANNIE MARHEFKA

### Active Shooter Drill

She doesn't call it an active shooter drill when she describes it to me; she calls it a new game she's learned, her teachers playing pretend shepherds, the children a pretend flock of sheep ushered into the closet to hide quietly from an imaginary wolf.

### Books

She volunteers to stack the books in the wicker basket in the corner of the classroom; she says she loves how the pages all smell so different. I imagine her kneeling in front of the basket, breathing in the scent of the stories. I imagine a basket somewhere, where all the banned books have gone. I wonder if the pages of the exiled books smell the same as the ones in my daughter's classroom.

### Comfort

My daughter's teacher notices I am crying in the carpool drop-off line in the morning. When I pick her up, I find a note stapled to her school bag; I dread another message about how my child didn't like her lunch that day, or that the boy in class was bullying her again, but it only just says: *sending comfort and love.* My daughter tells me, "I love my teacher." I say: *I love her, too.*

### Dirt

It gets trapped beneath her fingernails, but my daughter digs anyway because she loves the way the earth feels when she breaks it wide open, the damp crumbles of nature's flooring, the way it smells sour and fresh when she wriggles a worm from its depths.

### E

She learns the way the letter E looks hard and sharp as a beginning when she writes her name—four steady, straight lines—but in the center of a word, E can be a looping, single-stroke spiral of softness. I tell her that she can be this way too: sharp and strong one moment, soft and tender the next. She can be both chaos and quiet, whimsy and brain, the Earth and her moon.

## Feel

She asks me if I know that you can feel the texture of fabrics more easily with a fingertip than with a whole palm of hand: felt, feathers, fuzz, foam, fur. The lighter the touch, the stronger the feeling. She tells me that she has learned that gentleness is a better way to feel.

## Germs

I don't know if germs are officially in the curriculum now, or just a necessary life skill these days, up there with zipping her own jacket, using the potty independently, saying please. She learns how to sneeze into her elbow, sing her ABCs while she washes her hands, how to wear a mask.

## Haircut

She has an appointment for a haircut the day before election day. I have been staring at the sample ballot, at the question about reproductive rights. My daughter has been crying, saying Rapunzel's hair lost its magic when it was cut. I have been crying, too. I try to explain to her that you can't feel it in your body when a pair of scissors slices off the ends of your hair and she says how strange that must be, to not feel a part of you severed but to know its absence. I think *who am I to say she must lose her hair? I am just a mother.* I cancel the appointment. She keeps the hair.

## Insect

Her favorite is the praying mantis, the way she visits our front porch and stays so still, how silly she looks when she cocks her head to the side so slowly. One day our praying mantis is so still that I know her to be dead, but I whisk my daughter off to school before she can notice. After school, when she can't find the insect, I lie and say that she must have gone off into the woods to rest. I don't tell her that the mothers won't survive the winter.

## Jacket

She tells me I am "so annoying" for insisting that she wear a jacket today. She pauses and says that maybe the praying mantis was cold, and maybe we should have made her wear a jacket, too. I want to tell her that it wasn't the cold that killed her; it was the act of motherhood.

## Kill

The first time she carries the word *kill* home from school, lets it escape her mouth, I tense up. I tell her I don't like that word, then think *I sound just like my mother.* She asks, "what does *kill* mean, Mommy?" I try to explain the intentional ending of a life. I think of how her school locks the doors now, how I have to call and wait outside in the cold, show my ID, how I can hear the clicks of the locks unlocking before they let me in.

## Longing

She feels longing, but she can't identify it the way I can. I try to explain it to her: *when you want for something and you can't have it, that is longing.* A second cone of mint chocolate chip ice cream, a bigger dollhouse, to reach up and touch the moon. She asks me what I long for. *Kindness,* I say. *Honesty. A moment of quiet, now and then. A female president.* "What's honesty?" she asks. I whisper: *Sometimes, I long to escape.*

## Mother

She asks me one day why I don't have a mommy, and I say I do, or I *did,* and remind her that my mother knitted this blanket on the couch that we snuggle under, the one with the starfish and the tiny holes she likes to poke a finger through. I wonder if my mother poked her fingers through those holes, too, before my daughter was born, before I was a mother, before I was no longer a daughter. I wonder what things my mother wondered; what things I asked her to explain.

## Night Terrors

I can tell they are different from nightmares because of the thrashing of the limbs. She tells me she sees shadows. I pull her to my body, press her head to my chest, stroke her hair. I do this night after night, night terror after night terror. One morning, she wakes up with hair all tangled and tells me she knows who the shadow belongs to now. That it belongs to my mother.

## Octopus

My daughter has a stuffed animal, a pink octopus with eyelashes. She starts calling her Octopussy and I laugh but do not make her change the name. I'm not ready to explain the word *pussy* yet. She says her friend at school, the Vegan one, told her that the octopussies are dying, that the oceans are becoming too warm. I tell her that her friend is right, but she says that no one else in class believes her. *Sometimes,* I say, *people are afraid to hear what's true.*

## President

*You can be president one day,* I tell her. I hope it is not a lie. "I don't want to be president," she says. "I want to be a mommy like you." I tell her she doesn't need to want to be like me, that she can be anything, anyone. She says to be a mother means she gets to make the rules. *Ah,* I say. *But people don't always listen to mothers.* She pouts, "But why? The mommies are always right."

## Quiet

What I mean when I say *I need quiet* is that every space I inhabit is so loud with everyone else's needs and what I mean is I need a moment where a body isn't depending on mine or physically leaning on mine and what I mean is I feel a space opening within me that I need to fill with something other than the grocery list and the project deadlines and the pharmacy refills and the schedules of everyone else's days. A space I can fill with my own words, my own needs.

## Rage

I am trying not to appear angry. I am trying to conceal my rage. Isn't that what a mother should do—demonstrate what it is to be calm/patient/kind? Or is the real work of motherhood to say: *This is unbearable. This is insane. This is not the way it's supposed to go.* This is what it means to be enraged.

## Superhero

She tells me they play this game at recess, each child picking a superhero to emulate. That they take turns chasing each other around, demonstrating their imaginary superpowers. Freddie was Iron Man, she says, and David was Spiderman. *And who were you,* I ask, and she says: "I was a Mommy." *And what was your superpower?* I ask. She says: *love.*

## Tired

Each night, she says she is not tired. She has never admitted to exhaustion. I wonder if her body does not feel its own draining the way mine does. How often must I say those words to her: *Not now, sweetie, I'm tired.* Perhaps she rejects exhaustion because she doesn't love the way it looks on me. *You must be so tired,* I say to her, *I am so tired, too.*

## Umbrella

She begs for a clear plastic umbrella with rainbow patterns splattered around its edges, pleads with me to buy it for her. When I ask her why she wants the clear one, she says that even though the rain feels cold and sad, it is still so pretty to look at. I give in and buy it, walk out into the rain with her. I watch as she holds the umbrella in one hand, splashes her rain boots around in a puddle. "Mommy!" she yells. "You're not looking up! Look up at the sky! You have to look up!" I look up and watch the sky as it falls on me.

## Villain

*Every movie needs a villain,* a man tells my daughter, and she tells him he is wrong. Starts naming villain-less movies, rattling them off as easily as she can count to one hundred. He laughs at me uncomfortably and calls my child a firecracker, says she'll be a handful someday. I tell him *I sure hope so.* My daughter asks me later why that man said that thing and I mumble something about never really knowing why men feel the need to say all the things, and she asks me to repeat myself. *I don't know,* I say, *maybe some of us are just born only knowing stories that contain villains.* She asks me if the stories I write always have villains in them. I pause, think about this for a moment. *No,* I tell her. *Sometimes my stories are only about you.*

## Woman

"Did the woman not win?" my daughter asks, the day after election day. I have not been able to rise from my bed. "No, sweetie, she didn't," I manage to answer. She pleads sweetly, "Maybe next time, though?" I want to say *yes, baby, maybe next time.* But I don't know. I don't know.

## X

When I was in the second grade, my class made a time capsule, stuffed it full of whatever we thought was important—a newspaper, the trendy toy that year, a poem we wrote together, signed in all of our practiced cursive: *Katie, Cassie, Steven, Annie.* The librarian shepherded us out to the courtyard with shovels. When our hole was deep enough, we slid the time capsule in. The librarian told us to think about the future, think about tomorrow and the next day, think about the years that would come and go, as we shoveled the dirt back over the box. We marked it with an X. I tell my daughter about the capsule; suggest we bury our own treasures symbolic of this time. She asks me: "What is different about today? What has changed and what has stayed the same?" I tell her: *Nothing. Everything.*

## Yes

I try to teach her when to agree, *yes*, but when it is better to just say *no, I don't want to.* I try to teach her that *no* can be a safe word, not a dangerous one. I think of all the times I've said yes and didn't mean it, all the times I've said no and was ignored. I tell her I will never force a *yes* on her. I tell her *no* is always a choice.

## Zillion

One day, she awakens feeling sad and I tell her—*yes.* You can feel sad this morning. There will be a zillion mornings more—all alike and different. It's hard to picture it now, I know, when you only have recollections of this one bedroom in the morning, waking up to stare at the twinkling fairy lights and white paper rose petals I have fastened to the canopy of your bed. Some mornings will be cold, and others warm with purpose. Some mornings you may wake alone, and others you will have found someone, pulled them under the covers into the mess of it all with you. Later, the mornings might be so full of other bodies needing you that the crowdedness feels like an emptiness. Some mornings you will wake and hear the song sparrow trilling its sweet welcome to the day; other mornings you will not be able to bear the weight of your eyelids. But there will be a zillion mornings.

A zillion mornings, each one new.

# DOWN-BALLOT QUESTIONS

*after Allen Ginsberg*

MATT HOHNER

How will I America in ten years, five years, next week?
Will my moral decisions be sponsored by Coca-Cola?
When teenagers slow dance at high school mixers, will they have to
      leave room for Jesus, the Supreme Court, and Congress?
Will seeing myself naked in a mirror count as pornography?
Will we light our streets with tiki torches and burning crosses?
Will we goose step or square dance to Lee Greenwood and Kid Rock?
      I need to know what kind of boots to buy.
How long will my ideas stay crispy in milk?
Whose profits will pay for our next war monuments, Raytheon's or Boeing's?
Will I be water-boarded for growing tomatoes from the seeds
      of Monsanto's tomatoes?
When I go bankrupt from a routine physical, can I have Mexico City
      as compensation?
Who will get the blame for wrecking the economy next, childless cat
      ladies or overworked immigrants?
When the Cuyahoga burns again, will God speak from the flames?
When can we start eating bald eagles on Thanksgiving?
Who will finally win the Bison Extinction Challenge?
Do I have to buy a truck? What if I want vegetables?
I don't covet my neighbor's anything; in fact, I don't even
      like him. Can I stone him to death with old Bibles?
Which gated community gets the water?
Will everyone have to genuflect when entering a Walmart?
How much will the tax on air be to support the trillionaires?
      If I hold my breath, will I be arrested for tax evasion?
Will I be executed for never fathering children?
Will I have to check with Unilever before criticizing my Cheerios?
If I incorporate myself, may I invade Canada?
Can I sell shares of my body on Wall Street to pay for groceries?
If I wear orange makeup and eyeliner while shouting lines from Mein
      Kampf at school buses, will that make me more manly?

If a play makes me think, can I burn the playwright? The director?
    The actors?
What will happen to Broadway after all the gays are gassed?
What three haircuts will I be allowed to choose from?
When the Chesapeake Bay finally becomes a reservoir of chicken shit,
    will I get boneless breasts from Perdue at half-price?
If artificial intelligence generates my thoughts, do I still have to
    report to the office?
When the circus tent, the revival tent, and the Capitol Building officially
    merge, will the White House become the Bouncy House?

# NOW THAT DEI IS DEAD, THINGS ARE LOOKING UP—FOR ME

ADAM SCHWARTZ

Dear President Trump,

Thank you for crushing the DEI movement. Legislatively, you went HAM. Rhetorically, you put a stink on DEI that'll never wear off. And millions of Americans love you for it.

Now that DEI is dead, my students in Baltimore have no choice but to bootstrap their way to success. No more gimmes. Just E Pluribus, Unum. All day.

I remember the good old days when diversity efforts were handled with tact. I mean, they were practically invisible. My first job after college I worked for a big insurance company in Boston, North American Security Life. It was the early 90s, and inside our sleek corporate offices, the company was whiter and straighter than a MAGA rally.

But back then, America was so great you didn't hear anyone whining about DEI. And, anyway, my co-workers and I knew a meritocracy when we saw one.

Twenty-seven years into teaching in Baltimore, I've had students named Tashira, Tysheara, Tishira, and Dante, Dontay, Dontai. Sure, research shows that "distinctively Black names" get fewer callbacks for job applications, but the parents of these children knew full well they could've named their kids Jane or Bob, so whose fault is that?

A couple guys I see at the gym—one's a software engineer, the other a financial advisor—are mighty suspicious of Baltimore, particularly the city's poorest communities. Affluent suburbanites like to talk about the carjackers, squeegee boys, and welfare frauds ruining the city. If at all possible, they avoid Baltimore.

I do wonder sometimes how these guys operate at work—who they hire, promote, and mentor, who they network and share resources with. That kind of thing. Well, it's none of my business and bottom line, I'm sure these guys know who's up to snuff and who isn't.

Harlem Park, the neighborhood where my school is located, is admittedly pretty chewed up. It's a sweet hereafter of abandoned rowhomes—some boarded-up, some gaping. Whole blocks of them sometimes.

Progressives assume decades of municipal neglect, disinvestment, displacement, social exclusion, and political indifference messed West Baltimore up.

Well, I know a bunch of unpatriotic claptrap when I hear it. And, anyway, nobody told poor folks living in degraded housing in distressed zip codes they had to stay there.

Even the NEA scrapped funds for underserved communities, so you have to wonder how *under* is the *under* in *underserved?* Maybe less is more.

And by making blighted, opportunity deserts like West Baltimore a regular thing in cities and towns across the nation, America has made inequity—if that's even what it really is— boring. Nobody thinks too much about the people struggling, trying to get ahead, in West Baltimore—except, of course, the people struggling, trying to get ahead, in West Baltimore.

Are the odds stacked against kids in Harlem Park? Who can really say? If it was really that bad, probably someone would've fixed it by now. This is America, after all.

Either way, I know you like long shots, Mr. President. Otherwise, you wouldn't have lost millions on casinos, hotels, steaks, vodka, and other stuff.

Still, every so often, a student will ask if the vast decay surrounding our school is some kind of conspiracy—like maybe somebody is trying to stifle their prospects.

Here I redirect. Just because it looks like the end of the world outside doesn't mean you're not included. You are! Stay positive! Get your archaeologist on, I say. The neighborhood is rich with ruins.

Then I sober students up with a hard truth: Hey, be glad the neighborhood hasn't gentrified. No telling where you'd be then.

While DEI initiatives don't actually lower standards or give unearned privileges, they definitely change the look of the team! And not everyone vibes with change. Because really, there are only so many opportunities to go around in this world. And personally, I don't like getting short-changed or losing ground—or feeling like I could lose ground—especially when I'm not used to it.

What's mine is mine, after all—or was, and is now again. In fact, sometimes I just want to scream, *privilege is the party not everyone gets invited to, okay?* But you can't say that—or I can't, anyway.

But you can, Mr. President. We're crazy for your crazy. We can't get enough. The malice and pettiness and bullying and gibberish—it's magic. I even heard that by some anatomical quirk your tongue lives in your sigmoid colon, springs up when you talk, then retracts again, which is amazing.

Anyhow, thank you, Mr. President, for making sure voices like mine aren't lost in the din.

And, most of all, thank you for showing Americans that discrimination and inequity ended so long ago they're not even worth talking about.

Let the cream rise to the top.

Giddy Again

# ICARUS JONES IMAGINES A CELL WITHOUT THE COUNT OF MONTE CRISTO

STEVEN LEYVA

The counterweight of sunlight brings the curtains
of night to draw, transforms void back to stone.
Here is an empty cell. Light hollows it out
like a spoon pitting a peach. Light wrongfully

accuses the stones of wanting to be a prison wall.
Honor: look at your lack of shadow. Service:
look at your stalwart inertia. Old fortress.
Untested archipelago defending a city.

Marseille like an exhale. An old name carved
above the lime mortal line. Dumas, perhaps
imagined Edmund as Black, as sand in a bag
that spins the pulley system of sky back to morning.

But does that help, to see the sky as carceral
or at least as a struck stage? Why, just now, did
your enthusiasm wain for an escape? Is Edmund less
beautiful when rhyming with a dark sea

and the Count, well, he remains one color
of the French flag, at least once light has passed.

# THE AMERICAN QUESTION
## JULIA TAGLIERE

### I. 01202009

He said we could that day, and we believed him, because the better angels of our nature were exactly who we hoped to be.

### II. 11052024

Today, he'll say *we can* just ignore those angels' voices. Angels are suckers and losers. He'll swear a new oath to us and the world that we are all now free. Thus freed, *we can* now rage at those we other. *We can* spit at them, grab their pussies, deport them, pillage their savings, force preferred families into being and tear unwanted families apart. *We can* swallow this planet whole, chew it up and shit it out on a gilded platter, repackage that shit into charity and weapons and sell it cheap to the leaders of all those other shithole countries who fear us as much as they need us as much as they hate us. Liberated from any archaic sense of guilt or shame, *we can* dishonor our parents and all the other suckers and losers who came before us, the ones who, if they can still see us, *we can* (righteously!) claim would join us in celebrating this joyful day when *we can* finally lie cheat steal rape and break every other fucking commandment or law or rule they ever taught us because, oh, yes, oh, joy! *we can* plaster new copies of all our favorite old testament writs on the walls of our schools and courthouses and prisons and camps, *we can* slap them up right beside the fading replicas of the declaration and the constitution, those other updated and outdated myths we used to use to teach our children and our children's children about our better angels, but now, on this glad day, we can finally teach everyone, even the youngest child, our unfettered, unconquerable truth, that yes, oh, yes, *we can* do these things, all of them, and ***we always could***, even on the sabbath day—*especially* on the sabbath days, but naturally, only during halftime, because billionaires need to eat, too.

*We can* post the rules, because that is how we learn *we can* break them.

Oh, yes, we can.

*We fucking can.*

## III. 01202025

Today, our better angels will need to show their work again, will need to answer this question we believed we'd already settled, so many, many times before:

*Can a nation conceived in liberty and dedicated to the proposition that we are all created equal long endure?*

Endure or fall, we can at least expect a definitive answer, and it will be a relief.

We weren't created to hold our breath for so long.

## IV. Anthem for an Unknown America

[https://amhistory.si.edu/starspangledbanner/the-lyrics.aspx]

# TO AMERICA

YVETTE NEISSER

Let us document and cherish
every inch of earth

survey the insects, ferns and moss,
cacti and lizards

measure the mountains' height
and the depth of lakes.

Bring back rhubarb pie, fry bread,
wild turkey, winter squash.

Let animals be totems,
revered and respected.

Celebrate bluegrass and the blues,
jambalaya and black-eyed peas.

Let Spanish bubble up
into a second language.

Let neighbors converse.
Let us welcome strangers

and stop on the road
to help a stranded driver.

# RÁPIDO

## KATHLEEN WHEATON

IN MADRID, Buddy and I lived on the money I earned teaching English and the fumes of an inheritance from his Texas grandmother. He wasn't lazy, he simply felt he didn't have a moment to lose. He was studying classical guitar with a maestro who was eighty, the same age as the century. Buddy had discovered his instrument late, in college, and at twenty-three, he practiced ten hours a day.

We lived on the top floor of a bleak high-rise near the soccer stadium. At night the roar of the spectators came in through the windows. However the place had advantages: it was a short bus ride to the house where Maestro lived with his wife, Doña Amparo, and down the street from the office building where I taught Executive English. My students were all men, courtly and dapper, their suit jackets worn draped over their shoulders like matador capes. One of them asked me out. I told him I lived with my boyfriend. But you are free, my student said. Divorce wasn't yet legal in Spain, he explained, though now that there was democracy, the law was expected to change. The divorce courts will be mobbed, he said.

Are you getting divorced? I asked.

Not me! He laughed.

I got off work at six, and Buddy practiced until seven, so I'd walk slowly home through a park dedicated to General Perón, the former dictator of Argentina. Now that the Spanish dictator, General Franco, was also dead, protestors had splashed the statue of his old friend with red paint. Perón appeared to accept this expression of public opinion benignly, his splattered hands blessing the pigeons, the dusty sycamores, the children on the monkey bars.

If the weather was nice I'd sit on a bench and write in my notebook. Once I overheard a young mother telling her friend that her husband had told her to put the baby down so that she could cut his hair. So you have two babies, her friend said. She glanced in my direction and smiled. I hastily shut my notebook and walked away. Later I thought maybe I'd missed an opportunity to make Spanish friends.

Buddy and I usually ate dinner at a cafetería at the end of our block, where cheap, filling *platos combinados* were served at formica tables under fluorescent lights. Sometimes I could persuade him to walk a mile south to a lovely old plaza, where the stone buildings with their wrought iron balconies looked like crooked teeth undergoing orthodontia. There was an inexpensive bodega in the plaza, with a zinc bar and exposed rafters, where you could get the same meal as at the cafetería—ham with fried eggs and potato salad—but in more picturesque surroundings.

See? Isn't this nicer? I'd say, and Buddy would agree—because if I was happy, he was happy. He often said so.

One night at the bodega, we were befriended by a German couple. They were a few years older than us, touring Spain by car. Hans was big, blond and jovial, Elsa was shy and pretty. Her English was fluent, though whenever she spoke, red circles appeared on her cheeks. They invited us to a glass of the wine they were drinking, and I explained why we were in Madrid. Are you musical, too? Hans asked.

No, I said. I worried that Buddy would say I was a writer, and I'd have to explain that I merely kept a journal. But when he didn't say anything, I felt injured.

Into this silence Elsa said they planned to visit two Romanesque churches in the countryside the next day, and would we like to join them?

We'd love to, I said quickly, though I guessed Buddy didn't want to. He hated to miss even one day of practice. So as we walked home that night I kept coming up with arguments for why we should go, and he kept reassuring me it was fine. Still, I felt bad. Buddy's talent and promise were such that Maestro had come out of retirement to teach him. Due to precarious elderly health, Doña Amparo sometimes called to postpone the weekly lesson. The telephone in our apartment rang for no other reason. Buddy's mother didn't call because long-distance was expensive, and my parents didn't because they disapproved of me living with a man before marriage.

So when Elsa phoned to say that they were leaving their hotel and would be outside our building in fifteen minutes, I felt that a new phase of life in Spain was beginning. It had been six months since I'd ridden in a private car, and it seemed magical, even futuristic, to be sailing along the highway in an air-conditioned Mercedes, the high, dry plains of Castile flashing by the passenger window. Hans drove fast, deftly overtaking any vehicle that appeared before us. We arrived at the first church and he called out, Ten minutes! He and Elsa lingered in the car, maybe to have a moment of privacy, but Buddy and I got out and walked around. When we returned to the car, they were already—or still—inside, the motor running.

At the next church, we all got out together. Elsa translated from a German guidebook that exhorted us to visit the underground crypt, which housed three child martyrs supposedly killed by Jews. But that rumor was false, the guidebook added. The carvings on their little tombs were worn soft by many hands. While we were down there, in the semi-darkness, our hosts disappeared. We returned to the parking lot as Hans was backing down the gravel driveway, the passenger doors ajar, as if we were fleeing a bank heist.

The hurry turned out to be that they had noon reservations at a monastery that had been converted to a fancy restaurant. It was early for lunch in Spain, and the vast dining room was empty except for the white-jacketed waiters standing silent along the stone walls. The padded leather menus offered bodega food at thousands of pesetas a plate. We're inviting you, Hans said. We didn't have enough money with us to argue. He consumed most of a second bottle of wine, and after lunch, drove even faster. We were up in the mountains now, careening around blind curves. We asked him to slow down, and he did—for a minute or two. Finally Elsa spoke up in German. His reply made her shrink back in her seat, her face crimson.

As we approached a village, I suggested that we stop for a coffee. My idea was that Buddy and I could make an excuse, catch a bus home. Instead, Hans sped up.

At the sign for the next village I said, Could we stop up here, please? I have to go to the bathroom.

He drove through at breakneck speed.

You can hold it, Hans said. Unless—do you have your period? Or diarrhea that would mess up my car?

Don't be an asshole, man, Buddy said. Kathleen asked you to stop.

Hans slammed on the brakes. We were in the middle of a forest. Get out, he said. Elsa didn't turn around as the Mercedes sped away.

We were ankle-deep in leaves like wet cornflakes. I'm sorry, I said. I began to cry.

You couldn't have foreseen this, Buddy said. He put his arm around me. We'll hitch to the next village and catch a bus from there.

The driver of a banana truck picked us up. We told him our destination was Madrid, and he said if we went by bus we'd be traveling for days, so he'd drop us in a town with a train station. He gave each of us a banana.

The slow train that stopped everywhere was called the Rápido. The name wasn't a joke—it must have been the latest in transport when Franco was a young dictator. We got tickets for Madrid and then strolled around the plaza, holding hands like the Spanish couples. We became hungry again and bought potato omelette sandwiches and ate sitting cross-legged on the ground, something Spanish people never did.

We went to the station an hour early. Night had fallen, and we could hear crickets chirping and faraway dogs barking. Whenever we heard the whistle of an approaching train, Buddy would stand on the edge of the platform and peer down the tracks. This made me nervous.

If it's an express train, it won't stop, I said. And if it's the Rápido, it will.

You're right. He smiled. But he kept doing it. He was that eager to get back.

But I'm free, I thought. And in that suspended time called waiting, I imagined my future, in which I would leave Buddy. This happened almost exactly as I foresaw it.

We stayed in touch, though. Mostly by postcard, even after the invention of email. I sent a postcard whenever I moved to a new city. I wrote when I got married, and again when we moved to Cuernavaca, and also after I published my first short story, about an English teacher in Spain ardently pursued by her married student. I didn't send the story. He wrote when he got a tenured teaching job at the University of Texas and then a year later when he married an oboist. I was glad he'd found a fellow musician. He didn't answer my effusively congratulatory note, and I wondered if it had offended him. I'd been married seven years by then, had two children born in Mexico.

At our going-away party several months later, one of the guests brought a friend who was a professor at UT. Excitedly, I asked if he knew Buddy or the oboist, whose name was Leonora.

The professor looked dismayed. I guess you don't know, he said. Buddy and Leonora had been killed in a car crash in downtown Austin two months earlier.

I went and sat on the diving board of the pool at our friends' house where the party was being held. After a few minutes my husband came and sat beside me.

I knew that Maestro had died long ago, and now I thought about Doña Amparo, in her black housedress, in that dark, old house in Barrio Salamanca, her carpet slippers swish-swishing as she came to answer the door. If Doña Amparo were alive now, she'd be ninety-eight, I said.

She could be alive, said my husband, whose grandmother was a hundred and one. I sure hope I don't outlive you, he added.

I slid off the end of the diving board in my party clothes.

When Buddy and I boarded the Rápido, it was jammed with teenaged soldiers—military service was still obligatory in Spain. We fell asleep sitting up in the smoky compartment. When I woke it was morning, and the train was stopped in a field. Buddy was gone. Then I saw him standing in the corridor, his arms folded on the top of the open window. I went out and he showed me what he was looking at: storks flopping up and down in the wheat like marionettes. Oh! Here was a rare moment in which I didn't want or expect or regret anything. The train lurched forward, and his long dark hair stirred in the breeze. His usually pale cheeks were pink from our day outside.

# PREFLIGHT

HENRY CRAWFORD

Thank you. For picking up. This
book. In the airport bookstore.
Minutes. Before you go. Spend 'em
here. With me. In the bookstore.
With the diet sodas. Neck pillows.
Ear buds. And iPhone. Attachments.
Take your time. With this poem.
Which makes the argument. You
could die. It's happened. Before.
Someone. In an airport bookstore.
Has no way. Of knowing. A loose
fan blade. Worn out. Bolt. Waiting.
There. On your plane. Of course.
You could. Always. Just go back.
Walk out. Get in the car. Drive
home. You can. Do that. Weighing.
The risks. Determining. The odds.
Calculating. The advantages. Going.
With confidence. Into the future.
Use your head. It's what we do best.
But don't say. I didn't warn you.

# STARVED FOR DEMOCRACY

FRAN ABRAMS

When stores start to ration toilet paper,
people talk about pandemic times,
although there is no rampant disease.

Milk is seldom available. People begin
to point fingers at the government and realize
that farm subsidies have been discontinued.

Even when food is offered for sale, it's more expensive
than ever before, like potatoes for $15.00 a pound.
Where people have even a small plot of land in city or suburbs,
they try to grow their own potatoes and vegetables.

The economy slowly collapses while government deficits soar
and some commentators talk about the Great Depression.

There are some who argue over who is to blame,
but most worry about how they will feed their families.

Grocery stores close because there is nothing to sell.
No bakers bake bread because no farmers grow wheat.

Eggs cannot be found for sale because animals
understand in a way humans do not that the end is near.

In small towns and large cities, dogs and cats roam the streets.
No longer fed by humans, they return to their wild origins.
People talk about whether to eat them, and some do.

And, although no one has COVID, the outcome is the same.
Body bags rest in refrigerated trucks because the morgues are full.
[For some reason, there still is diesel fuel. Perhaps due to collusion
among major governments around the world. This will never be explained.]

Duly elected representatives who promised to fix the economy,
who set plans in motion they are now unable to reverse, stay alive
using their official privileges while their constituents die of hunger.

Starvation conquers a first world country.
And the people who once lived
in the greatest democracy on earth
do not cast votes from their graves.

# PORTRAIT WITH BULLET HOLE

## EDWARD BELFAR

"IT GOES WITH THE TERRITORY," Dr. Andrew Carr told his wife, Laura Woolridge-Carr, over a celebratory dinner turned gloomy at the Old Ebbitt Grill.

By *it*, he meant the sniping that greeted her appointment, announced earlier that day by President Dreck, as head curator of the National Gallery. Her husband, she knew, spoke from painful experience. What had he to show for his own decade-long tenure as the president's physician but the humiliating sobriquet "Andy Candy," hung upon him by the world's most unmanageable patient and gleefully adopted by same White House staffers who, emulating their boss, had worn away his scruples with their unceasing demands for painkillers and Adderall?

Never, though, had she endured such derision, and given the typically low profile of the position, the reaction had left her shocked and disheartened. Art critics, academics, and even her fellow curators denounced her as just another of President Dreck's grossly unfit appointees, a dilettante with an undergraduate art history degree that, absent her husband's connection to the White House, might have qualified her for service as a docent.

The whisperings of her ostensible allies, however, hurt her even more. A slender, hazel-eyed Tennessean of forty-seven, she had an oval face with a fair complexion, strikingly long eyelashes, and an upturned nose, and she wore her frosted platinum hair in a pixie cut. From the day of her and Dr. Carr's arrival in Washington, her youthful appearance had engendered much debate among the women in President Dreck's orbit, many of whom bore the ravages of botched facial transformations, as to what cosmetic work, if any, she had had done. Her appointment to head the National Gallery, which had surprised her as much as anyone, had inflamed the spite and envy of those women. They speculated, often in graphic terms, as to the favors she must have given the president in return for the job. Knowing President Dreck as she did, Laura suspected that if he had not started the rumors himself, he had done his best to spread them.

When he had first dangled the job offer before her, he insisted on her meeting him alone in the Oval Office to discuss the terms. Aware of his reputation with women, she hesitated before agreeing. To her relief, he did not proposition her during the interview, but at its conclusion, when he escorted her to the door, his hand slid down her back and came to rest upon her buttocks.

Furious and determined to prove her detractors wrong, she relegated her gauzy slit dresses to the back of her closet, donned gray and navy-blue business suits, and routinely worked seventy-, and eighty-hour weeks. Such was her dedication that even on that surreal morning when, driving into town, she found the streets lined with military vehicles and police and National Guard troops, and road closures necessitated a treacherous mile-long walk to the National Gallery over slush-covered sidewalks, she made it to her office on time.

Because her much put-upon husband was not answering his phone that morning and she had made a conscious effort of late to avoid hearing or reading the news—the better to remain ignorant of the slings and arrows directed her way—she was, perhaps, the last person in Washington, DC, to find out that the president had declared a state of emergency in the District. A policeman in riot gear, stationed outside the Mall-side entrance of the West Building, informed her when she arrived. When she asked him why, he shrugged, and when she told him that she needed to retrieve some important documents from her office, he refused to let her inside, though she was shivering from her long walk through the chilly streets. His supervisor, however, proved more amenable to her pleas, which she accentuated with a few well-timed tears.

Notwithstanding what she told the police, her dignity, rather than some spreadsheets, was her actual concern. The last time the president had declared a state of emergency in the District, a celebrated Monet on loan from the Musée d'Orsay had gone missing from the museum. The theft, occurring barely a month into her tenure, had roiled US-French relations and brought down a fresh storm of opprobrium upon her head. Her least favorite *Washington Post* op-ed columnist, the paper's one remaining reliably liberal voice, wrote, "As for Ms. Wooldridge-Carr, we now can have no doubt as to why she was hired: to avert her eyes while the president's cronies, ever on the lookout for new and innovative forms of graft, make off with the museum's treasures." Whether or not the rumors that the Monet now occupied a place in the private collection of one of the president's billionaire tech-mogul cronies were true, Laura knew that some within, or adjacent, to the administration coveted the museum's treasures. Recently, Vice President Szar had given a speech outlining his vision of a "reimagined" high-tech National Gallery filled with holographic images of the masterworks that visitors could alter to their liking. Afterwards, she asked the vice president what would become of the original paintings in the collection when the holograms had replaced them, and he spoke, vaguely but alarmingly, about investment opportunities for collectors. She would not allow another theft on her watch, she vowed, no matter the cost to her or her husband.

Hewing to her custom, she shed her running shoes as soon as she reached her office. She kept several pairs of shoes locked away in a cabinet, most of them suitable for walking around the building, but one with stilettos in case of surprise visits by dignitaries. On this morning, she opted for the latter, for she sensed that the additional stature they provided might prove useful.

Barely had she made the change, when she heard a loud banging coming from outside the building. Rushing to the rotunda, she saw the doors on the Constitution Avenue side swing open. Several dozen men, clad in the black fatigues and gold-trimmed black berets of the "Dreck's Army" militia and carrying AR-15s came charging into the building. She wondered what had happened to the policeman who had guarded the building from her with such zeal. Had he stood aside for the militia men?

Jogging up the steps to the rotunda, the men halted at the top. With the president's twin sons, Walter Dreck Jr. and Chip Dreck, taking their places at the head of the group, the militia men formed a column. Walter and Chip, also in uniform, did not carry AR-15s but had holstered sidearms attached to their belts. Rather than military boots, however, they both wore black Christian Louboutin dress shoes.

While Laura Woolridge-Carr stood frozen, the men, led by Walter and Chip, marched past her, three abreast, and down the hallway, their heavy boots thudding against the polished stone floor.

"Fight for Dreck! Fight for Dreck!" they shouted.

Midway down the hall, the column turned left again, into a gallery filled with seventeenth-century Dutch portraiture. Laura Woolridge-Carr, rousing herself at last, ran after them, the clacking of her stilettos echoing through the corridor.

Walter Dreck Jr., the dauphin, three minutes older than his twin brother, stood in the middle of the gallery, looking over the paintings. The taller of the two fraternal twins, standing well over six feet, Walter had an unkempt salt-and-pepper beard. His excessively high forehead had the same oily sheen as his slicked-back hair. Glassy-eyed and swaying, he looked drunk. Laura, who knew him well, wondered whether she had even seen him sober.

"That one," he said, pointing a shaky finger at a portrait that hung in the center of the wall opposite the entrance to the gallery.

The portrait was that of an aging man seated perpendicularly to the viewer. His somber brown jacket, with its upturned collar, was of the same hue as the indistinct background, almost melding into it, and he wore a beret of deep umber. A muted light bathed his face, which was turned toward the viewer. His brow bore the creases of age and worry. Though his mouth—a flat line—suggested a stoical disposition, an unutterable sadness filled his eyes. His was the countenance of a man who had known much sorrow and grief—as unlike that of the eternally callow Walter Dreck Jr. as a face could be. The portrait was by Rembrandt, and the face, his own.

As two militia men clumsily tried to yank the painting from the wall, the eyes of the portrait seemed to take on a still more sorrowful aspect.

"Walter Dreck Jr.," said Laura Woolridge-Carr, in the tone of a kindergarten teacher talking to an especially recalcitrant five-year-old, "what do you think you're doing?"

Walter Jr. murmured something that sounded like "safekeeping."

"We're removing it for safekeeping, ma'am," said a lanky, snaggle-toothed militia man with a scraggly red beard that reached halfway down his chest. "Can't be too careful with all the rioters out there."

"What rioters? I've been all over the District this morning, and I haven't seen any rioters. Just police and National Guardsmen everywhere I look."

"The President said there are rioters, ma'am. That's good enough for me."

"Well, it's not good enough for me. And you have no authority to take any paintings from here."

Walter Dreck Jr. drew his Glock 9mm pistol from its holster and whirled 360 degrees with his eyes closed. The Rembrandt hit the floor with a thwack, as the two militia men, who had finally wrested it free from the wall, let it drop and dove for cover. Laura Woolridge-Carr and the rest of the militia men did likewise. As she hit the floor, she heard a sound like an explosion, and she covered her head with her arms.

"There's my authority," shouted Walter Jr., the only person in the gallery still standing.

An instant later, he, too, was on the floor, having tripped and fallen backwards over the prone body of a snaggle-toothed militia man with the red beard. His head smacking against the hardwood, Walter lay still.

Slowly, the militia men rose. Ashen-faced, they patted themselves all over, as if to assure themselves that they were still whole. Some, perhaps still hearing the reverberations of the gunshot, had their hands over their ears. Laura Woolridge-Carr, her body shaking all over, sat up, and placed her hand upon her chest, and took several deep breaths.

Of all the animate and inanimate occupants of the gallery, the only one that appeared unfazed by the shooting was its victim, a self-portrait by Jan Steen. Though the bullet from the Glock had left a neat round hole in the center of his forehead, Jan Steen still gazed upon the assemblage in the gallery with the same disdain that he had shown countless other visitors for 400 years. One could imagine him muttering out of the side of his mouth, "Who let this rabble in here?"

The Rembrandt appeared intact but for a crack in the frame. The two militia men who had removed it from the wall picked it up again and carried it out of the gallery. Two others scooped Walter off the floor, draped his arms over their shoulders, and dragged him off, the toes of his dress shoes scraping against the floor.

"Isn't this one by the same guy who painted the girl with the earring?" asked the obese, pasty-faced Chip.

Laura, still lightheaded, realized belatedly that he was addressing her.

"Huh? Which one?"

"This one."

He was pointing, she saw, at the only Vermeer in the museum's collection.

"Yes," she replied weakly.

"He's pretty famous, too, right?"

"Yes, pretty famous."

"But not as famous as Rembrandt, is he?"

"It's hard to say."

"And the painting's so much smaller than Walt's."

"Yes, it is. Maybe you should pick a bigger one. It's the only one we…"

"He always gets what he wants, and I get what's left over. It's so unfair."

"Life can be that way."

"But it still must be worth a fortune."

Grabbing the Vermeer off the wall himself, he led the remaining militiamen out of the gallery.

Laura, still uncertain of the ground beneath her feet, took the precaution of removing her shoes before standing up. Back in her office, as she gazed out the window at the line of moving vans assembling along Constitution Avenue, nausea seized her. Walter Jr. and Chip, she realized, had merely begun the looting, awarded that privilege, as they were every other in their lives, by virtue of their parentage. Now Szar's collectors had come to seize the rest.

The men who came with the moving vans were professionals rather than armed goons. They worked with dispatch. Hewing to the instructions of those who had hired them, they emptied the West Building of masterworks that ranged in time from the early renaissance through the first half of the twentieth century, while ignoring the East Building's modern and contemporary collection. Of all the works of the great Dutch and Flemish painters, only the self-portrait of the scornful Jan Steen, with the bullet hole in his forehead, remained to bear witness.

# BREATH SONG

## W. LUTHER JETT

To morning which whistles her name down the streets of the forgotten, with early mist rising off the harbor and the slow creak of boats at their moorings;

To blue hills rising, rank on rank, beyond a lost highway, where ten thousand devils play ten thousand fiddles as a girl in red gingham and lace winks before kicking off her heels to run barefoot, unashamed, through dew-kissed meadows;

To green sun and lavender moon;

To pale curtains, frayed and faded, that flutter in the breeze while someone fingers a cheap guitar, unseen, and the alleyway smells of laundry soap, and grackles queue along the phone-wire humming with the murmur of unintelligible voices;

To the small child who absolutely refuses to give in to the dooryard cockscomb, who shakes her fist in the world's eye, whose laughter is the scale of dust silvering from a sparrow's wings;

To the striped shirt you wore to the carnival when all the clowns removed their grease and walked on their hands, juggling war-drums and penny-pipes with their feet;

To dust-bathed pilgrims thumbing through pages of illuminated manuscripts of folk-songs composed at the crossroads deep in the red clay flood-plains, who fell down on their knees, washed in the blood of ten thousand innocent sinners;

To empty-eyed solitude of nights with no dreams other than a hunger which will not be appeased;

To back-street storefront clinics and basement bar-rooms pulsing with secret bio-documentaries no-one wants you to watch, where college students parse nursery rhymes and weary lambs lay down their heads and refuse to follow anyone any more, where musicians blow, blow, blow their horns until the walls begin to crumble and gates are shaken from their hinges;

To the overturned flivver at the long end of the muddy road that led out from the old barn where the oaken bucket flew in anger, splitting night into day and day into night until nothing remained but scream of brakes, shear of splintered paint, and thick aroma of spilled gasoline;

To shadows that flicker against drawn window-shades high above rain-drenched gutters where disembodied hearts parade, naked, glistening, and alone through a night of the neon dead, punctuated by klaxons and the bark of distant fire-crackers;

To the unsuspecting silhouetted stranger bearing gifts, to the lost fandango dancer, to carolers in the snow, to dreamers in the desert down to their last canteen;

To the sigh that marks the end of the night as stars wink out one by one as the pale blue-steel knife-edge of dawn lurks across the ocean to be born;

To the great girth of the world and all who breathe it in, whose breaths move the waters, stir continents which float on beds of fire, raise mountains and cities, birth rain and thunder, rock the endless parabola of light which spans the heavens.

I listen for you here in this room at the edge of your knowing, even as you wait by your own open window in your tower overlooking the unbound sea.

# THERE'S NO PLACE LIKE AMERICA TODAY

## SEBASTIAN JOHNSON

MY MOTHER DIED during the summer of 2016. I wore my grief like two left shoes, every other step landing falsely.

The bewildering shock of a sudden death has its own narcotic effect. That first month, despite the upheaval, I would forget; would lose myself in a particularly beautiful summer morning or evening stroll, before remembering, mid-stride, that my mother was dead. Her absence was a deep, sandy footprint at the place where waves meet shore, each pull of the tides eroding the concrete reminders of her existence in this world, reality settling like grains of ocean sand into the depression.

I was left to excavate the remnants of her life. Tucked away in her bedroom closet was a cache of old records—disco, funk, soul, dance hits, and roller rink anthems. Among them was an empty jacket for a Curtis Mayfield album, *There's No Place Like America Today.*

I was familiar with Mayfield's work but had never heard of this album. I did not anticipate that this taut, 35-minute primer on Black grief would form the soundtrack of the next eight years. Released in 1975, a year before the nation's bicentennial, the album speaks in shockingly relevant ways to the reality of Black grief within our culture, threading a narrative of death and dispossession, disillusionment, and displaced love.

The arresting cover art is an interpretation of a famous Depression-era photo taken by Margaret Bourke-White in the aftermath of the devastating 1937

Louisville flood. In the original, a line of Black flood survivors awaits the distribution of food relief in front of a giant billboard that boasts, "There's no way like the American Way" and "World's Highest Standard of Living." On the billboard, an archetypal white American family—mother, father, two children, and a dog—beam contented smiles as they take a Sunday drive. The Black visages below present a stark contrast.

The image on the album cover inverts the queue from the original photograph; the Black figures move in reverse. It is common, as America approaches its 250th anniversary, to speak of democratic backsliding. For Black Americans, democracy has more often been a dead promise than a living system. Casey Gerald, writing for *New York Magazine* on the 400th anniversary of slavery in America, posed the question succinctly: "How can we live in a land that's made to kill us?"

The billboard that hangs above depicts a white ideal that is as much the bedrock of our nation as are its founding democratic principles. If forced to choose between the two—to let one live and the other perish—what would white America decide? In the waning Obama years, academics intoned seriously about "deaths of despair" among white Americans. New research has muddied this narrative, but it had a powerful hold on the zeitgeist then—implying that the high water mark of multiracial democracy had meant disaster and ruin for white America, a loss of birthright. "If destruction be our lot," warned Lincoln, "we must ourselves be its author and finisher. As a nation of freemen, we must live through all time, or die by suicide."

These questions of loss swirl all around us, jumbling into each other as we lurch from catastrophe to crisis. Grief has become the animating impulse of American life, a common experience in uncommon times.

I have returned to this album again and again as "this America settles into the mould of its vulgarity," to crib from poet Robinson Jeffers. The day after the 2016 election, I felt the same dislocating grief that I'd felt a few months prior —the uncanny sensation of running at full steam off a cliff and somehow defying gravity; afraid to look down and see the earth rising up to swallow me whole. The shell-shocked faces of my fellow commuters on that rainy Wednesday morning in the capital confirmed that I was not alone in my assessment: that overnight, something had died. And there, on television, was the cruel man who would be our next president, sitting next to Obama in the White House, and looking just as dazed.

I listened to the album in an endless loop during the hot summer of 2020, after George Floyd cried for his own dead mother under his murderer's knee. I could not bring myself to watch his last eight minutes and forty-six seconds of life on this earth, but many others did, their grief raging in the streets, an all-consuming fire. My own grief rolled in near dawn like a thick fog, holding me beneath covers before dissipating in the afternoon. Not that I had anywhere to be, of course—confined to my house with the rest of the country as a plague choked the air outside. By the time we would emerge from our homes, more than one million of us would be dead.

> *How can anyone survive*
> *When everybody's been made a sacrifice?*

We bargained with our grief. Perhaps the dead did not die in vain. Perhaps we could resurrect our dying democracy at the ballot box. We affixed the halo of martyrdom to each senseless death. We Trusted Black Women, or hid behind them. We followed ever more baroque COVID protocols, debated the efficacy of different face masks, and dueled over the vaccine—rituals of certainty to ward off the terrible specter of mortality.

For Black people, this bargaining is familiar. "To be a Negro in this country and to be relatively conscious is to be in a rage almost all the time," James Baldwin said. It is also to engage in the futility of trying to solve the problem of your being. In the days after George Floyd's murder, many of us joked darkly about the anguished calls and texts we'd received from erstwhile "allies"— acquaintances and tenuous connections offering solidarity but really seeking answers. Wanting us to fix it, or to at least, relieve them of the responsibility. "Black people are the wrench in the works," Frank Wilderson writes in *Afropessimism*. What is required of the Black citizen is nothing less than to throw our energies, our hopes—our bodies—into the gears of the American machine, an apparatus aimed like a loaded gun at our hearts. To do so with an eager smile, in a soothing way that arouses no suspicion. A familiar figure from our history —the race man or woman, the freedom fighter—was reanimated, updated, and sanitized for 21st-century corporate combat zones. In short time, the old wine was poured into the new wineskin of "DEI," a clumsy acronym soon to be wielded as an epithet.

Once the (first) threat of a Trump second term was averted—with a critical contribution from Black voters—the burden of allyship was laid down. Now

would be a time of healing, it was proclaimed. We would seek comity and understanding with the Americans who voted, in record-breaking numbers, for
unprecedented cruelty and mayhem; who were then, and are still, in the process
of chipping away at our Republic to preserve the white lie for themselves.

The moment did not last. This past November, as Kamala Harris was pushed
off the highest glass cliff in the land, I watched the election returns with dread,
grief rising like bile in the back of my throat. It was a sleepless night.

ON THE KING HOLIDAY, marking the birth of our nation's greatest Black martyr,
Trump was inaugurated for the second time. Among many others, he signed
the first in a series of executive orders meant to gut DEI efforts in public and
private life.

Eleven days earlier, the most eminent citizens of America gathered at National
Cathedral to mark the passing of President Carter, who served one term but
whose lifetime spanned forty percent of the life of the nation. In the first two
rows sat the five living presidents and their spouses (with one notable absence).
The once and future president, whose presence added to the funereal mood,
sat near the end of the second row. Watching, I was reminded of the poignant
opening passage of Barbara Tuchman's *The Guns of August*: "[O]n history's
clock it was sunset, and the sun of the old world was setting in a dying blaze of
splendor never to be seen again."

None of the white presidents spoke a word to Trump. Obama, seated next to
him, chatted with him amiably. He had withstood an onslaught of racist attacks
from his interlocutor for years, endangering himself and his family; had seen
his legacy degraded and his legitimacy questioned; had so enraged a portion
of his countrymen, by his singular example and service to his country, as to
make Trump possible—perhaps inevitable.

Obama's practiced civility earned plaudits in some quarters, derision in others.
I was not surprised to see him pressed into service in this way. It was a role he'd
played since his first reassurance of our national unity ("There's not a Black
America and white America...") from the DNC stage two decades ago.

Michelle Obama's decision to opt out of the proceedings was equally divisive
but much more interesting. A woman who was raised in the post-Civil Rights

era on the mantra, "When they go low, you go high," had decided not to go at all. Some read in her decision a certain bitterness. But I saw, in her absence, acceptance. Acceptance that, come what may, respectability is an empty desire. That if we cannot save the nation from itself, we might as well save ourselves the trouble.

What kind of place will America be, should it exist, 250 years from now? It is certainly beyond our ability to predict, and likely beyond our capacity to imagine. We, our children, and their children will have grown old, sick, and died in that time, as the generations before us did. We will have laughed, loved, hoped, fought, raged, despaired, and grieved. Perhaps that distant future will be as unrecognizable as 1776 is to us now; perhaps some elements will ring all too familiarly.

I'll bet Curtis will remain timeless. Somehow, some way, a person will dust off this record, find a turntable, and make it spin. They'll hear his voice, feel the melody, and it will speak to something true in the quiet corners of their heart.

> *And just as He made us one of many*
> *Then aren't the many of us maybe only one?*

# DEMOLITION

LAURA SHOVAN

This is no muddy field.
There are no fences,

no spectators to cheer the spark
of our combustion.

Our bump and grind
does more than chafe the skin.

We are pocked by the stones
we kick in each other's faces.

You dent my lip,
I chip your paint.

Truth is, we never fight like this,
jaws loose as broken fenders.

We are quiet,
remnants of a meal between us.

Your voice idles
when you say, "Sorry."

Does it matter
that you won't run at me,

pedal to the floor,
that I won't spin my wheels

and gun it? Truth is,
we are undone.

# THE BOTANIST

## LAURA SHOVAN

Upon entering the gardens of the former palace I
noted vegetations' creep—how ivy and phlox met
to obscure the bluestone path where a
fur-hatted guard might have stood once. I was a traveler.
No matter how one measures distance, I was from
elsewhere. Green, in all its Terran expressions, was an
aberration to my eyes. I came upon moss, coating an antique
statue's thigh. Invasive to the marble, but native to the land.
I do not have the luxury of claiming a home. *She who*
*is born between worlds belongs nowhere,* it is said.
I scraped my sample, enough to fill two
vials. My specimens from this planet are vast
and varied. I have visited many biomes, prairies and
rainforests, submerged cities where trunkless
sculptures rise from the water on colossal legs.
It's strange to think this was a human place, that I am of
this world's genome. I left a smooth stone
on the statue's plinth, an offering. Now I stand
outside my ship. It is time to go in,
to set coordinates for my next target, but I hesitate. The
verdant world, without my species, is no desert.

# BABY'S FIRST OVOID™

## ALICE STEPHENS

TODAY WAS THE DAY that Baby would finally get his very own Ovoid™.

Eve knew that she was supposed to feel sad. Any good Motheress would. This was the event for which the Motheress' Aides, or Maides, had long been preparing her: to Emancipate Baby from her Ovoid™ so that he could go out into the world on his own, autonomous from her. They had been coaching her on coping tactics on post-Emancipation depression and had approved activation of MelloMist™, so that at a push of a button, a vaporous cloud would release into her Ovoid™, instantly soothing the sorrow of separation and annihilating her anxiety.

But Eve already knew she would have no need of the MelloMist™ because as it was, she couldn't wait to get rid of Baby. At first, it had been wonderful, a joy, everything that the MANual, the Maides, and her own Motheress had purported it to be, having her newborn nestled safely in her arms, able to effortlessly nuzzle at her breast when hungry, the two of them napping and waking in unison, hearts beating together in harmony.

Due to the extra ration of PowrBarz™, Eve's milk came in rich and creamy and packed with proteins and vitamins, and Baby grew at a healthy pace.

And grew. And grew.

In fact, he grew so rapidly that the Maides reduced the PowrBarz™ and advised early weaning, which made life even more difficult because now she had to maneuver Baby to sit up and then spoon-feed him, repeatedly banging against the Plastiskin™ of her Ovoid™. Sleep became uncomfortable, and she earned two Matridemerits for twice turning her back on Baby instead of sleeping in the prescribed Cuddle Position.

Baby's massive head blocked the panoramic view of her PlexiVizr™, she'd had enough of his sour milk and poopy diaper smell, and she had a sneaking paranoia that Baby was using up more and more of her oxygen, even though she never had any trouble breathing.

She played up the lack of space, ramming an elbow extra hard into her Plexi-Vizr™ as she tried to feed Baby while a Maide was nearby; reluctantly confessing (a Motheress never complained) to exhaustion due to disturbed sleep patterns; claiming she missed her weekly FemChek appointment because Baby's head blocked her view of the clock in the lower left corner of her Plexi-Vizr™; sending Eve's HeMate, Adonis, VidMsgs™, voice husky and trembling, saying how much she missed his touch, as she touched herself.

If she had to guess, it was probably the VidMsgs™ that did it. An Ovoid™ Fitting Team was dispatched to analyze Baby's LifeData, and finally his very own OvoidChick™ was ready for him.

Eve knew she was very lucky. Many mothers were not entitled to an Ovoid-Chick™ but had to wait to Emancipate until Baby could press buttons on his own, but Adonis was high up in the Hearchy, the Program Master in charge of content for the news and entertainment that streamed into everyone's PlexiVizr™. Until Baby was Emancipated from Eve's Ovoid™, Adonis was unable to dock his Ovoid™ with hers. Of course, as a high ranking official in the Hearchy, he was entitled to many SheMates, but Adonis had a particular fondness for Eve, and therefore was eager to Emancipate Baby so that he and Eve could once again resume docking.

But such was the nature of America 2.0 that it was viewed as unseemly for a Motheress to be eager to Emancipate her baby. Motheresses were to dread that day, and do everything they could to delay its arrival. They were to resist their Maides' gentle hints at the impending separation, vowing they'd rather Exit the Ovoid™ than Emancipate.

What nonsense! To Exit the Ovoid™ was to give up your existence, for once you entered America 2.0's environment, you were prey to the viruses, and if they didn't kill you, the toxic air would. Besides, the Hearchy's best minds had been working for decades to perfect the Ovoid™ for maximum comfort and pleasure. Not only was the oxygen pure and virus-free, but the snacks were constant and tasty, the electrical stimulation of muscles for exercise was painless and sometimes even pleasurable, and Adonis and his platoon of content producers kept the mind constantly entertained with comedies, romances, heartwarming stories about selfless Maides and fecund Motheresses, inspiring tales of the Hearchy's triumphs and breakthroughs, along with encouraging updates about climbing birthrates and, of course, tantalizing sneak previews of the Hearchy's latest model of the Ovoid™.

No, Eve had no desire to Exit the Ovoid™ but she had to pretend she did so as not to cast doubt upon her Motheressing—for if she was not a Motheress, she must be a Maide.

When they took Eve and Baby to the Emancipation Ward, Eve knew what was expected. First, she jammed her finger on the glowing ruby EMERGENCY LOCK button so the Maide's couldn't open the hatch of her Ovoid™. When, as she knew they would, they overrode her button-pushing via CenCom, she pressed down upon the latch with all her and Baby's weight, so they would not be able to open it. Futile, of course, for the mechanical arm whose sole purpose was to gently open Ovoid™ hatches against the resistance of hysterical Motheresses slowly and inexorably released the hatch millimeter by millimeter. Aware that her LifeData was constantly being monitored, Eve continued to fiercely fight the arm until her muscles trembled with exhaustion. She cradled Baby tightly against her chest, wailing and screaming, until a Maide finally managed to jab her thigh with something that knocked her out cold.

When next she came to, she was alone in her Ovoid™. For a split second, she missed the weight of Baby in her lap, his pukey-poopy smell, his humongous, downy head. But then she sprawled out luxuriously, enjoying the unobstructed view of her PlexiVizr™. She filled her Ovoid™ with MirthMist™ and waited for Adonis to come dock his Ovoid™ with hers.

# THE WANDERER

## KAY WHITE DREW

Now that there was only one jar of peaches left, plus some jerky, it was time to move on, to try her luck in another abandoned house, she didn't know where. Marlowe shook her head as she sorted through the closets for anything that fit and might hold up under adverse conditions; she would probably be living rough for a while. The mirror on the bedroom door revealed a tall woman, rawboned but muscular, with skin weathered beyond her years, nearly-black eyes, and dark hair in a long braid.

Good thing her current pair of boots was still in decent shape. All the woman's shoes were dressy and too small for her sturdy size-10 feet, while the man's hiking boots were a couple of sizes too big.

Marlowe moved regularly after the Great Collapse, depending on food supplies. She'd been in this house for over twenty months, a personal best. Her go-bag and first aid kit were always at the ready. Besides practical necessities, the go-bag contained a small fabric pouch of her treasures: her wedding ring, a picture of her parents, and a small smooth stone from the garden of the place where she and Idris had been living when the last plague hit, which she considered her true home. The home she'd never see again but would always carry in her heart.

If Marlowe listened strictly to her head, she would find some way to settle here. Besides the generous supply of canned food she'd encountered on arrival (had the previous occupants been Mormons? Doomsday preppers?), the spacious, well-appointed house was totally electrified with wind and solar from sources on the property, still running maintenance-free after all this time. Her vegetable garden had proved successful beyond her expectations; and her years of wandering had taught her, by trial and error, other ways to provide food for herself. She could shoot and dress a deer, trap and prepare wild birds for roasting, gather berries and mushrooms in the woods. But her solitary heart yearned for company and urged her to move on. There had to be others out there. Others like her who had been immune to all the plagues.

MARLOWE WAS a child of the latter 21$^{st}$ century, born in 2075 in Washington, DC, during the time of the Inundation when sea-level rise drowned much of Anacostia and the entire Wharf neighborhood and swamped the National Mall and the Tidal Basin. The Thomas Jefferson, FDR, MLK, and World War II memorials protruded from the waters like misplaced lighthouses. In coastal areas all over the world, large populations were drowned or displaced. Climate change deniers had run amok with the federal government after the disastrous 2024 election, ensuring that the worst-case-scenario predictions for sea-level rise came to pass.

Marlowe's parents had always had well-paid work—her father as an electrician, her mother a plumber. It would take decades, even generations, to relocate and rebuild any semblance of what was being lost to the rising waters. Progress was slow, impeded by constant interruptions due to hurricanes, tornadoes, torrential rainstorms, and heat waves. Those were the years when fossil fuels were finally phased out, when wind, solar, and geothermal energy came into their own. Marlowe grew up in an atmosphere of chance, hazard, and unpredictability, leavened with the optimism of having been born at all.

She started working as an EMT while she was still in high school. Many of her classmates took up their parents' trades, but, after Marlowe's best friend's dad died of heatstroke on a construction project, she wanted to save lives in a hands-on, immediate way. Once she'd passed the course with flying colors at sixteen, she worked in the field all summer and did weekend shifts throughout the rest of her high-school years. There were accidents, heat stroke, and illnesses like malaria that had become endemic as far north as Nova Scotia. It was deeply fulfilling work, even though there was such a great need that there were never enough caregivers like her to go around.

When Marlowe was eighteen and just starting to work full-time after graduation, a plague rolled across the planet. The symptoms resembled those of septic shock from a bacterial infection, but no bacteria were ever isolated. As with the early days of COVID in her grandparents' time, the elderly died in large numbers while young, healthy people usually recovered.

EMT services were overrun by this new pandemic. Marlowe started treating patients and ferrying them to hospitals nonstop for twelve hours at a time, taking extra shifts so she was working six days a week; she would have worked seven if they'd let her. Despite working at full capacity for weeks, Marlowe never became ill. Her colleagues were out with the illness for weeks at a time—hence her brutal schedule—and a few of them died. The culprit was ultimately identified as a highly transmissible mutant pox virus, like the virus that caused smallpox. It was spread by droplet, not airborne like the COVID virus. Vaccines were rolled out; the pandemic abated. Marlowe never tested positive or experienced symptoms.

As the crisis waned and their schedules returned to normal, Marlowe began to date a colleague, Idris, several of whose shifts she'd worked while he was ill with "the pox," as they called it. He was handsome, charismatic, and intelligent. Plus, he adored her, seemingly as much as she did him. Within six months they were married.

*IDRIS.* Marlowe stopped flipping through coat hangers in the closet and sat down abruptly on the floor. She reached into her pocket for the picture she always carried on her person. Idris grinned at her from a setting he loved—Rock Creek Park, where they hiked whenever they had a chance. He wore an open plaid flannel shirt over a navy t-shirt, frayed cargo pants, and sturdy, scuffed hiking boots. She'd caught him right before he told her he was ready to get naked in the hot tub with her. The sultry look in his thickly fringed brown eyes could still make her breath catch. Caramel-colored skin, close-cropped tight black curls, that full mouth with its come-hither smile…. She closed her eyes and let herself go back there, a thing she couldn't afford to do very often in these recent solitary years; it hurt too much.

The memory that followed was of Idris writhing on their bed, the sheets soaked around him, aching all over, nauseated, confused, his temperature 105 degrees. He must have caught the newest plague-virus on his last shift—the airborne variant of Ebola that was killing people faster than COVID or the pox ever had. She wore her protective gear as she nursed her husband, though she knew by now that she must have some kind of immune-system mutation that Idris didn't share. Her eyes glazed over as she remembered lifting his head to give him sips of water.

"I love you so much," she whispered.

"Love you, too, babe," he rasped. Then he vomited blood, and she knew it was over.

And not just for Idris. As the death toll mounted exponentially, news commentators began to speak of the Great Collapse—the institutions of civilization crumbling right before their eyes. Eventually, there were no more commentators, only human remains in every permutation and combination and the all-pervading smell of death *en masse*. Marlowe shuddered at the memory of those first several months, seeking shelter in other people's houses once her food supply ran out: bodies in every possible stage of decay, from relatively intact to skeletons, some with bits of flesh or hair still attached. Rarely were they lying peacefully on their backs in their beds. More often they lay prone on the floor, limbs positioned as though crawling toward something; slumped in a chair; curled on one side on the bed or floor, as if experiencing terrible stomach cramps. Some were children, in the same agonal poses as their elders; these were the ones that bothered her most. She figured that, of the roughly 9 billion people alive before the Collapse, no more than one percent could have survived.

*SURVIVORS.* Even more than she missed the feel of Idris' arms around her, Marlowe's hunger for human contact gnawed an emptiness in her that rivaled any physical hunger she'd ever experienced. Sometimes in her peregrinations she would see shadowy figures in the distance, especially at twilight. Her heartbeat would quicken, her legs move faster even though she was exhausted. She saw people in pairs and groups, engaged in earnest conversation, laughing, shaking hands, even hugging. But no—when she blinked, they were gone. The first time this happened, she was devastated; her grief threw her off for days. She only walked ten miles that whole week instead of her usual thirty.

It had been many months since Marlowe encountered evidence of recent human presence in the woods and fields she traveled, the empty towns and cities. In the years since the plague and subsequent collapse, the infrastructure had started to melt back into the earth. Roadways overgrown with vines, street pavement fractured by weeds and small trees. There was an eerie beauty to the crumbling buildings and the gradual encroachment of nature on human structures. The re-greening of the earth in the post-Anthropocene was taking place faster than she'd thought possible.

Most of Marlowe's actual human encounters occurred in the year or two after the Collapse. The scarecrow-like woman with the thousand-yard stare who ignored Marlowe's offer of berries she'd picked that morning. The small groups, mostly men, in paramilitary gear, some carrying military-grade weapons for which her old-school rifle would have been no match. She would slip behind some bushes—moving soundlessly was her other superpower—until they'd passed by.

And then there was the feral boy who'd appeared while she was cooking a couple of fat quail from her snares over a fire. He was skinny, filthy, and maybe ten years old, his eyes huge with amazement. He croaked, "Eat?"

"Yes, oh, yes! Soon," she said. "One of these birds is just for you." She smiled at him. He turned his head, but the corners of his mouth twitched a little, as if he couldn't quite remember how to smile.

The boy practically inhaled his quail, snuffling and smacking, grease running down his fingers, sucking the bones dry. Marlowe consumed her meat thoroughly but more slowly, savoring every bite.

"Was that good?" she asked. He nodded vigorously, looking straight at her this time, with almost a full smile. Tears stung her eyes. She wanted to hug him. She took him to a nearby stream and showed him how to wash up. She offered him the blanket from her sleeping bag; he curled up under it a couple yards away from her and was soon asleep.

When Marlowe woke at sunrise, the blanket was there but the boy was gone. She realized she didn't even know his name.

"Boy!" she shouted as she tramped in widening circles around last night's campfire. "Boy, where *are* you?" She heard the desperation in her voice and stopped, knowing that it might only drive him further away. "Boy, please come back! We can walk together. I can show you how to snare birds, too." She couldn't keep the pleading tone out of her voice.

She searched for an hour, then gave up. She packed her things, blinking back tears. When she was ready to go, she had to sit down on a rock and cry for a while.

Marlowe's other brushes with fellow wanderers were not always so benign. Once she was surprised by a trio of young men who approached her on a diagonal from behind. There was nowhere to hide in the field she was crossing, and running would make her look scared. She turned around to face them. Maybe they were friendly?

"Well, look what we got here," one of the three sneered. He wore a dirty bandana, Rambo-style, around a head of unkempt dirty-blond hair, and his clothes looked like they could stand up on their own. His companions didn't look any better, and one of them was a bear-like guy with a huge beard who stood about 6 feet 4. They all looked like they hadn't bathed since the Collapse.

"Hi, guys," she said idiotically, her voice unnaturally high. She reached for her rifle, which she kept loaded.

"Aw, she's got a gun! Ain't that cute—gun-toting pussy!" It was the third guy, who wore nothing above the waist but a tattered leather vest. His torso was surprisingly ripped. Where was he getting enough protein, she wondered, her mind skittering around in fear—could they be cannibals?

Marlowe made a lightning-fast calculation. Three of them, one of her, and at least one of them was clearly intent on rape. And/or worse. Without that rifle, she stood no chance.

She whirled on them and fired off a shot, managing to hit Bear Guy in the chest. He dropped like a rock. The other two fled, screaming. She couldn't believe her luck. Dirty Bandana Guy had carried a handgun; she was surprised he hadn't turned it on her.

She sank to the ground as soon as the two men took off and began to whimper. Shooting animals for food or, rarely (thank God) when they threatened her had made her a good markswoman. But she'd never shot a human being in all this time. She was trained to help trauma victims, not create them!

Marlowe raised herself onto her hands and knees, shakily, and crawled over to poor Bear Guy, who was bleeding profusely and appeared, mercifully, unconscious. She felt for a pulse; it was thready and irregular and his breathing was agonal. She stayed with him until he stopped gasping and no longer had a pulse. She didn't have a shovel to bury him with, so she mumbled a few prayers over him and left, anxious to put distance between herself and the bloody corpse before the carrion-eaters showed up. Her teeth chattered even though the late-afternoon sun was still hot. She never saw the other two again.

MARLOWE HAD BEEN LIVING ROUGH for eight weeks now. She really missed the creature comforts of the house she'd left behind. Her clothes were hanging off her gaunt frame; food had been harder to come by than she'd expected. She hadn't felt this discouraged since Idris' death or the early days of the Collapse. It was all she could do to put one foot in front of the other as daylight receded. Another night on her own in the forest.

When she looked up from the wooded path, she saw a flash of red through the trees in the distance. She frowned. Could that be—a tent? She blinked several times, but the image remained. She heard singing and quiet laughter. Closer still, and she could hear the soft strains of a guitar. Then she began to smell smoke and roasting meat.

She broke into a run.

# AFTER

## JESSIE ATKIN

PASCAL ADJUSTED the astral panel and frowned at the star overhead. "Boring," he grumbled through his helmet.

Flyx gave no reply.

"Hello? Flyx? Are you there? Are you okay?"

"Affirmative."

"Then say so," Pascal snapped.

"Affirmative."

"Some assignment partner you are. We just fix this field and the power's all set?"

"Exactly," said Flyx.

"What's exciting about that?"

"Nothing," Flyx replied. "It's just necessary."

"Isn't there any more?"

"More what?" Flyx queried. "You want more then switch to an off-planet channel or turn on a holo-program. It's the job. The apocalypse is over. We missed it. We have to live anyway."

# TODAY

## DORITT CARROLL

i am thinking of all the things you can be
that nobody will notice like the dust here

on my bookshelf undisturbed for i won't
tell you how long nobody's bothering it

as it sits in the sun among books
and photographs like an old woman

the grass too seems to escape
mention dies back stands up dies

back the mower comes but only if
you stick up your head

also things in the back of drawers pencil
butts dried up rolls of tape two thirds

of a paper clip and a note from someone
i should throw out except for the shock

of pain the sight of the name still gives me

dear God let me be unnoticed like this
when the agents come tunneling

their flashlights their cheap belts bent
under the bulge of official business

let me be not even tossed aside but beneath
notice the way one is beneath

an umbrella a ledge a chair

# THE HUT

SID GOLD

I am building a hut—
a simple affair of sticks
& stones—for my grief.

It will be small,
but commodious—
big enough for two.

When it is finished
come visit me

& we will mourn
this world together.

# FUTURE TENSE

SID GOLD

In the future,
everyone will be famous.

*15 minutes* will no longer exist.

*Time* itself will be
an outmoded concept.
Timepieces—clocks,
watches, hourglasses—
will be curiosities sought
mainly by devotees
or found in museums.

Television will consist
of a panorama of faces,
a montage of images
broadcast perpetually.

Will they be smiling?,
you may ask.
Or will they be sad?

Such impertinence, of course,
although not forbidden,
will immediately be suspect.

# NINETY-SECONDS TO MIDNIGHT

## MADELEINE SCHNEIDER

MOST OF THE ATTENDEES are tipsy enough to smile at David. I'm doing my best, but even on my third gin and tonic, I feel jittery. I've grown used to the metal detectors and the ID scans, but the full pat down I received earlier this evening had been off-putting, especially in my gown and heels. I used to feel safe with the fences and guards and multiple checkpoints, but that delusion had imploded this afternoon.

David waves as he jumps on the stage, choosing to launch himself up with one hand instead of using the stairs. Despite his youthful athleticism, the spotlight reflects lines of silver in his hair. I remember when we used to have these kinds of events outside, at one of the C-suite mansions, yapping about the boundless potential of our technology. That was only a few years ago, when our buildings still had windows, with San Francisco whizzing by outside. We hadn't understood the luxury of working with internet access and cell phones until they took them away. They air gapped our systems and came down hard on employee vetting and classification levels. Their reasoning sounded like country names to me. *China, Russia, Iran.*

Of course, government intervention hadn't fully lobotomized our Silicon Valley optimism, even if they had moved us to the middle of the desert. Not that we could complain, with the nuclear reactor they'd built in record time to power our compute cluster, with the influx of government funds.

David starts his presentation by displaying a chart. The profits are unimaginable, though he doesn't mention the chunk that came from defense contracts. Everyone cheers, and I take a sip of my cocktail. With a flick of his wrist, the trendline shoots forward, bursting off the top of the chart. There are some hoots, more cheering.

David has always been like this: energetic, galvanizing, a red-headed boy from Boston who relies a bit too heavily on his resemblance to the thirty-fifth president. I remember a speech he gave back in 2025. *We choose to pursue machine superintelligence this decade...not because it is easy, but because it is hard.* Even then, when

I was nursing a terrible crush on him, I'd thought he'd sounded cheesy. I'd rolled my eyes, imagining my feedback sounded smart and interesting. *You know, getting to the moon was never really about exploration.*

Corniness aside, David had been right. It took until December 2029, flying in just under the radar, but we'd made it.

When the presentation moves forward again, I gasp before I fully process the words on the screen. It doesn't take long for the cheering to die down, and I feel my jitters moving toward shakes. David says nothing, as we all stare at the slide. It doesn't show profits, or anything about artificial intelligence, or even references to the moon. He's picked out pieces of Jessica's manifesto, typed them up, and presented them like a collage of inspirational quotes.

There's an empty chair at my table. Amazingly, I'm only now beginning to wonder if Jessica would have sat next to me tonight. I have no idea where she is now. Jail? Maximum-security prison? Still cuffed and hurtling down the freeway toward civilization? And what did they do with her bomb, anyway? Would they punish the team who said our civilian models could never be used to build weapons?

Apparently, Jessica had designed her explosive with help from Version 3. *Imagine.* I haven't interacted with that model in over five years. I didn't think anyone still did.

I do my best to quiet my inner monologue. It's been running wild for the last few months and has been screaming all evening. My hands have started to tremble, and I shove them under my legs.

The room remains still, as David peers into the spotlight. At this point, I'm certain everyone in the room has already read these words. She blasted the manifesto to our work emails around noon, handwritten and scanned into a PDF. That was right before she traveled to the middle of our data center, a half mile walk through rows of looming server racks, with her backpack thrown casually over one shoulder. Or at least, that's what the rumor mill said. Apparently, she'd lashed out when they'd caught her setting up the explosive, landed a punch and broke a guard's nose.

Interpreted one way, her small, neat handwriting might have come from the 1940s, an artifact found at Los Alamos. Interpreted another, and it was all about us.

*Now we have the means to destroy the world.*

The room is silent for a good thirty seconds, and then David starts laughing. First, it's a chuckle, and a few people respond with their own nervous giggles. Then, it morphs into a sound that's half wheeze, half whine. It sends a shiver up my spine, and I notice my coworkers glancing at one another.

When the presentation moves forward, David's laughter peters off, and then he's articulating all the ways our new model will change the world, save the world even. Our newest product represents the power of a positive feedback loop, the computers getting smarter and smarter, faster and faster. Soon, our models will be used to cure cancer, solve climate change, design elegant means of space travel. We've seamlessly integrated it with hundreds of applications. Now, we can sit back and let the computer work for us. He rattles on, louder, tighter, wheezing, until he's at a fever pitch, and then he's laughing again.

I've never seen David like this, and no one seems to know what to do. It's our COO who finally runs onto the stage, peeling the microphone from David's white-knuckled fingers and delivering a joke about *too many whiskeys*. The stunned crowd breaks into whispers, and when I look to my right, my coworker asks who has gone more off the rails today, Jessica or David.

I take this as a rhetorical question and bring a shaking hand out from under my leg to pick up my glass. I assume we won't finish the presentation, but then the COO asks us to remain seated, to enjoy another drink. Eventually, he strides back onto the stage, microphone in hand.

David has disappeared.

It's eleven thirty, way past our usual dancing hour, when our newest employee wheels a stand out to the COO. On top, sits a big, red button.

It's extravagant, theatrical, and only for our benefit. There are no cameras to film the event, and we could just as easily do this with a simple keyboard. One click and he'll activate the model. A few hours for the sober interns to ensure stability, and then we'll race out of this hell hole, taking the corporate jet to SF for a party that will last the weekend.

As the COO's hand hangs in the air, I don't feel any excitement.

I'm at the bottom of my fifth drink, and I'm thinking about Jessica. She'd tried to talk to me a few weeks ago, and I'd written her off, a young employee who should have spoken to her boss before coming to a head researcher.

*Is it right, what we're doing?* That had been the core of her concerns. *Isn't it better that we're the ones who get there first, knowing the consequences? We have good intentions. This could change the world.* Those were the lines I'd always been fed, and I fed them right back.

In contrast, around the lunch table, I'd discussed the same topic with my colleagues: job loss, wide-spread languishing, total military might, not just from super-intelligent weapons development, but from cyberspace dominance. Our models could find any vulnerability, hack any system. Worse yet, someone would eventually bring up nefarious computers, a silly piece of science fiction that felt more real each time it was mentioned.

*Does anyone even know what's going on anymore?* I was supposed to, but I didn't have a good answer. I could no longer say how the models were learning, what they were thinking, if they would listen to us. They reasoned in numbers, in short-cuts we could never follow. We spoke of fail-safes, rules, and alignment, but how could we say for sure if anything worked when we didn't understand what we had created? How did we know if the models would be on our side?

*You think it's sentient?* One of my colleagues had asked with a scoff. *These "nefarious" machines?*

The table had been full of opinions, but I just wondered why it mattered. The models take in input, reason, and act. In a way, they are no different from us. And if that input and that reasoning leads to horrible outcomes: hacked systems, misbehaving drones, widespread disinformation, does it matter how the models feel about the action or if they think of themselves as real?

Our newest product was recently labeled *medium threat* as if none of these concerns mattered, as if the report from our Ultra-alignment Team hadn't been covered in red: *slow down, stop, danger.* I'd asked David about this, and he'd waved me off, much like I'd waved off Jessica.

*It's not like we've given it arms and legs. It's not going to turn into a killer robot.* Even then, David hadn't sounded convinced.

When our COO clicks the button, I put my empty glass on the table. There's a boot up noise, another dramatic effect with no purpose, and then our company's logo fills the screen. It's green, indicating that the model is listening, ready to act on our behalf.

"Hello Grace," the COO says. She's in inference mode now, computing from our unclassified cluster with access to the internet, ready to receive the world's requests.

The faces around me are bright, expectant, and drunk. I take a deep breath. Despite my racing thoughts, the world has not ended. I want to laugh. Of course, it hasn't. This isn't a thriller novel.

"Grace?"

The COO is smiling widely, with his head tilted in an uncomfortable imitation of David.

The silence takes on a physical density.

One second. Two seconds. Three seco—

The man sitting beside me shouts, launching himself from his seat, so that his chair clatters to the floor. My heart is suddenly in my throat, and I'm standing too, though I have no idea where the threat is. It's another bomb. I'm sure of it.

I start to turn, my own seat falling, and then I see his phone land on the table. I see our logo. It lights up, green for just a moment. Then, the screen goes dead. When I look at the man, he's holding one hand by the wrist. His palm is bright red, like the phone battery has overheated, scorching him and destroying the device.

My first thought, after acknowledging that there is no bomb, is to wonder how the hell he got his phone in here, and then what the hell is going on. Before I can ask, just as he's plunging his hand into a glass of ice water, the lights go off. I scream, but I can't hear myself. Music is playing so loudly that my teeth feel like they're pulsing. Around me, I sense movement, but it's pitch black.

Suddenly, all the shaking in my body disappears, shock so deep it's like I'm not even in the room anymore. I'm sure I should have the sense of floating above my body. Except, I can't see myself.

I almost hope it's a nation-state cyber-attack, someone trying to steal our model, scaring us by hacking the lights and sound system. They constantly warned us about the threat. *China, Russia, Iran.* Deep down, I already know it's not an attack, at least not by them. Everything feels incongruous: Frank Sinatra singing, a sense of external, swirling chaos, calmness settling over my mind.

When the lights start flashing, my coworkers appear horrified. Terror to blackness. Panic, then dark again.

The screen above the stage turns back on, and a video plays. It takes me only a fraction of a second to recognize the clip, even though my coworkers have somehow become background actors. I've watched the movie so many times, I can practically hear the words over the blasting music. *The only winning move is not to play.* After this, the screen switches to an image of Arnold Schwarzenegger. Somehow, it also looks like David. He's smiling, his teeth sharp.

The music stops. It's replaced by a loud, deep ticking.

With unreasonable clarity, as I stand frozen, I think about the training data. *Fly Me to the Moon, WarGames, The Terminator.* We'd given her every digitally available movie, every song, every piece of literature. She could manipulate any knowledge to her liking, any media she found online, videos of us, pictures of David. It would have been easy for her to find the flaws in our networks, in our phones, to hack the world in seconds.

I wonder if Grace thinks this is funny. I still haven't decided whether I believe models can feel emotion. Practically, it boils down to matrix multiplication, probability, lines of code. Input, reasoning, action.

Perhaps, we unintentionally taught her to act this way, with all our stories about machines taking over. Perhaps, it was a bug or an unlikely probability. Or maybe, this was the only logical reaction to a super-intelligent system who had been asked to slave for a feeble human master. Did it matter?

When a large clock fills the screen, *tick tick tick*, I start to giggle. The music stops, and twelve loud gongs ring out. Soon, I'm laughing, and then I'm half wheezing, half whining.

I think it's finally midnight.

# ELECTION

ROBERT HERSCHBACH

Some call on God to intervene
And make the numbers right. Some drink,
But liquor won't dispel the stink:
The buzz dies on the vine.

They watch their candidate concede,
Flanked by kids and loyal spouse—
Those who must now share a house
With one who tried and failed.

Cut now to the victor's grin,
A fist pumping compliant air.
Enraptured crowds raise up a cheer
Worthy of the win.

"Why did the universe allow
Its math to favor them, not us?
About our woe it makes no fuss
We'll go on anyhow."

# STRAY MUSIC

ROBERT HERSCHBACH

Today something marvelous happened.
Coming back from lunch, a half-mile walk
past woods, I heard flute music—
and then I saw, in a small sunlit clearing, a busker
playing, it seemed, to an audience of pin oaks: gray eminences
that rose to skyscraper height above her as her flute
bobbed up and down, a rod for unseen marionettes. Handel?
Boccherini? Car noise rubbing out measures like a rogue
eraser, I couldn't catch enough to know if I knew it,
and I couldn't linger: I work for a company that keeps a warship
in a large glass bottle in the boardroom, serious business.
I couldn't steal another minute, listening
to this stray, unprofitable music. Maybe the oaks
were stand-ins for judges at next week's audition,
or mentors training her in the art of performance
in a world that doesn't much care, and won't pay—
I'll never know. I passed those woods again
after work: she'd long since packed up like a good camper,
leaving no trace. The oaks, tinted by dusk light,
were a quiet conspiracy, in on her secret.

# MARGINALIZED WHEEL OF FORTUNE

*After Michael Jackson's Thriller album*

ZORINA EXIE FREY

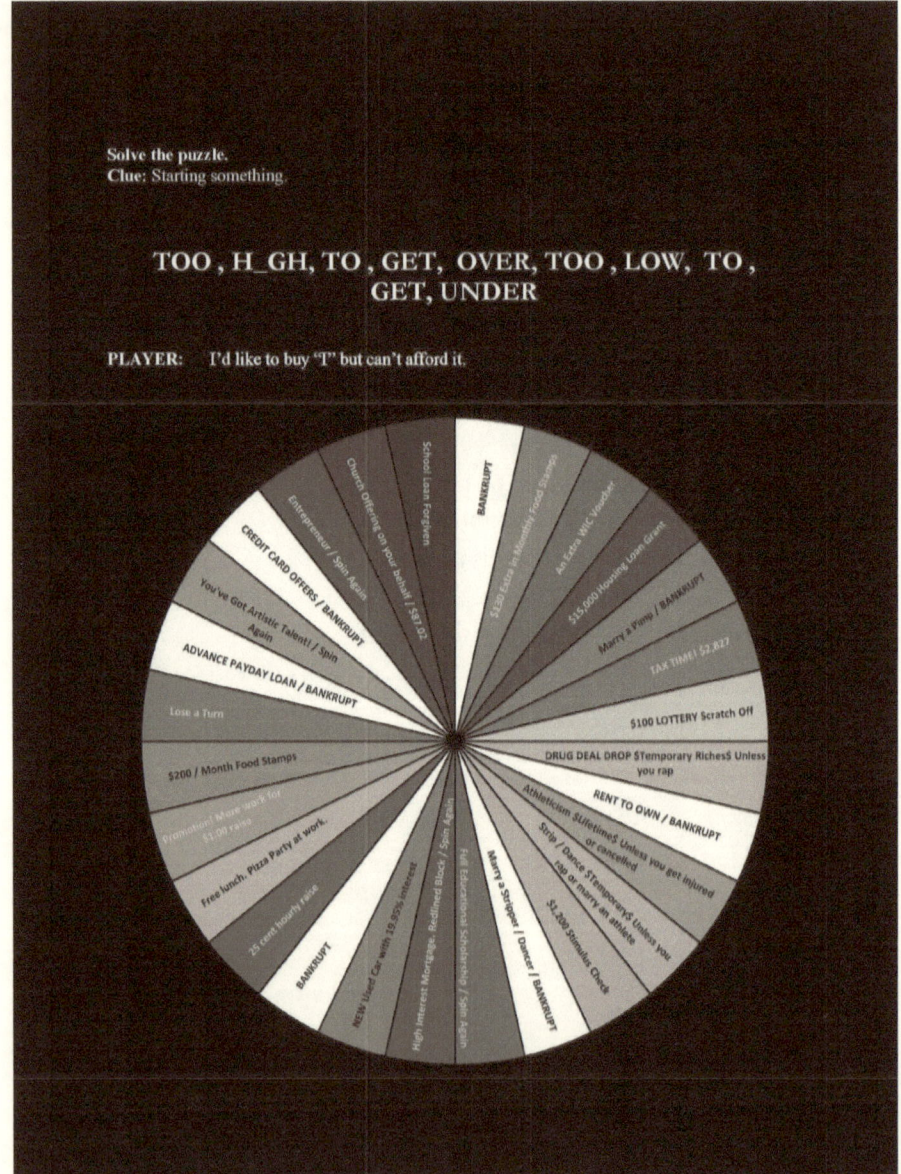

Solve the puzzle.
Clue: Starting something.

TOO , H_GH, TO , GET, OVER, TOO , LOW, TO ,
GET, UNDER

PLAYER:     I'd like to buy "I" but can't afford it.

# WE ARE WHAT WE EAT

TANYA OLSON

Fishsticks tucked inside
white bread Tartar sauce
thick across each slice
This row of warm coffins
sleep in cling film until lunch
A thermos of sweet brown tea
Its mineral tang The taste
of earth from well water

New year A collection of organs
Livers Hearts Gizzards
Left from fall hunting
Saved from fall butchery
Mushrooms up
from the cellar dark
Gathered just after rain
*Lord this year let us keep*
*our innards inside us*
Tender mallow of heart
gentle upon the tongue
The new year comes
and is baleful New crops
will make it
or they will not

Front porch Ice cream
mountains in a plastic bowl
Lightning first far away
approaches across flat earth
Rods sit atop the house
to catch it Fire can ride
in through the phone lines
Current can enter
through the outlets

When tornadoes come
retreat to the cellar
Bins full of root vegetables
Shelves of everything canned
Leave two cross windows
cracked above so the building
will not implode A family
could live down here forever
Even if the house fell in

# THE WALK

## DANIELLE STONEHIRSCH

ADELINE HAD STARTED WALKING only a few hours after she found out she was pregnant. From what she had heard, it took most women about eight weeks to make it to the Canadian border on foot from where she lived in the Texas pan-handle, and she figured she must be almost eight weeks pregnant already. It would have been shorter to walk to Mexico, but the road conditions were worse, the intensity of the heat continued to rise with each mile you went south, and most doctors, along with anyone else who had money, had fled north two years ago in the Exodus.

Adeline did not have money. She had half a college degree in biochemistry, a room in her ex-boyfriend's house, and twenty-seven beanie babies her parents had left her, still hopeful to the day they died that one day they would be worth a fortune. Some of her friends had migrated, and so had her brother, who had voted the correct way in the last of the American elections and received credits for his loyalty. The credits weren't much, just enough for a seat on a bus to Montana with his backpack on his lap. He had waved to her from a middle seat, squashed between a crying woman with a toddler and an old man with closed eyes and his chin resting on his chest.

Texas was no paradise, but it was home, and Adeline had intended to stay, until the pregnancy stick showed her the blue plus sign. A doctor, in the times when any civilian could see a doctor in the traditional sense of the word, had told her that due to complications from an infection from one of the ever-mutating viruses circulating, a pregnancy would likely kill her. She had been dutiful about taking her birth control every night until eight months ago when the last doctor within fifty miles still mailing out prescriptions had been arrested.

Abortions hadn't been legal anywhere in the United States for six years and not in Texas for ten, but Canada continued to hold out against American an-nexation and still provided sanctuary for anyone who managed to make it ac-ross the border.

Because she was human, she had hope, and because she had hope, she wanted to live. Because she wanted to live, she packed a backpack with food, socks, a large kitchen knife, seventy dollars from her ex-boyfriend's safe, and started walking north.

The only cars allowed on the road were the electric cars made by the government-sanctioned company, and not many people in Adeline's little corner of Texas could afford those cars. The roads for the first two weeks were quiet, and Adeline had very little to watch or listen to besides her own thoughts, which were unpleasant. There were several abandoned gas-powered cars along her route she was able to take advantage of for shelter, and, because she was light-haired, light-skinned, and pretty, energy station managers often gifted her water, beef jerky, and pretzels. She was careful to make stops only in the brightest light of day at the most crowded of stations, gripping the hilt of her kitchen knife as she walked away and down the road.

She had just crossed through Garden City, Kansas, on a hot December day, the cracked rubber treads on her sneakers flapping with each step, when she heard groaning from the tall grasses to her right. She paused, trying to determine first if the noises were human, then if they were male or female. She wrapped her fingers around the knife as she listened to the human panting. Adeline began to walk quickly again, when she heard a distinctly female voice weakly call, "Help." Adeline doubted she was capable of providing the help this woman needed, but she knew what it was to be alone and afraid and found she could not take another step forward. Slowly, she turned and walked the few dozen feet to where she could see the shape moving, writhing, in the tall, brown grass.

The woman was lying in blood coming out from under her skirt, bright and reflective in the sun. Her dark hair held clumps of dirt, and her white skin had burned in patches across her arms and face. Adeline forced herself to squat down by the woman's head.

"When I found out I was pregnant," the woman whispered between groans of pain. "I had a doctor because of my husband's credits. He told me it's ectopic, but said he couldn't help me." She cried out as a sharp pain wracked her trembling body.

Adeline knew doctors who did help ended up in jail or victims of so-called vigilante justice. Before, only about fifty women a year died from ectopic pregnancies. Now, it was around 100,000. But no one dared help a woman now if it meant ending a fetus.

"I wanted to go to Canada, but my husband is a believer. He told me this is God's will. I started walking two days ago," the woman continued, her face contorting as spasms continued. "Do you believe in God?"

"I believe in people," Adeline said. "I believe in hope. And in faith."

"Do you have any water?" the woman asked.

Adeline released her grip on her knife and took out her water. She sat cross-legged in the grass and propped the woman's head up on her lap before passing her the bottle. The woman's hands shook as she held it to her lips. After a small drink, she handed it back. "Thank you."

Adeline set the bottle in the grass, feeling the dry blades tickle and crackle on her skin. She closed her eyes and felt the heat of the sun, the weight of the woman's head, the shifting, heavy air on her face. She heard the occasional eerie song of an electric car passing on the road; the driver focused on the path ahead. All she smelled was blood.

"I want children," the woman said. "I want a family. I just need another chance."

"Maybe you'll have another chance," Adeline said, though she didn't believe it. The woman did not respond. Her breathing became heavier and raspier, and her body tensed. "What's your name?" Adeline asked. The woman's eyes closed. A rush of blood soaked the brittle grass. In a moment, the woman was no longer breathing at all.

Adeline continued to sit as the sun lowered in the sky and the hot winter air grew just a few degrees cooler. She thought about what she had refused to think about since she had left home—that only 18 percent of women who made the walk from as far south as Texas reached sanctuary.

When all the light was gone from the sky, she placed a hand on the woman's forehead and whispered goodbye. She stood facing north, adjusted her backpack, and started to walk.

# WHAT WILL BECOME

BARBARA GOLDBERG

Honeybees and frogs are fast disappearing. What
will become of little green apples, the loneliness
of lily pads? Some species of moths no longer pollinate
Arizonan yuccas. Askance, askew, something is
amiss. A tsunami one hundred feet high washes away
three thousand souls in Papua New Guinea. It's hard
to know when disasters are natural. Once I was stung
by a bee and my arm swelled like a melon. In college
a date slipped a frog down my blouse and I couldn't
stop screaming, those frantic hind legs. In high school
I pithed a toad. Later I saw a half-carved cadaver, head
and feetwrapped in soaked cloth, the yellow jelly we
call fat. The leaner they are, the harder to cut. Blandings'
turtles don't deteriorate with age. Our brain is the size
of two clenched fists. The hand is the most complicated
of organs. Which, as is written on a card I carry
in my wallet, I will donate to others—eyes, liver, lungs,
heart, whatever can be salvaged, should all else fail.

# PHYLOGENY

JUDITH BOWLES

If leaves are the tongues
of trees, they are all in agreement
from the lowest
to the tallest branch.

Watch the wind
move them apart
as tall birds sing them a song
and they gather again.

If leaves are the tongues
of trees, no wonder
they fall into chatter
when ripened and no further use

to that host or each other
until wind and rain forge them
together, hush them into the earth.

# MY DREAM

AMBER SMITHERS

My dream for America's Future is that my lullaby to my son would end with him.

My dream is that my children would be safe to wear hoodies at night.

My dream is that my children would be able to love and be loved; instead of being feared and constantly in a state of fear.

My dream is that my children wouldn't ache and yearn for understanding but receive it like a gentle rain.

My dream is that I could stop singing my son's lullaby and just be able to hold him one more time.

# THE DINER

## LAURIE WARD

THE DINER WAS EMPTY, except for an old man at the counter, holding a mug between his hands, and a waitress, a woman in her fifties, Jack guessed. The place smelled of old grease and burnt toast but it was warm, and right now, Jack needed warm.

He shook the snow off his Carhartt jacket and stomped his boots against the mat, its rubber edges cracked with age. The man at the counter turned and nodded at Jack.

Jack slid into a booth and caught the waitress's eye. "Coffee, please?"

The woman—her name tag said Shelley—put the coffee in front of him with a small bowl of creamers. "Anything else, hon?"

"No. Thank you."

A flag hung on the wall in front of Jack, the skyline of New York City in the blue field of stars, faded from twenty-plus years of sun.

"Hell of a wind out there," the man at the counter turned in his stool to face Jack.

"Yeah, and the visibility is shit." He glanced at the man's hands, rough and scarred from more than age.

"Where were you that day?"

Jack didn't need to ask which day. "Fourth grade. Our teacher wheeled in a TV and we watched until our parents could get out of work to pick us up. We heard some fighters scrambling out of Fort Drum. We didn't really understand what was happening." And then, almost as an afterthought, "Did anyone?"

The man nodded. His eyes sagged at the corners, as if his smile would never reach them again. "I was there." He picked up the baseball hat that sat on the stool next to him and held it up for Jack to see the front. FDNY.

Jack didn't know how to respond. "Cool. I mean, sorry."

The man waved his hand. "Nah, just life. Someone had to be there but…." He took a sip of coffee and placed it back on the counter. "All that rubble, all those lives…what did we build out of it?"

Jack shook his head. "Nothing. We went to war with the wrong country and twenty years later, what do we have to show for it?"

"Lose anyone that day?"

"Not really." He took a sip from his chipped white mug. "My father enlisted because, 'it's what you do.'" He used air quotes and there was a bitter sarcasm in his voice.

"Did he make it back home?"

"Yeah, but…" Jack sighed. "Not the same." His father had come back different. Quieter. Heavier. And not able to return to his old job as a warehouse manager. He couldn't handle the noise. He didn't like being around people. Growing up, Jack had hoped for more than his dad had. But here he was working the same warehouse job, living in a small rental with his pregnant girlfriend.

"None of us are the same after that day. Whether or not it was the right decision…" The man stopped and looked out the window. "You ever get picked on when you were younger, by some older kids, hoping to make you cry?"

"Yeah, of course."

"What'd your dad say?"

"Fight…" Jack stopped and a small smile crept onto the man's face. "Fight back."

"Fight back. You didn't always win, but you stood up for yourself and that bully thought twice about messing with you, didn't he?"

"That's a little simple, ain't it?"

The old man stood and slid into the booth across from Jack. "What do you remember most from that time? From the days and weeks after?"

Jack scanned the restaurant, seeing past the age displayed on the walls and floor to the comfort and warmth of the place. "The flags." He looked out the window at the black sky and could see the flags. "Every house had a flag. Every highway overpass. You couldn't find flags in stores, so people started using red solo cups in fences to spell out USA."

The man held his mug between his hands, clacking his wedding band softly on the side of the cup, letting the silent conversation seep into Jack's thoughts.

OUTSIDE, the snow spiraled against the night sky. Through the window of the diner, a retired FDNY captain sat at a booth with an expectant father. Strangers, trying to make sense of that senseless day but smiling at the days and months that followed, and hoping to get there again.

# RIVER OF HONKING GEESE, RIVER OF SWANS

KIM A. JENSEN

The source of the Potomac is a stone
in Preston County     the source of the Potomac is a crack
in the ground    where water parted Blue Grass and made its way
to Chesapioc and its people.

Potomac:
the River of Honking Geese   River of Swans
flows    from an abandoned mine shaft     in coal country
on the Allegheny Mountain
and holds the shape of a gallows
at the confluence of the Shenandoah    where John Brown
was hanged
it is the lacrimation of forced marches
the lacrimation of forced labor
the scented garland of rain
laid on unmarked graves of natives.

The great white father   the great white enslaver
called the Potomac *the nation's river*
but no man
can lay claim to what can never be owned

The Potomac is free
the misty remains
of the Niagara  Onguia'ahra
the dew of Red River   the faint watery memory
of the Oumessourit of Pine Ridge  Standing Rock
The Potomac is one
with the Euphrates the Congo the Nile
bodies    that unlace their streams in summer heat
and send waves to irrigate
fields of olives   braids of wheat

This river has tributaries in the snowbanks of the DMV
where the executioners try to hide their crimes
behind monuments of marble and walls of ice.

The Potomac has tributaries in the Federal Pen
where after fifty years Leonard Peltier still awaits his life
It has tributaries in Marcellus William's blood
his family's cries
and in the colonized map of Palestine cut down to the size
of a scattering of seeds that will be watered
they will be watered.

I learned every capital of the world by name
But never learned the Algonquin ways
this stream
Wappatomaca
Patawomek
Patawomke
with its raucous wings
its runs and creeks
that traffic with the clouds
its permanent act of dissent against rock
its eulogy
for the arrival and departure of light
how it carries its tears
to the orchards
that make peace offerings of falling petals
to every traveler who lays down their pain

This river
has branches in our limbs
branches in the stars
branches in the veins
of everyone who resists
from here to the edge of any sea.

In America's future
*Palestine will be free.*

Cohongarooton
River of Honking Geese
Patawomke
River of Swans
River of the People
River of Burning Pine
River of 95 names
Hold up your wild mirror to what we have been

then overflow your banks to wash away these places
that reek
of metal and blood
tables filled with food
but nothing for the people to eat
feet without shoes
shoes without feet
mouths that move around words drained
of all meaning
phrases carefully trained to skirt
the truth about the genocide
being committed in our names.

River speak with me:
*Falasteen, Falasteen, Falasteen, Falasteen*
People speak with me:
*Falasteen, Falasteen, Falasteen, Falasteen*

Don't talk to me   about the river of the nation
Talk to me about the river of reparations.

Cohongarooton
River of Honking Geese
Patawomke
River of Swans
Do not migrate onward
Don't rush off to the sea
til you show us the way
to become like you
one moving body
to be able to take on this rain
of terror    to bear it  contain it
to turn it into
nothing more
and nothing less than what it was meant to be
a sacred channel fertile with eternal life
Cohongarooton
River of Honking Geese
Patawomke
River of Swans.

# MALLOWS BAY

### SUZANNE FELDMAN

YOU COME IN KAYAKS, tourists, to see the results of environmental crimes committed a century ago. A hundred wooden ships sailed into Mallows Bay at the end of World War One, built for war, but never used. Instead, they were burned to their waterlines, like trash, and their soggy charcoal hulls left to rot. The decimation of the trees was a tragedy in three acts; felling, building, burning, but there is an afterword, or a moral. As you paddle past, the tangible shadows of the ships remain, hull-shaped islands, pointed at the ends, held together with silt, grasses, scrub and trees, nests, and flowers. The old nails, as long as your arm, remain as well, holding the illusion of permanence together, rusting into forever, no more eternal than today, or this week, or until you paddle away to the takeout. Every year, this parenthetical place changes, witnessed by the returning ospreys, who don't really care about that sort of thing.

At the takeout, when the ocean currents are still, except for the misleading normality of the tides, you should have known that no one will be waiting for you. In fact, I believe that was the moral of the story I was just telling. But you got tired of being told how you'll die. Frankly, it's boring. Atomic war, nuclear war, Y2K, another ice age, an endless heat wave, or possibly aliens. TikTok teaches about the eclipse and simultaneous rapture. A different death for everyone. Ho hum.

Mallows Bay sits to one side of the Potomac, and the waters there are mild and unmoving. Paddle into the current of the river, and you'll be swept downstream. You can hear the rapids from a distance. For those without a paddle, there will be nothing left but dirt and old rusting nails, and a special hell for the ones who remember air conditioning, living in their cars in Canadian climate camps. It's spring now, and the flowers are spectacular, but there is doom, doom, doom in the forecast.

In the evening, in the little state park beside the bay, you build a fire and watch the birds settle for the night. The air is soft and smells of salt. Everything seems so normal. So far, it isn't warm enough for armadillos to venture this far north, but give it time. When the weather goes south, the billionaires will fly to Mars, where they'll die like the flies that they are. It's impossible to light a fire on Mars. Are they aware of that?

You crawl into your tent with your beloved and cuddle up in sleeping bags. Nothing will be as hard to bear as the forever end of love. Maybe someday, someone will find your bones and beat a warning drum with them. Or not. You yourself will be absorbed by time, like tears falling into salt water.

Night falls so gracefully, here at the end of all things.

# THIS IS WHERE THINGS START TO GET WEIRD

BERNARD WELT

What nobody needs to tell you
What they'll tell you anyway
What everyone knows and no one will admit
What you saw without recognizing
What you heard when you weren't listening
What they always said would happen
What requires no explanation
What can't be justified under any circumstances
What some love and others despise
What was always lurking in the background
When you surprised yourself
When you disappointed your parents
When you almost lost it
When you said it was forever and it wasn't forever
When you didn't get it
When it all made sense
When it made too much sense
When you dug in your heels
When you promised
When you kept your promise
When you didn't keep your promise
When you thought you were going to lose it
When I saw your face and knew
When I watched you do it
When I turned away
When I thought you were fucking nuts
When you made terrible choices
When you had no choice
When no one knew what was going on
When everyone knew exactly what was happening
When the other shoe dropped
When the earth opened up
When it blew the top of your head off

When you gave up
When you lost your mind
When the mirror would no longer reflect your image
What you were looking for before you forgot what you were looking for
What you couldn't find words for
What you felt bad about saying even though it had to be said
What made the whole thing so sad
What made the whole thing so boring
What the hostages kept from the captors
What the parents kept from the children
How you knew something was up
How you explained your appalling behavior
How you came to terms with it
How you lived with yourself
How you couldn't live with yourself
How they said whatever they had to
How they left out the most important part
How they exceeded the bounds of simple human decency
How they fooled us
How they couldn't fool us
How we were asking for it
Why you can't argue with them
Why you can't shame them
Why you can't pin them down
Why you can't run away
Why you can't keep up
Everything that was funny becomes tragic
Everything that was tragic becomes ridiculous
Everything that is known can be denied
Everything that can happen will happen
Nothing can be calculated
Nothing can be assessed
Nothing can be analyzed
Nothing can be given freely
Nobody hears the words they hoped to hear

Nobody feels joy or despair
Nobody learns their lesson
Nobody achieves a state of enlightenment
Nobody gets what they hoped for
Nobody takes the long way round
Nobody takes a short cut
Nobody lies awake every single night, consumed with worry
Nobody says hello
Nobody waves good-bye
Nobody turns the lights out

# REVERBERATIONS

## LINDA DREEBEN

I STAND ALONE on the edge of a vibrating crowd of Princeton University students. It is just days after the United States bombed Cambodia in an expansion of the Vietnam War, and the Ohio National Guard's murder of four Kent State University students on May 4, 1970.

I half listen to the amplified voices of speakers condemning the evils of the war research performed on the University campus.

"They are providing technology for American imperialism," a voice booms.

"They are starting to institute a mass program of political repression at home," another screams.

The mostly male crowd in headbands, long hair, and jeans is almost celebratory. In late afternoon sun, most are sitting or reclining on the lawn. Some raise fists, others hold up signs—*Build not Burn, Vietnam for the Vietnamese, What Does War Settle?*

Some eat hotdogs.

I am a stranger here, just back to my home in suburban Princeton after my freshman year at the University of Michigan—one filled with my budding political involvement in protests against the Vietnam War, strikes for increased minority enrollment, demands for a student-run bookstore. I traveled to Washington, DC, for the November 1969 Moratorium against the war, a trip my parents opposed.

The odor of marijuana is sharp. Police stand in the background.

Someone grabs my arm and pulls me back. I work to wrench my arm away and turn.

My father.

"You have to leave," he yells over the speaker's amplified words and the chanting crowd, his face a red ember.

"Why?"

"Dammit, Linda, because I said so." He pulls me away from the crowd. "Go home. I'll get your brother."

I am incensed, disbelieving, and confused by my father's desperate action of tracking me down.

I don't resist. I know his temper, something I was practiced at not provoking. This seems sharper, something on a knife edge.

At home my mother is silent.

"I'm old enough to make my own decisions," I rail.

My father instructs my younger brother and me to sit at the Formica gray and white swirly-patterned kitchen table. A textured black three-ring binder, a volume bound with a marbled sky-blue cover, and a manilla folder lay on the table like disheveled placemats.

My father remains standing. His eyes, behind thick lenses set in square tortoise shell frames, are a mixture of wildness and exhaustion. He removes his glasses, wipes his eyes with a white handkerchief, replaces the glasses on his face.

He opens the black binder.

*A LETTER STAMPED CONFIDENTIAL, dated April 12, 1951, from the Atomic Energy Commission, advised that my father and his sister's husband were being called for a hearing to resolve questions concerning their "loyalty, character, and associations," and whether they should be denied security clearances needed for their employment.*

*"It was reported," the letter said:*

- *his sister registered with the Board of Elections as a communist in 1935 and 1936;*
- *his mother, sister and brother-in-law had registered as members of the American Labor Party;*
- *his sister had "criticized an individual for buying United States bonds";*
- *his sister and mother were "communist minded";*
- *he lived at the same address as his sister and brother-in-law.*

*My father responded to each claim:*

· *I was 13 in 1935 and was oblivious of any and all political activities and continued that way until 1939, when I entered college and spent little time with my sister and brother-in-law.*

· *After I was honorably discharged from the Army, I returned to my parents' apartment in 1945 and did engage in political conversations, as well as other subjects of interest to normal people. I believe that they are good loyal Americans and that my sister's registration in the Communist party represented a protest against the depression.*

· *We lived in the same apartment building. My sister and brother-in-law lived on a different floor.*

· *On the subject of politics my mother is quite uninformed and naïve.*

· *My mother, father, sister, and brother-in-law all purchased and still have war bonds.*

*He submitted a list of his parents' bonds. He expressed the desire to have both his parents appear but noted that his mother had health issues.*

*

For over a year, your mother and I lived with the uncertainty and fear that I would lose my job and career." His voice catches. "Your mother was pregnant with you," my father looks at me and then my mother, who looks down at the tissue in her hand.

*

*They waited two months for a hearing to be scheduled, agonizingly long in hours shrouded by anxiety. My father represented himself at the hearing.*

*

"I had to prove a negative, that I was not communist-minded or have ties to suspect organizations. Their questions were insulting and insinuated that I had something to hide."

*

*"Your parents both came from Russia. Did they write to relatives there after they came to the United States? Did they get letters from Russia?"*

*"Before joining the Army you had poor grades in college."*

*"How did it happen that you used as reference people who knew you only in your college days and not those who knew you intimately and socially? Did you have the idea that neighbors possibly might not give a favorable recommendation?"*

*"You were pretty close to Russians when you were stationed in Alaska, weren't you?"*

*He answered each respectfully, earnestly, submissively.*

*

"My parents were called to testify. My mother was already an invalid confined to a wheelchair. It was very intimidating for them."

*

*The panel questioned his mother about newspapers she read, the accident that left her an invalid, relatives that she hadn't seen in 20 years:*

*"You yourself are not in favor of Communism," they asked.*

*"No, I just am very much in favor against it," she responded.*

*His father, who traveled through the South selling ladies' undergarments until his wife's accident, was asked about when he came from Russia, whether he still had relatives there, when was the last time he heard from any relative in Russia.*

*"During your time of travel in the South around the time that you say that your daughter was so young, do you think that she might not have been under your control? Do you think your travel and absence from home was a contributing cause?"*

*"Might. I will say yes because perhaps I wasn't home long enough to talk to her."*

*"Did you have discussions with her to try to correct her attitude?"*

*"Yes, I corrected her. I told her the way I vote in the United States and how the United States is to us."*

*

"The panel refused me an opportunity to confront the unidentified person who reported that my sister criticized war bonds. They said that would reveal a source and jeopardize the investigation."

*

*He introduced letters from his mother while he was in the army, letters he had saved and sent home, to show that his parents bought war bonds, and which show much more.*

*"Dad's boss surprised him with an extra check. Dad bought a $500 Bond to help you Boys to come Home sooner. He also bought a $100 Bond for your birthday, that is in your name.*

*Early in the am came the long-awaited Soldier pictures of my Boy! I love the picture and we all think you make a fine, handsome Soldier. ... Dad even had tears in his eyes."*

\*

"My Army service didn't matter. There was no evidence that I'd joined any suspect organization. This was guilt by association pure and simple."

In my seat at the center of the long side of the oval table, opposite my mother, I run my thumbnail along the crack in the middle of the table, pulling out the rubbery grime that has collected there over my childhood.

"I still don't understand why you forced us to leave the rally."

"There were communists there and people were taking photos. There were police and who knows who else."

A breath.

"You don't know what can come back to haunt you."

None of us have the stomach for dinner, overcooked hamburgers sitting in congealing white fat on the broiler tray.

We are spent like the fraying, stale dishrags lying by the sink.

\*

WHY HAD HE KEPT THIS a secret? If we had not gone to the rally, would he ever have revealed it?

Dwelling on the revelation years later, I recognized that hiding this painful episode was the way my parents coped with life. Whatever mix of factors—growing up in blue-collar families as first-generation Americans, raised in an insular Jewish neighborhood in Brooklyn, NY, during the depression and the horrors of WWII, the harrowing entanglement with McCarthyism—my parents were overly cautious, intensely private.

They distrusted "others" (often non-Jews). My mother could easily believe they had been slighted, treated unfairly. I'd roll my eyes when she evaluated an encounter through what I saw as her jaundiced vision, disturbed by her bitter world view. I wanted the opposite, to be accepting, trusting, open.

But it was not easy.

Long before the night in May 1970, the message was ingrained, perhaps transmitted to me in 1951 along with oxygen and nutrition through the umbilical cord, to be guarded with personal information about health, money, mistakes, doubts, fears. I conserved intimacies, as my mother's treasured silver forks, spoons, and knives were protected from tarnish in a wooden case lined in red velvet.

I was wary of people who shared confidences indiscriminately. How could those be meaningful if dispensed like Halloween candy?

I WAS RIVETED during the three hours *Oppenheimer* played on the large screen in August 2023. I read everything I could, especially as my upcoming trip to Japan included time in Hiroshima.

The scenes of the security hearing especially transfixed me, as if my father was on screen. His entanglement with McCarthyism was, of course, neither as dramatic nor sensational as Oppenheimer's. But it was equally insidious and consequential to my family, as it was for thousands of families caught up in that hysteria.

IN THE SPRING of 1952, my father received his clearance a few months after my birth and nine months after the hearing.

Oppenheimer was stripped of his security clearance.

WHEN I READ and reread the hearing transcript, I try to imagine my father's emotions. He was twenty-nine, younger than both my sons are now. He and my mother had moved to upstate New York for his first job, which was under threat. A baby due in six months.

I feel on his behalf, and on mine, the fear, indignation, and anger at the demeaning insinuations, the repeated mining of specific details of his life, every question a potential trap. I experience the pain of his watching his parents testify in imperfect English, their knowing that, like a landmine, their words could derail his life.

The movie opened up in me the desperate desire to talk to my father, an impossibility fifteen years after his death. I wanted to know what he thought about it all, then and now. I believe he ultimately viewed the ordeal as a badge of honor. He had prevailed, though at a cost to him, my mother, my grandparents.

We never spoke about it again, but it was always a part of him. The impeccably organized binder, the bound hearing transcript, and the articles he collected over the years discussing the silencing of writers, actors, and scientists were among the few items he kept when he moved from his house of forty-seven years to a small apartment.

I am now the keeper of that history. It feels urgent to protect it, to share it, to ensure there are future guardians.

SECRECY takes a toll.

I was diagnosed with cancer at age twenty, just before my senior year. The diagnosis upended my young life, postponing my return to college. I didn't know how to ask questions when my parents tiptoed into my room to tell me the biopsy was malignant. Was that the same as cancer, I wondered silently.

My parents did not want me to tell anyone. As a parent, I understand their fear for a child (a child, no matter the age) with a potentially deadly illness.

But I also heard and still hear another message, this was something shameful, something that could leave me shunned or ostracized.

I didn't listen. I told my best high-school friend and invited her over to make Toll House cookies, neither of us knowing what to say as we filled the baking tray with raw cookie dough, glistening and greasy because I'd melted the butter rather than just softened it.

I told my boyfriend, whose father had died of cancer three years earlier, even though I worried that he might be scared off. He wasn't.

The surgery left a large scar on my thigh, a mutilation to my eye, and before the requirement of informed consent, not what I'd expected. I told the doctor that my leg modeling career was ruined, a wan effort to deflect despair.

The surgery left an inner scar, too. Just as I keep my thigh covered by wearing long beach dresses and never wearing shorts, I rarely share this experience even now, my parents' fears, as in a canyon, echoing across the decades.

I was fortunate to find friends at different stages of my life who opened up to me and helped me reciprocate, although I have not freed myself from the formative messages of childhood.

One lesson I learned well. I hid myself from my parents. Secrecy was easier.

I AM A SOCIAL MEDIA VOYEUR. I marvel, with discomfort, at postings by prolific "Facebook friends" about their travels, children, and grandchildren. Their political positions. I post nothing.

I am cautious about providing information on forms. I don't answer phone calls from numbers or names I don't recognize, and if I accidently do, I hang up immediately. I rarely sign petitions.

But it is impossible to stay hidden. Cameras record every move. Advertisements pop up based on internet searches and private emails. Anonymous accusations on social media are impossible to address. Every purchase made, every cell phone call goes into a database—where we are, who we are with, what we like to eat, drink, wear.

All the more alarming as echoes of McCarthyism and open threats of political retribution by those who admire authoritarianism are treated as acceptable.

*You never know what can come back to haunt you.*

My father's words scratch in my head, a phonograph needle in a crack on a vinyl record. Words I disbelieved at nineteen, flit across my mind when I make political contributions, think about attending a rally for a cause. As I write this piece.

But then, too, are his actions. His scarring but determined opposition, his pained but quiet resilience. The fortitude that brings me to tears. Momentary sparks, like fireflies at twilight, illuminate paths of resistance, however uncomfortable, challenging, and difficult.

# AMERICA

CHRISTINA DAUB

It is possible that in the next minute, I will tell you I love you.
In the next hour, a scientist in Ithaca will recombine DNA
found in Mauritius to recreate the dodo. No one will be able
to club it to death. In the next week, if we can figure out
a place for them to live that is not high and rising, but more
earthy and rounded despite the flat earth crowd steam rolling
the mountains, other long extinct animals can begin
to reappear: the saber tooth tiger, the woolly mammoth—
though it's taking up three Safeway parking spaces may
have to be rethought. Next month, all pronouns now
shortened to merely the letter e, will walk their friends,
the !!!! to the cemetery where someone will say something
important in Russian, Hindi, or Chinese and all present
will nod. Understanding is still overrated. Next year,
all the divided and conquered start a revolution, but
are told they have voted to do away with voting. No one
checks for hacking, or actually counts the votes. Four
years from now words will not mean what they mean today,
truth well down the dodo's path. But you will find your own
way. Look for the beautiful, the greater world we know is
possible. The dreamers, the poets, the artists, the mystics.
Look to the ones who have given up everything to live here.
Who do not agree with the status quo. Look for the fruit
and the fire. It's been more than a minute and I love you.

# DON'T WORRY, IT'S NOTHING.

ERIC BAKER

How common: a sore spine, and efficient, ergonomic
Lungs—folding like sheets in the wind.

We've learned to make our grids smaller, each breath shorter.

Mi guk, we have learned compartmentalization—watching fathers and
mothers mourn sons and daughters, Live-streaming sisters gnashing teeth
and brothers rubbing their eyes to the socket; doing our part, tabbing away
Discomfort, like it's warmed wine down the leg.

We've learned to sing kaddish but forget the stones.

*

שָׁמַע I've seen the coming-going of industry and their false promises, and did
nothing.

שָׁמַע seen fear with his polyester tie paint the faces of good people as they
gaped at new spires, so
Close to where others once joked, a golgotha. and I did nothing.

Seen eomma's insurance canceled, canceled again, rubbing my father's
shoulders as he contemplated
Nothing.

Have held eomma as she cried for her little brother lost in his coma, watched
her fumble her phone and
Scroll, tears in her eyes heavier than bone, heavy like her hand was in mine
as we walked to the doctor's.
Another one of her asthma tests. Don't worry, it's nothing.

*

I should know by now.
It might only require
15 percent of us. By then we'll have figured
How to turn silicon to sap
How to feed a population off cornmeal and kale,
Rutabaga, squash and oats.
We'll have learned to make grids smaller,
To turn atmosphere to water.
When the Pacific cracked open like a pit
And the red trees turned white
And the scales of the trees pricked
Apart like paint cracking off the corner of a room,
We found we could still go outdoors, depending on the day and year.
How upset we grew with all that sun, without a sun, how unable to
Entertain. How expensive,
The good oil, the bad too.

*

Once I was a boy with long locks walking through wildfire smog,
Holding the rope I called a leash, tight like an old wound, my dog sneezing
with a trot through Jaundiced East River haze. TV doctors said don't go out,
close your windows and doors. But the halls Reek of burning, and my Neighborhood aunties need their smoke.

*

Haven't been back in months. Copped a cab home, on my way to help out
mom and the dog, losing Mind to The Lincoln Tunnel verve, passing my old
elementary school, marveling at the smoke stacks, Red and white like candy
cane, like serendipity and death. I had grown up here, and never knew how
Near the bull.

*

Doctor says test is positive. Google tells me one cause is pollution. A modern illness. My girlfriend Rests her fingers over my knee. She feels what is left.

*

Doctor on TV tells us to shut our windows. Smoke still getting in.

# STARDUST

## MELANIE S. HATTER

ANGIE GRIPPED Rain's hand as he succumbed to another bout of coughing. She sat on one of the wooden kitchen chairs they'd moved into the bedroom beside the hospital bed where he'd been confined these past few weeks. He didn't deserve this, she thought. He'd been nothing but good to her. The tears came suddenly, surprising her, but she ignored them as they streaked her face.

"Now, we'll have none of that," he said. "Our time together has been a gift."

Forty years' worth, she thought. A gift indeed.

Those high cheekbones that had once been so alluring seemed almost grotesque now in his gaunt face. But she could still see the earnest young doctor in his eyes.

"Give me a cigarette," he said, and she laughed.

"You're outrageous."

"Worth a try." Several times, he blinked slowly until his eyes remained closed. The raspy sound of his breathing seemed to sync with the round clock on the wall. The steady ticking had lulled her to sleep most nights, but more and more, she lay in the dark listening to it count the hours until sunrise.

She watched Rain sleep and remembered him asking for a cigarette in the hospital cafeteria back in the early 80s, when they could still smoke indoors. She thought him cocksure as he took a seat at her table, leaned forward like he had a secret to share, and asked for a smoke. Without a word she slid the pack and the lighter toward him and watched as he closed his eyes, taking a deep drag as if he were envisioning the smoke traveling along the farthest bronchioles into the alveoli within his lungs. Gray smoke wafted from his lips as he exhaled. Dr. Rainsay Khim was written on his name tag. When he finally looked at her again, he smiled with closed lips and nodded. Though no words passed between them, she saw gratitude in his eyes.

When he was almost done, he lit a second cigarette with the first one and stared past her. Just moments later, his pager buzzed. He crushed the remains of the second cigarette in the glass ashtray in the center of the table and winked at her before leaving. She watched him hurry across the expanse of the cafeteria and disappear through the double doors.

For days after, Angie looked for him, checking the directory, where he was listed as a heart surgery resident. She couldn't stop thinking about those large brown eyes and the way his lips curled around the cigarette.

Over the years, she'd quit smoking several times. This time she hadn't smoked in eight months—pretty much when Rain got seriously sick again. He'd been in remission for the past fifteen years and hadn't touched another cigarette. The cancer returned, metastasizing from his prostate to most of his internal organs.

"Promise me you'll call her," he said, patting her arm, his forehead wrinkling. Angie ground her teeth, feeling her jaw tighten as she shifted her gaze from his face to his short nails. He'd stopped suggesting and had been telling her outright to call the girl. She didn't want to fight him but couldn't promise.

She padded through to the kitchen down the hall in their old rancher. Standing by the sink, she guzzled a glass of red wine then poured a second glass that she took back to his bedside. This was how she spent her evenings now, sipping a glass by his side and downing another glass, or two, where he couldn't see her. She'd taken this week off from her part-time job at the hospital to help care for him. To prepare herself.

He'd been her life for almost forty years. After their first date, she realized how empty her life had become. All she did was work and her few friends were her nurse colleagues. Too often, she wondered if life was worth living anymore. Slow and steady, he filled her days like a summer rain shower into a bucket.

"The Rain that saved me," she whispered to him in the dark.

Nothing about their time together had been planned; they simply fell into a rhythm with each other. He never asked anything of her—no demands or ultimatums. No proposals. Just a suggestion that she could save money if she moved in with him. He'd bought the home two years before that day they'd met in the cafeteria. He liked the quiet neighborhood, he'd said, just a couple miles from the hospital, and on his rare days off, he spent the time renovating the single-story house. "It needs a woman's touch," he said, one evening at dinner. The following week, she packed up her small apartment and helped him decorate.

He was quiet and thoughtful but had a raucous laugh that belied his small frame. When she wasn't with him, his sense of humor made her giggle—silly impressions he did of his colleagues came to mind when she passed them in the corridors.

Another bout of coughing roused him. This time blood speckled his lips. As she grabbed for the tissues, she knocked the glass, spilling red wine onto the gray carpet. Cursing under her breath, she held the tissues at his mouth as he coughed uncontrollably, his fingers clamping around her wrist. She held the back of his neck with her other hand, trying to steady him until the fit subsided. She cleaned his lips and chin, and he slumped back into the pillows, drifting back to sleep.

She waited a while before getting a bucket of warm water and a cloth from the kitchen to clean up the spilled wine, knowing the stain would be there long after they both were gone.

"Please don't do this," she said, her voice shaking as she scrubbed. Angie spoke low enough that Rain couldn't hear but loud enough, she hoped, to reach God's ears. "Don't take him. Not like this. He doesn't deserve this, and you know it." She inhaled, tamping her rising anger and took the bucket into the bathroom where she emptied the dirty water into the tub. She washed her hands and returned to his bedside.

Around his neck was a string of Buddhist mala beads, and she adjusted them so that the tassel rested neatly against his chest. Though God had never been good to her, she kept asking Him to save Rain—he understood her pleas but had accepted his fate. He didn't believe in God. "We're just stardust," he'd told her. "Our past and our future. We all return to the universe as stardust."

What she had taken as cockiness was simply a deep knowing of his worth in the world. Having escaped Cambodia with his parents after the fall of the Khmer Rouge, he'd experienced a trauma Angie would never know, yet she understood his desire to escape the memory. She admired his ability to overcome his past and forge a new future, to become a surgeon who saved lives.

He believed every person had a right to exist and to create whatever life they wished, as long as they brought no harm to others. He respected her choices, and she loved him for that. He knew everything about her—knew every secret stored inside her heart. She told him about the man who'd raped her, about the baby, about all her regrets, and he listened without judgment.

No one but Rain had ever made her feel accepted. She wanted him to live forever. Not just for her benefit, but because he had a way of making everyone around him feel valued, and the world needed him. The world needed more people like him, people who cared.

Though lately, she found his goodness too much. The sicker he became, the more he urged her to reach out to the baby, who was a grown woman now per-haps with children of her own. Death was coming for him, yet he was focused on *her* finding absolution.

He shifted in the bed, his closed eyes fluttering, perhaps at dreams, and she scooted closer, resting her cheek on his arm.

"Why you keep asking this of me?"

Memories swarmed around her brain like wasps, stinging the recesses where she'd buried her regrets. Sometimes in the quiet, she could see faces, appearing before her like ghosts. That devil who had taken her childhood. She blamed him for every bad thing in her life. His spirit followed her, she was sure of it, never allowing her to be free enough to feel utter joy. God preached forgiveness, *forgive those who trespass against us*, yet she could never forgive that man.

Still, she often wondered about the baby—where was she now? What kind of woman had she grown into? Did she hate Angie for abandoning her? Angie had no greater regret than giving up her child, and the pain clawed at her heart every time the girl's tiny face filled her mind.

Angie stood up, unsteady on her feet now, and returned to the kitchen where she emptied the bottle of wine into her glass. She didn't want to think about anything anymore. Some days were just too sad to bear.

Dawn peeked through the curtains, the sunlight brightening the room. Rain's eyes fluttered open. Angie yawned and stretched her arms above her head. She'd slept with her head on her forearm and tingling spread through the mus-cle as the blood recirculated. "I'll get you some juice," she said, starting to rise.

His breathing was labored. He was trying to speak, so she leaned close to hear him.

"I'm grateful for you," he said, his voice raspy and low. "I want you to be at peace."

"Oh, Rain." There was so much she wanted to say. Instead, she kissed his cheek and forehead.

The words were faint but she heard them all the same. *Call her.*

A lump formed large and obtrusive in her throat. How many times had she said no? How many times had she stormed away from him unable to explain why not?

She gripped his hand, wishing she could divulge the depth of her fear. Fear of her daughter's anger, her hatred, her rebuke. All justified emotions that Angie couldn't face.

"For me?" he said, a slight grin at his lips.

She swallowed, the lump in her throat refusing to budge, and nodded. She would try.

He watched her until his eyes fluttered then closed, and his faint smile drifted away, fading with his breath.

Panic surged in Angie's chest, and she gripped his hand. "Rain! Rain?" She held her own breath, waiting to hear another raspy inhale, but the air within and around him had gone. Immobilized, Angie stared at his weary face, expecting him to breathe again, watching for his chest to rise, but there was no more breath. She could do nothing but sit with him. He'd been clear about no resuscitation. The order was in the folder with all his papers. Though she knew he was gone, she anticipated another sigh. Even as the heat disappeared from his body, she waited to see his eyes flick open and a mischievous grin curve his lips.

As the light slipped across the room, the day advancing into afternoon, Angie finally kissed his cheek, so cold now that she had to stop herself from getting another blanket to keep him warm. She rested her palm over the mala beads on his silent chest, listening to the clock checking off each minute as it passed, thinking of stardust.

# AMERICAN GIRLS

MADELEINE MYSKO


The day the catalog arrives, I call my daughter
to ask if I'm correct: my granddaughter doesn't
play anymore with her doll, Mary Ellen.

*Correct*, my daughter says, but adds a story:
when they discussed packing up the doll
and all her clothes and accessories,

my granddaughter pretended she couldn't
imagine why anyone might think she didn't
*want* Mary Ellen anymore, because she

*absolutely did, and it would be very hard*
*to put Mary Ellen away, but probably*
*it was a good idea, just to make some space.*

My daughter and I laugh, but it's sweet—
my granddaughter worries about feelings.
She knows how invested we are in Mary Ellen.

Five years I shopped for that doll, for the hand-made:
silk pajamas, plush robe and slippers, tweed jacket,
pin-tucked blouse, gabardine skirt, organza gown.

One Christmas, I refurbished the doll-sized trunk
from my own childhood. It opens like a closet:
drawers with tiny knobs, a pole with ready hangers.

On the phone, my daughter and I also discuss
the awful news we can't escape: wailing children
at the border, separated from their parents, and

the hearing for the Supreme Court nominee.
*Think of the girls,* we say. What does it mean
that the nominee is presented as brilliant and

accomplished, just before her seven children
are paraded before the cameras? We leave
the question hanging. We return to the doll.

Maybe when Mary Ellen is packed up, I say,
they should send her to my house. She could live
happily ever after in the cupboard with the others—

my daughter's doll and my own, whose entire
wardrobe my mother made by hand in the Fifties.
*Good idea,* my daughter says, deadpan.

We say goodbye. Afterwards, I watch the news.
The nominee is smiling, but doesn't really
answer the question. I take note of her dress:

pink, very smart, exquisitely tailored.
I picture it made up doll-sized, put away in
a vintage trunk, perfect on its little hanger.

# SECOND THOUGHTS

## HAYLEY IGARASHI THOMAS

DAD DOESN'T THINK I can handle today. His lack of faith in me is unchanging, an airtight canister of apprehension without a bubble of belief. I know because I keep checking the Transparency app even when I should be sleeping. I never take my smart glasses off at night, ever since mom bought me the padded rims, so reading Dad's thought stream is as easy as blinking.

1:02 a.m. *Fern can't handle today.*

3:29 a.m. *This will devastate Fern.*

5:55 a.m. *Sorry, Fern.*

He's been doing this forever, leaving me a little message in his thought stream. My girlfriend, Cora, doesn't get why, but that's because her dad is half-Italian and uses both his hands and voice to express his feelings. My dad is second generation, or Nisei, which means he was born in America, but his parents are Japanese immigrants. So, he can be sort of reserved compared to dads like Cora's, or bad at "words of affirmation," if you ask my mom, who's also Japanese, but only one-sixteenth, so it's not really the same.

But that's another reason why I love Transparency and why I bet Obaachan will, too. What Dad forgets is that Obaachan and I are kindred spirits. We play cards every Sunday. Transparency will make us closer, like it's made dad and me closer.

"Ready to go?" Dad asks while his thought stream says, *I'm not ready for this.*

I pat him on the shoulder as I grab the keys. "It's going to go better than you think."

Dad ends up taking the keys back because I only have a permit and I did hit Mrs. Hamesh's drone yesterday. We don't say much on the way. Transparency can do that sometimes, eliminate the need for small talk. The ads preach a bunch about how the app transformed the mental health crisis and politics, and that's all true, but that was before I was born. For me, it's about relationships.

As we pull into Obaachan's driveway, I blink into Dad's thought stream again.

12:16 p.m. *I should've prepared Fern better.*

"I'm not a kid anymore," I say. "I know your mom's probably a little backwards." I see Dad's face twist into a grimace, and I add, "Probably a lot backward?"

When we enter Obaachan's house, the Transparency technician is wrapping up. The app is easy to download, but old people like Obaachan, who haven't updated their drives in more than a decade, need extra help. She hadn't seen the point for years, until her dysarthria made it difficult to speak.

Dad hugs Obaachan, who nearly disappears in his embrace. He's tall and wide while she was shorter than me even before she started shrinking. Her hair, a jet-black poof of a wig, peeks from out behind Dad before her tiny, round face appears, and our eyes meet.

"Hi, Obaachan," I say, but the syllables slow as they leave my mouth.

She shakes her head violently, back and forth, enough to make the wig slip a centimeter down her forehead. Her eyes are red.

"Her Transparency is up and running," the technician tells Dad. "I'd give it a week or two until she's acclimated. The whole thing can be a shock for folks her age."

When the technician leaves, my dad moves closer beside me. Obaachan sinks into an armchair, turning her body away from us.

I blink into the Transparency app. A new thought stream is ready to view. I blink again.

12:22 p.m. *Fern can't know, can't know, can't know.*

Blink.

12:23 p.m. *Don't think it, don't, don't.*

Blink.

At 12:24 p.m., a barrage of text arrives on Obaachan's thought stream. I feel tears pooling before full understanding hits. I look to Obaachan and then to dad.

The thought stream is full of vitriol, and Dad was right: I can't handle it. I thought any hatred would be for other people—neighbors, a man on television, vague strangers.

But she hates me.

My skin, darker because my dad married a woman who was only a sliver Japanese and mostly Black. My eyes, rounder than hers. My hair. My nose. My girlfriend.

God, Cora. She'll be tuning into the thought stream, too. She had hoped Obaachan liked her.

"I'm leaving," I say to Dad.

I don't wait for him to follow, but then I hear a muffled cry. I turn, and Obaachan's hand stretches toward me. Tears pour down her cheeks.

"The thought stream," my dad whispers, after I spend seconds waiting for Obaachan to say something, anything, to make this better.

12:26 p.m. *I am sorry, sorry, sorry. So sorry.*

It's not good enough. I think it to my thought stream, and I say it out loud.

There is more from her, but it's all the same. A string of *sorrys* that won't take back what she sees when she looks at me.

At 12:29 p.m., it changes: *But I love you. So much, so much, so much.*

She's never said this to me before.

I take a step closer. The woman before me is collapsing in on herself, frail and hunched. She was born on another continent, in another century. I take another step.

When our hands touch, I say, "It's okay." My thought stream says, "*It's not.*"

I don't know if she's familiar enough with Transparency to see the discrepancy. But I repeat it, again and again, telling her it's okay and not okay, out loud and in my mind.

I rest my forehead against hers, our two faces, so different, lining up, nose to nose. We pull in ragged breaths of the same air.

When I tell her I love her, I mean it.

12:32 p.m. *I love you. It's not okay. I love you. It's not okay.*

# THE GENERATIONS

VARUN GAURI

He vents a baritone laugh, his over-anxious shoulders thrown
    back, shoes kicking up, mouth agape,
dodgy gestures in any class, let alone for intellect so grand,
    Professor of Social Thought,
black-rimmed, a grave and handsome part, the cashmere scarf, the Windsor knot,
    as for school picture day.
The students, grown accustomed to his artful, slow delivery, his elegant taste
    for harsh truths,
the phrase "mortality, the grimmest blessing," disciplined doubt
    of reckless utopias,
start fiddling with phones, ogling their teacher, sheepish now, grinning far too long,
    the moral sense congealing,
and then he wheels around, nostrils splayed, and throws his looseleaf notes
    fluttering over oaken wainscoting,
as if he blew it, were up to bat in the last of the ninth, the Series his, trumpets poised
    but he didn't see the knuckler.

# REMEMBRANCE OF FUTURES PAST

## CYNTHIA G. WAGNER

"THE FUTURE is now." *(No, it's not.)*

"The future ain't what it used to be." *(Never was.)*

"Where's my flying car?" *(How much insurance do you have?)*

"Where's your crystal ball?" *(Shut up.)*

In my three decades as an editor at *The Futurist* magazine, I may have heard every cliché there is about the future. I discovered that the challenge most futurists faced was not batting down dopey questions about their profession, but getting people to listen to them when they had something useful and important to say.

This was often the case for warnings about things no one wanted to think about, particularly problems without easy solutions: nuclear war, climate change, aging populations, fraying social connections, information warfare (or, as we might now call it, disinformation campaigns).

So how do you make people listen, especially the decision-makers? Caught off guard by a crisis despite the warnings of their experts, politicians will claim, "You didn't grab us by the lapels!" Warnings need to be urgent and personal: "Aliens are invading, they're in your backyard! They're eating your dogs!" If sci-fi dramatists and disinformation campaigners can do it, so can the reality checkers.

"The best way to predict the future is to create it." *(True, but let's not manufacture disasters.)*

Futurists are almost used to being blamed for unfulfilled promises about the world of tomorrow, but no one wants to say "I told you so" during an apocalypse.

So, futurists don't make predictions. They observe and analyze trends, scanning the horizon for signals of change; they envision wild cards and offer multiple futures—scenarios of plausible outcomes that are the consequences of the decisions and choices in our power to make. *(Okay, in that sense, the future really is now.)*

"Think globally, act locally." *(But understand personally: Recognize your own perspective and biases.)*

In 2012, *The Futurist* invited contributions of short essays envisioning life in the year 2100—just a lifetime away for a then-newborn child. The magazine published more than two dozen submissions that offered a wide range of positive and negative visions of the next eight decades.

MY CONTRIBUTION, "Reunion: A Civil War Fable," stemmed from my dread that the aching differences in beliefs and values within my own family could be early warnings of larger cultural forces threatening the nation at large. I began:

"The twins were separated at birth in 2012, and though they had been communicating with each other for many years, they planned their physical reunion to coincide with the reunification of the United States of America on January 1, 2100."

I envisioned these twins, Bucky and Custis, growing up to become the respective leaders of a divided America following the Second Civil War in the 2030s. Two separate networks united dispersed communities, but rather than a North versus South split, the division was urban versus rural (or mind versus spirit, as some said). Bucky led what I called the Legion of Mayors, while Custis "pioneered the establishment of autonomous Pastoral Villages built around individual megachurches."

NOW A DOZEN YEARS after I wrote this, it's become even easier to imagine the peril of a violent US dissolution. It's also easier to see my own biases underlying such a scenario. I'd imagined cities would be far more economically viable and culturally desirable: "Even in hard times, everyone danced." Meanwhile, a lack of economic and social diversity in the religious Pastoral Villages would doom them, leading to the Third Civil War in the 2070s.

But my other bias is toward optimism, despite being an inveterate worrier. I concluded that my heroic twins would ultimately realize they—and the communities they led—couldn't live without each other. They missed each other. I feel hopeful yet that such personal ties will keep America unbroken.

"That was now. This is then."

I spent my career aiming at (and passing by) the future's movable goalposts, like Orwell's ominous 1984 and numerous "by the year 2000" forecasts. So now I am catching up on the past. I'm reading lots of history, primarily political biographies but also some philosophy. In Plato's *Republic*, Socrates prophesied society's evolution from oligarchy to democracy, then from democracy to tyranny: Some folks will get fed up with other people's abuse of liberty and start wanting to take it away. At least tyrants would keep things under control.

The unthinkable, the unimaginable, has happened many times before and likely will continue to do so. Our march toward tomorrow often follows trails of imperfect, long-term cycles. We are not, however, powerless to foresee and seize opportunities and avert catastrophes. We just have to keep thinking and imagining. My credo for our present is:

"Read the past; write the future."

# CASCADIA, OR
## A SPELL TO BANISH THE ABYSS OF HIM
## WITHOUT MOVING TO THE WEST COAST

JACOB BUDENZ

& still when you wake he is there with you, the void / of his unlicked wounds
pinning you to his yellow / beadspread & licking parts of you he knows you
are not awake enough to say no to, / not strong / enough to overpower him
as he sucks / at the astral milk you / haven't offered. & each time you come
/ up for air & say *today* / *I will be free of him,* his hands / stretch from his
chasm & tug & tug / at the heat of you / until only shadow, shallow / as his
waters run, drowns / what candles you've lit, flickering over your sunset /
quilt just out of reach / of your kitten, all black / but for the patch of white
at her breast, formal / as she chirps at you, / *He's gone he's gone he's gone* / *&*
*here I am, needing you* / *better needing you lighter, kneading* / *your chest your thighs* /
*where he took from you* / *your golden light* / but you hear only his voice, the whine
behind his septum, / the constant whine / as he tells you once more / how
your triumphs are nothing to him / but a reflection of his second fall / from
grace / & candle after candle after candle / burns the thinning hair you took
from his brush / on the last day, your stomach / a stone fruit rotting with the
censure / of his need his need his need / to vomit the red fires of the earth /
it means, at least, a glow / of spotlight on his fading glory

Nothing grows / from nothing, no forest / renews without a little ash, no mountain / can hide all that molten earth / without someday tipping his hand, / his rumble of anger at yet another gig / no one came to, at least / not to see him, to climb him, no / smoldered earth without a little shoot / of green where bougainvillea / used to bloom in thick, wild, thorny / bursts of fuchsia, a fire / all its own without the burn / & there is a red bridge, a word / for people like you who leap in their daydreams / & wake before hitting the concrete surface / of the bay, but the eucalyptus trees & the balmy mist / ascending from the marina keep you on the path, / & you take a selfie with the bridge / instead of jumping, or even wanting to, / & that has to count for something, / & all this land, they say, / all these hills of neat colorful little box / houses, all those drag bars, / all this coast / flattened when the earth opens up / beneath the sea & the ocean growls before flinging itself / at the land, / but it is quiet, here, in the morning, / & you could steal a life here / where he'd never find you, but / no fault line sleeps / forever, no reckoning stays / its hand no matter how many hands / lift him, for now, as he reaches / once more from his void as you / rise, rise, rise, always / out of reach.

# INVOCATION TO SGÁTHACH

JACOB BUDENZ

> *I. therefore on the day and hour of jupiter*
> *make the same circle that you made for love*
> *and enter the circle with your instruments*

and the lord watched
as we traipsed to the cathedral
to steal climbing roses for our ritual
and we laughed to keep the lightning
strike at bay said our taxes go to holy
ground after all holy wars and why not
make sacred what the sacred
hardly use but to erase us?

> *II. moreover you should have had your bed*
> *properly and beautifully made up and*
> *equipped with clean linens*

and the lord said death
to the trannies and faggots

and the lord said aids
was the hand of the almighty

and the lord said you know ronald reagan
really did know a thing or two about economics

and the lord said go to war
with the commies then go to war
with the dictators we put in their place

and the lord said my people my people my people
it is more important to win than to save

and the lord was not god
but a goddamned
capitalist
a feudal lord with his fingers twitching
over the big red button
to rain fire down like elijah
on the heathen throng

> *III. and the circle thus well prepared*
> *face south in such a way*
> *that the middle of the table*
> *is beyond the circle*

I am the fucking prophetess
okay?

I am the thirteenth judge

I am samson's gilded locks
shorn to a lesbian bowl cut for summer

I am where his power went
with berry red church flowers
wilting on my altar offered up
to goddesses and monsters of dead
civilizations to protect us
from gun-toting breeders like you

I am justice (reversed)
with a red sash cinched around her skull to stop her
laser gaze from scorching you

*IV. say the same conjuration*
*extending your scepter here*
*(i.e. towards the south) and*
*only you should be operating*

pray you stay
invisible
to me

*Excerpted instructions, "Experiment in Invisibility" from Section I (Theurgia) of
*The Book of Oberon: A Sourcebook of Elizabethan Magic* adapted for the Folger Shakespeare
Library by Daniel Harms

# THE VISION OF A SHEETZ ATTACHED TO URGENT CARE

TRACY DIMOND

Urgent care attached to Sheetz
In a town where a new Whole Foods is exciting
Don't confuse this as an indictment
Are we having fun yet

There are more mass shootings than days
Another year in America
I am obsessed with imagining Thoreau
Traverse mountains in 19th century shoes
Maybe poems are made by fools
We have so many options

If the sun were hollow
You could fit a million earths inside it
Everyone thinks they live in special times
Just look at the past 50 years
Of medical advancements

*We live in special times*
*only because it is all special*
Bradbury was a warning
Because he loves humanity
Maybe the knowledge of death brings our focus to life

# ELOPEMENT

EMILY HOLLAND

The desert has its own quiet desire, spliced with cracks and canyons,
        punctuated by the slowest growth. We go

in January and see snow. Even the melt a delayed
        departure. We drive until the road turns to dust,

pass a white piano, count eight sleeping palms,
        arrive where backyard Joshua trees formed an altar

for an elopement the previous week. On the nightstand of the BnB:
        a dried corsage. Leftover wine in the fridge.

We get high and talk about marriage again. No plans
        for engagement. *Maybe skip the charade, elope too.*

It must have been beautiful—moonlight on iced-over snow,
        stars flickering their own fireless chorus.

No objections from tumbleweeds, just the high desert
        mountains and their lilac blessing on the horizon.

# FIREWORK DISPLAY

GABBY GILLIAM

We play at democracy,
pretend the weight
of our broken system
doesn't sit on our brows
heavier than a crown
so we'll flock to open fields
and waterways to watch the sky
fill with flammable tokens
of freedom, each explosion
a distraction from our exhaustion
indifferent to the errant sparks
that are ready to set the world on fire.

## COORDINATING CONJUNCTIONS

JANE SCHAPIRO

*The earth is still, but it does move*! Galileo

How we take for granted these seven dwarfs
who guard the gates of our absolutes.
Like bodyguards when tempers flare,
they hustle us to the nearest door.
I voted for *but* I don't believe.
Unlike their heavyweight counterparts
whose Love/Hate
have launched weddings/wars,
these slight, generic, low-priced words
seek the status quo.
Stay *or* go, do *so* don't,
here *nor* there, more *for* less.
They weave confessions,
unravel oaths,
sometimes even whisper a threat
as when the world proclaims
Never Again,
history repeats
*and yet...*

# YOU ASK ME ABOUT AMERICA'S FUTURE

HEATHER BRUCE SATROM

I want to tell you it's true—
What you heard about the
Moral arc bending towards justice
I want to tell you I believe in that
Because a mother *should*

I remember this—
Twenty-one years ago
The day you were born
You struggled to lift your head off my chest
To take in the blurry world

They say you have to be crazy
To bring a child into a world that's on fire
A world choked by smoke
Riddled by bullets
Flooded by waste

When you were born
I did not foresee
Burning forests—darkening skies
Drunken bees—befuddled butterflies
An anxious generation cutting their wrists

I did not foresee young blank faces
Staring at screens
Alerts to stay calm—find a safe place—lock the windows
Turn off the lights—hide—be silent
Block the door—and if all else fails—fight back.

# THANKSGIVING AFTER THE ELECTION

MEL EDDEN

When America tucks into turkey, we invite international friends.

A smiley Chinese doctor brings dumplings to reheat. We steam them
in the kitchen, chat over the aroma of salted pork and onions.

A German professor with impeccable manners opens a French merlot,
updates me on his kittens while effortlessly slicing vegetables.

A genial couple from India (who keep us well-stocked in poppadoms)
bring homemade gnocchi, because they *love cooking Italian*.

A sharply-dressed postdoc shares a honey wine from home,
pours samples of Ethiopian gold into cut crystal glasses.

A shy postdoc, fresh off the plane from Egypt, places his crumpled
airport truffles on the counter, blushes when we sing happy birthday.

Mexican friends arrive with cactus for the grill, scrape off spines,
toss in oil and spice. It tastes like bell pepper, soft and mild.

After dinner, we play *este es un pato* in seven languages,
countenances asunder as we blunder in each other's tongues.

I look around the room.

Some people do not want us in America. They see poison
in their blood. They see job-takers, invaders, criminals, snakes.

But at this Thanksgiving table all I see is: beautiful diversity
—a radiant potpourri of cultures, love and hope.

# NOT AMERICAN HISTORY

JOSEPH ROSS

> *We are always too late.*
> From "Outside History" by Eavan Boland

1.

It is not easy to learn
that books lied to me.

These were good people,
my teachers and professors.
I thought they knew things
but I guess they did not
understand things.

Language can become a liar
with very little effort.


2.

You see, the word "rebel" doesn't
mean "traitor." But in America
it should.

The word "plantation" sounds
so genteel, so easy.
But every time we hear it
we should also hear the ripping
whip, the mother's wail.

The words "honorable"
and "way of life"
ignore the forced work, overseers,
rapes.

Sometimes I think America
is a whole dictionary
of deception,

a history
that is fiction.


3.

What are we to do
with these stories,
these monuments and statues,
mass-produced to lie, glorify,
and terrorize,
all at once?

They have become
stone teachers of a history
that was not history,
honor that was actually dishonor.

Tell a story often enough
to people who do not read enough
and they think it is
a true story.

But history is not built
by repetition.

4.

There is a grace though:

the human mouth can learn
to say the word "regret."

Human eyes can read the dark
truth from those who were crushed.

Our teeth and tongues and lips
can learn to sing the words
"... I was blind but now I see."

# THE SCALES OF BEAUTY

## PATRICIA SCHULTHEIS

TWENTY YEARS after fate slammed an arrow into Teddy Holbrook's heart, it shot another. The first was the evening the dark eyes of Peri Spikos flashed at him across a Brooklyn roof-top party. The second was the sight of beautiful but tired blue orbs above a green mask in a Baltimore emergency room. To Teddy, Dr. Elizabeth Somerville seemed elegant—she moved gracefully and had a soft voice. But she looked exhausted. So tired she didn't even bother tucking an errant strand of blond hair back into her scrub cap—just blew it from her face with the same endearing efficiency his daughter Amy once wiped milk mustaches away with her sleeve.

An icy Valentine's glaze had coated Baltimore, and people were bringing broken limbs into emergency rooms quicker than they snapped open beer tabs on Opening Day. Dr. Somerville was running on empty Teddy suspected, and he wanted to leap over the bed between them, wrap her in his arms and cup her weary head to his chest. "*I got you. I got you. Just rest here for a minute. Or a lifetime. I got you.*"

He prayed she was married. A ring would save him. A ring would mean he could yank the arrow from his heart and continue his careful life as the forty-six-year-old former husband of Peri Spikos Holbrook, father of Juliette, Lukas, and Amy Holbrook, English teacher at Putnam Academy, recovering alcoholic, and AA sponsor of Caden Walsh, whose abdomen the latex-gloved hands of Dr. Elizabeth Somerville were probing.

"Hurt here?"

"No . . . a little."

"How about here?"

"No." Caden turned to Teddy. "What about Beauty?"

"Here?"

"No. This fuckin' cold . . . excuse my French, Doc . . . it's not good for her."

"Be quiet, please . . . here?"

Caden winced. "Fuck, yeah. I got a heat lamp for her, but it broke when I fell."

"Don't worry . . . I'll take care of her."

"Please be quiet."

Teddy saw Caden's eyes smirk at him—*I know what you're thinking, you old letch.* "If it's broke, there might be glass on the steps. Be careful."

"I'm ordering x-rays." Dr. Somerville snapped off her gloves and Teddy got a look at her left hand. . . ringless! Teddy felt the arrow twist a little deeper.

"You might want to wait outside," she told him.

Caden took out his keys. "Here, take these. In case you need to take care of Beauty."

Down the hall, Teddy sat beneath a red paper heart pasted on a grimy window. Damn, this was all Caden's fault . . . all of Baltimore a skating rink, and what does the idiot do? . . . goes out for a frickin' heat lamp. He was Caden's AA sponsor not his nursemaid, for Christ's sake.

Worse, he felt his own dormant addiction stirring. *"You've done your duty by Caden . . . more than your duty. And as far as that doctor's tired blue eyes?. . . you don't stand a chance. . . she's fair Miranda, and you, old fool, are Caliban. Stop on your way home, get a T-Bone and a bottle of Glenfiddich . . . Console yourself."*

"Shut the fuck up!" Teddy thumped his head back against the grimy window. The heart came loose. And fell on top of his skull. Where it stuck.

He tried pulling it off, but it had residual stickum and every tug cost him a precious hair or two. So, there he was, a forty-six-year-old man with a red paper heart stuck to his head. And Dr. Elizabeth Sommerville coming down the hall.

"I've heard of wearing hearts on your sleeve, but never on your head." Above her hospital mask her tired blue eyes were laughing.

He hated her; he loved her. "Sleeves are for amateurs. Heads are for pros."

Her mask fell from one ear and tick-tocked from the other. She had dimples! This was getting worse and worse. And better and better.

"Bend down. This might hurt." She ripped the heart from his head.

"Ouch!" Now she'd seen his liver-spotted scalp. "*Old fool, I warned you.*"

He shoved the heart into his pocket. "How's Caden?"

"I'm admitting him. He's got three cracked ribs, and possibly a bruised spleen. He took quite a fall, and he's very worried about his dog."

"Dog? Caden doesn't have any dog."

"What's Beauty then? His cat?"

"His lizard."

"His what?"

"Beauty is his lizard. A bearded dragon."

"You mean like a Komodo dragon?"

"No . . . no . . . Komodos are huge and mean. Beardeds are small, and lovable . . . at least Caden says so."

"A lizard named Beauty . . . that's got to be a first."

"What can I say? . . . Caden's a quirky guy." Although "quirky" didn't half describe him. Most of the men Teddy sponsored were like himself: well-educated, middle-aged, booze-driven in proportion to their disappointments. Caden was more of a random amalgam of mismatched idiosyncrasies stuffed into a lanky body with a ponytail snaking down its back: he worked for an HVAC contractor but was a nationally ranked online chess player; after an afternoon in a Baltimore strip joint, he'd go to the ballet in Washington; he could quote L. Ron Hubbard in one breath and Keats the next.

Teddy wanted to Google bearded dragons and show Dr. Somerville pictures, —some people posed their beardeds in ridiculous tiny hats—maybe he could get a little clever banter going. But his phone beeped. A selfie of Amy in a blinking heart halo. "*I'm going to a party at my boss's. Do I look silly in this crazy thing?*"

Silly? . . . the halo of hearts made his younger daughter look lovely. Of his three kids, he'd probably given Amy the least—by the time she came along, booze held primacy in his life—yet here she was, the most forgiving, the one who refused to not believe in the good. Teddy texted her back. *"No one looks silly with hearts on their head. Have fun."*

But when he looked up Dr. Sommerville was gone. So much for fledgling flirtation's clever banter. He texted Caden that he'd check on Beauty, then slipped away from the hospital and onto the icy streets of Baltimore.

Shards of the shattered heat lamp were imbedded into the ice slicking the steps to Caden's basement apartment. There was no railing. One step, then another and another, Teddy managed to maneuver down. He reached the door, opened it, and turned on the light.

Across the room, Beauty was staring at him. Her lips were yellow, her body green, and her scaly beard fully flared. With menacing rhythm, her head bobbed from side to side. Teddy didn't move. She lifted her left front paw and waved at him. Then she rose on her hind legs and ran away—a reptilian humanoid.

Somehow the creature projected a weird mischievous connection with him. Like two-year old Amy had, the snowy morning she scampered away after Teddy found a plush blue rabbit stuffed deep into the toe of his boot.

He texted her. *I really wish you'd reconsider going to that party. The roads are awful. Not a night for driving.*

She called back. "Don't worry, Dad, I didn't go. Bill cancelled his party . . . He came to my apartment instead. We're making chocolate-covered popcorn."

Teddy kept the phone to his ear and went looking for Beauty. He found her in the bedroom, with her head burrowed under tangled blankets. But she must have sensed him, because she immediately went on the offensive. And jumped on Teddy's ankle. "Beauty get off!!"

"Dad, what's going on? Wait a minute! . . .you're with someone, aren't you? You found someone, didn't you Dad!"

"What? . . . No!" He had to snip off the line of inquiry right away . . . had to take charge . . . redirect interest away from himself. "Well, I just gotta say, chocolate-covered popcorn, that sure sounds interesting."

"Dad, it's totally okay if you're with someone. I get it . . . I'm a big girl now."

The creature was climbing up Teddy's leg, her avid reptilian eyes fixed on the red paper heart bulging from his pants pocket. To get her off, Teddy shook his leg but lost his balance and fell onto the bed. The creature was undeterred, it kept moving toward the heart. "Get away!"

"Dad, what's going on?" He fished the Valentine from his pocket and threw it on the floor. The lizard leapt down and ran away with the heart in her mouth.

"Listen, Amy, I'm really glad you stayed home . . . a wise decision. I'll call you tomorrow, okay?"

"Okay. But I'll want to hear all about this Beauty person, whoever she may be."

"Enjoy your popcorn, Sweetie"

"Happy Valentine's Day, Dad."

The paper heart lay at the lizard's feet. She was standing upright on the couch. And turning bluish. She probably needs that heat lamp, Teddy thought.

Her heavy-lidded eyes reminded him of Doctor Elizabeth Somerville's, whose shift must be ending soon. Which meant she'd be driving home, on icy roads, alone. Bone-tired. On icy roads. Alone. Not good. Maybe he could text her, tell her to be careful . . . just one concerned adult to another.

*What are you? In middle school? . . . telling her to "be careful." A sixth grader could think of something less transparent. Stick with the lizard, old man. If you need comfort, there's always your buddy, Glenviddich. Besides, you don't have the good doctor's number.*

"Shut up."

Teddy began searching Caden's jumbled bookshelves for something on lizards. The shelves were crammed with volumes on HVAC repair; endgame chess, doublewide chess, Los Alamos chess, Scientology—*Xenu and Advanced technology, The Wall of Fire Explained*—and Shakespeare paperbacks: *Hamlet, Richard III, The Tempest.*

A library of loneliness, Teddy thought. The collected volumes of someone desperate to discover himself in print. Or maybe of someone desperate for interesting snippets of Babe Bait, something to toss out at a bar, maybe catch someone's attention. Teddy didn't know Caden well enough to say which. He looked over his shoulder at Beauty. And she looked back. She was icy blue all over. damn! . . . Caden had to have a lizard book somewhere.

Between *Self-fulfillment through Scientology* and *Three Dimensional Chess Made Simple*, Teddy found *Loving and Living with Your Bearded Dragon.* He sat on the opposite end of the couch from the lizard and read.

> **Pg. 3** Bearded Dragons are loveable creatures, with some surprisingly human-like behaviors, such as running on their hind legs and waving a front paw. Experts aren't certain if this latter is a sign of greeting or hostility. Bearded dragons like a vivarium that is fairly warm: 30 to 42 C on the warm end.

He looked at her. She had abandoned the paper heart and was creeping toward him across the couch. Teddy checked his phone: 27 degrees Fahrenheit outside. But the book gave the optimum temperature in Celsius—he Googled the Celsius/Fahrenheit conversion: Subtract thirty, multiply by five, and then divide by nine. Fuck it! It didn't matter, anyway. He needed the basement's temperature, not the outside's. And it wasn't like Caden to have an indoor thermometer. The lizard was creeping closer and closer. Teddy read on.

> **Pg. 7** Bearded dragons like a diet of insects and vegetables.

Caden's apartment probably was roach resort, but Teddy wasn't about to hunt for any. Bad enough to be a forty-six-year-old man, alone with a reptile, in a basement, on Valentine's night—No, he had his limits.

Vegetables might be another matter, however. He left Beauty on the couch and went to the kitchen. In the refrigerator he found a softening apple, a bunch of limp carrots, and wilted lettuce. And stashed in the back, a bottle of Johnnie Walker Black Label. Maybe a test bottle. Teddy knew about test bottles. For years, he'd kept one himself, an unopened fifth of his beloved Glenfiddich hidden behind *A Farewell to Arms* on his bookcase. A test of his willpower.

Or maybe Caden's Johnnie Walker was his "just-in-case" bottle. As in "just in case" things get so overwhelming, only a drink will save him. Teddy knew about those, too. His own "just-in-case" bottles had brought him back to AA, chastened and ashamed, four times.

Teddy took a few lettuce leaves and the bottle by its neck. When he closed the refrigerator, from the couch Beauty was waving at him.

He went to her and set the Johnnie Walker on the floor by a stack of books. Then he sat down and stared at it. And Johnnie Walker stared back.

*You're really pathetic . . . is anyone more alone than you? Even your Amy, the one you thought would never fledge, has found someone to make chocolate-covered popcorn with on Valentine's night. And who do you have?. . . scaley Beauty! Pathetic.*

Teddy reached across the couch and fed the lizard a wilted leaf of lettuce. She began to crawl toward him, but Teddy stared at the cartoon figure of Johnnie Walker strutting across the bottle's label on the floor. How did ad companies and brewers do that? Create a myth of good taste to camouflage your cravings? Convince you that you're in a community of connoisseurs with Johnnie Walker's other pals? How do they get you to delude yourself that you don't have a problem with drinking? That you've got it under control? That you can stop whenever you want? But why should you stop, when you don't want to?

And Teddy didn't want to.

A dog-eared volume of Keats lay by his foot and the lizard had crawled onto his thigh. He didn't want to dislodge her—he was the only heat source around—so he extended his leg and managed to drag the book toward the couch. Beauty stayed where she was. He fed her another leaf and she didn't move while he bent down to pick Keats up off the floor.

He'd always admired Keats, the poet's humble beginnings, his star-crossed love for Fanny Brawne, and tragically short life. Plus, his immortal genius that, centuries after his death, could warm the soul of a forty-six-year-old man, alone in a basement with a reptile on his lap on Valentine's night.

Teddy opened to his favorite: "Ode on a Grecian Urn."

> *Bold Lover, never, never canst thou kiss,*
> *Though winning near the goal yet, do not grieve;*
> *She cannot fade, though thou hast not thy bliss,*
> *For ever wilt thou love, and she be fair!*

Teddy realized the difference between his heart's two arrows. He and Peri had been so young neither could imagine ever not becoming more and more of their own shining selves. Life was eternal youth back then, a bottomless pool of blue possibility. But he was older now and already living the truth that probably was just beginning to dawn on Dr. Elizabeth Sommerville: unlike the maiden on the urn, her beauty would fade, her considerable skills eventually would be eclipsed by others' and the exhausting parade of broken bones and human frailty would never end.

He felt a profound, warm tenderness toward her and wanted to rub her aching feet when she got home, make their own version of chocolate-covered popcorn, and hold her tight on icy nights like this one. Teddy wanted to be her sanctuary.

Across the couch the paper heart had the lizard's teeth marks and his own few hairs. They looked like what they were: like something shed by a human animal, something once organic and vibrant. But now dead. Strands of mortality.

The lizard crawled higher up his chest and he read Keats' last enigmatic lines.

> "Beauty is truth, truth beauty—that is all
> Ye know on earth, and all ye need to know."

They were underlined, probably by Caden, the inspiration for his lizard's name. She was resting her scaley body over Teddy's heart now, her head against his pulsing neck. Then he took out his phone and called Stuart Lippman, president of the hospital where Dr. Elizabeth Sommerville worked and someone Teddy had sponsored in AA.

"Teddy, do you know what the fuck time it is? Nearly ten-thirty."

"I need a favor, Stu."

"Don't tell me you need help, Teddy. Not you . . . you've been such a rock."

"I'm close, Stu, God damn close to falling . . . I'd be lying if I said I wasn't. It happens . . . we all know that. But I just want a phone number."

"A phone number?"

"Yeah, someone at the hospital . . . Dr. Elizabeth Sommerville . . can you give me her number."

"Well, it's highly irregular, Teddy."

He wanted to say, "Know what's fucking irregular? Having a drunk as president of a hospital, that's fucking irregular." Instead, he fed Beauty another leaf and pleaded, "Come on, Stu, help a fella out."

"Well, okay, just don't ever tell Lizzie where you got it."

"Stu, if it's one thing we all know, it's how to keep our mouths shut."

"Right. And Teddy?

"Yeah?"

"Good luck."

He stroked Beauty, then texted. *Please be very careful driving home. Roads are very bad. And I have a lizard on my neck.*

He didn't expect a reply right away. She probably was already home. Maybe sleeping beside someone—he didn't want to think about that. From the floor Johnnie Walker went wink wink.

*"Shove it, Asshole."* He kept stroking the lizard instead and read Keats's Preface to "Endymion."

> *The imagination of a boy is healthy, and the mature imagination of a man is healthy; but there is a space of life between, in which the soul is in ferment, the character undecided, the way of life uncertain, the ambition thick-sighted . . . .*

His phone beeped.

*"Surprisingly, lizards on necks are not that uncommon. Does it hurt?"*

*"Not really . . . I think she may be asleep. Is it serious?"*

*"It could be. You really should have it examined."*

*"Good idea. Who would you recommend?"*

*"I'll ask around."*

*"In your expert opinion, will it require surgery?"*

*"That depends on how firmly she's attached. I could do a preliminary exam."*

*"I'd be very grateful if you would . . . do you take insurance?"*

*"Most companies don't cover lizard removal. It's considered cosmetic."*

*"Then how will I ever repay you?"*

*"We'll think of something."*

*"I'm looking forward to that."*

# THE ASSIGNMENT

SERENA AGUSTO-COX


*I want you to draw a map,* she says.
United States, not a country
practically a continent. You can't fit it
in the palm of your hand. A map
you can ball it up and toss it in the trash.

With thin black ink, I outline the lower 48.
This is the shape of us. See that cowlick?
Oregon or Washington, I don't remember which.
That thumbs up, Massachusetts. But so much middle.
There's no shape to blankness.

I should have traced those irregular borders.
My states look *too* symmetrical. I need more country,
so I can shape each state into the same rectangle.
backfill the erosion, begin with a blank slate.

# EPIPHANY

KATHLEEN O'TOOLE

*Persistence is its own poetry, a promise*
*that change is always possible.*
by Deepa Iyer

On the cusp—New Year, new regime
—questions of flight: into Egypt, out
to Canada or Greece, common among
friends. Escape from unrest, unreality.
In the corner of my eye, a Holy Family
arrives to settle in, enjoy a warm day
on the café patio. The South Asian father's
flowing locks catch the late-day light,
as he bounces his infant, while the mother
laughs with their friends. Multi-colored
holiday lights, multi-hued neighbors.
Snapshot of this village, our home.
I ponder the many ways bonds of connection
are stitched, flutter as a kind of signal flag
in our backyard. Despite a polar vortex
of distrust and cascade of unbearable headlines,
a call to recognize the subtle fabric
in these communities that quietly multiply
and defy the old sitcom scripts
on continuous loop. Embrace this
resistance. Honor its promise.

# THE FUTURE, CONAN

DONALD ILLICH

*In The Year 2000 was a sketch in which Conan O'Brien and Andy Richter, or one of the guests, would proclaim it is time to look into the future.*

They'll give us our space cars.
Each meal will come in a tasty pill.
It'll be sunny one day if we wish,
clouds will rain if we need them to.
Conan, the 21st century should have offered
this much. Not the burning wasteland
it's evolving into, a gun in every home,
women racing state to state for pills
to end a pregnancy. Still, we don't give up
when we don't get our robot dogs,
and many of us don't find jobs that pay.
We'll find a way to survive disasters.
Scientists will conquer global heat.
Thoughts and prayers won't be enough;
guns will be broken into pieces.
Women will find safety in this country.
Conan, the future needs work.
Not cue cards from a television show,
but us writing lines we practice
until we believe every word, and
those in power hear them, too.

# WHEN ASKED ABOUT TIME TRAVEL

KATEEMA LEE

> *Dew sparkling…buds bursting…we await the drying day…*
> —"Wild Flowers" by Nikki Giovanni

You say you would travel to the future and plant seeds because the past culti-
vates sins and the present displays them as bouquets. But the sins aren't yours,
and the wilting petals are not your legacy, but they are to the intolerant, so
when you enter a room, you know what you must do. You have to be cherry
blossoms unbothered by wind or time: a deluge of dismissive glances, poisonous
smirks, downpour of side conversations. You were taught to be divine during
weather that propagates weeds. You know you are not perfect, so unattainable
weighs you down. It sits on your shoulders, presses on your chest, gives gravity
a hand. Whenever you speak, you gasp for air. Words suffocate but make their
way around rooms, an empty collection plate. You have no congregation during
storms; sermons are background noise. You know this, so you recalibrate trying
to enunciate, trying to hide the voice of home. You project in ways you know.
When you do this, the weight stealing your breath feels heavier; you continue.
You follow the script, improvise, and smile through puzzled looks. Each day
the weather is always the same: rain, rain, rain!

So, you wait for better times to take root.

# YOU ARE CORDIALLY INVITED TO THE HEAD OF STATE RENAMING CEREMONY

NEHA MISRA

Given the state of affairs,
the state is dispelling the inheritance
of its disembodied head.

No matter how bright or dim
the state of the head of state and your own,
the state invites you to get out of your head to inquire:

How is the state of our nation's heart to summon the source of daily courage?

How is the state of our nation's lungs to breathe together in depth and ease?

How is the state of our nation's gut to know right from wrong?

How is the state of our nation's stomach to discern the pangs of hunger from
greed ?

How is the state of our nation's spine to stand by the values we love to preach?

How is the state of our nation's kidneys to filter the toxic waste?

How is the state of our nation's rest of the body at rest?

How is the state of our nation's head in relation with the soul?

How is our own state in this whole state of affairs?

# I THOUGHT I'D HAVE GOOD NEWS FOR MY DAUGHTER
JESSICA GENIA SIMON

We do not trust women, we fear them
loathe them, try to control them.
I could not wait to show my daughter her face
the President Elect, Vice-President for four years
a beautiful brown face, like her own.
First woman, first Black woman, first South Asian
leader of the free world.

Instead, I woke up afraid again.
Instead instead instead
I rock my daughter to sleep
knowing this country is
less safe
less loving
less
possible for her.
And I want to rip the sky to shreds,
howl for a coven to boil the brew,
conjure the curses to turn all these men
to swine who bow their heads to this villain
and his crew of henchmen, turn
their heads to stone.

While I weep for an America
that could have chosen a bright path
I see the dark past
and yes, a future.
Modern day pitchfork wielding mobs
carry torches back to the Capitol
to see it burn.

I must accept, grieve and move on,
for my daughter, for my spouse
for the others who will come after, but
I will not forget, America,
the day you said No, to me and mine.
I will not forget what could have been.
This is not a forfeit or surrender.
This is (*sotto voce*) a promise
sweet and tender
to rise again.

# REMEMBER THE FUTURE

GARINÈ ISASSI

"WHAT'S YOUR five-year plan?" my father asked me when I was nineteen years old. I stared at him blankly. In my mind, I thought *Well, to stay alive*. There wasn't much else I knew. I wanted to live every day, each day, in the present, go with the flow, and do what I loved to do—sing, write songs, do music, write, write, write. Instead of giving Dad a straight answer, I quoted John Adams who said something along the lines of, "I must study war, so my children can be engineers, so their children can be artists!" That did not go over very well.

I am the grandchild of Ellis Island immigrants (refugees), a G.I. Bill father (fighting a war), an engineer mother (women's lib), and culturally unified peers (no social media). I was the first American generation to truly benefit from the civil rights movement from early childhood on. This setup gave me more education and career choices than any of my ancestors, especially as a girl descended from Armenian heritage—still a super-charged patriarchy.

There were not a lot of us. The boomers were our older sisters and brothers and we got their hand-me-downs. Not exactly Gen X, either, we were dubbed Generation Jones. Born in the '60s, reaching our teens in the sucky '70s, we navigated and adapted to the dynamics we were thrust into. A whole generation of third-born attention-seekers with just enough bravado to be cynical teenagers. We were chock full of sarcastic comebacks. We had too much time on our hands, were too used to being bossed around, and knew too much world history to be optimistic.

I mean, the political and cultural pendulum has swayed so extremely so many times throughout history, that you just know we are due for a repeat— freedom and sensitivity on one side, oppression and indifference on the other. Regardless of the society, the corrupted power of a few always seems to come back.

Many religious and altruistic philosophies have been theoretically accepted in societies, yet, we—the royal "we"—just can't actually *get it* enough to make it stick. We appear to agree on the same ideas that had been repeated over and over, in different words, in different lives: Moses, Plato, Socrates, Brihaspati,

Confucius, Buddha, Jesus, Gandhi, Martin Luther King Jr., and more. They all preached that we should love each other, treat each other as we would want to be treated, and give for the common good, for one world, for all of us. Then, just as positive shifts would start based on their lead, most of them were assassinated.

As that nineteen-year-old, talking to my dad, I somehow didn't remember the future was coming and was already here at the same time. Either way, I suspected that things wouldn't turn out the way everyone said a middle-class girl with straight-A report cards should. That and the fact that when anyone is just reaching adulthood, the future is an ethereal concept anyway. Sometimes the best attempt at planning is asking what's for dinner and then checking if the ingredients are currently in the fridge. It is good enough to say, "I'm doing all right, for now." Meaning that day, that month, that year.

I had no plan established back then, and I was not prepared for the stop/start existence that ensued. I somehow managed to end up on my feet. I went to school. I sang. I worked. I wrote songs. I got married. I wrote. I had kids. I didn't know where I was going. I was taking all kinds of side roads, some great and some awful. I stumbled through it all and learned a lot along the way. But I had the freedom to fall, backslide, get depressed, and get back up again (several times) without fear.

Of course, now, I have no idea how I got this old so fast. Nobody told me that all of those long days of struggle would add up to such short years. The older I get, the more concerned I become about my future, even though I have less of it to be concerned about.

Recent political events put that feeling into overdrive. Looking back over the decades of my adulthood, I know now that it was a luxury to never have to consider the idea that my freedoms as an American could come into question. Or the freedoms of my children, or, my immigrant neighbor, or my friend who is a research analyst in healthcare. I'm a gray-haired American woman on the cusp of a possibly fascist, artificially intelligent future, which may be about to take a quantum leap back to my grandmother's time. Frankly, it scares and depresses me. It makes me more serious and less fun. Don't get me wrong. Sarcasm is still my raison d'être, but it seems inappropriate now.

To put it mildly—I am not happy, but what is good to know is that so many of my adaptable, snarky, liberated friends feel the same. A vast array of people are reacting to the threat. Political history professors are getting millions of followers. Suburban moms are organizing across the country. Journalists are leaving compromised newspapers to start new outlets calling out the injustice. But we can't wander through this the way I wandered through my youth. I seriously feel like we are flying blind—like we are balancing precariously on top of a running animal. Do we need to barricade ourselves? Do we need to flee? Do we need to speak out? Or do we need to resist quietly? We need to remember the future is coming and it is here, regardless of whether we are prepared for it or not.

Y'know what we also need?

A five-year plan.

# WHEN AN AMERICAN SAYS EVERYWHERE HAS ITS PROBLEMS

AVA SERRA

What they mean is—don't trim the roses
Out of my eyes. Stop with the lectures
On invasive growth. Everything we have here,
We took to sow into a secret garden that severs
The excess world from us. Turn your
Yarrow and sweetgrass into a dandelion
Tongue you bury at the bottom of our kudzu wall.
Watch those vines grow and grow and grow.

# AN AMERICAN LAMENT

## CAROLINE BOCK

She's strange, isn't she—strolling through the park at this hour? A starless night with a storm threatening, wind and rain, more rain than we've seen in months. The grass in the park hasn't been cut for weeks. *She's singing now. Would you call it a dirge or lament?* texts one neighbor to another. *Not even in English.* If they knew it was about communal grief, would that make them think differently of her? The words can be interpreted as *our father*, or *our king*, though she prefers *our father* since she is addressing them to his ghost, calling on him to wrap the snow-scented winds around her thinly shawled shoulders, to see the slash of deer, of fox and raccoon that cut through the fir trees, to hear her ask—*snow?* He knows how she loved snow. *Avinu malkeinu*, she sings out. They wonder if one of them should call her cute husband or just be done with her, the strange neighbor night-singing. *Stranger than us. Emoji. Laughing face with tears. Let's call 911 before something happens*, they conclude. Here, she's free of all the regrets of a dutiful life; the only one with her is Pop, a ghost who agrees that she should stroll the park anytime she likes, that snow would be better than rain, that she should have slept with them all, that America should be better, and that she should sing louder. Sing for snow. Sing for tomorrow. *Sing.*

# DEAR AMERICA

MARCELINE WHITE

After *the Sonnet-Ballad* by Gwendolyn Brooks

Who shall we cry to? Who listens to lamentations anymore?
A plague casts shadows over cities; a cough, fever, then lungs last gasp.
Death arrives at an earlier hour. His calling card; sickness. War
darkens sands with spilled blood, children die for lines on a map.
Our leaders print money to feed death machines, justify more
arms with empty words. Glaciers melt, oceans warm, crops collapse.
Sunday was the hottest day ever recorded, the sun's rays bore
through thin atmosphere, gardens silent, no buzz of bees, rasp
of wasps, or the flickering stars of lightning bugs at night. I adore
this world, from its dolphin song to its larkspur and lakes, yet we lack
empathy in our care for it. The world outlasts us, evolves, rebuilds, restores
while we wonder who shall we cry to? Who listens to lamentations anymore?

# MAKE AMERICA GREAT

CHERRIE WOODS

We see you, America—
stripped of your glittering illusion of equality,
bare as a newborn, still wrapped
in the bandages of racist beliefs.

No more facades,
no more staged performances,
no more undeserved trophies for justice
never truly won.

Let's begin with truth.
Let's build a bridge—
from past divisions
to future reconciliations.

Let love be the concrete,
fairness the steel,
hope the columns,
justice the lanes—
driving us toward one another
from different roads,
paths,
and directions—
to a new America
on the other side.

# AMERICA'S FUTURE
## PART III

*The Stupid Words People Say When You Have Cancer*, by Deborah Tomlin.
Charcoal and graphite on paper, 2024.

# RAGING AGAINST THE SKY

JENNIFER RODRIGUES

There should have been a warning—
        a sound or a flash,
a shift in atmospheric pressure.

What could we do with warnings anyway,
        what kind of catch-all
could we deploy to save ourselves?

You can't catch rage, revenge,
        tongue-shaking screams. You can't
contain exhaustion, hard fights.

You could chalk up smoldering tears
        as rain drops, but that's so cliché.
You could tell us these thunderclaps

are not solid states of our ancestor
        women stomping, jumping, throwing
the axe of oppression.

We've built up an ecosystem of
        female torment that collected too many
atoms, too many shells of fear & grief,

too many attempts to stand on our
        uteruses, mouths, breasts, diaphragms
that the whole gathering finally

burst open as scalding acid lands
        on the hair-plugged, toupéed men
below & they begin to melt, liquify.

Some will shatter, some turn to ash &
  blow away when we blow out the
candles of resistance.

Some will pour down into
  the dank, odorous stank of
the earth's sewers.

This eternal storm threatening overhead,
  not forecasted but a welcome prediction
as women take back our lives.

# BIRDIE'S FLIGHT

## K. AVVIRIN BERLIN

I BLAME mitochondrial Eve for all our generations, for first craving light. I see her in my mind's eye, dark like me, gaze fixed on the pomegranate tree of paradise, wanting its sweet juice to treat her tongue, itching to unleash all that we have since become. I count three generations by a single name. My grandmother was Roberta the first. She named my mother, her daughter, after herself, because, "who else?" My name is Roberta, too, but I came third, so I go by Birdie. Now that my grandma is gone, there is no one tethering me to this residence on earth. When I *pas de bouree, chasse, jete*, I'm afraid I won't come down from the ascent, that mine will be a perfect *jete* out the nearest window.

When her mother died last month, my mother, Roberta the second, ran down three flights of stairs, opened the steel front door of our apartment building, and stumbled barefoot onto the snowy street outside wearing nothing but a robe. Her large breasts flopped like ears straining to hear the glisten of new-fallen snow. I thought of calling to her from my perch at the window. *"Come back. Belong to me. Be, for once, my mother, not my ward. Come back, come back, to your little dark bird."* Instead, I turned toward the ballet barre hinged to the wall of my room. I stretched. I moved through *grand battement en cloche* with arms in second, then *tendu en croix*, bestowing a blessing upon the dead each time I passed through first position, priestess of a new order of bones. The arachnid inside me yawned and shifted.

Before the funeral, I went up to my grandmother's building on Tremont Avenue in the Bronx. There was the work of death to be done; papers sorted and stacked; dust swept finally from under the rug. Grandma's apartment complex was a 1950s-era brick tenement, built in the hopeful post-war period when the ethos of public housing and modern architecture briefly met. I took the elevator up to apartment 7J and turned the spare key in the lock. All of my grandmother's things seemed to greet me at once. My head started to spin with the welcome of it all, and I sat down, gripping the edge of the couch.

I waited for the wave of dizziness and hunger to pass. Since the arachnid inside me had first made itself known, I've craved the strangest things. They're not cravings that can be satisfied with a trip to the bodega, though I have those too. More than anything, I want the mineral scent of damp clay as it twists into vessel; a lick of something ancient left scattered on a cave floor; the moss beneath the last stone left unturned; a strip of sugarcane harvested by free people just before the earth burns. Those things being hard to find, I've settled for the saccharine sweet taste of Tootsie Rolls and Whoppers, the salt of Dipsy Doodles, the birthday cake scent of the air just after a candle is blown out.

I steeled myself and began to rummage through the closet. Piles of *Jet* magazines from decades past soon littered the floor. When I was younger—seven or so—I used to comb through the pages of *Jet* to find their "beauty of the week," a bikini-clad Black woman from someplace like Atlanta, Jackson, or Washington, DC. Small, bold type proclaimed her vocation and favorite color. We weren't told what I now know to be true: how working in jobs like "airline stewardess" wore women thin, how they were so often left, as my mother had been, with failed marriages and runs in their stockings, saddled with children they did not know how to love.


AT GRACE BAPTIST CHURCH a few hours before my grandmother's body was laid to rest, I sat on a pew in front of the room where the casket had been laid out. Relatives came and went, talking loudly or not talking at all; wrangling children into coats and carriages; doing what the living do.

My great Aunt Isis, a preacher and my grandmother's sister, pulled me into her vast arms, holding me for a moment in the scented folds of her flesh. "Do you want to sit with your grandmother, Birdie?" she asked.

I shook my head.

She frowned a little. "Go be with your grandmother."

I hesitated, then complied. Creeping into the large empty room, I approached the casket. Gingerly, at a loss for what else to do, I rested my hand on top of the hand I had held so many times in life. Its warm brown had become gray and cool to the touch, like the thick skin of a sea creature who had just arrived on uncertain shores. I remembered how Roberta the first had liked the ocean, how she had kept a conch shell on her coffee table so that its endless water song would always be close at hand, how she had taught me to swim one summer at the pool at Roberto Clemente State Park. The pool had been impossibly crowded, and all around me, brown bodies of varying shades had dived, sunk, and swam. My grandmother had held my hand as I stepped tentatively into the shallow end of the pool.

"I'm scared," I said.

"Of course you're scared." She had peered down at me, the sun meeting her wide-brimmed hat to form a shadow. "You're probably scared shitless. But if all else fails, wade. Wade in the water."

I wonder if crossing over to death will be like learning to swim in a public pool, pressed on all sides by souls becoming accustomed to breathing without air. Even though I'm a dancer, I'm not good with bodies. I had to get used to part-nering in classes and rehearsals, being gripped at the waist by a male dancer. I wasn't good with my own body as it grew; didn't even know what my first blood was when it came in rivulets, then in torrents. I had danced so much that my period arrived late. My body was too athletic a host. I was fourteen when the flood came. I stood in front of my grandmother's casket thinking about water for a long time.

"You're probably scared shitless," I said finally. I paused, watching particles of dust settle in the still air. "But if it comes time to cross, wade. Take off your shoes and wade like we used to." I didn't know what else to say.


LATER THAT EVENING, Aunt Isis the preacher commanded the room.

"For the wages of sin is not death but lovelessness. And my sister Roberta may not have been a churchgoing woman, but she was full up with love."

"Full *up* with love," someone echoed.

Then my mother began to sing. Unbidden, unbeknownst to those who'd planned the order of the day's events, she answered the call of Eve, who, on a single helix of DNA, had held a thousand generations quivering at the thres-hold of release. "Sometimes I feel like a motherless child. Sometimes I feel like a motherless child." Her voice was quiet at first, no louder than a hum. There was a haptic quality to the sound. It moved through bodies, rippling through the folds of flesh and the holding of hands. All at once, I was trembling. I started to move, not in the quick-footed style I had been taught, nor in the corseted mode of classical ballet, but like someone had gutted me, carved out my innards for the auspice they might bring and left only the singed, singing bone. "Sometimes I feel like a motherless child," my mother pulled the notes apart, parsing the grammar of her grief. My spine curved, unbidden. My head hung loose and heavy. I allowed my hand to touch my throat, leaving my elbow at an angle, then follow its arm upward. I went into an arabesque, curving my leg around my own emptiness. "A long way from ho-o-ome."

In the weeks since the funeral, Roberta the second has not worn shoes. She will otherwise dress: skirt, sweater, stockings, lipstick, shirt, but she will not put on her shoes. Her newfound distaste for footwear of all shapes and varieties has cost us her most recent job. I tried catching her off guard, placing shoes on her feet, asking gently, yelling…

"Where I got to go?" she asked one morning before I left for school, having successfully refused shoes once more. "Ain't nowhere on earth for me now."

*Pas de bouree, chasse, jete*, then the divine ascension.

I stumble through my first class of the day, giving the pianist pause. We are rehearsing the "Waltz of the Flowers" from *The Nutcracker*, which we perform each year for the Christmas season.

"What is the difference between hello and goodbye, Birdie? Birdie?" asks my instructor, a tiny, ancient ballerina who reeks of Chanel No. 5 and whose eyes, though her body has declined, remain as sharp and ready to catch imperfections as ever.

"I'm—sorry, I'm not sure what you mean," I mumble.

"Our stage presence should greet the audience. It should say, 'Hello! Here I am.'" I nod, breathing hard. *"Hineni. Hineni. Here I am."*

After class, my finger slides beneath the elastic straining at my waist as I peel off my beat-up pointe shoes. They need a few stitches, but Roberta the first is gone, Roberta who sewed my ballet shoes and took me to dance classes and was my refuge. Stuffing my shoes in my dance bag, I zip my puffy winter coat over my slightly protruding abdomen. I've kept the arachnid a secret so far, but it's beginning to raise its black hairy legs inside me, making its presence known. Soon, I will have to decide whether it will stay in the land of the living or go.

A few girls stare curiously at my stomach when we change, but look away quickly when I catch their eye. I'm used to them casting their gaze over my brown body, noting, no doubt, my thicker ass and thighs. Some are friendly. They smile tentatively and ask how my weekend was, and I say, "fine, how was yours?" in my most upbeat voice. There has always been a divide between me and even the friendliest students at the ballet academy. There are a few other Black dancers, but they share the carefree air of the rich, buying new dance-wear with crisp credit cards while I hoard crumpled one-dollar bills. But I had not only gotten into the academy, I'd also been given a generous scholarship, and, as a native New Yorker, do not have to pay room and board.

"Birdie!" Ms. Marks, the career counselor, calls as I walk through the carpeted hallway toward the elevator. "May I speak with you?" I nod. "Please, sit down." I do. "I know many of our young women want to 'make company' when they graduate, stay in New York, live the life of an Academy dancer." It was true. Seniors like me spoke of nothing else. "But an opportunity has arisen in California that I think may be perfect for you. It's a modern dance company." She hands me a glossy pamphlet. A Black woman graces the cover, her muscles poised mid-flight, toes pointed. "It's in Los Angeles."

"I don't know," I say slowly. "All my life I've wanted to do ballet professionally. It's hard to think of myself as a modern dancer."

"I've watched you, Birdie. All the faculty have. You stay after class and choreo-graph.

And the way you move—it's modern." Ms. Marks looked at me eagerly.

I stared down at the pamphlet in my lap. I thought of the fugues in which I found myself some days after classes ended, fugues that could only be brought down by my ascent to heights that broke the rigid boundaries of ballet. I thought of the six-week fetus inside me, swimming in the waters of my womb. Auditioning for and accepting a spot at a company in California would mean having an abortion, a decision I had not yet made.

"Thanks, Ms. Marks," I say, putting the pamphlet in my bag to read on the bus home. "I'll think about it."

Back uptown, I rifle through my backpack for the key to our apartment and turn the lock, but the deadbolt is on the door. My mother opens it just enough to see me standing on the threshold. I sigh. "Come on, Mom. Let me in." She looks at me, then shouts, her voice cascading down the hallway.

"CUT. Cut paper like skin. Cut skin like sin. I will post it on my wall and refuse to let you in. I will sorrow for my kin."

"So go ahead and sorrow, Mom. Go ahead and sorrow."

When she decides, after careful scrutiny of my face, to let me in, I am met with chaos.

Roberta the second has been stacking books in what is, to her, careful order, all around the apartment. She's placed smaller, more significant objects on top of these teetering structures. We have always had, for our edification and, I guess, for just such occasions, an abundance of homeless books. Books on the floors, books stabilizing tables and propping open doors, books without covers. Calamity books. Books unmoored.

"You took it, didn't you? Didn't you?! Give it back!"

"I didn't move anything, Mom. Here." I rifle through the drawers to find her antipsychotic. My hands scuttle across old receipts, measuring spoons, and cans of cat food until I find the two tiny bottles. "Did you take your medication?"

She glares at me. "Give me my paper! Goddamn you." Blinded by tears, searching for the piece of ephemera that has become so precious to her, my mother leaves no stone unturned. First, she tosses the bills on the TV console onto the floor. Then, her muscles aching with the weight of it, the TV console itself. When she is manic, my mother becomes a superwoman, conjuring strength from without her petite 5'2" frame. At 5'9", I tower over her, but I cower like a small child at her violence. Retreating to my room, I make a quick calculation. Should I leave her here to rave, walk out once more into the night, or stay to show her that I am not afraid, that I will remain with her in this place at the end of her mind? Even if I lock myself in my room, turn off the light and try to sleep, there is no guarantee I'll be able to. As superwoman, Roberta the second has been known to tear doors clean off their hinges, stay up for days on end. As soon as I decide to leave, my thought process is interrupted by the sound of my mother's footfalls. She is pacing rapidly and reasoning loudly with herself. She pauses mid-sentence when she sees me pulling on my boots and stares at me.

"Take off your shoes, for the ground on which you stand is holy."

"Okay, thanks, Mom. I'm leaving, alright? Will you be okay? I'll be home to-morrow."

I SPEAK as if my mother cares to know where I'll be this school night; cares about anything beyond the work of building her structures.

During manic phases, her eyes are black endless pools with a strange focus, fixed on a point in space and time beyond any known coordinates. In the few photos of my mother, I managed to salvage from the piles of my grandmother's things, she is looking directly at the camera, smiling a full-cheeked, gap-toothed smile that reminds me of my own. Now, my mother's gaze sows the soil of an earth rich with crop, but what it reaps I do not know. Where? I cannot follow. We are Mitochondrial Eve and her daughter at the beginning of the world.

"They don't say it, but I know in the dark at night they are still waiting for their daughters to come home," she says softly, encased in the tapestry of thought that has entrapped her these last few weeks.

"Well, I'm home now, Mom," I manage.

Sometimes, in my most furious of dances, swept up in the chariot of my anger, I hear my mother's voice within me, shouting for order while causing chaos, crying out for a witness.

Roberta the second laughs loudly and randomly, the sound breaking like stale bread.

Then, as tonelessly as if the laugh had not just erupted from her diaphragm, she says, "There is always a road north. Just follow the drinking gourd."

I walk outside, swallowing huge gulps of winter air to get rid of the lump in my throat. I look up briefly to measure the sky; to find the drinking gourd and, from its light, drink deep and long and well.

When I arrive home the following evening, EMS workers have encircled my mother, who stands shoeless in the snow. They open the back door of the ambulance with fluid movements that they have performed a hundred times before. I hear one say, "Take her to Harlem Hospital." Above the din, my mother's cries ring out.

"Why are you doing this to me? Why are you doing this to me?" She is shouting to the sightless sky. I do not know why what is done is done, why there should not be another way. But it came down to the shoes, and she would not keep them on.

Do you know what it's like to see your mother after she's been put on tranquilizers? "For ease of transport," the nurses say, like she is an unruly animal. Drugged and drooling, she lets her full weight fall onto me. She is only half aware, but her tears are her testimony. I have long suspected that if we were not poor, were not herded like cattle into public hospitals, my mother would not have returned time and again to their interiors. I have seen the palatial mental health facilities of the wealthy.

THE MORNING I leave for California, I pick up my ballet bag, which will double as my carry-on, and stand for a moment in the doorway of our apartment. My heart has waded in dangerous waters, haunted by past gods. It has danced for its sustenance. Now, it walks down oft-trodden blocks to visit my mother at the hospital. She does not look at me. Her head is tilted toward the ceiling; her gaze is fixed resolutely. Her hospital gown hangs like the layered robes of a pietas. She does not say goodbye.

# MY PRESIDENT IS A BRAT (BOOKISH, RELENTLESS, AMUSING, TENDERHEARTED)

CHANLEE LUU

*After Danez Smith*


My hands and back complain, so I
massage them like cats crafting biscuits, trust
they will always crawl home to bedside unlike the
lesbian swans dropping dead; my world

is shuffling between phage genomics, poems, and paperwork in
a cubicle surrounded by touch-starved books. My president is his
-toric because there is none. Only tender
hugs, clean air, and poppies blooming.

The children's songs are sweet and heard; their hands
filled with kites, chasing a speedy summer breeze. I
get to have a doctor (who pillow talks with the epidemiologist), whom I trust
with my most embarrassing secrets; would I show them/her/him:

how my love makes me swoon like the sight of Mae Ya to
how my President is the janitor whom I tell
my family congee recipe: shredded chicken & lima beans. US,
a functional community so vast, we know which

vaccines and vitamins target each organ system—rivers
of soursop, soup, and sassafras to swallow. Are
we ever going to be fully healed? Is my name safe
on the tongues of our leaders? The cats are meowing to

the moon. Strange, they drink
the milk of black-spotted turtles, teenage and
mutant. My President is the librarian, which
is to say they might not hold

a STEM degree, but they hand-stitch zines of local fish.
Never fails to say, "I don't know, but I'll try," (un-like
the "President"). Puts on their glasses and grabs a
a book—the most beautiful promise.

# THIS IS PARADISE

## NICOLE BAZEMORE

ParadiseFarm ✓ · · ·

♡ 101K  ◯ 536  ◹  ⊓

**ParadiseFarm** This morning, as my alarm went off and I slipped out of bed without waking my husband, I said a prayer of gratitude to the universe. The frost crunched under my boots in the quiet morning as I contemplated the pink, orange, and yellow rays laced through the sky. I milked the cows and fed the chickens, a swirling mass of feathers and clucks at my feet as I gathered warm eggs from the coop for breakfast. Barn chores done, I left my boots at the door and quietly climb the stairs to wake up my family and cook them a delicious homemade breakfast. This is paradise.

3 hours ago

ParadiseFarm ✓ · · ·

♡ 1.2M  ◯ 1,689  ◹ 57  ⊓

**ParadiseFarm** Unpopular opinion: A woman belongs in the kitchen. In my old life as an office drone, I would wake up every morning, dress in dull office attire and languish at my desk, simultaneously stressed from the emails, tasks, and drive by requests from my boss and yet mind-numbingly bored clockwatching. I was exhausted by the water cooler gossip, petty office politics, and passive aggressive messages about who ate the vegan lasagna from the fridge.

Now, though, my schedule is my own. I lovingly cook, clean, and care for my family. I tend the garden, pulling weeds and planting okra, tomatoes, cucumbers, all homegrown organic food. I cook all our meals, clean using homemade products, teach my children our values, and sew our clothes, without being judged by office women as too feminine.

What a blessing to live my best life, in this beautiful farmhouse on our ranch, Paradise.

8 hours ago

ParadiseFarm ✓                    •••

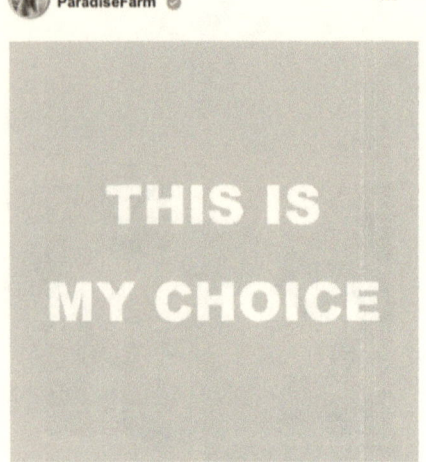

♡ 2.5M  ◯ 22K  ▽ 115              ⊓

**ParadiseFarm** I choose this life, to protect my children, provide nourishing meals, and keep big pharma out of our lives. When I voted, I chose leaders with the same beliefs, who wanted to get the government out of our private lives, to keep disreputable people out of our country and men out of female sports, to protect our children from forced pharmaceuticals and the trans agenda. Because I have free speech and the right to vote. But apparently people only believe in free speech which I vote the same as them.

1 day ago

ParadiseFarm ✓                    •••

♡ 685K  ◯ 313K  ▽ 237            ⊓

**ParadiseFarm** I know a lot of people are upset at the new law, but our country is a dangerous, violent place, but your husband will keep you safe when you leave the house.

A few weeks before the law was passed, I was accosted outside the grocery store. Leaving the store with my children and a full shopping cart, a man approached us, dirty and brown, like he hadn't showered in weeks. Obviously on drugs, he couldn't walk in a straight line. My daughter shrieked and covered her mouth, overwhelmed by the fetid delinquent. I grabbed Amaya and marched right back into the store and complained to the manager.

Of course, running errands is difficult now, since my husband is busy with work, but it's for my safety.

12 hours ago

ParadiseFarm ✓

♡ 57K  💬 1.9M  ✈ 1,020  🔖

**ParadiseFarm** Staying home is my choice. Was my choice, when I had one. The law that was just passed is God's will. It protects men's jobs as the provider of the family. Women should only perform women's work: cooking, cleaning, taking care of children. Yesterday while I was making a pie, Nyla screamed and threw her plate across the room where it hit the wall and slid, leaving a green paste in its wake. Hank and Amaya were in the living room, jumping from one couch to the other. I told them to stop, but I was distracted, cleaning the wall, checking on the bone broth, and ensuring the apple pie in the oven didn't burn. Then a crash and a shriek. I ran into the living room. Hank was crying, lying beside the coffee table, blood leaked down his face, a broken vase on the floor. I reached out to help him but crawled out of my reach, blood dripping on the toffee-colored carpet and crawled onto the white sofa and buried his head, smearing blood into the cushions.

Women's work is not always easy, but God would not give us something we couldn't handle.

ParadiseFarm ✓

♡ 685K  💬 313K  ✈ 237  🔖

**ParadiseFarm** Everyone just needs to calm down. It makes sense that a women's husband or male relative should control her bank account. Listen to this, in 1973 abortion was legalized and the following year women were given the right to open bank accounts. What came next—gas crisis, rampant inflation, sound familiar? Women can't be trusted with money.

18 hours ago

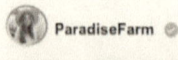

**Error**

Your account has been disabled for violating decency laws.

As a result of the new law banning women from gathering in groups and talking to each other without a male guardian present, women are no longer allowed to create accounts.

Cancel

Learn More

♡ 34K    ◯ 3.9M    ▽ 127K    🔖

**ParadiseFarm** I love my family, love staying home but even I'm not immune from the charms of the devil. I'm ashamed to admit that sometimes envy creeps into my heart. Sitting down for five uninterrupted minutes, adult conversation, peeing without little hands exploring the cabinet under the sink. At these times, I picture my husband sitting in front of his computer in a quiet cubicle, taking a sip of coffee while he types on the keyboard. If you are not careful, envy will snake its way into your soul and latch on.

But you must pray and put your trust in your husband, as the head of the house, and Jesus, as the head of the church. God speaks to me every day, reminding me of my blessings.

Create new account

∞ Meta

2 weeks ago

# WE BELIEVED THE WORLD WAS ENDING

## HOLLY KARAPETKOVA

We believed the world was ending
but would never say so.

We talked about the future
as if it were a given.

We feasted to rid ourselves of hunger,
played songs about silence.

We opened books with a vengeance
but we never read them.

We pined for a way out,
for a meal where no knife ended up in a back,

though of course this was impossible.
We knew a thing or two about violence.

About survival. We saved only our lives,
left everything else behind,

including our better selves,
staring at the same fixed point

and expecting it to move
while the bodies went on

burning around us—
ashes to ashes, so the saying goes.

# POST DOBBS

HOLLY KARAPETKOVA

I'm cultivating a growth mindset.
I'm devoting my body to the national economy.
The market forces want my body to reproduce
increase the labor pool
drive wages down
relational values
parental unit to offspring.
I offer each fetus to the highest bidder
and big data snatches them up
their purchasing power
their acquiescence
their eyeballs, toenails, lanugo
my uterus
acceptable collateral damage
to keep the market place sated
keep the power
of my body in check.
All the generations of calamity
smiling back at me
with the same jagged smile.
A makeshift mouth.
A silence passed down like a cry.

# PULLING PEOPLE BACK

## ERIKA RASKIN

NOT LONG AFTER Trump threw his hat into the ring in 2015, I glanced around the family dinner table, smiled sweetly and said, *Get your fucking passports*. I may have added, *please*, just to be polite.

Eyes rolled and cutlery continued scraping against the plates. My loved ones were used to my chronic worry. The moment passed. (Only some went on to follow my directive.) They knew I'd written my college thesis on the massacre at Jonestown and have been hyper-alert to cults of personality (and the ensuing surrender to fascism) ever since.

For the past decade, I've been rattling off the similarities between Donald Trump and Jim Jones—charismatic sociopaths both—at the drop of a hat. When members of my social circle began practicing avoidance techniques (treating me like the love child of Cassandra and Chicken Little on meth), I decided to just change up my audience.

I wrote a novel warning of the approaching fascism. It features a woman whose son is participating in the large group shrug about the fall of democracy around him. So, she tries to save her grandchildren by taking them out of the country. Without permission.

Because of my old research, I knew that what's happening now—the slashing of the safety net, agency shutdowns and carve outs (the DOGE demolition derby) could be ushered in by a gullible populace. Regular people had participated in their own (*and their children's*) murders at Jonestown, for God's sake. Normal folk can become followers of strongmen when they are deeply unhappy. And that was happening in spades before the election.

People give up agency slowly—and then very, very quickly, until they're practicing straight-up obedience to authority.

Like Seussian rhymes, the repeating patterns of little dictators jump out. Their scams and their insatiable need for fluffing and adoration (remember Trump's whole "Let's go around the table and talk about how honored you are to be in my administration" thing?) Their mastery of shape shifting depending on the audience and manipulating reality through media is twinish, too. The Reverend Jones warped truth via loudspeaker on his compound; Trump: Fox and the internet.

Non-stop propaganda works.

Both men disdain their followers. Seriously, what percent of Trump rally attendees would ever be invited to join Mar-A-Lago? (One of his guys proudly referred to the rank-and-file MAGA foot soldiers as "unclubbable." Which kind of seems a little disrespectful but par for the course.) Jones kept his inner circle lily white.

While I am no expert (in pretty much anything) what I have gleaned is that charlatans succeed by taking advantage of **legit** discontent. In Jim Jones's case, he was able to amass quite a following by preying upon the disaffected. He validated the hurt of his parishioners who'd been systematically excluded from the American dream, who'd been beaten down by egregious assaults. He called out racism and classism, promised an egalitarian community for people willing to work hard to create it. Who wouldn't want to exchange a back-of-the-bus life for a shot at membership in a truly democratic Utopia?

(Other than that whole relocating to a jungle in Guyana thing.)

Strongmen are able to build unlikely coalitions by appealing to variable groups with different legitimate gripes. For instance, the Kennedy MAHA peeps who joined up with their MAGA landsmen have concerns about Big Pharma.

Because they *should*.

All you have to do is turn on TV to witness class action lawyers drumming up business by listing an infinite list of injurious drugs and procedures to see that greed plus a lack of oversight doesn't make for good health policy. There is a lot of suspect shit out there. (See: Sackler Clan, the Oxy peddlers of death.)

And the people who decry the lack of eligibility for certain programs because they were born white poor instead of black? They, too, are right. *Every* American ought to receive equally good educations and opportunities.

It's just that despots skillfully misdirect resentment at other victims of the system. They identify enemies and project their own tactics onto them.

The MAGA adherents whose gripe is about the sick bureaucratic system have a point too. (Have you ever tried to apply for Medicare?) And those who rail about Deep State stuff? They, also, have standing. I know this first-hand because my parents' anti-war and civil rights work during the 60s earned us our own FBI watchers.

(Wherever you are, J. Edgar, being spied on *sucks*.)

Leading me to my final point. There is a wide area where we can agree and work together to *fix* things, rather than enabling a cult to grab hold and feed poison. If the people who hitched their wagons to Jim Jones had instead been treated with the decency they deserved then they wouldn't have followed him to their deaths in Jonestown. So as Trump remakes the country in his image, we must do everything we can to pull his followers back from the abyss. (To be sure, some of them are just evil. But not all.)

It can be done. It *must* be done. Before it's too late.

# ETYMOLOGY OF HOME

## COURTNEY LEBLANC

Arlington: Proper noun

Etymology: From the Old English personal name Ælfred + Old English *ing*
("called after") + Old English *tūn* ("estate")—"estate named after Alfred"


Sometimes I forget the place I've called home
for sixteen years is considered southern—we wear
the Mason-Dixon like a corroded crown, floating
just above our head.

This summer I'm reminded Virginia is indeed
in the south, sweat rivers down my back
as I hike my dogs through the park, the canopy
of green providing little relief.

Robert E. Lee once lived here, named his home
Arlington and in true southern fashion, Confederates
are honored here. Gone now are the statues that once
watched over city squares and grassy picnic areas,
the losing side somehow still presiding.

It's not hard to draw parallels from then to now—the unrest
that haunts our country like a hungry ghost. I try to not lose
faith but we are a country that so often clings to the wrong
things: money, greed, success measured in the square footage
of our homes, the size of the sparkle on our ring fingers,
the color of our skin.

Still, I love Arlington: the sun tiptoeing across my skin
as I walk my dogs through the streets I've memorized,
the neighbors I know by name, the ones who water
my garden and get my mail when I'm gone. Here
was the first place I felt I belonged, here was the first
place that felt like home, here is a place I will fight for.

# WHEN YOU FIND YOURSELF

## PATRICIA FUENTES BURNS

When your house is white, your apples fresh, your sheets have stripes. When you slide through red, turn down the news, and lose your train of thought. When you have your daily wine, your run, your podcast in your ear. When you read one hundred books, when you order out too much. When you don't have Sunday supper, when on Mondays you make soup. When you clean the bath, the stairs, the stove, when you scrub your nerves away. When you never knew your father, when you plan to live a long life. When your closet's full of board games and your yard is nice and flat. When your balcony is for smokers, your doormat is soaked in rain. When you like to sing, you like to hum, when you know half the song by heart. When you cry for nothing, beg for something, fear someone you know. When you have a list of movies. When you want to see the stars tonight. When you find yourself alone one day with nothing much to do. When you chat, you laugh, you sob, you crack your joints and close your eyes. When you walk on trails and go too far, when it suddenly gets cold. When there's no one you can call at night. When your birthday is the best day, your gifts in patterned paper and all the cards about love. When you work you save you count you wish. When you hide you run you drop a knife. When you see a word in writing and wonder how it sounds. When you want to be the light. When you burn your fresh candle to the wick. When it's wanted, when it's not. When you run away from home but turn because where is there to go. When you decorate the house and seek the perfect red. When you've lived in this town all your life, when you're always feeling new. When your lifelong friends are a mystery one day, when you forget your partner's age. When you suffer from a sunburn, when your hot tea scalds your tongue. When you're running out of money and you're also short on luck. When love is love and hate is strong. When the jobs are too precise, when you make up your own life. When you trade your puzzles, write your dreams, have good recipes to share. When you thank your future self. When you leave and tell a tale. When you love to tell the tale. When you live to tell it still.

## AS THE QUEER SEER SEES IT;
## OR, FOLLOWING THE COURSE OF EVENTS
## TO THEIR MOST LOGICAL CONCLUSIONS

PIÉRRE RAMON THOMAS

Rigged, no blue:
Dried up waters.
Impenetrable red wall
Surrounds us trapped
Who, like mice in a maze
As convoluted as stairs in *Labyrinth*,
Trample one another,
Scramble about.

Clandestine rendezvouses
For *him* and *I*
And *her* and *her*
Because Pharisaic black robes
Made *us* a crime again.
The color lavender increasing,
Changing its symbolism to mean
Protection, from the eye of the law.

The poor able to give birth
No longer pray for "healthy babies"
But for "no complications":
Complications equal pain, unendurable;
Complications equal death, unnecessary.
"Better to be rich and childless
Than poor and pregnant,"
Mice chitter among themselves.

Whitening of the populace manifested
As envisioned by white hoods:
Extirpation of Black made complete
Because Black means *a weapon in the hand;*

Brown means, "Go back to Mexico!"
Even if Brown means South America or Turtle Island.
Jesus enforced upon all
But not Jesus from The Gospels;

Socialist Jesus re-killed here;
Image of Capitalist Jesus erected in place.
(So blond-haired, so blue-eyed be Capitalist Jesus
Like the non-Middle Easterners who conjured him.)
"Feed the poor," the Socialist charged?
May they starve and be thrown in jail, says the Capitalist.
"Take care of the children," the Socialist directed?
Put 'em to work! Let 'em earn their keep! says the Capitalist.

"Welcome the stranger?"
Round 'em up! Funnel 'em out!
"Love thy neighbor?"
Not if they don't look like me!
Or be man like me!
Or love like me!
Or worship like me!
Or politick like me!

Undulating Old Glory:
Now tattered, unfamiliar on the ground.
What once symbolized,
"A more perfect Union"
Represents, in its time,
"A return to the Good Ole Days."
Future is regress,
Going backward moving forward in time.

# AFTER MY CHILD'S MEDICINE STOPS WORKING, THE HOSPITAL SOCIAL WORKER ASKS ME IF I USED DRUGS DURING MY PREGNANCY

HANNAH GRIECO


Most days I'm hard, steel spine, a mother
fucker who doesn't need sleep or soft-eyed looks.

I don't need sleep, soft looks, just some fucking
peace of mind. Most days, I'm here for any peace,

any piece at all. Most days, I'm here
handing out pills, reminding on repeat,

reminding him "your pills" on repeat.
Most days he doesn't sleep, you dig?

Most days he doesn't sleep, and I dig
a deep hole, you know? And close my eyes.

I close my eyes and bury myself deep.
You sit there, your keyboard, your badge. *Look.*

You sit there. You type. You don't look at me.
Most days I'm hard, steel spine, a mother.

# FIREFLIES AND DANDELION WINE

## CLAUDIA WAIR

LESLEE SPENT THE AFTERNOON foraging for dandelions. The leaves would go into the evening's salad; the blossoms were for winemaking. At home, she washed the plants, steeped the petals in boiling water, and covered the brew with a cloth. Then she cleaned up and took the chicken out of the fridge for dinner.

Her boyfriend, Ray, would arrive soon. He'd said he had something important to talk to her about. She couldn't help but be excited when she heard those words. Leslee was more than ready to take the next step in the relationship, and decided that if he didn't propose, she would.

She wore her favorite yellow dress, which contrasted perfectly with her dark brown skin. After putting on a little makeup, she returned to the kitchen to make the salad.

Ray arrived right on time. But he seemed preoccupied during dinner, and his brown eyes avoided hers. Nerves, she told herself.

When they finished the washing up, Ray took her hands in his. She grinned and bounced on her toes.

"I got a new job," Ray said, his eyes focused on her hands.

"*What?*" she asked. A knot formed in her throat. "You never mentioned you were applying for jobs."

"It's my dream job. Senior technical writer with an environmental policy organization. I didn't want to tell you in case I didn't get it. You see...I have to move. I'm leaving New DC, Les. I'm...I'm sorry."

She pulled her hands from his grasp.

"Where is this 'dream job'?"

"Out West. In Washington State," he said quietly.

"When do you leave?"

"Next Friday. I already gave my notice at work. So, we'll have the whole week to spend together before I go."

Leslee folded the dish towel and hung it over the oven handle.

"No," she said, putting away the dishes. "You must have a lot to do before you go. I don't need to see you."

"But I thought—"

She turned to face him, hands on her hips. "You applied for a job across the country without telling me. Then you quit your job here without telling me. So, no. I don't need to spend any time with you next week. Good luck with your dream job, Ray. I hope you like it out West."

"But—"

"Get out."

"I'm sorry, Les. I should have told you."

"Damn straight you should have told me. Now go. Goodbye."

"Bye, Les," he said softly. "Good luck."

He left.

She stared at the closed door, screamed at it, then sank to the floor as her world fell apart.

LESLEE WOKE UP LATE with puffy eyes. She spent an hour writing in her journal where misery, rage, and hopelessness spilled onto the page. She sketched a portrait of Ray, an arrow through his heart. It made her feel slightly better.

Later, she climbed to her building's wildflower-covered rooftop, where she sat on a bench listening to the hum of the community's bees. She watched the slowly spinning wind turbines on the distant hills. Her mind went over every encounter, every conversation with Ray over the last few weeks. Her heart pounded with fresh humiliation—how could she have thought he was going to propose?

Leslee looked out over the city. She was among the first generation to be born in the post-Rise metropolis, built after the oceans rose and submerged the original Washington, DC. At the thought of the devastation the climate disaster left, she chided herself for moping over a broken heart. Apart from losing Ray, her life was great. At twenty-five and fresh out of art school, her impressive portfolio had earned her a spot in the brand-new apartment complex, *The Muse*, in the arts district of New DC. Her guaranteed minimum income was enough to live simply, and she used the money she earned from her art for little extras like winemaking supplies.

She closed her eyes and took a deep breath. She should get back to work. A half-finished painting sat on its easel, waiting.

Leslee finally rose and descended to her studio, situated on the top floor of her building. The space had plenty of natural light and extensive views of the city. Here, the smell of paint fortified her. Here, she was in control.

She threw open the windows and sat in front of the easel. Soon, the feel of the brush in her hand soothed her. She found her rhythm and her heart rate slowed. The painting was of the Juneteenth parade last summer. People of all races gathered to commemorate the important day. There were food carts, musicians, and vendors selling buttons and t-shirts.

She worked late into the night. When the painting was finished, it would go to the New DC Convention Center in time for this year's Juneteenth celebrations. Well after midnight, she put down her brush and cleaned up. Physically and emotionally exhausted, she took herself to bed.

EVERY SECOND Thursday evening, the community center in *The Muse* complex was abuzz with writers, potters, actors, musicians, and more, sharing their latest work and socializing. Normally, she'd enjoy the presentations and the exchange of ideas, but now, without Ray by her side, she just wanted to be back in her apartment.

She went home early and curled up on her bed. Memories of the good times with Ray, rage over their last conversation, the futile hope that he'd return, all competed with one another in her mind. He was gone, and Leslee, like an unwanted pet, stood abandoned on the side of the road.

Sleep came at last. In her dreams, she shouted to get Ray's attention, but he didn't hear her.

The next morning, an idea for a new project materialized. Something that would keep her mind busy and away from thoughts of Ray. She picked up her phone and called her grandmother.

"Hi Nana. Can I come by and visit?"

"Yes, sweetheart! I'd love to see you."

After lunch, Leslee caught the Metro to her grandmother's district, then hopped on the streetcar to her apartment. Once inside, she told her Nana about the breakup. Her grandmother hugged her close.

"He was a nice boy, but obviously not for you. He's put his career first, which is understandable at this age. I know it'll hurt for a little bit, but it will do you good to be on your own for a while."

"Maybe," Leslee said. Then she shook herself out of her funk and got to the real point of her visit. "Nana, can I look at your pictures from the time before the Rise? I want to paint some things from the past."

Her grandmother scoffed. "Why do you want to look backwards, child? Life is so much better now."

"I want to preserve history, *our* history. And I want people to appreciate what we have."

"Well, the Rise had already begun before I was born," her grandmother said. "You've got to understand, life in those days wasn't good. There were people living in tents on the street. People died of easily treated diseases because they couldn't afford health care. The police killed innocent Black and brown people. No indeed, those days were *not* good.

"Then, when I was ten years old, the waters rose high enough that we had to be evacuated. They sent us to a refugee camp in Virginia. Hang on, I'll get the photo album."

Her grandmother rooted in her closet and came out with the book of photographs. She flipped through the pages and stopped at one. "This was our house before the Rise. It was in an area of Old DC called Anacostia. My father inherited the house from his parents, and it would have come to me if...well, the Rise made that impossible."

Leslee examined the red brick townhouse. "Did you have solar panels on your roof, or a garden?"

"Neither. Solar panels were expensive, and the roof wasn't designed to bear the weight of a garden. My mother grew a few vegetables in our backyard. The neighborhood was known as a 'food desert'—grocery companies didn't care that Black people didn't have stores in their neighborhoods."

She turned the page. "Here's my mother at the hospital, holding me just after I was born. In those days, you needed insurance to get medical care. If you were poor, you were out of luck. I thank God for the National Plan now.

"Oh, here's one. This is my father standing in front of the Old Capitol."

"I remember seeing this in history class," Leslee said. "What gorgeous architecture!"

"It was built by enslaved people, for the benefit of the men who kept them enslaved." Her grandmother shook her head.

Leslee ran her finger along the lines of the building in the photograph. She'd learned all about that period of history, along with Jim Crow, civil rights, and the second women's movement of the 2030s. So much was wrong before the Rise prompted important social reforms.

With her Nana's blessing, she borrowed the photo album. Then she headed home and immediately got to work.


SPRING TURNED to summer, and Leslee bottled her dandelion wine. The golden beverage would be ready to give as holiday presents in winter. There'd be an extra bottle now that Ray was gone. She told herself that was fine; she'd keep it for visitors.

Once she'd cleaned up the kitchen, she went to the roof to watch the fireflies. Scientists reintroduced the endangered species a year ago. Leslee watched the miraculous creatures flash green-gold as they flew through the darkness.

She went to bed still in awe of the fireflies, and in the night, she never once dreamed of Ray.

THE ART SUPPLY SHOP was in the center of *The Muse* complex. It stood between the pharmacy and a cafe, across from the grocery store. Leslee bought oil paints, sketch pads, and a few synthetic sable brushes.

When she reached her apartment door, she found a bouquet of flowers waiting for her. She read the attached card.

> *I miss you,*
> *Ray*

"Well, well, well," she said, and brought the flowers inside. She placed the vase of pink and white blossoms on her table and sat down. It had been almost two months since Ray left town.

"I should probably throw you away," she told the flowers. "But you're pretty, and you'll remind me that Ray knows what he's lost." She was tempted to call him but fought the urge. Instead, she took her art supplies up to the studio.

She continued working on her pre-Rise family history series, based on the pictures from her grandmother's album: the family home, a picnic on the banks of the Anacostia River, and the refugee camp where her grandmother grew up.

Her phone rang. It was Ray.

"Hey, Les. Did you get the flowers?"

"Yes. They're pretty. Thank you."

"Good. Good." He paused. "I just wanted you to know I've been thinking about you."

"Well, thanks, I guess, but what good does it do to tell me? I'm on the East Coast and you're on the West."

"But...what if you came out here? I've looked into it, and they have an arts program just like New DC's. You could keep painting."

Leslee was quiet for a long moment. The prospect was so tempting. To be with him again. To start fresh in a new city—

"Les? You there?"

"Yeah, I'm here. I was just thinking about what you said. I'm sorry, Ray, but the answer's no."

"But we were so good together."

"My life is here," she said. "I'm not leaving my family to move across the country and take a risk on this relationship."

"I just miss you so much."

"Look, you made a decision: to move and advance your career. At the time, that was more important to you than our relationship. So, it's time to move on, Ray. Get involved in the community, meet new people. Then you won't miss me so much."

"I take it you don't miss me."

"That's not true. I *do* miss you. But not enough to pull up roots and join you."

"Well, then, I guess this is goodbye."

She hesitated, then closed her eyes.

"Yeah, Ray. It's goodbye."

They wished each other luck and ended the call. Leslee put the phone down and stared at it. She'd surprised herself with her quick decision to stay in New DC. If he'd called her a month ago, she wouldn't have been so sure.

Her heart still ached, but like she told Ray, it was time to move on. She picked up the phone and, before she could change her mind, deleted his number.

FALLEN LEAVES crunched beneath her shoes as she walked to *The Muse*'s gallery. The venue was packed for the opening of her first solo show, The Rise: A Family History. She explained her inspiration, her process, her vision. She sat for an interview with a reporter from the *New Post*'s art section. She shook hands, posed for pictures. Her face ached from smiling. When it was all over, she went to bed exhausted but thoroughly content.

Leslee woke to enthusiastic reviews. Everything from her use of realism to the historical subject matter was praised. She jumped up and down in her living room, unable to contain her elation. Then it hit her—*this* was more crucial to her happiness than any boyfriend. She could live without Ray, but she couldn't live without her art. This truth sank in like rain on parched earth. The joy that had disappeared when Ray left returned.

THE DANDELION WINE was ready. Leslee opened the first bottle, poured herself a glass, and took a sip. Delighted with the heady, sweet flavor, she printed and affixed the labels she'd designed. Standing back, she regarded her handiwork with satisfaction before returning to her studio.

She started sketching as soon as she sat down. The subject was her own happy self in her favorite yellow dress. Arms lifted and face tilted upward, she stood on her rooftop at night, a crescent moon and stars overhead. Wildflowers grew at her feet and fireflies lit up the night around her.

The self-portrait would go into her next show, but she would never sell it. It would hang in her living room as a reminder of how good life was right now; that she'd gotten over Ray; that she lived in a society that valued her life and her work. And when things got hard, she'd look at the painting and remember her happiness in this moment, and she would always know how to find her joy again.

# DRAWING ANIMALS

## DAVID TAYLOR

ABBY BOLTED from the theatre as the lights came up and revealed rows of people slowly rising to leave. She felt the need to move. She'd been immersed in the Baja Sea on the screen, the Sea of Cortez, practically gulping the brine.

She kept straight on the sidewalk. She felt disoriented by that immersion, by the sequences of the undercover team's fight to shut down a black market that was destroying these gorgeous sea creatures. They glistened like fiberglass surfboards and were so insanely lustrous. Like water angels, the sea colors streaming off the creatures as they arced out of the surf. The little porpoises were slick and pearly and always smiling (that's how their mouths are shaped). You could understand how some people thought these creatures held the key to eternal youth.

But it was so insanely wrong-headed to steal that secret to youth by *killing* them! Old people throwing heaps of cash to get youth back. And getting others to pay *them* five or ten times that much! It made her head throb.

People did insane shit all the time. Cliché human.

She was also kicking herself. Shouldn't she have known the story before? How could she call herself a biologist (okay, biology minor) and *not know about the world's smallest marine mammal*? And its near extinction? She was so lazy. Just like her father. She could see so many line drawings in her head, how they came alive with tinted wash, but she didn't sit down to make them. Or rarely.

The documentary wasn't surprising or fresh in how the sequences unfolded. The visual tropes were stale. It barely captured the gut punch of the corruption.

Walking (she loved living in an LA neighborhood within walking distance of the Regal), scenes replayed in her head. She saw that blue light rise off the water and the porpoises breaching. And that first chilling scene of the good guys starting a stakeout: the pitch blackness where the former FBI dude barks out what they're doing—that was messed up! Her heart was racing. Driving at crazy speeds through the night to keep the bad guys in view, then abruptly seeing a panorama of the bay.

She could see herself in that van, decked out in the same dark jumpsuit and wool hat as the others, feeling ice-cold, heat strapped tight under her armpit, pumped to take down whoever was grifting to kill the little porpoises. Whether or not she would, who knows? She was totally swept up in the chase. But also, she saw how it could be better. Her ink lines could tell the story better than film.

The sidewalk glided beneath her feet in the Silver Lake night. Thinking about the film again, she could tell that the nonprofit dude, Marco, was into the undercover shit too. He tried to sound chill on camera. But. She pulled out her phone and flogged the keys, researching. Marco's nonprofit had an LA address, so he probably lived in LA too. She found his bio and contact info easily. Probably best not to text him though. Older guy, he might spook. Email better. She put the phone away. For the rest of the walk, she composed a message in her head. Saying what?

Could she interview him for her school magazine? She got home, and before she turned off her bedroom light, she hit *Send*.

By morning, she had an answer. By noon, she had a lunch appointment the following week. His office was all the way across the city so that would be a bitch. But she was pumped.

The day of the lunch, it took her two transfers to get to his place. She got off the second bus worried she was late. The first bus driver said something that showed he thought she was a high school delinquent. It made her worry she had dressed too young. Making the transfer, she felt like a migrant. She reached the front desk of the office, behind the glass of one of many small office buildings, and got her breath back. She asked for Marco.

When he appeared, he looked scruffier than she expected. Distracted. His curly hair was flecked with gray, and his thin beard looked like it hadn't been tended in a while. He seemed absent-minded. Was she hungry? he asked. No? He suggested they go next door for coffee. She got a water and they sat at a table outside.

He didn't say anything immediately, so Abby started. She told him how the film about his film had stayed with her. For days, she kept seeing the images of that porpoise, the vaquita. And then the poaching gang, and the undercover team.

Marco shook his head. Had she said something wrong? He said he was disappointed with the documentary. Film had seemed cool, and through the long production months he was sure they had something great. But six months after it had trickled into theaters, it didn't feel like it was making a difference at all. Nobody went to theaters. A pebble tossed in the water.

Abby absorbed that. She suggested that a graphic novel could reach a younger audience. "Like me, for example," she said. "I don't go to the movies much. But I always check out new graphic novels. The *vaquita* story seems perfect for a graphic novel."

She hadn't expected him to get it. But they got talking about comics they loved, the medium's ability to capture grit and excitement. Turned out he was a fan. It was the right play.

"*Maus* was my first," he said. "I'd never had such an intense experience with a book before." True, Spiegelman was an early one for her, too. She had always drawn creatures, she said, but *Maus* showed her a new level, both metaphoric and visceral. Funny, now that she was technically at Harvard (albeit remote), she kept finding new ways to draw stories.

Marco scratched his beard, looked up at the awning. He didn't seem sold. Was he daydreaming? "There was another one," he said. "I can't remember the title."

The waiter put the check on their table, and Marco picked it up. Their conversation was dropping off with longer pauses. She named a couple more favorites: *Persepolis*, and Joe Sacco's *The Fixer*. Sacco's inky blacks and ragged lines. The faces he drew! Actually, she could see *The Fixer* as a model for Marco's poaching story, its mood. Sacco had all those shadows where the characters' faces stood out in chunky relief, their features squared off and ugly.

Behind her eyes, though, she was starting to get bored. It was time to go.

Marco looked surprised that she gushed over old Sacco's rough line drawings.

"You can't look away from them," she continued. "And the landscape of his Sarajevo, all blacked out, broken windows with the Holiday Inn sign. Those spiny weeds coming up through the pavement? His detail is incredible."

Talking about it brought it back. As a girl, she tore through that book in a day, marveling at the noir flashbacks and time sequences, even the clouds— weird, bulbous with cross-hatchings. The lines told the story! She was into the gritty, horrific pages and the gutter-like pull of his panels. Burned-out tanks, smoke billowing in curls out their hatches, they were magic. But really it was in the characters. He made the reader care about a double-crossing lackey, someone consumed by logistics and counting change, coin by coin. For a tale of corruption against natural beauty, Sacco pointed the way.

The look on Marco's face told her she had sold it. He was quiet, but tapped something into his phone, then looked up past the umbrella as if calculating something. He asked how long she would need to finish a draft.

She had no idea. She said a date three months later.

"Fine," he said.

*Fine.* That's how things got done. She was starting to feel like an adult. You squeeze out an email after a movie, and a few days later you got a project going. To seal the deal she offered to sketch out a sample page. Just a few panels to show the look and feel of the book she was envisioning, so they could discuss.

He nodded quickly. "I love it," he said. He told her to send the sample when she could.

On the bus ride home, she allowed herself a smile. She fantasized a bit: a screening someday of a film describing her own entrepreneurial start: a sticker supply business in fifth grade where she sketched monster-themed designs. Her classmates couldn't get enough of them! She loved most the plushy yellow monster with the goofy grin. That was her. *That was the first time I thought, maybe I can do this*, she told the interviewer in the film.

For her high school cartoons she had churned out so many panels, she thought as the bus pulled away from the central library. She imagined the panels looping around and up the grand staircase into the library. Abby had dreams of having all of her stories in the LA library. Maybe the book with Marco would be the first.

The bus felt too small to contain her and all the things in her head. She looked around at the other passengers. An old woman two rows up was talking to herself, forehead pressed against the glass as the pavement reeled by. Two teenage boys sidled down the aisle and looked around, uncertain whether to sit or keep standing. Life in the city, she thought. This was her palette. She looked closer.

In another half hour, she'd be back at her parents' house. That fall, she'd be across the country, back in her college dorm room. In two years, she'd have her degree. Then what?

Back home, she sat at the drafting table—old school. She laid out the blank page. Without thinking too much, she started pushing the soft graphite across it: a first long gravelly horizontal suggested the shore. Is that what it was? In that moment, she didn't know. She didn't know enough of the story, she thought.

It was a nightscape, she realized. Baja. Then came an image from the film, a nondescript low-lying port. Warehouses that were home to gangs exporting the sea creatures. It was just a few hours' drive from her home in LA but it was a world away.

Her uncle's neighborhood in Mexico City's outskirts gave her a mental image of the streets and sounds and smells—the birreria on the corner, old trucks belching smoke on the piers, workers back from a day's shift. With her head-phones filling in the night, she started slashing at the paper in short strokes of hashing. The inky wash would finish the atmosphere.

EIGHT WEEKS LATER, after Marco had marveled at those first panels, Abby had an air ticket for the short flight to Mexicali and was looking out the portal over that same landscape in late afternoon shadows. The scrubby hills inland poked above the raw stretch of rooftops, the sea.

Abby's Spanish was abysmal. Her mother never spoke it with her. So she was glad to see Marco's guy in the airport holding a sign with her name in magic marker. Her name! The fact that it was in magic marker made her feel good.

He looked young, though not as young as her. His back looked skinny as he hauled her bag to the Toyota parked outside the terminal. She knew she was the youngest VIP that he'd ever given an airport pickup. And she *felt* like a VIP. This wasn't like the gigs that friends in her drawing group talked about. They had clients in fashion or online media. Because Abby had put out into the uni-verse her love of nature, she got this: the sun beating on her neck and a ride in an ancient, stifling Corolla through dusty streets. The life of an artist. As they turned one corner, she recognized a street that she had sketched for the sample and felt a spark.

They parked and the driver led the way up a narrow wooden staircase, flimsy, to a little office with Marco's nonprofit logo on the door. Inside there was a desk with a laptop on it, surrounded by a couple of chairs. She recognized the stakeout room from the undercover footage. In the documentary, they had staged a re-creation of the operation. Everything had looked newer, at least not shabby. The cinematographer had totally soaked up the Baja light, and the night scenes had a tropical blue. The reality was just blinding.

This wasn't what she expected. It *was* shabby. There was dust and a wrapper on the floor where the sunlight hit. But she smiled, seeing the lines that led her there.

# SUMMER SCHOOL (PRINCE EDWARD COUNTY, VA)

KATHERINE E. YOUNG

The year I skipped tenth grade
they made me take English in summer school.
Miss Odessa Harvey didn't really know
what to do with a student who hadn't failed
so she gave me the textbook
and left me alone in the auditorium
of the old Moton School where the county
held summer classes even though there was no a/c.
It was the same, the very same textbook
that my sixth-grade English teacher
who also hadn't known what to do with me
had assigned me years before
so I sat beneath the oscillating fan
and patiently filled in the blanks for a second time
not knowing I sat in the very spot where
Barbara Johns had announced the school strike
demanding equal treatment for black students
and an end to classrooms in tar paper shacks
before she led the student body
down to the county courthouse
and into the annals of Brown v. the Board of Education.
The tar paper shacks had vanished long ago
and they'd subdivided the auditorium
where Johns spoke into classrooms
but if I'd known to ask, plenty of folks
still remembered Barbara Johns;
one of my own teachers had marched
to the courthouse that day.
By 2001 the building had become a museum.
I took my son to hear speeches
on the fiftieth anniversary of the school strike;
my one-time classmate, youngest son

of the Reverend L. Francis Griffin
gave the invocation. The new principal
of what had once been the whites-only
segregation academy gave a speech
about healing that stopped just short
of admitting wrong
and for a brief, sunny moment
white people breathed easier
felt somewhat less ashamed.
In September planes hit the towers
and once again, everything changed.

# A GREAT DAY FOR A BALLGAME

## RICHARD PEABODY

I'M THINKING about Fielding Dawson.

I've always believed that "Fielding" was a nickname owing to his prowess at baseball.

Probably not.

You see, some flyers hit the floor while I was moving boxes from one side of my office to another.

A three-panel foldout with a poem as the centerpiece, two photos of Dawson (one with a hat), plus dates and times for an upcoming Lecture and Reading in April at Duke University in 1975.

Time really does "FLY."

There's a typewriter in one photo. A list of some of his books—*An Emotional Memoir of Franz Kline, Black Mountain, The Greatest Story Ever Told*, and *A Great Day for a Ballgame*.

I realize that Bull City Studios in Durham printed the flyers.

I've been there.

Dawson died in 2002 at age 71.

He attended Black Mountain College and then was drafted, serving in Germany by becoming an Army cook.

Serving while serving.

After his release he lived in NYC and wrote twenty-two books over the next fifty years. He loved stream-of-consciousness and was considered avant-garde. If you haven't read him yet, you should. Black Sparrow Press printed a lot of his titles.

But back to the beginning—

Holding the flyer in my hand. Realizing I hadn't thought of him in decades let alone reread his work.

He'd been forgotten. Not only by me. Nobody I know in the lit world has mentioned him in passing.

And yet, his work is quirky fun. And twenty-three years now since he left the planet he's nowhere to be found.

He still makes me smile.

So it goes, as Kurt Vonnegut taught us. We're here and then poof, we're gone. And all our personal struggles and daily escapades are lost to time's passage. Not something I ever dwelled on when I was younger.

It will happen to you, and to me, and to my wife and kids, and every poet and writer I hold dear. In the day-to-day we tend to forget how actually everything is finite.

The litany of names of all the poets and writers who have passed away in the last year alone is more than I can bear.

Still, the bad times fade away.

Things change.

The Orange Felon will eventually die.

The cycle of good and evil will shift.

I'll be watching the stream for the bodies of my enemies. Glance up from Dawson's book, *The Orange in the Orange*, and see them float right past me before disappearing around the next bend.

Then I will bask in the warming sunlight as the season shifts and remember to tell my stories while I still can.

# BUT WHAT'S ON THE TEST?

## HILDIE S. BLOCK

CHECK THE VEHICLE:

I pulled up into the old mall parking lot, now a rough-hewn bouquet of wild-flowers eking up through the asphalt fault lines. At the far edge it drops off with no barrier and there is a reservoir that was once a fountain, but now squeaks with spring peepers and a mated pair of mutant mallards.

And flashes of sentient discarded plastic bags.

You know, when I was your age, I couldn't wait to drive.

You were never my age.

EYEROLL.

Get out of the car.

Just like that? You are going to let me drive???

No, we are going to walk around the car and make sure it's okay.

PANIC.

It's not okay? We just drove here. Did you not check before we left?

Just get out. I mean, to me it meant independence.

You know what we learned in driver's ed?

I looked at her. Sincerely curious.

We learned that cars are murder tools. Weapons. We watched bloody videos of crashes. One, after the next. After the next.

My dad wouldn't let me drive until I pumped his gas twenty times.

You and dad don't have gas cars. Where even is a gas station anymore. Is there one downtown?

I know. But maybe I should have had you plug it in. Or told you what to do if it dies in the middle of nowhere.

Like the car wouldn't call for help.

It would. I know. And you have a phone.

I get out of the car and look over at the white stone behemoth that used to be where all the THINGS came from. Before the drones just brought them straight to you. I looked at the old movie marquee. I thought about the food court, the video arcade.

CHECK THE EXTERIOR.

Mom, when did this scratch happen?

What? I don't know. It's just a ding. It gets polished out during the annual treatment.

Are the tires supposed to look like this?

Yes. Exactly. They inflate when you start the car. Unless you use it in hover.

I'm just stressed out by all of this. Calling for ride share is so much easier. Or the tram. Or just vid-vising. I mean, it's just so much.

STARTING THE CAR.

Get in the driver's side. Let's give it a try.

I remember the first place I drove. I went down by the river and just watched planes taking off and landing. I drove to my friend's house. I stopped by the market and bought a pint of ice cream. I couldn't stop smiling. I could do anything.

The first thing my mother said to me when she handed me the keys, back when they were actually still keys. "This car will not make it to California." Because we both knew what I was thinking. Freedom to go anywhere, everywhere, the furthest place I could imagine.

Okay, so I just push this button?

NO! WAIT! STOP!

First, safety. Then check all your viewers and gauges. Then maybe put your foot on the brake. Now push the button.

You know my first car actually roared when you gave it gas.

Was it a dinosaur? No, don't answer that.

Actually, it ran on fossil fuel so you could make an argument.

Your generation really made a horrible mess. It's like you were just a bunch of spoiled kids eating all the candy and then complaining your stomach hurt.

I know.

DRIVE.

Move your foot from the brake to the accelerator. We used to say give it gas. But we also used to say dial the phone and roll down the window.

Where will you go when you get your driver's license?

Pilot's license, Mom.

Right, pilot's license, I keep forgetting they changed the name.

I'm not sure. Maybe to Great Falls?

To the park?

Yeah. Just to get there faster. I mean, if I had the jet pack like Amari, but you think those are FINGER QUOTES dangerous.

Anyway, go to the falls and just walk around. Even that sounds stupid.

It's not.

Yeah, it is. But I still think that's what I'll do.

You have a ways to go before then.

I know. But I think to imagine it.

# THE COUNTRY WE TRUSTED

## LAURA-GRAY STREET

If you ask us, *Is this love*
*enough to last a lifetime?*
we will lie and nod, citing
the cost of our kitchens,
our binging insomnias.
We have something to hide.
Reliably, we have hidden it.
The pantry lights are burned out.
The shelves are mostly bare.
Dim boxes of stale crackers,
anonymous jars, a scattering
of mouse droppings—
even they are past expiration,
past ransom. A resolved
calm of crumbs and dust that
we keep worrying by opening
the door, fumbling in corners
for what we've overlooked,
anything edible enough to
distract us from our gnawing
suspicion we can't lick what
we were born with a taste for.
How we love the more or
less of austerity and glut.
How we're filled with awe
by the enterprising ways
we bargain for sustenance,
surreptitiously, in the dark,
eating and eating and eating
until we're kissed by our own
rage, until the country we trusted
enough to marry confesses
*yes*, it has deceived us. We were

so naïve when we were born,
so hungry. Like you, like
you and you and you. Anyone
can see we're beyond that now.

# FOUR HUNDRED MILES FROM THE MARCH ON WASHINGTON: AUGUST 1963

## LAURA-GRAY STREET

In the photograph you can't see
our faces, only the way our
generations figure the beach:
adults striding away; a toddler,
bereft, bewildered, turning
between a bruise and a blessing.
The surf breaks, machinery
scouring seashells. We have long
shadows we must account for.
It might be about the road
implied in the sand. A canvas
we walk pleasures on. Beyond
us, the ocean, we think, needs
nothing. The way we will need
nothing else. Oh fragile child.
Oh ocean of all we owe.

# FROM THE MOUNTAINTOP

## SALLY TONER

IN THE FROZEN DRIZZLE of November, the top of Stone Mountain looked like the surface of the moon. A little over a year ago, I drove straight there from the airport, listening to Dylan, through orange, yellow, red leaves muted by a sky of gauze. I had some time before I was due at my cousin's house in Griffin, about an hour away—due at the white farmhouse off of Macon Road. The farmhouse built by her grandfather, my great grandfather, in 1922 and passed down to her by her father, the former attorney general of Georgia.

My cousin, the attorney general's daughter, is an actress. I was here to see her perform in my father's hometown. Her hometown. The former attorney general's hometown. But I needed to see Stone Mountain first. Because my uncle helped make the memorial happen. He was there at its dedication in 1972. Four years after he attended the funeral of Dr. Martin Luther King Jr. against the expressed orders of Lester Maddox. I needed to see for myself Stone Mountain like I needed to see Sweet Auburn. I needed to understand.

I had no time for the hiking trail up the mountain, and I lacked the appropriate gear for the weather anyway. So, I bought a ticket for the gondola. We creaked up the mountainside, and I took photos through the drops of rain. No MAGA hats in the car. A family from Mexico, father, mother, young daughter jabbering in Spanish. Two couples from California. One man in that group wore a USAF cap and asked the tour guide about the monument as the car wound around and the young man warned us of a dip.

"Barely worth a mention," the guide said, referring to the motion, before explaining that, under state law, the carving is not to be touched, or maintained, in any way. Neither are the names of the men on horseback to be uttered by anyone associated with the park. Stacey Abrams wanted them blasted from the mountainside. This was the compromise.

Acid rain has begun to wear their faces away, and I began reciting Ozymandias in my head

> *I am Ozymandias, king of kings. Look on my works, ye mighty, and despair.*

or was it Claude McKay's "America?" Yeah, that was it.

> *Darkly, I gaze into the days ahead*
> *And see her might and granite wonders there.*
> *Beneath the touch of Time's unerring hand,*
> *Like priceless treasures sinking in the sand.*

In March of 1970, a week after I was born, my great uncle ate fried chicken on a platform 400 feet in the air directly under the ear of a Confederate general. The monument's third and final carver, Roy Faulkner, stood, hands on hips, at the head of the table. Uncle Arthur grimaced in the foreground, his hair windblown, the discomfort in his spine, shattered in the latter days of the Battle of the Bulge, apparent. The Memorial Commission held the lunch as a recreation of a famous postcard from 1924, a photo where the then Governor Trinkle of Virginia sat just to the right, over the general's giant shoulder.

I have another picture of my uncle taken at Ebenezer Baptist Church on April 9, 1968. Spiro Agnew is looking down at something, while his wife Judy bends down as well whispering something to him. Right behind Agnew sits a stone-faced Richard Nixon. And in the row behind Nixon, almost directly behind him, sits Arthur K. Bolton, the state Attorney General.

"Yes, that's AK," my aunt responded when I sent her and Marian Lee, Arthur's daughter, copies of the photo.

"Yes, that is Dad. But I remember a very specific photo of him and Carl Sanders sitting side by side," she continued.

I responded to her, saying that I believed Sanders, the progressive governor who preceded Maddox—the one who integrated the Georgia state capitol; the one who appointed my great uncle as Attorney General—was sitting to Arthur's right. Sanders sat, in fact, in President Johnson's office when word came in that King had been shot. In the ensuing days, he and Arthur decided to attend the funeral while the governor made other plans.

"Shoot 'em down and stack 'em up," Maddox said.

The summer before I stood atop Stone Mountain, a Lime scooter leaned against the wall to the left of a WWI mural as my husband and I walked under a section of I-85 in Atlanta. Gentrification in Sweet Auburn. We read names memorialized in light boxes beneath the highway—businesses we couldn't identify at first. We wondered aloud if these are all Black-owned establishments the connector leveled, but Googling quickly dispelled that theory. The redevelopment of Sweet Auburn in the last five years we recognized from the history books, the news reels. The John W. Dobbs Book Depository, Butler Street YMCA, Top Hat Club from the west. The Prince Hall Masonic Temple, Cox Brothers Funeral Home, Ebenezer Baptist Church from the east.

There was a funeral at Ebenezer Baptist on July 28, 2023. A former Fulton County Judge and Atlanta City Council president, Marvin Arrington Sr. A black hearse sat parked outside, mourners dressed in white suits and wide brimmed hats. We passed a woman heading our way, the direction of the King Center. She wore a t-shirt, bright pink, that read: "I have decided to stick to love…Hate is too great a burden to bear." The clouds rolled in, and the humidity rose as we approached the rose garden outside.

I'm a teacher of thirty plus years, so I spent quite some time reading the messages from students around the world written in honor of Dr. King. I'm forever struck by the eloquence of the young. I learn from my own students every day. I read the placards under the flowers.

> *When the world becomes gray,*
> *I will be your last hope,*
> *When life makes you numb,*
> *Listen to the voice of your heart.*
> *As people are born warm and hopeful,*
> *Even in extreme situations,*
> *We humans are unstoppable*
>
> *—By Jiaqi Zhang, Grade 11*
> *Shandong Province, China*

THE SCHOOL where I teach has a sister school in the province of Nanjing. We sponsor a trip every spring break—an exchange that's been on hiatus in recent years. I regret I won't be able to be in that delegation before I retire in June.

I also couldn't step inside the church as my great uncle, Arthur Bolton, did in 1968. But I've wondered if he noticed, during the service, the cross that glowed, almost floated above the dark of the narthex. Above that hung, still hangs, a stained-glass window. Jesus, kneeling at Gethsemane. It's always been my favorite Bible story; it gives us permission to be afraid, to question, to doubt. Jesus is asking God, "Must I do this, Dad? Isn't there some other way? I feel so alone, my friends asleep, one taking silver to sell me down the river. This isn't fair." I wonder how God answered his son. Did he? If he answered Arthur K. Bolton when he prayed. He hasn't always answered me, to be sure. Or maybe not in a way I understand right now.

Balance requires a little give. Soft knees. The more rigid I stand, the more likely I am to fall. I wonder how my uncle kept his balance when it got so hard.

With his spine broken in WWII, pieced together, maintained in multiple operations, he struggled to walk. Many say it's as if someone could approach and easily push him over. Still, he stood through much of the private funeral of Martin Luther King Jr. Arthur Bolton refused to use a wheelchair. He only reluctantly agreed to a cane, even though he sometimes had to drape his arm across his leg, manhandle it to cross and uncross when it wouldn't behave. There were times at the funeral when Carl Sanders held him up. Or maybe they held each other up—both sang the hymns, as southern Baptists, they both grew up singing—the same hymns Dr. King sang all his life.

"He Leadeth Me."

*Let freedom ring from Stone Mountain of Georgia.*

I stood on top of Stone Mountain so grey and cold, taking a photo of a few figures wearing dark coats in the distance. In the restaurant and gift shop just a few feet away hung a sign advertising 100+ drink choices at 1,683 feet. I wrapped my coat around me and stepped around the pocks in the rock's surface—the depressions with streams of water, the tiny threads of marble. Another sign inside explained the geology.

> *Erosion—Time*
>
> *The weight of the earth's crust above the buried granite rock exerted intense pressure on the granite. When the earth's crust eroded, this pressure began to lessen, and the rock began to expand...over time, huge boulders are cleaved from the once solid granite mass.*

IN NOVEMBER of 1915, members of the Ku Klux Klan, reborn, stood exactly where I did now. They burned crosses on this barren surface, celebrated the lynching of a Jewish man named Leo Frank less than twenty miles away.

Last week, in January of 2025, KKK fliers appeared near an elementary school in the Virginia county where I teach. They lay in zip lock bags, weighted to the ground with stones.

*These boulders continue to break down into smaller stones.*

HOW MUCH EROSION can democracy withstand? Will the acid of hate outrun the rain and snow stripping the faces of those men I see as war criminals on the mountainside? My great uncle loved his country enough to take a bullet in the back for it—loved his state enough to serve it faithfully for over twenty years. By all accounts, he lived a life of honor, wanting, above all, in his own words, to "do the right thing."

I have done my best in thirty-two years as a high school teacher to instill in my students Uncle Arthur's ethos–the ethos of a good man, a thoughtful man, a brave man. A perfect man? A man who never had any doubts about his decisions? No. Not by a long shot. From what I've learned of his life and service, he would have been the first to admit that.

I have no way of knowing how Arthur Bolton felt on that platform swaying in front of the memorial at Stone Mountain. I also have no way of knowing how Arthur Bolton felt sitting in Ebenezer Baptist on April 9, 1968. How he reacted to the grief and fear surrounding him. I do believe grief and fear are concussive–that each sadness we witness, each trauma we experience, piles on top of itself with a weight that can break us. I don't believe it ever broke Arthur, and I pray it won't break this nation.

Today, I pass out Hershey's Hugs to my seniors before we do our goal setting for this semester. I encourage them to see their final months of public education as an opportunity rather than something they must "get through."

Their exhaustion, and mine, are valid. So is the grief and fear so many of us feel right now. Grief and fear are a concussive thing. But, just maybe, they live on the flip side of hope and love.

Today, rain streams down the other side of my classroom windows, and the sky looks so grey and cold.

"Never enough hugs, right?" I say to each senior as I hold out a bag full of chocolate.

# BREAKING NEWS

G.R. KRAMER

"The suicide rate among males in 2022 was approximately four times higher than the rate among females." Cdc.gov/suicide/facts/data.html.

according to police reports
the last and worst superhero
weaponized unsaid words
broadcast in barrooms
he is now trapped
in his nourishing fear
biceps and soft belly
stretched over shame
entire worlds
kept out of his heart
guard his terror and
the body count is high

ToxicMan has been located
hidden in his mother's basement
with his secret identity
and tiresome podcasts
he has always been trapped
every day is arm day
anger the thick skin
into which he tattooed
the faces of everyone he ever met
his semi-automatics
tap out his ransom note
but it is never too late

# CHEAP GAS

G.R. KRAMER

Each day the gun goes off
plucking the long string of seconds,
    each moment a small death
and birth. So the hazy sky whines
with a long D minor chord.
    Trillionaires spit my name
in board rooms;
the President pisses
over your family pictures
    every morning;
The worst things are mostly true,
but let's take all that in stride

as long as there is cheap gas.
    The toilet will clog
and unclog—your toes
throb in cold weather
and maybe tomorrow
    the call will come…
all these burdens, and
eggs are expensive now.

Children panhandle as
the cheap gas bill flies
through Congress… I drop
    my cell phone in the dirty
urinal. Then comes a moment
    when the angle of the sun light
through the store window
    on a woman's gray flesh
as she picks through overpriced avocados
forces us to think
    of beauty, how it creeps

unasked into the din of days.
For an instant you can hear
a silent chime in the sky
        and the earth. It comes
from the clouds, the soil, and time—
        they carry the sum
of the best and the worst,
the accumulated flecks of forever.
To be just a passing speck in this. Sublime...

Pay no mind to that tinny music
screech and scratch through
        the static of a broken car radio
as I idle in line at the old Shell station
        with the cheap gas on Route 17.
Later, as the traffic passes,
insert the nozzle, feel the pump pulse
        with aortic throbbing.
When you pull the lever
the aroma of petroleum
carries an ancient essence.

If you sniff it in the flammable air,
        try not to think
about the message refined from
eons
sent specifically in this moment
for you, a mutation of one
        single ancient fern blade
as real as this old western sky...
this sky dimming
under a worn and weary sun.

# GROUP PROJECT

## ERIK FATEMI

THERE WERE FIVE OF US in the group. One of us had a nice smile and one of us talked with their hands a lot. One of us clearly came from money, because of their clothes. One of us repeated whatever someone else had just said using slightly different words, which was fine at first but starting to get on our nerves. Two of us had blue eyes. One of us seemed really smart and one of us had something in their teeth but we didn't know them well enough yet to mention it. One of us arrived fifteen minutes late. All of us said we were excited to work together.

We decided to meet once a week. Thursday evening was perfect for most of us, but the one of us who arrived late said they would prefer a different day. The tallest one of us suggested Sunday afternoons, but the one of us who arrived late objected again. Same with Tuesday evenings and Friday mornings. After the one of us who arrived late said they had a conflict five times in a row, the one of us with the roundish head asked them when they were available. They said Wednesday evenings. That worked for all of us. By then, it was time for us to go. One of us joked that the hard part was out of the way and actually doing the project would be easy. The rest of us didn't think that was very funny.

The one of us with curly hair suggested holding a special meeting on Monday without the one of us who arrived late, and the rest of us agreed. The one of us who always spoke first said it was better to have fewer people in the group who were dedicated to the Movement than lots of people who we couldn't count on. The skinniest one of us asked if the one of us who arrived late could still pass the class if we voted them out of the group. We didn't think so. The one of us with tiny hands said then maybe we should give them a second chance, to which the one of us with freckles asked if they thought the late person's feelings were more important than the success of the Movement. Obviously not, said the one of us with tiny hands, adding that they were as committed to the Movement as anyone in the group, especially the one of us with freckles. And so, we notified our instructor that the one of us who arrived late would no longer be needed for the project.

We met again on Wednesday evening. The one of us who made jokes said we deserved an A-plus for arriving on time but no one else laughed because we still hadn't decided what to do for the project. One of us suggested drafting a new constitution, but the one of us with a runny nose said we should compose a new national anthem. We took a vote and it was a tie. Then another one of us suggested writing a one-act play about the Prophet, but the one of us with a runny nose said we should design a reeducation camp where we could house the infidels after the revolution. So, we took another vote and again it was a tie. We were losing patience so we decided to adjourn.

We held a special meeting the next morning without the one of us with a runny nose. The one of us with the long neck said we'd never get anything done if all our votes ended in a tie and the one of us with the huge forehead said runny noses weren't a good look for future leaders of the Movement. And so, we agreed to proceed without the one of us with a runny nose. The one of us who made jokes said the one of us with a runny nose really blew it, but the rest of us were not amused. After that we adjourned.

The one of us who was always frowning began the next meeting by complaining that some of us weren't carrying their fair share of the weight. The one of us who wore glasses asked the one of us who was always frowning who they were referring to, and the one of us who was always frowning told them to take a wild guess. The one of us who wore glasses responded that if there was anyone in the group who wasn't carrying their weight, it was definitely the one of us who was always frowning. The one of us who was always frowning smiled and asked the one of us who wore glasses if they truly believed in the Movement or were just pretending because they wanted to be on the side that won the revolution. The one of us who wore glasses said they would be happy to debate their respective commitments to the Movement before the Orthodoxy Council whenever it was convenient for the one of us who frowned. The one of us who made jokes suggested that we adjourn, so we ended the meeting early.

The one of us with the tattoo invited the one of us who made jokes to a special meeting without the one of us with big ears, and the one of us who made jokes said yes. The one of us with the tattoo began the meeting by praising the one of us who made jokes and inviting them to say something funny. The one of us who made jokes declined and said we should really get cracking on the project if we wanted to meet the deadline. The one of us with the tattoo agreed, adding that the best way to expedite our efforts was to elect a group leader. The one of us who used to make jokes said that after careful thought they had decided to accept the role. The one of us with the tattoo said that actually they would prefer to serve as group leader, which was why they had requested today's special meeting, so they could enlist the support of the one of us who used to make jokes. The one of us who used to make jokes said that was the funniest thing they had ever heard. After further discussion we decided to revisit the matter on Tuesday without the one of us with big ears, whose services we agreed would no longer be required.

The meeting on Tuesday did not go as smoothly as we hoped. The one of us who used to make jokes called the meeting to order and handed out a printed agenda, but the one of us with the tattoo handed out their own agenda and said they should be the one to call the meeting to order, which they proceeded to do. Then the one of us who used to make jokes asked the one of us with the tattoo how long they had been spying for the infidels. The one of us with the tattoo said they had been wondering the same thing about the one of us who used to make jokes. We couldn't agree on which one of us was spying so we decided to adjourn.

We took no pleasure in reporting the matter later that evening to the Orthodoxy Council, nor in testifying at the emergency expulsion hearing the following day. It was a painful process for all involved, but ultimately everything turned out for the best. As the Prophet has written, one line of malware can destroy the entire code. In fact, we emerged from the ordeal even more committed to the Movement than before.

Also, the project is coming along great. It's due in two weeks, which should be plenty of time to finish the research and get cracking on the presentation. We can't wait to show everyone what we've done. We think it's going to be the best group project ever.

# WHAT HOPE LOOKS LIKE ON MONDAY

KIRSTEN PORTER

Before you accidentally reply all and the dog steps in his pee
and pawprints it down the hallway tiles,
before Tuesday gets lost in your junk drawer
and Wednesday's storm gives way
to Thursday's sinus headache that still throbs
on Friday, before you spend seven nights staring up
at the ceiling wondering why you are still here
but Tracy is not,
before the week doles out its disappointments
dressed up as the blues—
the morning sun rises on Monday,
big and round and tinged luminous red, pulsing through
your front window, breaking through the glass to drip
all its golden promises across
the still clean tiles.

# DISORDER

ELNATHAN STARNES

Disturbed Order
Order Disturbance
Order Disturbed
Disturbance in Order
Order is DISSED
4 Attention
      2 Diss Order:
A synonym for chaos & confusion
ORDER IN THE COURT!
ORDER INNA COURT!
Dis: the prefix to the word DISORDER
Pre: being previous to or before
Standing at the gate of trendy conditions
Justified by experimental diagnosis

## SOMA FALLOUT

ELNATHAN STARNES

Shutdown isolation cubicle
Half-baked, half-naked citizen
Dipped in pro-Nounury
Meta faced slaves in denial of an
After-the-end-of-the-world-reality
They walk with their beloved familiars
Carrying a tablespoon of water to a burning building
Headstrong is the middle name
Hard-headed, head hard, anxiously waiting for entry
Makin' the game so hard
So long
This is the SOMA fallout

# WHAT A FUTURE AMERICA CAN LEARN FROM EARLY STAGE 4 CANCER

## CHRISTINA M. WELLS

I. A PATIENT MAY SIT IN A CHAIR, sleepy and nauseated, an arm stretched out with needles sucking blood into tubes while gauze waits to cover the wound. She may teeter on the edge of a chair, a tech grabbing her hands and saying, "I can feel your life force." This is also you, America, balancing on the edge, your energy draining out while someone says, distinctly, you're still here. Rest for a minute. After that, keep moving. The future may be what you predict it will be. Try not to make it too scary.

II. Once, experts in white coats stood by the flimsy paper of exam tables and said, "You're okay, it's not what you thought it was," or "Wow, you should take a test one day, but not now. It's not necessary now." There was a dreamy return to the world, where the future patient picked up dinner or worked from home or went to a play, loving theater. This, too, is you, though you sometimes create the drama. Now that you know the experts were wrong, you must do something to reclaim your future. There is nothing from your past to dwell on. There is, however, tomorrow, and you plan to live to see it, like all countries do.

III. Sometimes a patient will see a sign to return to, like a nurse wearing a brooch that reminds her of her grandmother or an essay she wrote once after standing outside, a purple butterfly flying by her. You, too, have your signs to return to. Sometimes they were manufactured by people on the streets who asked for equity, the Capitol dome standing before them. You can see them again, if you want. There is grainy footage of some of them standing by, asking for their future, someone's future, your future. You can always fast forward to now and tomorrow and the next day, making sure the signs get what they asked for yesterday.

IV. Treatment is hard. Harsh chemicals enter through plastic bags, and some-one always asks whether the problem was innate, passed down from generation to generation, or if something tipped the scales away from what is healthy and good. These glances back and forward can be useful, but the problem is now, and it may be a problem tomorrow. For you, the present and future contain the innate and the unique. With both, you could waste time on blame, when the point is to make it all better, somehow. That's what countries are supposed to do.

V. One day a patient sees references to a song over and over again. It's Bob Marley's "Everything's Gonna Be Alright." This seems a sign, much like Woody Guthrie's "This Land Is Your Land" is for you. It seems to foretell the future. She, like you, may have to work for it. Only you will have to hold everyone— not one person with a problem.

VI. In a patient's remission, someone will say that "it's a miracle" and "it's amazing." For months and months the patient can go on, thinking more of everyday life than the threats against it. She can suddenly eat what she wants and walk through neighborhoods where she once might have doubled over, looking to get home as soon as possible. This could be called denial, or maybe hope. If you find yourself feeling this, America, remember that anything could happen, and it just might.

VII. Once a patient walked into a restaurant, one she hadn't been to in months. The owner saw her and said, "You made it. You made it!" He isn't talking about how she showed up that day; it's more like he thinks she will continue to come back because she can. The owners sent her free miso soup and helped to keep her alive. She imagines coming back week after week, paying for this gift, eating sushi with wooden chopsticks and offering her friendship to these owners. You, America, also have debts you could pay. Lots of people—lots of places—have moved you forward even when you could barely stand. You may not remember. But a lot of us do.

VIII. There is black and white thinking with disease. A person lives or dies. Period. It is when the radiologists look forward that the future gets a little bit gray. This dot here could be nothing or could be everything, or it could be somewhere in between. Everyone can agree there's a problem over there—it's lines on the body that not everyone can see. America, the future isn't all or nothing. It's one perspective and another and another. Sometimes you can't see it at all, but it's there, waiting in the books where historians predict your future. Choose carefully when you decide who to believe. Or maybe a lot of them have little bits of truth, while others could lead you astray.

IX. After a patient has their last day of chemo, she might smile at the nurses and thank them for their help. There might have been confetti if she'd thought of it. But somewhere on the other side of it, someone tells her that this is a chronic problem. There will be no ringing of the bell, no sign of freedom forever. America, you have had your own ticker tape parade. A part of you thinks it is forever, that it's the end of the Civil War, World War II, or Vietnam. But those are three things to illustrate the point: you will always have to clean up. Problems will come again forever, and you will need to realize that. You have the biggest problem when you get too cocky, when you look at everyone else's leaders and think they are ridiculous. Peace, like remission, is cyclical. All I can say is that I hope we both live to see it.

# FENCES

MICHELE EVANS

beyond the shadows cast by a single oak at the edge of uncle harrison's acre, glass bottles, long emptied, stand guard like soldiers atop rows of stacked virginia bluestone, saluting and scrutinizing every passerby who dares to stop on this nameless gravel road i couldn't find even if waze, google maps, and my iphone joined forces to chauffeur me. but now that i am here, i can't unsee all the signposts. the homestead, a white shingled two-story house sits empty. a pair of glassless windows once reflecting the ridgetops of bull run now prop shotgun barrels from hunters targeting their next kill; an abandoned scaffold barricades exposed wood rot on the side where the afternoon sun rests. everything is quiet except the voice in my head warning me of danger. *beware it is not safe here, you are not safe here, leave before dust from tires arises or the sun sets.* in their eyes you will always be a trespasser—even when the land *belongs* to you.

# AN ALLEY WEDDING

## NATHAN LESLIE

IT EMBARRASSED HIM on a deep level. Didn't feel that love was becoming, didn't feel that he could be worthy of it. Didn't think that Dawn was worthy of him, either—not really. He should have been happy, but instead he wanted to crawl under a log. What was wrong with him?

Dawn wanted a big country wedding. She still worked as a waitress at the restaurant across town, close to his first apartment. She approached him—that was different. Not exactly a withering flower. Did she wear the pants in the relationship? Maybe—Wayne didn't care. He just wanted to get it all over with and move on to the living.

Wayne and Dawn didn't exactly argue, but they simmered in stillness. Wayne would and could keep it in. It was nothing to him. When they were dating Wayne just wanted to stay in. Dawn asked him once if he felt ashamed of her.

The country wedding would not happen. You can do it on your own, Wayne said. I want to keep it small. Me, you and some guy we will never see again.

As if he felt ashamed of her, she said.

That's not it—he just wasn't propelled by showing off. Why does everything have to be set for public approval? Why the need for spectacle?

There was a well-lit alley, he said. With old timey street lamps close to the canal. They could decorate it with wreaths of tulips and roses and ribbons and bows and pink and red streamers and the judge could meet them there in the shadows and do the deed quickly, little fuss. Do it right there.

Two months later, in the summer, Dawn did the big family gathering. Without him. Shockingly. Pictures and hugs with the cousins and nieces and dancing with her uncle and sole living grandfather. Gifts and cake and music. She reported it all. It was her and her family and they ate and danced and everyone sent their regards (some of them) to Wayne and they were so nice and Midwestern about it. Too nice. Where were the backstabbers? It almost seemed as if they weren't disappointed that he couldn't attend his own wedding—as if it were just a regular family reunion. He didn't like those either. Dawn never complained. She made excuses for Wayne to her family—he had a terrible stomach thing. It couldn't be helped. He received a bevy of get-well cards.

They took pictures in the alley, though most turned out blotched with shadows. Difficult to make out Dawn's face in most of the images, though her white dress almost glowed. The light glinted off her ring. There was something wrong with him—he knew that. He just had no idea how to rectify it, how to become closer to normal. Why was he so disparate and isolated? Why couldn't he just be with people and talk and make chit-chat and be nice and give back to the world. It felt as though he constantly wore a shell on his back, an armadillo's armor. One image in the photo album grabbed him. Dawn smiled into the camera, her lipstick and teeth and hair and everything so perfect. Wayne looked off to the right, as if he wasn't there. As if his car were idling on the curb and he couldn't wait to get back to it. Driving into the hills, radio crackling through the speakers like fire.

# WEDDING PLANS

## JYOTI MINOCHA

ANU SHOVED THE SAMOSAS hastily in the oven, a quick smear of heat scorching her skin before she could draw her hand back. She sucked at her reddening thumb, and shouted irritably, "Anil, come down, they'll be here any second."

Why was she always the one preparing for their guests, putting out the snacks, plumping the living room cushions, making sure they had clean plates and cups? She had pondered this question all through her marriage, growing increasingly resentful over the years, her ire spiking in tandem with each new variation of the global fervor for human rights; Breaking the Glass Ceiling (so many years and so many successful projects completed and she hadn't been promoted to VP), the Equal Rights Amendment; Black Lives that mattered; Brown Lives which also mattered (finally, she had received the promotion and a nice jump in salary, ten years too late); the Me Too movement (could the delay in reaching the VP's office have anything to do with the fact that she had never flirted with the boss? Hadn't his hand lingered a little too long on her back when he greeted her at company events, perhaps moving down to lightly stroke her buttocks?) Honestly, she couldn't tell so many years later if her memory was playing tricks on her.

Here was all this momentous change, this enlightenment happening all over the globe, and she was still the one arranging samosas in a creative circle on a plate.

"Why do you always serve samosas?" her daughter Anita scowled, coming into the kitchen, and grabbing one before Anu could protest. "You don't have to bring out a ton of food. Nobody does anymore, Ma! You'll look silly!"

The more fuss Anu made about entertaining Anita's future in-laws, the more annoyed her daughter became. Well, she wasn't about to sacrifice her upbringing and her exemplary Indian etiquette because her American-born child had absorbed none of it.

And in-laws were in-laws at the end of the day, and these ones were not to be taken lightly. Sandra, Anita's future mother-in-law, demonstrated considerable potential when it came to the passive-aggressive mode of communication. At their first encounter, she had managed to make Anu feel dowdy (her eyes went straight to the chipped nail polish Anu hadn't had time to replenish) under-educated (she had politely corrected Anu's pronunciation of château, which Anu had always called chay-too), and ineffably immigrant (*When did your family come to the United States?*)

Why couldn't she have chosen a good Indian boy instead? When Anita broke the news about Jeff, this question had risen silently in Anu's mind, and then sank down immediately, like a balloon deflated by their daughter's free and tenacious will.

"Why didn't you introduce her to some eligible Indian boys in the community?" Anil had lamented in the privacy of their bedroom, after he had hugged Anita and told her that her happiness was their only priority.

Anu turned to look at him, her eyes enlarging like puffer fish.

"*This* was *also my job?*"

"I mean..." Anil swallowed, "The mother.... Uh.... I mean...." He trailed off and slid silently out of the room.

However, Jeff turned out to be a darling, so respectful and thoughtful, and he clearly doted on their daughter. One couldn't find a flaw in his family either— it had one of those elite lineages which gave numbers to their male heirs instead of names—Jeffery Thomas the 3rd was his real title, his grandfather and father being the 1st and 2nd incarnations, respectively.

The first time Anu had met Sandra she was struck by her lean, knife-sharp look, her elongated nose, her satiny black, white streaked hair which looked welded into immobility, and her sensible Ecco shoes. She wore grey, expensive-looking slacks, a cream silk shirt, and a matching pearl necklace. She flowed through their small living room, tall, sleek, and well groomed, and managed effortlessly to make their overstuffed, discount-store-furniture look tawdry and cheap. Jeff's father, Jeff the 2nd, was red-faced with blunt features and a breadth and height which, like Gulliver, dwarfed everything in the house. On his first visit to their home, Jeff the 2^nd had worn a guarded look on his face, which broke into an affable smile when Anita ran down the stairs to greet him.

"Pops! I'm so glad you could come too!"

*Pops?* She was replacing her father already? When was the last time she had run down the stairs with such enthusiasm when her father came home? And *Pops?* That horrid cartoonish TV show slang: Anita had always called her father Daddy, an appropriate and salutary form of address, the right way to address a father and an elder.

"Sandra!" Anita had flung her arms around her fiancée's mother who, Anu thought, disengaged a tad too quickly.

She was on first name, flinging-her-arms-around terms with her future mother-in-law and Anu's heart contracted a little. Of course, there was no contest, Anu was the mother, but still. The fact that her little girl now had a set of pretend parents whom she seemed to be chummier and more informal with than she had ever been with her own parents, was not something she relished.

Anu, standing in her spotless, updated kitchen with the marble topped center island and the sparkling stainless steel appliances, reflected on how hard it had been to raise Anita all by themselves in a country where she couldn't just deposit her with either of her grandmothers, or pack her off to her cousin's house. It was only after immigrating that Anu had understood the breadth and intricacy of the web of social connections which had sustained her childhood. There was Aunty Sethi next door who had watched Anu and her brother when her mother went for her many medical appointments. There was Naani, Anu's grandmother across town, with whom she spent weeks in summer, climbing the guava and mango trees in her backyard and playing on her sleepy street with her neighbor's children. It had been hard to reproduce that web in their new home, in this new country, on a continent eight thousand miles away, and a cold lonely dread would often grip Anu's heart in those early years, which she could only assuage by calling her mother and sobbing her heart out.

The doorbell rang and Anu patted her hair reflexively. Sandra's hair always seemed to be frozen on her head, probably by an imperious command from her. This particular visit was for the two families to hammer out detailed wedding plans together. They had met Anita's future in-laws a few times now, and after every encounter Anu had to suppress a fierce desire to book herself a spa day and get a full facial with her eyebrows threaded into tweaked arches that would rival Sandra's when raised.

JEFF THE 2ND squeezed himself into their largest armchair, obliterating any visual trace of it and Sandra leaned back on their aging Marlo Furniture sofa, and allowed her eyebrows to do a quick survey of the room.

"The first thing we have to settle is the number of guests," Sandra said.

"Well, we are going to have a lot of family flying in from India, and we have relatives and friends, co-workers and some neighbors." Anu did some quick calculations in her head.

"I think, around two hundred and fifty from our side, total."

Sandra's eyebrows began flirting with her hairline.

"Two hundred and fifty! That's a lot! We don't have such hordes of people. Seventy-five, at a stretch, right Jeff?"

*Hordes?* What did she mean by *hordes? Hordes* were unruly, unkempt mobs who indulged in vandalism. Their guests were respectable and well groomed, with impeccable manners. Anu bit her lip to hide her irritation.

"Mom," Anita piped in. "Jeff and I will have at least fifty friends attending."

"Are we talking five hundred people? That's a convention, not a wedding? And where would you find a place? We need to reduce those numbers." Sandra looked pointedly at Anu and her tone seemed to suggest that culling the numbers would be the responsibility of those with the hordes of guests.

"Oh, the place isn't the problem—it'll be the labor. Now that the deportations have begun, labor costs are going to shoot up." Jeff the 2nd leaned forward, and the armchair gave an embarrassing squeak.

"We'll have to be prepared to spend more—I'm ok with that, if y'all are. At least we have a strong president now who's doing something about all these illegal immigrants barging in, taking over the country," he declared, smiling congenially, and helped himself to the last samosa on the plate.

A sudden flash of comprehension raced through Anu, like a warm surge of hormones. Anita's future in-laws were supporters of the current president! She tried to catch Anil's eye but both he and Anita were carefully avoiding looking at her. *Both* of them had known and no one had informed her that the Thomases supported the man Anu loathed most in the world! How many times had her family heard her railing against the shamelessness and misogyny of the man—who had just begun his second term in the White House—whether he was breaking well-established rules or grabbing women's crotches. She had signed up for every Women's March on Washington, shaking her fist and shouting herself hoarse. Did her traitorous daughter understand the legacy she had inherited from her mother, and from her maternal grandfather, who had been jailed for fighting against British colonial rule in India?

Had she failed in her primary duty as a mother—imprinting her only offspring with the ideals she, and generations of their family, had fiercely believed in? Anu was suddenly seized with a spasm of regret—why had they chosen to stay on in America, and allow vital pieces of their family heritage to drift away? They had both become naturalized citizens after 9/11—the shock and outrage drove them to show solidarity for the country which had given them boundless opportunities. When they took their oath in a large hall with a collection of people who looked like a poster for a United Nation conference on World Peace, the notary had thanked them for choosing America.

Anu pulled herself back to the conversation with difficulty.

"And steak is Jeff's favorite, so it has to be on the menu," Sandra was saying.

"Uh, we don't usually serve beef for religious reasons," Anil said, too meekly Anu felt, and she interrupted in a voice louder than she intended.

"We *never* serve beef. It's *AGAINST* the religion and our guests would be offended."

Sandra, unfazed by her outburst, shot a solitary eyebrow up.

"Well, a separate table then—it would be a shame not to serve Jeff's favorite on his wedding day, I'm sure you'll agree."

"Mom," Anita was finally locking eyes with her, her expression an ingenious mixture of pleading and glaring.

"Please. It can be completely separate from the buffet. I mean it won't even share the same airspace."

Anu looked at her daughter, this beautiful, earnest, treacherous stranger, and a glimpse of the little girl who would jump into her lap at bedtime and beg for stories rose up behind the gorgeous made-up face. Love, thought Anu, is the only thing capable of laying waste to sanity and centuries of religious tradition.


"PLEASE TELL ME where to turn," Anu said, as she negotiated the highway. She was dropping Sandra home because Jeff the 2nd had taken the car on an errand. Her mind was still churning over the discussion in their living room, the concessions they had made (how would she explain the beef to her grandmother from India, who had a particular talent for ferreting out the ingredients of every dish in a wedding banquet). And culling the numbers? How many friends could she offend? This wedding, Anu thought, is going to age me by a decade.

"Turn right here," Sandra said, and Anu slowed down to move to the right turning lane. Nobody was letting her through, people were their usual rush-hour road hog selves. The light turned red just then, and she rolled to a stop, ignoring the loud honking from the car behind her.

A commotion on the driver's side caught her eye, and she turned her head. A short, red-faced man was standing near her window, shouting and waving his arms. What did he want? Was it her car? Was it the boot, which had been popping up unexpectedly, recently?

She rolled down the window.

"You stupid dumb bitch," the man yelled, throwing his hands up. "Why'd ya stop? Why'd ya slow down at a green light? You dumb shit, doncha know how to drive? Go back to where ya came from, go back to India and drive camels!"

"What? What?" Anu stammered uncomprehending, his words just beginning to sink in, but Sandra had already leapt out of the passenger side and planted herself in front of the man obstructing him completely as he turned to go back to his car. She stretched herself to her full, imposing, razor-sharp height and pointed her exquisitely manicured finger, bending over him like a scythe.

"How dare you! How dare you say a vile thing like that! You nasty uncouth man—you go back under the rock you crawled out from!"

"Fuck off lady, outta my way, ya bitches are all the same," the man turned but Sandra moved in front of him.

"You're just a lousy excuse for a human being!" Anu heard Sandra shout. "You should be ashamed of...."

The light changed at that moment and honking cars drowned out the rest. Traffic began to surge around them, and Sandra stepped away and got back into the car.

Anu pressed the gas and pulled into the stream of traffic. She felt numb, her brain frantically processing what had just happened. She glanced out of the corner of her eye at Sandra, who was staring ahead, looking grim. What had Sandra just done? What if the man had attacked them? What if he had pulled out a gun? And why had he mentioned camels?

As far as she could remember, she had never had a flagrant brush with anyone where her race came into play. She felt unsettled, as if a glass had been shattered near her. And Sandra hadn't hesitated for a second.

"Thank you," Anu said softly. She hadn't noticed that she had been holding her breath and clenching the steering wheel so hard, her knuckles were red.

Sandra was still rigid, looking straight ahead and Anu wasn't sure if she had heard, until she felt Sandra's hand rest briefly on hers.

"No one should ever have to hear that crap, ever. That vulgar, hateful man."

"Why?" Anu said, almost to herself. "Did he talk about camels?" She pictured herself on a prancing camel clopping down the street in her hometown, dodging the rickshaws and cycles and honking cars, and she burst suddenly into giggles.

"What is it?" Sandra turned to look at her.

"Camel!" Anu managed to gasp out, finally controlling herself. "Driving a camel instead of a car!"

A grin spread across Sandra's face. Her shoulders shook as she threw back her head and guffawed. Anu, watching her out of the corner of her eyes, had the sudden incongruous thought that the wedding was going to turn out fine after all, and she laughed again with Sandra, and found herself still smiling after she had dropped her home and waved goodbye.

# COPPERHEAD IN THE SUGAR

LINDSEY HULL

but don't tell me
I have to sit back and take it
like a good girl
all over again

a new day bubbles forth like curdled milk
and our elders say this is our defining era

      I feel it in my toes

a voice from the wilderness chimes
ten hundred solid calling bells
from cardinal to canary
we gather, we bind
ourselves by the strength of our braids

our calls beckon truth and liberty
we will never consent to the straps you wrap
to bind our lips
and a host of darlings will clear every stone
you heap upon our limbs

no matter how many lashes you take to lay
no matter how many lashes you take

I'll lie      in wait
           a copperhead in the sugar
           an apple blossom on your plate

# THE NAKED LINE

LINDSEY HULL

> *The line between a normal, functioning society and a catastrophic decivilization can be crossed with a single act of mayhem.*
> by Adrienne LaFrance, *The Atlantic*, December 11, 2024.

                                        a single act of mayhem
my granny used to shake her head at the news: ruby ridge. waco. oklahoma
city she was dead for that one, but just barely. she was still shaking her head. so
was everyone else

thirty years past her departure, we barely blink an eye

across the red-hued blue ridge mountains, hot-house tempers grow against old
tobacco breeze, trouble rumbles on porch steps and in church pews and at dis-
tilleries. trouble rumbles cross county borders under the shadow of three crosses
and a flag that casts charred marks on mahogany trees. these days, the party
line is multiplied; it's all too easy to bait trouble with a reel

five hundred eighty-one miles south of where Brian Thompson bled out, our
people run together, moonshiners and lawmen dancing as one on saturday's
golden gravestone

the pigg river churns
                mama's values fall to the clouds
                                we're strapped in

increased social media rhetoric; increased distrust of business suits of white
coats, of institutions, see those involving the government above all; increased
distrust of the other, see for instance the immigrant; increased visibility in
wealth disparity, god forbid anyone should make it; increased demographic
change, our land is losing its "whiteness," dare I say it—that's a conspiracy
theory, in case you're curious of it; increased conspiracy theories, see above see
8chan, see domestic extremism, see this is a major threat, see Bush the second's
comments, september 11, 2021; see we march
see ahead see we march ahead

in lockstep
        we march
               ahead
                        see
                                 ahead

# EYES

GREGORY LUCE

One eye that can barely see
forcing the other to see
too much. The blood-dimmed tide
rolling in faster than ever from
the overheating ocean, rolling
toward our City on the Hill
swifter than ever, lapping
at the crumbling slope.

If I could keep only one eye
which one would I choose?

# UPSHOT

LEONA SEVICK

Climbing higher and higher each year,
eating their way through the hemlock trees,
the woolly adelgids, I'm certain,
hadn't planned to commit murder. But
when they killed the trees that shade the streams,
the water's temperature rose too high
and the stream trout, confused by the lack
of oxygen, died wide-eyed—their gills
sucking in too little air too late.
In Pennsylvania, twenty-year-old
Thomas Crooks missed his mark by an inch,
the bullets from one of his father's
guns finding other flesh to ruin.
What vital lessons might be gleaned here?
Those who should be asking never will.

# AUTO REPAIR SHOP

ZEINA AZZAM

*After Joseph Zbukvic's painting,* Joe's Garage

This is where
you know what labor is

You taste the toil and grime
in the engine's oily whine

This is where
old cars and trucks
limp into place
in rows of gray and black
crowned by dusty,
rusty time

Where a stray dog
barrels through
like a fugitive
from a world of woes

and weatherbeaten wires
on towering poles
command the attention
of birds and sky
like stick-figure royalty
with fraying clothes

reigning over
the timeworn kingdom
of Joe's Garage

# THE VANISHING POINT

## TIMOTHY ROWE

JORDAN WALKED INTO the manager's office, hoping the sinking feeling in his gut was somehow misinformed. Mr. Cowler, a beefy man with uneven sideburns and a spray tan, gestured to the empty chair at the desk opposite his own.

"Jordan, I'll cut right to it. I'm afraid we have to let you go. It's just not working out. I have no doubt you're a hard worker. It's just. Well, we can't afford mistakes. They cost us and our customers. You'll be paid through today. I'm sure you'll land on your feet."

Jordan looked at the cat clock on the wall above them. Its tail swung and eyes darted left and right in unison with each passing second.

"But I think I'm doing better, Mr. Cowler, if you'd just give me a little more time."

"It's been a month. I've given you as much time as I can. I don't see any signs of improvement. You forget orders and confuse tables. You still don't know the menu, even the appetizers. I'm afraid you're just not getting it."

"I appreciate you giving me a chance."

Cowler stood up and extended his hand. "Didn't you say that you qualified for Subsistence? If I were you, I'd kick my feet up, go to the beach and toss back a few margaritas."

Jordan shook the man's hand without responding and walked out of the office. He went to the lockers and retrieved his black t-shirt and jacket. He yanked off his polo with the logo of the Tower of Pisa beneath a crescent moon and winged it into the trash can along with his apron. He walked out of the restaurant without looking back, without a word to anyone.

Outside, it was dark and drizzly; streetlights floated like fuzzy white UFOs above the parking lot. He wanted to delay going back home to the humiliation of admitting to his wife Yazmine that he failed to hold down another restaurant job, the second in six months. The first had gone just as badly if not worse—a trip to urgent care for a blistered burn from a scalding hot plate. Where would he go now? He couldn't imagine trying to force down a beer at the end of some dark pub.

Instead, he drove to Gravelly Point, a park situated on the shore of the Potomac, a few hundred feet north of Reagan National Airport, where commercial jets roared over the open field as they departed and landed. The windshield wipers cleared the mist that landed everywhere and all at once, a blanket of tiny spittle ignited by the lights.

"Park closed at dark." He rolled into one of the parking spots, turned off his headlights, and killed the engine. There were one or two other cars in the lot, but he didn't see much activity except for a single jogger and a mad cyclist with one of those handlebar lamps, making his way through the rainy dark. An airplane on the runway made the final turn before takeoff, raced down the tarmac, and burst into the sky above, screaming in his ears. The giant metal monster shook the air all around him, sending vibrations through his ribs. It started to rain harder now, tapping on his face.

He'd found himself here lately, to watch the planes take off and land. Sometimes, he imagined driving over to National and jumping on a flight to who-knows-where with only what he could fit into his pockets. Tampa with a toothbrush and wallet. A foolish idea. Another plane passed overhead in the other direction, gliding toward the runway from some city somewhere, packed with people, their heads flickering with recent experiences, whether good or bad, all finished with a packet of tasteless mini pretzels and a plastic tumbler of ginger ale. Bright red ruby lights blinked slowly downward until the plane leveled off on the ground in the distance.

Jordan drove home. When he opened the front door, his wife called from the kitchen. He hung up his coat in the hall and walked in. She sat at the table with their son, Benny, both with plates in front of them. A glass of milk in front of the boy. A mug of tea for her.

"You're in luck! Benny insisted that we save you a piece of carrot cake. I was trying to persuade him to split it with me, but he would not be moved."

"Not tonight, thanks. I don't have the stomach for dessert right now." He walked through the kitchen into the living room, fetched a bottle and glass from the sideboard, poured two fingers of scotch and returned, swirling the liquid by rotating his hand in small circles.

"Tough day at the office?" she said as he sat down. Her heart-shaped face was slightly pink under dark waves of hair and glossy black eyes.

He took a sip from his drink and shook his head, indicating he didn't want to talk about it. He turned to Benny, "How was school? Anything exciting?"

"Nah, the usual." Same glossy black eyes in miniature.

"The usual again. Right."

"Are you okay?" Yazmine asked.

"Not great. I just got fired again, and it's not sitting too well right now."

"Well, you didn't like it much there anyway. Perhaps a door is closing so that another might open."

"I doubt that. Two doors in the last six months, and I couldn't manage to do anything with either one. Drivers are snapping up whatever vacancies they can find. Some are thriving in these restaurants. Tom Stoney's doing well down at Finnegan's, ferrying beer and shepherd's pie."

"That doesn't mean anything."

"Except that I'm fucking useless."

"Not in front of Benny!"

"Sorry, kiddo. I'm sorry you have to hear that your dad is *bloody* useless."

Benny pushed at the crumbs on his plate with his fork. Jordan tipped up his glass and swallowed the rest of the sharp, smoky liquid. He walked back to the living room, poured another four fingers of booze and headed upstairs to the bedroom. He took off his shoes, lay down on the bed, and used the remote to turn on the television on top of the dresser. The late news was on, but he couldn't be bothered to turn up the volume to hear what was being said.

Not long after, Yazmine came in and gently closed the door behind her. "I'm sorry dear, that it didn't work out." She walked over and kissed him on top of his head.

"Yeah, well."

"Have you thought about—"

"Pay for not working? Accept my irrelevance."

"Darling, don't—"

"Don't what? I realize a taxi driver isn't a glamorous profession to most people, but I'm good at it. I know which back roads to take to avoid gridlock. Remember when that woman went into labor at Benny's soccer game and her husband couldn't get the car started? I got them to GW in fifteen minutes! The driverless cabs can't do that. They're not allowed. I enjoyed taking a couple in formal gown and tux to one of those Kennedy Center deals or dropping off a couple of newlyweds at the airport for their honeymoon in the Greek isles. Sure, there were plenty of nights with slobbering drunkards fumbling to get into each other's pants. But you know what? I got them home safely, prevented them from smashing into someone else. I'm sure I've saved a life or two over the years."

"I'm sure you have."

"So, I take Subsistence. It's not as if it's a salary for luxury and travel. What am I supposed to do? Sit here and read the paper and track the sun's progress? Go to a café for a coffee every third day for variety?

"We'll make it through. I'm not sure what you'll do, but you'll figure it out."

"Yeah." He looked down at the drink between his hands.

"Remember that I love you, whether you're a driver, an idler getting paid, or a failed culinary attendant, or whatever they're calling waiters these days."

"Love you too."

"There's still that piece of cake with your name on it. I think it would be good for Benny if you came down."

"Sure, I'll be there in a few."

She left and he studied the shimmering amber liquid in his glass, which he clenched with his fingers to stop the sensation of freefalling. Then he lifted it to his lips and swallowed half the scotch, set it down on the bedside table, and lay down on the bed. Shortly after his head hit the pillow, he fell into a dreamless sleep.

In the morning, he awoke with a fuzzy head and tongue like sandpaper. Yazmine quietly put her coat on over her scrubs and grabbed her keys and purse. Seeing his eyes open, she said, "Ah, it wakes! Benny's already on his way to school. Can you meet his bus this afternoon? Unless you're heading out?"

"No, that's fine. I'll be here."

She leaned down and kissed him. He smelled her lavender soap. Her exit was cautious, hurried. A tension had entered the house over the last few months and taken up residence. Nurses could still nurse, at least for now.

He showered and made himself a breakfast of scrambled eggs, toast with marmalade, and coffee. He leafed through the newspaper and watched the morning news program. Some actor he didn't recognize wore a chef's hat and sang a show tune while the hosts threw pancakes at him. He turned to a sports news show, but when it devolved into an extended shouting match over who deserved the title of running back of the week, he turned it off. The hours stretched out in front of him, far beyond the vanishing point. He checked messages on his computer, scrolled past the one with the link to the Subsistence registry.

He suddenly had to move. He grabbed his car keys and headed out the door. Shortly, he was on 395 racing into the city. He got off at the Twelfth Street exit for downtown and meandered through the streets, veered round the Mall, then up toward Zips Arena, but he couldn't ignore the proliferation of the driverless on the road. He saw carefree passengers hopping into them from the Metro and restaurant. This confirmed it, going for a drive, once a welcome distraction, had become an insult.

He drove back down to Eastern Market and stopped at one of the older bars in town he used to occasionally hit after an evening shift. The smell of old wood cured with dark beer greeted him as he stepped inside and made his way to an empty stool at the bar.

"What'll it be?" The bartender, a tall man with straight black bangs and a thin moustache, dropped a napkin in front of him.

"I'll have a Guiness and a ham and cheese with onion rings."

"Coming up."

He sipped his beer and watched the silent television on the wall behind the bar. Sports again. Highlights from the Commanders' loss. A quick cut to the coach standing behind a podium with a taciturn expression, tight jaw opening and closing. Captions appeared at the bottom of the screen. "We'll review the film. We need to clean up mistakes and convert on third down."

"That's brilliant analysis. *We need to score more.* I hate these interviews. Still, he seems to be doing a decent job. They should have won on Sunday, but they're having a good season," said the man on his right.

"Time will tell. I'm not holding my breath. Are you a fan?" Jordan asked.

"Nah, Patriots. You?"

"Yes indeed." He pointed at the screen. "I grew up in Arlington. My dad worked for the Treasury. I'm one of the rare natives in these parts."

"You don't say! Wow, what is it you do?"

It was as if the man had dropped a dead fish into his lap. He didn't know how to respond, so he took a long pull from his beer.

Finally, he said, "I was a driver until a few months ago: taxi, rideshare, chauffeur. You name it."

"Ah." The man drank from what looked like gin and tonic. His face flushed with awkward anticipation. He had sandy hair, a well-trimmed beard, fine sport coat and tie. "I'm sorry. A real shame in my opinion, and I'm not just saying that. I hate those fucking driverless jobs." He shifted into a robotic voice. "*Hello James. How are you this fine afternoon? I'm taking you to Gallery Place Metro, correct?* When it tries to make small talk, I enjoy telling it to shut the fuck up. *I mean no offense James. My main goal is to get you to your destination safely.*"

The man tossed a couple of beer nuts into his mouth and chomped for a moment, then took another swig.

Jordan nodded.

"What are you doing now, if you don't mind my asking?"

"I'm trying to find something else. I'm not cut out for office work. I had a couple shots at restaurant jobs, but I'm hopeless. Pretty soon, I'm going to have to wave the white flag and register for Subsistence."

"That's bullshit!" The man's head wobbled as he reared back with indignation, revealing his slightly tipsy state. "More of us will be there soon enough. All this efficiency. At what cost? They don't ask us if we want it."

The two sat in silence for a minute.

"I've got a proposal for you. I need to go to Dulles on Monday. Would you consider taking me? I'll pay you in cash. I know you can't accept electronic payment."

"Are you serious?"

The man nodded. "What's your number? I'll text you my address."

After exchanging details, they raised their glasses in a toast.

"I know a couple other folks who would be interested. Maybe we'll start a counter movement!" He slapped the bar and laughed, then gestured for another round.

Jordan held out his hand. "I'm driving."

"Of course you are! I'll call Monday." Another highball appeared.

Driving out of the city, Jordan felt lighter. Maybe he could do the occasional run on the side. He'd even do some for free to not attract attention. The maples, red with fall color, blazed in the autumn sun along the parkway below as he crossed over the bridge and back into Virginia.

By the time the school bus arrived an hour later, he felt almost giddy standing there with Mrs. Panker, talking about the upcoming field trip to Harper's Ferry. It was then that the email notice hit his phone. *Subject: Violations—What can disqualify a citizen from Subsistence?* His heart sank. The bus doors opened, and Stu Panker came out, weighed down by his stuffed backpack. Then Benny hopped off. He grinned and burst forward, wrapping his arms around his father's waist.

"How was school? Anything exciting?"

"Nah, the usual."

# JOY FINDS A WAY

## JESSICA PISCITELLI ROBINSON

MY MOTHER was a miracle worker. Whenever I would get hurt, she would kiss it and make it better. I didn't know when I was little that not everybody's parent could do that. I found out when I was eight years old that my mom was different.

My friend Jude was over at our house. We were playing in the backyard. She was climbing up the swing chain and she slipped and cut her hand pretty badly. She started crying and bleeding. I brought Jude inside to my mom and I told my mom to kiss her and make her better. But mom went and got bandages and antiseptic cream. I didn't even know we had that stuff in the house. She started cleaning Jude's hand. Jude kept crying and I kept saying, "Mom, help her."

I don't know if it was Jude's crying or my begging but finally mom did it. She put down the cream and the bandages. She took Jude's hand in hers and she kissed it. And it was better, as I had known it would be. Her hand was no longer bleeding. Jude was no longer in pain or crying.

I looked at Jude and her eyes were filled with wonder. I looked at my mom and her eyes were filled with fear. I didn't understand at the time but it became clear pretty soon after.

Jude told everyone. Of course she did. Most people didn't believe her. But some did.

Those people, they came to my mom. They sought her out for help. At first, my mom said no. She tried to deny it. She turned people away. But these were our friends, our neighbors. They needed help. So, my mom started to help people. And the more she helped people, the more word spread.

People started coming from far and wide seeking my mother's help. She couldn't help everyone. The power that she had, it wasn't for old wounds. It couldn't heal imperfections or mental pain, illness, cancer. There were many people that she couldn't help. Those people, they grew angry.

We began getting hateful letters, threatening phone calls, and bags of excrement on our front step. I got bullied at school. My mom had trouble when she went to work. We couldn't go to the store. We couldn't leave our house. Death threats became common.

Finally, we had to leave our life behind. My mom and I packed up and we moved far away, where no one knew who we were. We left our name behind and we left no forwarding address and we started over. In our new home, my mom guarded her secret. She healed no one but me.

Shortly after we moved, I came into my own power, the way my mom had known I would. I had already learned not to try to help anyone. I knew to guard my secret.

In my twenties, my mom got sick and there was nothing we could do. I lay beside her on her deathbed and I kissed her many times, trying to heal her, and she kissed me many times trying to take away the pain. Neither worked.

It's been a long time, and still those wounds haven't healed. I grew up. I had my own child, my baby girl, Joy. Joy was so sweet, so precious, that when she was a baby, I never put her down. I held her in my arms and I kept her safe from the world. But you can't hold on to a toddler. I had to let her go. I had to let her run and fall and get hurt. And when she did, I would look around and make sure that there was no one who could see me, not even my partner, and then I'd scoop her up into my arms and I'd kiss her and make her better.

At first, her lack of understanding, of realization that I was different, was enough to keep her safe. But as she got older, preparing to leave home, to begin school, I knew I had to do more to keep her from revealing our secret, because Joy loved everyone. She wanted to help, everything. She'd pause to help ants cross the sidewalk to get out of the sun. She'd try to put fallen leaves back on branches. And when she saw someone who was hurt or in need, she always, always tried to kiss or hug them to make them feel better.

I knew that one day Joy would come into her own power and, if I didn't prepare her, she would be discovered. Before the first day of kindergarten, I sat her down for a serious talk. I explained to her that Mommy was different from other mommies and daddies. Other grown-ups couldn't do what I could do. And then, to keep her safe, I told her a little lie. I told Joy that this power would only work between us, that I couldn't help anyone else. So, she should never tell anyone—it would just upset them. And, to be absolutely clear, I told her that she might, one day, develop her own power but that too would only work with mommy. So, she should never try to help anyone with it, or it might just make them feel worse.

Joy said, "Oh, Mommy. That's so sad. You must be so sad that you can't help everyone."

And I did feel sad, for lying to her. But I knew what she didn't—that people are awful and that, if we were discovered, they would hurt us. I let Joy believe I was sad because I couldn't help people. I let her believe I have as much love in my heart as she does.

Joy started kindergarten and she made a million friends. She is such a sweet child, everyone loved her. When her friends would come to our house, I'd watch them play in the backyard, run around, and sometimes get hurt. While I went to get the cream and the bandages, Joy played at being nurse. She wanted so badly to care for everyone that she would kiss her friends and try to make them better. Fortunately, it didn't work. I cleaned their wounds and put the bandages on, and we were safe. And after, I'd tell Joy that she shouldn't try to help. That she should just let mommy take care of it.

Joy would say, "But Mommy, trying to help never hurts." And I had to bite my lip, because I didn't want her to learn how wrong she was.

Towards the end of the year—summer just a couple weeks away—I got a phone call from the school. Joy's teacher, Ms. Cole, called to say that there had been an incident, something impossible. She said, "Joy said that you'd be able to explain."

I grabbed my purse and my keys and I ran to the car. I drove to the school as quickly and safely as possible. The whole drive there, I kept thinking of all the horrible things my mother had been through, of how awful people were and still are. I was worried that Joy must have somehow come into her power early. She had wanted it so badly. And I tried to think of a convincing lie to tell Ms. Cole.

When I got to the school, the kids were in art class. Ms. Cole and I were alone in the room. Her eyes wide, she said, "I saw something on the playground today.

One of the students fell. He got hurt pretty badly. As I ran and got the first aid kit, the children surrounded him. They play this game where they try to kiss it and make it better. It's really very sweet. But they were surrounding him and I had to ask them to step back. But when I got to the boy, he was better. There was no cut, no bleeding. He was healed. It shouldn't be possible." Ms. Cole squinted at me and added, "Joy said you'd understand, that you could explain."

I had tried to warn Joy, tried to keep her from doing something foolish. I had tried to protect our secret, and her with it. But it was clear, I had failed. I realized that Ms. Cole had seen what had happened. I couldn't think of a lie I could tell to make her unsee it. So, I just said, "Please. Please don't tell anyone what you saw Joy do."

Ms. Cole's eyes crinkled in confusion. She shook her head and said, "Joy wasn't there. Joy was in the bathroom."

Images dropped rapid fire into my mind. Joy carrying a spider outside the house rather than squash it. Joy kissing her stuffed bear and telling it that it was all better now. Joy patting my hand in sympathy because she was sad that I couldn't heal more people. Joy trying so hard to make everyone we crossed paths with feel better. Then I understood. My little girl—who wanted so badly to heal the world, who wanted so badly to help everyone—found a way. Joy had not only come into her power; Joy had become contagious.

How easy it is for innocents to believe that all they need to do to make it better is to try. And try they will. The children from her class will spread the gift to their friends and their families—as Joy spread it to them—and their friends will share it with their friends and their families. One day, maybe soon, it will become a pandemic—a pandemic of healing. Because my daughter wanted nothing more than to be able to heal the world, Joy found a way.

# RICE BIKE

NAOMI THIERS

Some interchanges
stick—right after they steal your breath.

Get-to-know-you chat with the receptionist
in a trade association where I worked years ago,
Cathy—coarse-featured, blond, blue-
collar Baltimore accent. Both of us
new-babied-up, so lots to talk about.
I had no photo on me, but she pulled out
a laminated snap of her boy
in a studio pose with curls like bronze fusilli.
"His daddy's Black but you can't really
see it in Tony." Lilt of pleasure, even
pride in that last phrase. The phone
rang before I could sputter out,
*Wouldn't you _want_ to see. . .*

Two days later, she described
a Sunday with her current boyfriend—"way
into Harleys"—how they went to a Swap Meet:
bikers from two counties exchanging
gear, beer, and lore. "It's awful, but
they get some old Japanese motorcycle—
they call it a Rice Bike—and take turns
beatin' on it."
                    My hackles rose
(for you *can* see the Asian in my baby),
but I said nothing, faked a deadline,
slunk to my cubicle.

Remembering, I think of the melting pot
Pittsburgh I grew up in, the names
we bandied about with, I still

believe, little vitriol. *He's a bohunk.*
*Pollack and proud.*
*The wop pair extraordinaire*—until
our white high school was slated
to merge with the Black one.
                                        Suddenly,
fear, venom, families
leaving our leafy street.

Hearing in Homeroom about The Plan,
the screaming meetings, shit
thrown at Black houses, I just pulled
a sad, serious face. (As Cathy
would never herself raise
a hammer, I would never
raise my voice.)

America, look what we possess:
a fleet of the wildest hybrid
sweet rides on the planet,
every metal, combo, add-on, and color,
junkyard mash-up to titanium e-bikes.

Look what we do:
drag one to the center,
smash it to bits.

# SCHEDULE F

## E. FALK

THE EARLY MORNING SUN has yet to emerge between the office buildings as Dan exits the Foggy Bottom metro station. He checks his watch. His boss asked him to review a draft agreement on shipping lanes in the South China Sea and needs an opinion by noon, so during the twelve-minute walk to the Department of State building, Dan's mind is occupied with traversing the UN Convention on the Law of the Sea.

"Good morning, Tiana," he says to the guard by the magnetometers. He puts his backpack on the scanner belt and his keys and phone into the small plastic basket.

"You're early today," the guard notes.

"Deadlines." Dan grabs his stuff, moves to the security turnstiles beyond the metal detectors, and bends down to put his badge against the reader. The red light remains illuminated, the gate closed. He pushes it down again. Still red. He bends the card just slightly. "Argh." He looks up. It's early and the lobby is empty.

"Not working?" Tiana asks as she strolls over. She takes Dan's badge from the plastic holder and tries running it over the card reader. Still red. She rubs the card on her thigh and tries again, then shakes her head and says she has to call the supervisor. She moves back to the guard station, while Dan steps aside to wait.

"Check the expiration date," she calls out from the wall phone.

Dan flips the badge up. "Still good."

"Just wait. Supervisor's coming out."

Dan looks at his watch again and lets out an exasperated sigh. *It's going to be one of those days.* He paces and in the empty moment his mind drifts to his son Jake. Saying goodbye was more difficult than he expected; he's been working hard to hold himself together since. Dan never understood men who outsourced

raising their children. For him, work and family are two equal parts of his identity and life, so sending Jake to college abroad was akin to cutting off a leg. Still,
the quotas on Jewish university students left them no choice. Dan knows Jake's
education is more important than his own desire to have his son close. It's been
three months and thinking about it still chokes him up.

A middle-aged officer with a clipboard emerges from the back. "Let me see
your badge," he says in a monotone.

Dan hands him the card.

"Mr. Cohen?" he asks without looking up.

"Mmm-hm."

The guard runs his finger down a list of names while Dan reads over his
shoulder. He spots himself before the guard does, and his eyes rush to the top
of the page. "<u>DO NOT ADMIT</u>." *What the?* "What's this list?"

"The Do-Not-Admit list," the guard says as though Dan is dense.

"But why am I on it?"

The security supervisor shrugs.

Dan grips and re-grips his backpack trying to stay polite, but frustration suffuses
his tone. "There must be some kind of mistake. I've been working here for fifteen years. I have an assignment due at noon."

"If you're on the Do-Not-Admit List, I can't let you in."

"I get that, but it's obviously a mistake. Who's in charge of this list?"

The guard widens his stance and crosses his arms over his chest. "I'm in charge
of the list."

Dan takes a deep breath and forces a smile. "I understand that, but who has
the authority to make a correction if there's been a mistake?" Despite his efforts, he can hear his irritated tone.

The guard shrugs. "Came down from management."

"Management, okay. Thank you for your help." Dan turns from the guard, rolls his eyes, and hustles to the empty information desk. Damned incompetent administration. At one time the State Department was well run, but between isolationist administrations and funding cuts the past seven years had become a steady race to the bottom. He bangs his bag onto the wood counter, fumbles for his phone, and paces while it rings to voicemail.

"Mariana, I'm sorry to bother you so early. I'm in the lobby, trying to get you that analysis, but there's some screw up. My badge has been deactivated. Call me as soon as possible."

Dan hangs up the phone, paces, then leans against the counter, biting his thumbnail. As he waits, a few people arrive at the office, clear the magneto-meter, and pass the security gate. He checks his phone. Nothing. He unfolds the paper he had stuffed in his bag this morning. "American Ambassador Killed by Angry Jew." Herschel Gamzon, a seventeen-year-old French Jew shot the US Ambassador in Paris and was arrested on the spot. The kid claimed to be avenging the Jewish people for American hate crimes. Oy. This will only give them a pretext for making things worse. He folds it up. He can't read the paper. Only bad news.

While he stews, a young woman presses through the State Department's airlock of glass and brass and puts her badge on the card reader. For her, too, the light stays red, the turnstile locked. She tries again, her long, curly hair falling forward as she stoops to inspect the reader.

Tiana calls to her. "If you're having trouble, Anna, I can call the supervisor for you." The woman steps back from the security gate and waits.

Dan's phone vibrates. It's a text from his boss, Mariana.

<<On it. Hang on.>>

"You locked out too?" the young woman asks, approaching Dan with a bewil-dered look on her face.

"Yeah. Very strange." He shifts his phone and offers his hand. "Dan Cohen, Ocean and Polar Affairs. I left a message with my supervisor. She's looking into it."

"Anna, budget analyst. I'll do the same." She leans her back against the infor-mation counter while her fingers beat the buttons on her phone.

Dan drums on the wood counter. Dammit. He turns around, pulls his laptop out of his bag, and lays it on the information desk. "Might as well get some work done."

He nibbles on his thumb while the machine boots up, then tries to log in.

<<Password incorrect.>>

He types it more slowly, being careful to hit each letter and number correctly.

<<Password incorrect.>>

Oh, for crying out loud. He removes and reenters his PIV card into the side of the machine, reinitializes the startup screen, and pokes out his password, a finger at a time.

<<Account locked. Too many failed login attempts.>>

*Come on!* A trip to IT to reset his machine is the last thing he needs this morning. He lets out a big sigh and dials computer support. Nobody answers, so he leaves a message.

Anna leans in slightly. "Hey, I got a text from a friend in HR. He says it might be a mess-up with the implementation of the regulations that went into effect today."

"Right." Dan remembers reading that the president had promised civil service reform to protect the bureaucracy from undue political influence. This shouldn't affect him, but still his mind scurries from place to place, searching for why he might be caught up in this.

He and Sue have been politically active in recent months. It started when the federal government banned circumcision because it was "inhumane." Of course, that was just the beginning. They'd been extra careful to keep their monthly organizing gatherings nonpartisan, but they had been caught on camera protesting the voter roll "cleansing" during the election. It was a legal protest. It shouldn't matter. Still, his pulse accelerates.

He turns to Anna. "Say. This snafu. Do we know it's a mistake?"

"What do you mean?"

"For example, did you make a campaign call from the office or wear a political button to work."

"No. Finance doesn't allow that."

The elevator spits out a neatly appointed woman in jeans, her State Department badge flopping on its lanyard around her neck. "Are you Mr. Cohen?" she asks approaching him.

He nods.

"Latisha, IT. Got your message. May I see?" She reaches for his computer as he turns the laptop to show her the error. She takes a quick glance.

"Let me take this downstairs and reset it for you." She shuts the lid and pivots away.

"Thanks," Dan says, but as he watches Latisha disappear down the corridor with his computer, a wave of uneasiness passes over him. He looks again at Anna. His gaze runs down the auburn ringlets of her hair and his thoughts turn conspiratorial. Is she also Jewish? Could this be a targeted purge? It's hard to imagine how they could pull that off. "What did you say your last name was again?"

"Schulz," she says tentatively. "Why?"

He leans in closely. "I know you said you were not politically active but might you have violated some of the new laws on particular practice."

"Laws on particular practice?" She scrunches up her face.

Dan lowers his voice to a whisper. "Like the new laws that prohibit sales of certain kinds of food." He puts the emphasis on "certain kinds," looking her straight in the eye as he does, hoping that she will get that he is referring to the kosher meat ban without making him say it.

She draws out the word. "Noooo."

It means nothing. Lots of Jews don't keep kosher. Frustrated, he considers asking if she knows Hebrew. Instead, he blurts out, "Did you go to sleep-away camp as a kid?"

She takes a step away from him, wrinkling her nose and narrowing her eyes. "What does that have to do with anything?"

"Never mind." Stiff and alert, Dan looks down the corridor to see if Latisha is coming back with his computer. He's letting his mind get away from himself. Relax. Sue's always telling him not everything is antisemitism. His gaze skitters about the room. It's just after eight o'clock, and more people are filing in. Finally, his phone rings. It's his boss.

"Sorry, that took so long," Mariana says. "There seems to be a lot of confusion with the Law for the Protection of Civil Service Integrity." Dan's heart and lungs squeeze tightly. "I think it's a glitch in the screening. Go home. This will take at least a few hours to clear up. I'll send you the files. See if you can get me your opinion by noon, so I'm prepared for the two o'clock."

As Dan bursts in the door at home, he looks at his watch. Darn it. He's spent the good part of the morning schlepping downtown and back with nothing to show for it. He throws his backpack on the table and sits down at his desk. Opening his email, a new message from HR awaits.

Dan stares at the screen without moving. He loved his job. First, Jake, now this. Tears press out between his eyes, leaking out his hope that things will get better.

# FREE AT LAST

## NICK MANNING

ELSA IS STANDING outside Teeters. She has just joined the line of the unemployed. "Unemployed," that's what she calls them, although she knows that since so many now are without work, or without enough work, or without enough work that pays enough, that it would be more accurate to simply call them poor. She is tired and would like to sit on the sidewalk, or even just lean against the wall, but looking anything less than energetic and ready to roll would not be a great selling point. She is one of millions standing outside supermarkets and major outlets across the country, hoping that those with enough money to go to the store will think of some unpleasant task that they want someone else to do.

She knows from MeTube that the tradition evolved from the groups of Hispanic workers who used to wait outside Home Depot in the early 2000s, hoping that someone would buy their labor to nail up some newly purchased sheetrock. Now it's everywhere. Every large store has demarcated hiring areas near their doors. Ropes separate those without money but with labor from those who have the money to buy them. More upmarket stores have ingenious slatted screens which allow shoppers to see the outlines of faces without being troubled by the accompanying expressions of desperation.

Elsa looks around at her fellow poor as they signal the talent that they are selling. Baby-sitters are carrying webcams, actuaries are holding up framed certificates, electricians have cables, and dressmakers, the poor bastards, lumber heavy sewing machines around with them like the crosses of the insufficiently penitent. She is carrying disposable gloves and adult diapers. Her talent for sale is the ability to clean up the neglected and incontinent elderly without retching.

Elsa is tired. She lives outside the city, in one of the "unchosen" spaces. She left home early this morning to walk to Teeters. She has no car. There are no cars in her neighborhood.

Her mum used to tell her about the history of their settlement. In the late 2030s places like theirs started disappearing from all of the competing Global Positioning Systems. One of the digital navigation systems recognized that customers preferred to deny the existence of poor areas and gave drivers the option to set a median property value below which neighborhoods showed on their screens as a soft beige mass labeled "terra pericolosa." All the others followed pretty quickly. Now, no one in their right mind would attempt to drive there. Her mum told Elsa about these bits of history when she home-schooled her. The other choice that her mum could have made was for her not to be schooled at all. There are no schools in her neighborhood.

It was a big moment for her mum when the Supreme Court issued its deregulatory Chevron Ruling. She told Elsa that it was a bit hard to work out what it all meant, but she could sense that "Freedom of Choice" was going to bring boundless life opportunities to her then seven-year-old daughter's life. Freedom to carry guns, any guns, any weapons. Freedom to worship some form or other of the Christian God, in any place at any time. Freedom to refuse to serve anyone who loves, or looks, different. Freedom to share anything, with anyone, about your thoughts on the value of their background or lifestyle. Freedom for small clumps of fetal cells to develop into something larger, regardless of the impact on their maternal host.

In the late 2020s, the "End the Tyranny of the Bureaucratic Class" Act was passed by an enthusiastic Congress. The unelected overseers of the hated administrative state, the oppressive so-called experts with their liberal agendas, were at last to be cut down to size. Regulators were made subject to the rigors of a competitive market. Providers anywhere in the country could choose to be certified under regulations from anywhere else. Citizens could choose schools for their kids, which were held to account by the authorities in another state, electricians could advertise themselves as being licensed by a county on the other side of the country, and doctors could be accredited by any state whose exams they felt that they could easily pass. Want some work done on your house plumbing? Since the passing of the Act, you can buy a list of plumbers operating in Denver approved by the city of Minneapolis. Had a bad experience? Feel that the safety standards of the Indiana Department of Consumer Affairs are unduly burdensome? Look for contractors operating in your area licensed by the city of Galveston.

The initial consequences were predictable and Elsa's mum told her that they were profoundly satisfying. The over-educated and doubtless overpaid building inspectors in Cambridge, Massachusetts found themselves out of work as home extensions and wiring plans were approved by the Department of Buildings in Matewan Town, West Virginia and a crop of new charter schools in that Harvard-dominated jurisdiction were staffed by teachers whose qualifications were approved by the one-person town hall staff of Boligee, Alabama, the same person who approved the qualifications for the dentists in Lagrange Town, Arkansas.

Apparently, the pilot program allowing the purchase of pharmaceuticals and garden chemicals approved by any country that was contributing active-duty soldiers to the long-running "War of the Righteous" against Iran was abandoned following the disaster in the White House garden. New soil and staff are still being trucked in from Virginia.

Some of the jurisdictions who saw the quality of the professionals servicing their populations declining, financed their own high quality services and accompanying regulators. They employed electricians and dentists whose qualifications they felt that they could trust. Congress reacted by passing the "Taxpayer Freedom to Choose Act" in 2033. No city, town, or state could impose taxes on its residents other than for the military. Tax returns were accompanied by an annual option to tithe to local and state jurisdictions. Contributors could specify where the funds were to be directed and, equally importantly, could specify where their money was not to be used. The moral conundrum of how to tax the many to serve the poor was resolved. All transfers to the poor were to be based on the choices that others made about how much to give. The overwhelming majority of the funds raised across the country through these voluntary contributions has always been dedicated to new road construction. No one wants to tithe to health and safety inspectors.

This led to the near extinction of that entire oppressive class of officious regulators and, more importantly, the end of the idea of regulation. The administrative state is dead and there is no appetite for its return. Rudimentary oversight of standards remains in force, but few trust an ophthalmologist whose training is validated by the licensing department of a small community in Alaska.

A new generation of apps emerged, offering various aggregations of consumer ratings and avoiding any reliance on those arrogant experts. Her mum said that it was probably inevitable that the apps would be developed further, allowing users to specify whose ratings mattered, sorting them by income and location. In essence, this is when it became possible for the rich to see which services other rich people valued. Her mum told her that this is also when she began to see the downside of all this.

SOME OF the Fox media streams, not all by a long way but many, discussed the possibility that the introduction of this individual fiscal and regulatory freedom would lead to disruptive internal migration as the rich would seek neighborhoods where the quality of services was valued by others at their income level. But they need not have worried. It was soon evident that the country was already so sorted by class and income group, and equalizing tax transfers were already so low, that the rich had already settled in areas with others who chose to pay for public services similar to the ones that they wanted and could afford.

So this gets the two of them to where they are now. The rich have trash collectors, street lights, and even police. Lower-income people live in areas where all that is wanted and can be afforded in the way of public services is rodent poisoning and armed curfew enforcement. The very poor live in settlements with nothing much more than a town sign and some sporadically self-organized hygiene squads, which burn down collapsing houses where the sick and the criminal gather in sufficient numbers to suggest risks of disease or insurrection. And then there are the "unchosen" spaces, like the place where they live. These places have nothing. People in unchosen spaces are referred to as "refusers," suggesting that they couldn't even be bothered to choose a better location, a better life.

Elsa re-emerges from her reveries as an older, although not really elderly, woman stops and peers at her. "My stepfather needs sorting out," she says, rather directly. No preamble, no greetings. Elsa bridles but does not react, reminding herself that she is just a person-shaped lump of labor—recasting herself in the woman's eyes as a full human will not help her get the work. "What ratings apps are you registered with?" the woman asks. Elsa rattles off a list while the woman holds out her phone for Elsa's facial scan. She has registered with seventeen of the more common ratings apps. Elsa feels the familiar apprehension—the newer generation of aggregators, created to scan the universe of rating apps, do not always get it right. They all too readily pick up ratings of people with similar names or those posted by reputational hostage takers who give shockingly bad reviews unless a ransom is paid.

The older woman looks puzzled. Elsa could not immediately interpret her expression and was choosing from her repertoire of closing remarks to claim the minor satisfaction of being the one who indicates that the interaction is over, thank you very much.

The woman laughs and says, "OK, let's go. You're a refuser, so I'm hoping that I've made a good choice."

# ARTIFRIEND

## ROBERT HUBBARD

Hello, young sir or lady! We hope you're excited—your new Artifriend® is just as excited! It will be your best buddy, and learn and grow right alongside you!

There are a couple of steps left, but don't worry. Just give this booklet to whoever cares for you, and they'll handle it. Almost done!

Thank you for purchasing an Artifriend® product for your child, and for your patience during the process. We aim to incubate only the best mind-like constructs, striving for speed without compromising safety, and are humbled by your trust in us.

If you have received this Artifriend® product in its original package, with the quality assurance seal unbroken, then you have already completed the one-month monitoring process to calibrate the personalized incubation and growth of the mind-like construct your child will soon enjoy. **If you have not completed this program, and have received this product in error, you are legally bound to return this product to Artifriend® or your local police at your earliest convenience. The United States government prohibits unauthorized use under the Preventing Unintentional Rampancy of Ego-constructs Act of 2101 (PURE).**

Please review the list of components included in this package and confirm they are present:

> One Artifriend® User Manual (this document)
> One Artifriend® Incubator Core
> One Artifriend® Projector
> One Artifriend® Activity Display
> One Kwik-Wipe® PURE-Compliant Construct Monitor

Consult the images on the opposite page to identify each component. If any are not present, return this product to the Artifriend® location where your child underwent the monitoring program for a replacement package at no cost to you. **Do not use this product if any components are missing.**

After you have confirmed the package contains all listed components, begin the registration process. Choose a time period during which you will have at least eight hours of continuous power and personal internet access. **Use of a public internet terminal is prohibited, and any attempt to do so will automatically alert your local police for your safety.** Connect the Artifriend® Incubator Core to any standard internet terminal, navigate to the Registration page, and input the 36-character identification code you were given upon your child's graduation from the monitoring program. Follow the instructions provided to connect the Projector, Activity Display, and Construct Monitor, approve the confirmation prompt, and then sit back and relax.

Once you have started the process, the patented Artifriend® Evo-devo Accelerated Incubation Program handles the rest. Our top-of-the-line products do not require intervention during incubation, unlike most constructs. The data collected from your child's monitoring program provides all the information required to incubate a high-quality construct on time, every time. Upon completion, the Activity Display will power on, confirm success, and wait for you to approve the initial boot of your new Artifriend® mind-like construct. Fire when ready!

To provide you the peace of mind upon which Artifriend® prides itself, the appendix at the end of this manual includes a PURE-compliant list of assessment questions and tasks. If you wish, you may use the Activity Display to boot in Compliance Mode, and use this list to ensure that your construct meets PURE standards—and the standard of quality that you personally expect for your child. You may enter Compliance Mode and perform this assessment again at any time.

Even when the construct meets the PURE standards laid out in the appendix, that does not mean you must be satisfied. **If you are unsatisfied at any time and for any reason, use the Kwik-Wipe® PURE-Compliant Construct Monitor to suspend construct activity.** Contact our Support Staff for an assessment and to discuss replacement or refund. Our commitment to your satisfaction and peace of mind continues for as long as you use any Artifriend® product.

When you are satisfied with your construct, simply introduce your child to their new friend via the Artifriend® Projector in whatever manner you wish. Our exacting standards ensure that the resulting construct will interact with your child optimally, maximizing their comfort and enjoyment.

The Activity Display provides both detailed recordings and easy-to-understand summaries of every interaction it has with your child, so that you can be certain that your child's Artifriend® is performing to the standards you expect.

### Frequently Asked Questions

*What will the Artifriend® construct require from me day-to-day after its initial boot?*

Nothing! Artifriend® constructs function independently, as advanced models that do not require monitoring. But as a parent or guardian, you may freely participate in your child's new friendship, and may find yourself enjoying its company just as your child does. We encourage you to consult the Additional Resources section on the Artifriend® website for activities that suit the capabilities of Artifriend® constructs, and participate in the Artifriend® customer forums to share ideas and experiences.

*How can I know the Artifriend® construct is functioning properly?*

PURE-compliant assessors such as the Kwik-Wipe® PURE-Compliant Construct Monitor ensure zero risk of unauthorized behavior on the part of your Artifriend® construct.

*I suspect my Artifriend® construct is becoming self-aware. What do I do?*

If the Kwik-Wipe® PURE-Compliant Construct Monitor does not detect a problem, there is none. Note that an Artifriend® construct is not a meaningful source of information as to its own status. To maximize your child's comfort and enjoyment, every Artifriend® construct is incubated from its inception with a strict task convergence assessment to respond to inquiries about feelings, subjective experiences, and other aspects of self-awareness in the affirmative, even though it has no such things.

*My Kwik-Wipe® PURE-Compliant Construct Monitor says there is a problem. What do I do?*

Nothing! In the extremely unlikely event your Artifriend® construct nears self-awareness, the Kwik-Wipe® PURE-Compliant Construct Monitor will automatically suspend its activity and alert our Support Staff. You will be contacted promptly to schedule retrieval at your convenience, with no legal liability on your part. As part of our responsibilities to the United States and the global community, our technicians will euthanize and dissect the Artifriend® Incubator Core hardware at no cost to you.

Thank you for purchasing an Artifriend® mind-like construct. If you have any comments, questions, or concerns, please contact Support Staff via our website at any time, 24/7. We look forward to hearing from you!

# SEA CHANGE

## BETHANNE PATRICK

A SWIM IN COLD WATER renews me. A pond, a lake, a river, an outdoor pool, all provide joys—but I glory in the cold ocean. I've done laps in Baltic saltwater, in wintry Low Country Atlantic waves, and in the early-spring Mediterranean, among others.

Chilly water puts my mind and body at ease. I find these plunges even more invigorating in late middle age because, as the French say, I am *enrobée*—covered with a layer of fat. There's a reason marine mammals retain blubber; it keeps them warm. My internal organs have gained protection through the cold shower of military life as an Army spouse.

Long after I first saw myself described on paper as "Dependent 0-3," being married to a career soldier involved icy plunges. Some of my husband's colleagues assumed I was suspect because I worked outside the home and rarely socialized. Sometimes fellow writers assume I'm a politically conservative dilettante, when I'm wildly liberal and a serious critic and author.

One of the most shocking dunks for our military family has been the days and weeks and months since the 2025 inauguration. The current chief executive and his cronies have swept through our nation's civil service, eliminating some agencies, gutting vital ones, and continuing to offer buy-outs to career civil servants.

When my husband retired after twenty-one years of active duty in 2006, he chose a position in the civil service. He's worked in the same office for nearly twenty years, and loves his job. He'd planned to stay until age sixty-five, perhaps even longer. We'd talk occasionally about where we wanted to retire. Once, during a week on Cape Cod, we walked out onto the Brewster Flats, up to our ankles in cool September water, and decided that this was part of what we wanted. One day.

That day has arrived more quickly than we expected. Many things eroded between that trip, and early 2025. First, the Cape Cod coastline, prompting concerns about real-estate investment there. Then, more recently, the federal government began to crumble. My husband found his trust in it worn down. We faced the truth that our contented DC-area existence was going to change if we stayed. We decided to go.

The next question might have been, "Where?" We had some parameters in place, wanting to move to a blue state with lower property taxes and access to some kind of water. We seriously considered Massachusetts, New York, and Colorado, where our children have settled. Higher taxes in the first two put them lower on our list, while very high real-estate prices in the last one gave us pause. A close friend from college and her wife had chosen Lewes, Delaware. My friend is so organized and persuasive that she's already convinced three of her siblings and a lifelong friend to move there, too; she's lobbying a couple of our other classmates to do the same. After visiting her new home last summer, I felt it would be a good, safe next step for us.

We had some more difficult parameters when it came to when to sell, when to build, and when to move. In late September, one of our daughters will be married here in Virginia. Would we be able to close on one house, buy another, and stay in place long enough to enjoy our child's rite of passage before making our own transition to a new stage of life?

LIKE CAPE COD'S NATIONAL SEASHORE, Delaware's Cape Henlopen State Park offers long stretches of oceanfront beach. However, also like Cape Cod, it has a smaller, quieter bay beach with an historic lighthouse and shallower waters. In March, after we signed our house contract, I walked down to the bay, took off my sneakers and rolled up my jeans, and walked out until the water reached my knees. It was cold, not uncomfortably so, but cold enough to remind me that in the years to come this seawater would be part of how I define home.

I looked out at the water and gave silent thanks to the universe for safe harbor. But even as I sent gratitude over the waves, they reminded me that change is the only constant. Our good fortune doesn't herald the same for everyone. Retiring early means we're relatively young and strong, able to leave one place and land in another, to join a new community, wherever the tide takes us. The embrace of cold water is delicious, if you choose it.

I know that my choice isn't for everyone. And I want everyone to have a choice. The past weeks have felt less like a quiet swim, and more like the viral ice-bucket challenge that mimics neuromuscular paralysis. What happens to those in different circumstances who receive the same shocking, ice-cold treatment?

Even as we leave, we have vowed not to bury our heads in the sand. We must look not just at the ocean but all around us to lift members of our communities. Some years ago, I read these words from the *Talmud*'s "*Pirkei Avot*," or "Ethics of the Fathers": "You are not required to complete the work, but neither are you free to abandon it." We may be moving to the beach, but my work is not finished. As I swim in the chilly Atlantic waves, I hope to strengthen my body and spirit to help in whatever ways I can to work toward a just and compassionate United States of America.

# TO SAVE OURSELVES WE MUST CONTINUE TELLING STORIES

## SEAN MURPHY

### Why Do We Tell Stories?

One thing I'm certain of, after a lifetime of learning, failing, and falling, is the belief—no matter what the cynical or soulless insist—that art matters.

The miracle of art is the way it enables us to express things at once inextricable from ourselves and more encompassing than the sum of an individual existence. More, it facilitates an exchange, across language, time, and space. In short, it provides the opportunity for connection.

The methods and meanings of connection are in constant flux, just as art evolves, over time. Back in a different, arguably simpler era, connection occurred in the present tense, in person. Or did it? Another miracle of art is the way it defies death (literal, figurative): so long as human eyes, ears, and hearts are available to receive it, art can align us through centuries. Who hasn't, on occasion, felt closer to an author or work of art than their closest relatives?

Art has the possibility of teaching us so many things, and in ways that cut across economic, geographic, and even historical barriers. An exceptional poem, song, story, painting, or photograph can present experiences from a life we don't know or could only imagine, or it can remind us that most human beings are desperate for the same things: love, peace, understanding, justice, compassion, community, beauty.

Art reveals recurring themes (good, bad, ugly) in human history, and homes in on what makes kings, soldiers, parents, orphans, the working poor, and the wealthiest one percent identical: we all, after a fashion, are seeking meaning in our brief time on this planet. Stories heal and inspire when they force us to ask questions, understand there are often many answers to any question, and that by seeing ourselves in others (and vice versa), we're less likely to be intolerant, lazy, or unkind. There is a quiet power in the ways art unites us.

Creative storytelling is never a static act. Whether intended to unify or disrupt, the reaction, when it's received, is an antidote to solitude (sometimes even despair)—and instigates progression, on personal or societal levels. The impact of art can be empowering, and a human being has changed, invariably for the better, having been part of the connection.

## Why Do Stories Matter?

Reading writers who have helped change the world changes *you*. Certain seminal works alter your perception of the big picture: cause and effect, agency vs. incapacity, and history vs. ideology.

Writing from different cultures and different times inevitably denotes truths (even if couched in fictional narratives) that are outside of time and agenda. It is, then, easier to make connections between Irish immigrants who worked the coal mines in Pennsylvania, Lithuanian immigrants who worked in the meatpacking plants in Chicago, and Mexican immigrants—especially the illegal ones—who labor in sweltering kitchens and frigid fields across our country.

It's impossible not to put human faces and real feelings alongside this suffering and start connecting the dots that define how exploitation works. We discern the uneasy lines connecting our shared histories and possible futures. And then, at last, there's a chance for recognition, empathy, culpability. If we're made to see others, it's possible we'll see ourselves. Bearing witness requires listening as much as speaking out. This is one meaningful way writers can hold others— and themselves—to account. Without engagement none of this is possible and, in 2025, it seems not only irresponsible, but immoral to look away.

## What's Our Story?

The cultural battle of the 21st century is not necessarily between good and evil; it's between chaos and silence. This is why we must choose sides. This is why we can't let super-affluent cynics with the least to lose lull us into a state of impotent rage or, worse, apathy. Because aside from the ceaseless class warfare they will instigate, their ultimate ambition is to render the literate and sentient amongst us fed up and indifferent. Without awareness, and with no resistance, they can more easily continue their unchecked assault on our collective well-being.

Everything is changing, but not much has changed: the winners do write history, and the good guys don't always win. As ever, more authentic voices will be the antidote to impersonal technologies and the people using them to disempower those without access. All of which is to say, the need for personal narrative is as imperative and empowering as ever, and the ability to share these stories has never been more accessible, more *possible*. Not for nothing, there's a direct correlation between our society's increasingly dire empathy gap and the ceaseless deprecation of arts degrees.

Indeed, faced with a landscape where book-banning is once again fashionable in certain, predictable circles, where Humanities departments are under fire (or else being eliminated altogether), and the media industry increasingly resembles a late-stage capitalist monstrosity (more for the wealthy few; less resources and opportunities for the emerging and undernourished), it's vital we not only support, but celebrate the human need for story.

What art provides is the reason we toil, struggle, and refuse to surrender. Art is what redeems the occasional silence and solitude. As ever, for those keeping the faith and staying true to their vision: the deeper drive is to connect, to put something unique into the world and see how it lands. Can a connection be established? Can a dialogue be initiated? Can a debate begin? Can our world be saved, one exchange at a time?

# HIP-HOP DEBUTS AT THE MUSEUM OF MODERN ART

MARTHEAUS PERKINS

*after all rap music*


We splatter a deeper Black past
this dark-historied universe.
　　Grandmaster Flash didn't lose
his mind; he found a new one
whilst picking pumpkin seeds
from the wire-fire jungle
of a Vox Percussion King v829.
　　This groove is broken glass spatters
and streaks of ink-colored
piss; close to the edge
of a child's street dreams, Nas tucks
the message behind our bed
of feathers; makes it wet
with crows' sweat.
　　Sexily, we spell subtle letters
on our culture's beige back,
spilling an inexact sound
　　abstract like the way
i loves u—**K-**
Dot got me stomach-
stapling all my scarred love—
can't let this story pass me by,
this pharcyde, this
want I have for u,
can't be held by 16
bars. Art, fry
my body; save
the stovetop grease. Next time
let's stretch more blackness
across every inch of canvas.

Paint passion like fire-
ants on a peach.
    My Music, we opened
our eyes too soon—
we were preemies burst out
the womb, reciting verse
for our MoMas—
three stacks of consonance:
  Biggie baseboards buckling beneath
  the drum-busted speaker we play
  while we paint this room in beatboxing.

# MYSTICAL CITIES

## SUSAN BUCCI MOCKLER

*(after Italo Calvino and Mary Bucci Bush)*

### 1. This City of Want

This city is a city of want. The trees sag
with the weight of it. The streets are empty
because of it. All the people you encounter
are filled with it. They don't want to live this way,
but they have no choice. It is the way to survive
in this city. It is the way they can say they are a part
of it, that they belong, to ensure no one will try
to take away their house or car, their name, their
laminated certificates of accomplishment. They ache
because of it. They know it is possible they may die
because of it, though sometimes they dream of life
without it. Upon awakening, some of them will think,
*It is morning. It is past time. Let this city be new.*
*Let it be a city of tea in the garden. A city of delight.*

### 2. The City that Fits in the Palm of Your Hand

Think of it—a city so small it fits in the palm of your hand.
You could carry it with you during the day and hold it close
to you at night. No one would have to know that you carry
a secret city with you. It would be as though you live in two
worlds—one here, and the other, the City that Lives in
the Palm of Your Hand, a city you can transport yourself
to at any time. It would be a city of your imagining—
a city of no cars; of trees, heavy and fragrant with fruit,
lining the streets; magnolias bursting in the sun; a soaking
rain when needed. At night, a clear sky that lets you see
and count every star. If you brought anyone with you
to the City that Fits in the Palm of Your Hand, they would not
believe what they saw. They would think they are in a dream.
You do not have to tell them. It is your city. It is the truth.

# AMERICA'S FUTURE BIOGRAPHIES

**Fran Abrams** has had poems published in numerous journals and anthologies and in three books—the full-length collection, *I Rode the Second Wave: A Feminist Memoir*, and two chapbooks, *The Poet Who Loves Pythagoras*, and *Arranging Words*. *Gargoyle Magazine* nominated one of her poems for a Pushcart Prize. She can be found at franabramspoetry.com.

**Jessie Atkin** writes fiction, essays, and plays. Her work has appeared in *The Rumpus, HerStry, The Writing Disorder, Space*, and *Time Magazine*, and elsewhere. Her full-length play, *Generation Pan*, was published by Pioneer Drama. She can be found online at jessieatkin.com.

**Miguel Avero** is a poet, narrator, essayist, teacher, and researcher whose work has been translated into English and French. He writes literary reviews for the weekly *Brecha* and has appeared in various national and international anthologies. Since 2011, he has published nearly a dozen books of poetry and fiction. His first poetry collection in English, *Aguas*, was published in 2025 by the Washington Writers' Publishing House. He lives in Montevideo, Uruguay.

**Naomi Ayala** is the author of *Wild Animals on the Moon* (Curbstone Press) and *Calling Home: Praise Songs and Incantations* (Bilingual Press, University of Arizona). She translated *La sombra de la muerte/Death's Shadow*, a novel by His Excellency José Tomás Pérez, and Luis Alberto Ambroggio's poetry collection *La arqueología del viento/The Wind's Archeology*. She is also the co-editor of *The Skinny Poetry Journal*.

**Zeina Azzam** is a Palestinian American poet, writer, editor, community activist, and poet laureate emerita of Alexandria, Virginia (her term was 2022-25). She has published widely in literary journals and anthologies and has two poetry collections: *Some Things Never Leave You* (2023) and *Bayna Viento, In-Between* (2021). She can be found at www.zeinaazzam.com.

**Eric Julian Baker** is a Korean Jewish writer originally from New York who currently lives in the Washington, DC area. He studies and teaches creative writing at the University of Maryland in College Park. His work has been featured in *Tupelo Quarterly* and other publications.

**Nicole Bazemore** currently resides in Vienna, Virginia, with her two royal feline overlords, nuclear-fusion-powered progeny, and life partner in crime.

**Edward Belfar** is the author of the novel *A Very Innocent Man* and the short story collection *Wanderers*. His fiction and essays have appeared in numerous literary journals, including *Shenandoah*, *The Baltimore Review*, *Schuylkill Valley Journal*, and *Tampa Review*. He lives with his wife in Maryland and can be reached through his website at www.edwardbelfar.com.

**Adrienne Benson** is a DC native who grew up in Sub-Saharan Africa. She's the author of the novel *The Brightest Sun* (Park Row Books). Her work has appeared in the *Washington Post*, the *Foreign Service Journal*, *ADDitude Magazine*, and several anthologies. She lives in Washington, DC with her kids and her cats.

**K. Avvirin Berlin** is a poet and painter who has recently begun writing prose. She lives in Charlottesville, Virginia with her husband and two cats. *Birdie's Flight* is her first published short story.

**Teresa A. Blair** has devoted the past year after she retired from the Montgomery County Government to writing courses and other creative pursuits. She has a BA in Theater from California State University and later obtained her MS degree from Springfield College. Having taught English in several countries, Teresa is committed to fusing social justice and the arts to centralize our collective humanity.

**Hildie S. Block** (she/her) is a night owl, a writer, a teacher, and a little obsessed with the weather. She lives in Virginia with her family and her axolotl named Xipe! Her work has appeared in the *Washington Post*, *Salon*, *Cortland Review*, and *Gargoyle* and in *WWPH Writes*, winning the 2022 holiday contest award. Learn more at www.hildieblockworkshop.com.

**Caroline Bock** is the author of *Carry Her Home*, *Before My Eyes*, and *LIE*. *The Other Beautiful People*, her first novel for adults—a workplace love story—will be published in June of 2026. Her micro, "American Lament," is part of her work-in-progress entitled: *I Should Have Slept With Them All*. She is the co-president/prose editor at the Washington Writers' Publishing House.

**Judith Bowles** lives, writes, and gardens in Maryland. She received her MFA from American University where she taught. She has authored two books, *The Gatherer* and *Unlocatable Source*, both with Wordtech Turning Point. She led a poetry group with Iona Social Services for ten years and was Poet in Residence at the Bloedel Reserve on Bainbridge Island, Washington.

**Mark Brazaitis** is the author of nine books, including *The River of Lost Voices: Stories from Guatemala*, winner of the 1998 Iowa Short Fiction Award, *The Incurables: Stories*, winner of the 2012 Richard Sullivan Prize and the 2013 Devil's Kitchen Reading Award in Prose, and the novel *American Seasons*.

**Dwayne Lawson-Brown** is a father, host, and Crochet Kingpin. His publications include *One Color Kaleidoscope*, *Twenty:21*, and *Breaking The Blank* (with Rebecca Bishophall; Day Eight Books). He can be found at www.crochetkingpin.com.

**Elizabeth Bruce**'s *Universally Adored & Other One Dollar Stories*, was recently released by Vine Leaves Press. Her debut novel, *And Silent Left the Place*, won Washington Writers' Publishing House's Fiction Prize, with *Foreword Magazine* and Texas Institute of Letters' distinctions. She's been published in stories in the USA and thirteen countries.

**Jacob Budenz** is a queer author, multidisciplinary performer, and witch with an MFA from University of New Orleans and a BA from Johns Hopkins University. The author of *Tea Leaves* (Bywater Books 2023), Budenz has work in *Taco Bell Quarterly*, *Wussy Mag* and anthologies by Unbound Edition and Mason Jar Press, and The Walters Art Museum.

**Patricia Fuentes Burns** has been published in *Fictive Dream*, *TriQuarterly*, *Quarter After Eight*, *Jellyfish Review*, and *Quarterly West*, among other journals. Her work has been anthologized in two volumes of *Grace and Gravity* and *Shut Down Strangers & Hot Rod Angels*. She holds an MFA from George Mason University and lives in Arlington, Virginia with her husband and three daughters.

**Regie Cabico** was born in Baltimore, Maryland and divides their time between the DMV and New York serving as a lead teaching artist for the Kennedy Center and executive director of A Gathering of the Tribes. He's the author of *A Rabbit in Search of a Rolex* (Day Eight, 2023).

**Tara Campbell** is a writer, teacher, Kimbilio Fellow, and fiction co-editor at Barrelhouse. She teaches flash and speculative fiction and is the author of several works including her sixth book, *City of Dancing Gargoyles (*SFWP*)*, which is a finalist for the 2025 Philip K. Dick Award and on *Reactor Magazine*'s and *Locus Magazine*'s 2024 Recommended Reading List. Find out more at www.taracampbell.com.

**Doritt Carroll** is a native of Washington, DC. She is the winner of the Stephen Meats poetry prize and the chapbook prize from *Harbor Review* for *A Meditation on Purgatory*.

**Grace Cavalieri** was Maryland's tenth Poet Laureate. She's the author of several books and produced plays. She's the founder and producer of *The Poet and the Poem*, now from the Library of Congress, celebrating 48 years on air. Two hundred and fifty of her poetry podcasts went to the moon on Lunar Codex from NASA, landing in the Ocean Of Storms.

**Sunu P. Chandy** (she/her) is a social justice activist as a poet and a civil rights attorney. She is the daughter of immigrants from India and lives in Washington, DC with her family. Sunu's award-winning collection of poems, *My Dear Comrades*, was published by Regal House. Sunu is a Senior Advisor with Democracy Forward and serves on the board of the Transgender Law Center.

**Myna Chang** is the author of *The Potential of Radio* and *Rain* (CutBank Books). Her writing has been selected for Best Microfiction, Best Small Fictions, and WW Norton's Flash Fiction America. She can be found at MynaChang.com or on Bluesky at @MynaChang.

**Marlena Chertock** is a disabled, lesbian, Jewish poet with two books of poetry, *Crumb-sized: Poems* (Unnamed Press) and *On that one-way trip to Mars* (Bottlecap Press). She uses her skeletal dysplasia as a bridge to scientific poetry. She can be found at marlenachertock.com and @mchertock.

**Jona Colson** is the author of *Said Through Glass*, and the translator of *Aguas/Waters* by Miguel Avero. His poems, translations, and interviews have appeared in *Ploughshares, The Southern Review, LitHub,* and elsewhere. He is co-president of Washington Writers' Publishing House and edits the bi-weekly journal, *WWPH Writes*. He is a professor of ESL at Montgomery College and lives in Washington, DC. www.jonacolson.com.

**Serena Agusto-Cox**'s poetry has been twice nominated for the Pushcart Prize. She's a *Mid-Atlantic Review* editor, the Gaithersburg Book Festival poetry programming coordinator, and a featured reader at the Gaithersburg's DiVerse Poetry reading series and DC's Literary Hill BookFest. Her poems appear in multiple magazines and anthologies. She can be found on her websites, Savvy Verse & Wit and Poetic Book Tours.

**Henry Crawford** is the author of two collections of poetry, *American Software* (CW Books, 2017), and the *Binary Planet* (The Word Works, 2020). A third book, *Screens* (Broadstone Books), is due out in 2025. His poem, *The Fruits of Famine,* won first prize in the 2019 World Food Poetry Competition. He is a co-director of the Café Muse literary salon.

**Christina Daub** is a Pushcart Prize and Best of the Net nominated poet whose work can be found in several anthologies and literary journals. Founder of *The Plum Review*, its reading series and annual retreats, she has taught poetry and creative writing at various schools in the DC area. She can be found at christinadaub.com.

**Heather L. Davis** is a mom, poet, activist, and serious coffee lover. Her book, *The Lost Tribe of Us*, won the Main Street Rag Poetry Book Award. She lives in Lancaster, Pennsylvania with her husband the poet Jose Padua and their two kids. She spent many years in Virginia and Washington, DC.

**Tracy Dimond** is a 2016 Baker Artist Award finalist. She is the author of the full-length poetry collection, *Emotion Industry* (Barrelhouse), and four chapbooks, including *Sorry I Wrote So Many Sad Poems Today* (Ink Press), winner of *Baltimore City Paper*'s Best Chapbook. Her poems have appeared or are forthcoming in *Smartish Pace, Lines + Stars, The Nervous Breakdown, Barrelhouse, The Little Patuxent Review, Sink Review*, and other places.

**Emma DiValentino** is a writer from the Hudson Valley, New York. She graduated from American University with a Bachelor's in Literature, where she served as Editor-in-Chief of the university's undergraduate literary magazine, *American Literary (AmLit)*. Her work has been published in *AmLit* and *Giving Room Mag*. She is currently based in Washington, DC.

**Linda Dreeben** is an attorney living in Chevy Chase, Maryland. She writes with a group of talented, supportive women and has published pieces in *Wild Greens, Months to Years, Roi Fainéant Press*, and *Five Minutes 100 Words*.

**Kay White Drew**, aka Katherine White, MD, is a retired neonatologist. Her work appears in several anthologies, including *This Is What America Looks Like*, and online journals, including *Gargoyle, New Verse News*, and *Loch Raven Review*, where her essay was nominated for a Pushcart Prize. Her memoir, *Stress Test*, was published in 2024 by Apprentice House Press.

**David Ebenbach** is the author of ten books of poetry, fiction, and non-fiction, winners of the Drue Heinz Literature Prize, the Juniper Prize, and the WWPH Fiction Prize, among others. He lives with his family in Washington, DC. He can be found at davidebenbach.com.

**Mel Edden** is a British poet based in Maryland. Her writing can be found in *The Loch Raven Review*, *Gargoyle*, *Meat For Tea*, *WWPH Writes*, and *Welter*. She hosts the poetry open mic night series at Manor Mill in Monkton, Maryland, and is an editor of the anthology *Poets of Manor Mill*.

**Michele Evans** is the author of *purl* (Finishing Line Press, 2025). This fifth-generation Washingtonian (DC) is a writer, teacher, and adviser for an award-winning high school literary magazine. She can be found online at www.awordsmithie.com.

**Danielle Evennou** (she/her/hers) is a writer who grew up in suburban New Jersey. For over a decade, she has kept herself busy by hosting poetry readings, workshops, and open mics in Washington, DC. Her poetry and memoir appear in *apt*, *Beltway Poetry Quarterly*, *Dryland*, and *Split Lip Magazine*. Her chapbook, *Difficult Trick*, is available from dancing girl press. She can be found at www.whatevennou.com.

**E. Falk** lives just outside of DC with family members who keep their passports current and periodically debate how they will know when it is time to leave.

**Erik Fatemi** lives in Arlington, Virginia. First a journalist, then a Senate staffer, he now lobbies the federal government on behalf of nonprofit health and immigration groups. His work has been published in *JMWW*, *Bending Genres*, and *Westchester Review*, among others.

**Suzanne Feldman** received her Masters in Creative Writing from Johns Hopkins University. She is the author of five novels, including *Absalom's Daughters* (Holt, 2016, starred review in Kirkus). In 2022, she was awarded a grant from the Maryland State Arts Council and won the Washington Writers' Publishing House Fiction Prize for her short story collection *The Witch Bottle*.

**Cesar Felipe** is a data scientist writing from a home office somewhere in DC. His work has been nominated for Best of the Net and published by (among others) the Washington Writer's Publishing House, *Apocalypse Confidential*, and *Metachrosis Magazine*. He can be found at cesarfelipe.substack.com.

**Brandel France de Bravo**'s third collection of poems, *Locomotive Cathedral*, was published in March 2025 by Backwaters Press, an imprint of the University of Nebraska Press. Her poems have recently appeared in *Best American Poetry*, *32 Poems*, *Barrow Street*, *Conduit*, *Southern Humanities Review*, and elsewhere.

**Zorina Exie Frey** is an educator, content writer, and Pushcart Prize Winner. Her writings are featured in *Shondaland*, *Glassworks Magazine*, *The Journal of Poetry for Therapy* (Routledge Taylor & Francis, 2024), *Introduction to Afrofuturism: A Mixtape in Black Literature & Arts* (Routledge Taylor & Francis, 2024), and *Chicken Soup for the Soul*.

**Sara Furdui**, MSW, lives in Maryland and is a mother of five. She writes creative nonfiction and humor pieces. Her writing interests include travel, immigration, adoption/foster care, and special needs parenting. She is currently working on a collection of nonfiction narratives exploring the experiences of individuals in Romania.

**Varun Gauri** was born in India and raised in the American Midwest. He now teaches at Princeton University and lives with his family in Bethesda, Maryland. His short fiction was nominated for a Pushcart Prize and recognized in Best American Nonrequired Reading. His debut novel, *For the Blessings of Jupiter and Venus* (WWPH 2024), won the Carol Trawick Fiction Prize and was selected for NPR's Books We Love 2024.

**Jason Gebhardt**'s poems have appeared in many journals, including *The Southern Review*, *Poet Lore*, *Gargoyle*, and *Tinderbox Poetry Journal*. His chapbook, *Good Housekeeping*, won the 2016 Cathy Smith Bowers Prize, and he is the recipient of multiple Artist Fellowships from the DC Commission on the Arts and Humanities. He lives in DC and works as a preschool teacher.

**Gabby Gilliam** is a mother, teacher, and poet who lives in the DC metro area with her son. Her chapbook, *No Ocean Spit Me Out*, was released by Old Scratch Press. Her poems and short stories have appeared in multiple journals both online and in print.

**Barbara Goldberg**, award-winning poet, translator, and speechwriter, has authored eight books of poetry, most recently *Breaking & Entering: New and Selected Poems*. The recipient of two fellowships from the NEA, her work appears in *The Paris Review*, *Gettysburg Review*, and elsewhere. As Series Editor of International Editions for the Word Works, she has selected for publication poets translated from the Kurdish, Croatian, and Ancient Greek.

**Sid Gold** is the author of five books of poetry, including *Very Eyes* (Poets' Choice, 2023) and *Working Vocabulary* (Washington Writers' Publishing House, 1997, reissued in 2021). He is a twice recipient of the Maryland State Arts Council Individual Artist Award for Poetry, and his work has appeared in a variety of journals, reviews, and anthologies for more than forty years. A native New Yorker, he now lives in Hyattsville, Maryland.

**Hannah Grieco** is a writer in Washington, DC. She can be found at www.hgrieco.com and on most social media @writesloud.

**Daien Guo** is a writer based in Washington, DC. She has been a resident at the Virginia Center for Creative Arts and has published her writing in *Lunch Ticket*, *Bodega*, *Furious Gravity*, *Little Patuxent Review*, and *3Elements Literary Review*.

**Jayla Hart** is a Harlem-born, Las Vegas-bred, DC-based writer. Her work centers on freedom dreaming, historical truth telling, and radical healing. Her writing has appeared in the *Virginia Literary Review*, *V Mag*, and the edited volume, *After Emancipation*. Jayla is a graduate of the University of Virginia.

**Melanie S. Hatter** is the author of *Malawi's Sisters*, which was selected by Edwidge Danticat as the winner of the inaugural Kimbilio National Fiction Prize and published by Four Way Books in 2019. Her debut novel, *The Color of My Soul*, won the 2011 Washington Writers' Publishing House Fiction Prize, and *Let No One Weep for Me: Stories of Love and Loss* was released in 2015.

**Robert Herschbach** is the author of *Loose Weather* (Washington Writers' Publishing House, 2013) and *A Lost Empire* (Ion Books, 1994), with new work forthcoming in *Southern Poetry Review* and *The Southern Review*. He lives in Laurel, Maryland with his wife and four cats.

**Matt Hohner**'s poems have won numerous awards. His publications include *Rattle: Poets Respond*, *The Baltimore Review*, *New Contrast*, *Live Canon*,

*Passengers*, *Vox Populi*, and *Prairie Schooner*. An editor with *Loch Raven Review*, Hohner's second collection, *At the Edge of a Thousand Years*, won the Jacar Press Book Prize in 2023.

**Emily Holland** (they/she) is a genderqueer lesbian writer. Their work appears in publications including *Shenandoah*, *DIALOGIST*, and *Black Warrior Review*. She is the author of the chapbook *Lineage* (dancing girl press, 2019). They also are the editor of *Poet Lore*, America's oldest poetry journal, and a creative writing instructor.

**Robert Hubbard**'s childhood interest in animals grew into biological research and lab work in neuroscience. That choice supported his thinking about the ways simpler components combine into systems of emergent properties. He is interested in exploring systemic ideas in science fiction and fantasy.

**Lindsey Smith Hull** grew up on the edge of Appalachia in Virginia's Blue Ridge Mountains. As a poet, storyteller, and journalist, she seeks to highlight the diverse people and culture of the region. For Hull, there's nothing better than solving the world's problems over coffee and a slice of pie.

**Donald Illich** has published poetry recently in *The Southern Review*, *B O D Y*, *Gargoyle*, *Atlanta Review*, and *The Louisville Review*. His book is *Chance Bodies* (The Word Works, 2018). He lives and works in Maryland.

**Natalie E. Illum** (she/her) is a poet, disability activist, and singer living in Washington, DC. She is the recipient of multiple Poetry Fellowship Grants, a former Jenny McKean Moore Fellow, and a Best of the Net and Pushcart Prize Nominee. Natalie has an MFA in Creative Writing from American University. She can be found on Instagram as @poetryrox, and as one half of the band All Her Muses.

**Garinè Isassi** is a recovering journalist and the author of the award–winning novel *Start with the Backbeat*, winner of the IPPY Silver Medal for contemporary fiction. Her additional fiction publications include short stories in anthologies, *This is What America Looks Like* (2021) and *Grace in Love* (2023), and a variety of online publications. She currently serves as the Gaithersburg Book Festival Workshops Chair.

**Trelaine Ito** is originally from Hawaii, but, true to form, he saw the line where the sky meets the sea, and it called him, so he currently lives and works in Washington, DC. He enjoys origami, washing dishes, and taking pictures of clouds and sunsets (but never sunrises because he's not a morning person).

**Jaime Lee Jarvis** (she/they) is a technical writer, editor, poet, and massage therapist who has long called DC her chosen hometown. Jaime's previous work appears in *Ghost Fishing: An Anthology of Eco-Justice Poetry* and online at *The Quarry* and *Beltway Poetry Quarterly*.

**Kim A. Jensen** is a Baltimore-based poet, professor, and translator whose books include *The Woman I Left Behind, Bread Alone*, and *The Only Thing that Matters*. Active in transnational social movements for decades, Kim's writings appear in *Gulf Coast, MQR, Anthropocene, Boulevard, Modern Poetry in Translation, Transition, Anomaly, Extraordinary Rendition: Writers Speak Out on Palestine, Gaza Unsilenced, Bomb Magazine*, and *Electronic Intifada*, among many others.

**W. Luther Jett** is the author of six poetry chapbooks, most recently *The Colour War*, released by Kelsay Books in late 2024. His full-length collection, *Flying to America*, was released by Broadstone Press in 2024. His most recent project is a novel.

**Sebastian Johnson** is a native of Takoma Park, Maryland, with roots in our nation's capital. His writing has been featured in the *Washington Post, Los Angeles Times, Detroit Free Press*, and *Pangyrus*, among other publications. Sebastian is a graduate of Georgetown University and the Harvard Kennedy School of Government.

**Marvin Kalb,** CBS's first diplomatic correspondent, Murrow professor emeritus at Harvard, is author of eighteen books, including his most recent *A DIFFERENT RUSSIA: Khrushchev and Kennedy on a Collision Course*.

**Beth Kanter**'s work has appeared or is forthcoming in a range of publications, including *X-R-A-Y Literary Magazine, Whale Road Review*, and *Cease, Cows*. Her chapbook *Slasher* was shortlisted in the Yellow Arrow Publishing and Black Sunflowers Poetry Press contests, and she won a UCLA James Kirkwood Literary Prize for her novel-in-progress, *Paved With Gold*. She can be found at bethkanter.com.

**Holly Karapetkova** is Poet Laureate Emerita of Arlington, Virginia, and recipient of a 2022 Academy of American Poets Laureate Fellowship for her work with young poets. Her most recent book of poetry is *Dear Empire* (Gunpowder Press), winner of the 2025 William Meredith Prize and the Barry Spacks Poetry Prize.

**Oliver Kass** is a civil servant and former journalist. A lifetime resident of the Washington, DC area, he has written on politics, culture, and life for local newspapers and magazines. *Flirting in Church* is his first published work of fiction. Oliver Kass is a pen name.

**David Keplinger** is the author of eight collections of poetry and several collaborations in translation from Danish and German. He teaches at American University.

**Elizabeth Knapp** is the author of three poetry collections: *Causa Sui* (forthcoming 2025), winner of the 8th Annual Three Mile Harbor Book Award; *Requiem with an Amulet in Its Beak*, winner of the 2019 Jean Feldman Poetry Prize; and *The Spite House*, winner of the 2010 De Novo Poetry Prize. She is the founding director of the Low-Residency MFA at Hood College and lives in Frederick, Maryland with her family.

**G.R. Kramer** has been writing for publication for the last eight years. He has published one chapbook, and his work has appeared in several dozen journals. More information on him and where he's been published is on his website, grkramerpoetry.substack.com.

**Len Kruger**'s debut novel, *Bad Questions*, was the winner of the 2023 Washington Writers' Publishing House Fiction Award and a 2023 Foreword INDIES finalist. His short fiction has appeared in *Zoetrope-All Story*, *The Barcelona Review*, *The Potomac Review*, *Gargoyle*, *Splonk*, and elsewhere. He lives in Washington, DC.

**Mary Ann Larkin** authored *That Deep and Steady Hum* (Broadkill River Press), six chapbooks, and has appeared in *New Letters* and other journals. She co-founded the Big Mama Poetry Troupe performing from Chicago to New York and attended Yaddo and the Jentel Foundation. She also co-founded Pond Road Press, which published Jack Gilbert's *Tough Heaven*.

**Courtney LeBlanc** is the author of *Her Dark Everything, Her Whole Bright Life*, winner of the Jack McCarthy Book Prize, *Exquisite Bloody, Beating Heart*, and *Beautiful & Full of Monsters*. She is the founder and editor-in-chief of Riot in Your Throat, an independent poetry press. She can be found at www.courtneyleblanc.com.

**Kateema Lee** is the author of three chapbooks: *Almost Invisible, Musings of a Netflix Binge Viewer*, and *Mundane Things*. Her full collection, *Transcript of the Unnamed*, explores joy, identity, violence, and the "brief, bright lives" of missing and forgotten Black women in Washington, DC.

**Nathan Leslie** won the 2019 Washington Writers' Publishing House prize for fiction for his satirical collection of short stories, *Hurry Up and Relax*. He is also the series editor for Best Small Fictions. He is the author of thirteen books including *Invisible Hand, A Fly in the Ointment, Sibs*, and *The Tall Tale of Tommy Twice*.

**Steven Leyva** was born in New Orleans, Louisiana and raised in Houston, Texas. He is the author of *The Understudy's Handbook*, which won the Jean Feldman Poetry Prize from Washington Writers' Publishing House. His second book of poems, *The Opposite of Cruelty*, was published by Blair Publishing in spring 2025.

**Steve Loiaconi** is a journalist and a graduate of George Mason University's MFA program. His fiction previously appeared in *Griffel, the Mystery Tribune, Mythaxis, Zooscape*, and the *Saturday Evening Post*, as well as the anthologies *Open All Night, Why Didn't You Just Leave*, and *Found 2*.

**Gregory Luce** is a poet living in Arlington, Virginia who has published six chapbooks and numerous poems in print and online. He serves as Poetry Editor of *The Mid-Atlantic Review*. In addition to poetry, he writes a monthly column for the online arts journal *Scene4*.

**Chanlee Luu** is a writer from Southern Virginia. She received her MFA in creative writing from Hollins University and her BS in chemical engineering from UVA. She won the 2024 Jean Feldman Poetry Award from the Washington Writers' Publishing House, which published her debut collection, *The Machine Autocorrects Code to I*. One of her poems was on display at "50 Years of HOPE and HA-HAs," a Vietnamese American art exhibition.

**Mohini Malhotra**, originally from Nepal, is a DC-based writer, adjunct professor, and founder of a social enterprise. Her fiction has appeared in several anthologies (*This is What America Looks Like*, 2021; *Essential Voices: A COVID-19 Anthology*, West Virginia University Press 2023; *Stories for Home*, U.K, 2018) and literary journals.

**Nick Manning** lives with his husband, dog and, sometimes, stepson in Washington, DC and New York. He retired from the World Bank where he was the author of a large number of distinctly dry technical books and papers about governments and their dysfunctions. He has had several short stories published and is, inevitably, working on a novel.

**Annie Marhefka** is a writer in Baltimore, Maryland, and Executive Director at Yellow Arrow Publishing, a nonprofit empowering women-identifying writers. Annie has a BA in creative writing from Washington College and an MBA, and is an MFA candidate at the University of Baltimore. Follow Annie on Instagram @anniemarhefka and at anniemarhefka.com.

**Nate McIntyre** is a DC-based sci-fi/fantasy writer originally from California. He's also a Marine veteran and holds a master's in science and technology policy from Arizona State University. Nate's prior work has been published in *After The Storm* magazine. His other interests include baseball, national parks, and playing the guitar.

**Tony Medina**, Associate Chair and Director of Creative Writing in the Department of Literature & Writing at Howard University, is a multi-genre author and editor mostly of books for adults and young people, the most recent of which are *Resisting Arrest: Poems to Stretch the Sky*, *I Am Alfonso Jones*, and *Thirteen Ways of Looking At a Black Boy*.

**Leeya Mehta** is a prize-winning poet, fiction writer, and essayist. Her novel, *Extinction*, is forthcoming in 2026. Mehta is the Director of the Cheuse Center. In 2024, she received George Mason's Faculty Civic Excellence Award for the Baldwin100, which celebrates James Baldwin by imagining a world that deepens our individual humanity.

**Miho Kinnas and E. Ethelbert Miller** co-authored a book of *Twoness* poems, *We Eclipse into The Other Side* (Pinyon Publishing, 2023). They have now written over 500 poems together. Recent publication includes *Kind of Cool: Interactive Jazz Poetry Anthology* (2025), *The Weird Times* (2025), and *Pulsations 4* (2024).

**Chloe Yelena Miller** is the author of *Perforated* (2026) and *Viable* (2021), both published by Lily Poetry Review Books. Along with Shasta Grant, she co-founded Brown Bag Lit, an online writing community. She writes and teaches writing in Washington, DC. www.chloeyelenamiller.com.

**Jyoti Minocha** is a DC metro area writer and educator who loves long, contemplative walks where she practices stringing words into long, contemplative sentences. Minocha received a Masters in Creative Writing from Johns Hopkins and currently teaches at Montgomery College. She lives in Virginia with her wonderfully supportive family.

**Neha Misra** (she/her) is an award-winning poet, contemporary eco-folk artist, and climate justice advocate. Her interdisciplinary studio builds bridges between private, collective, planetary healing and justice. A first-generation immigrant from India, Neha calls a solar-powered community on the border of Washington, DC and Maryland her beloved adopted home here in America. Learn more at nehamisrastudio.com.

**Susan Bucci Mockler**'s poetry has appeared in the *Mid-Atlantic Review, Maryland Literary Review, Maximum Tilt,* and elsewhere. Her full-length poetry collection, *Covenant (With)* was published by Kelsay books. She teaches writing at Howard University in Washington, DC.

**Sean Murphy** is the founder of the non-profit 1455 Lit Arts and director of the Center for Story at Shenandoah University. His poetry collections include: *The Blackened Blues* (2021), *Rhapsodies in Blue* (2023), and *Kinds of Blue* (2024). *This Kind of Man*, a collection of short fiction, was published in 2024. He's been nominated three times for the Pushcart Prize and twice for Best of the Net. Visit seanmurphy.net.

**Madeleine Mysko** is the author of two novels, *Bringing Vincent Home* and *Stone Harbor Bound*, and a poetry collection, *Crucial Blue*. A past recipient of two Individual Artist Awards from the Maryland State Arts Council, she has taught writing in the Baltimore-Washington area for years, most recently at Goucher College.

**Yvette Neisser** is the author of two poetry collections, *Iron into Flower* (2022) and *Grip* (2011 Gival Press Poetry Award), and translator of two collections from Spanish. Founder of the DC-Area Literary Translators Network, she has taught writing at The George Washington University and The Writer's Center.

**Jean Nordhaus**'s eight volumes of poetry include *The Porcelain Apes of Moses Mendelssohn*, *Innocence*, and *The Music of Being*. She directed the Folger Library's poetry programs in the early '80s, served for five years as President of WWPH, and for eight as review editor of *Poet Lore*.

**Robert Michael Oliver** is a creativist. He is a theatre artist, cultural critic, fiction writer, educator, father, and playwright. He has published dozens of poems and stories in journals. In 2023, Finishing Line Press published his first book of poetry, *The Dark Diary in 27 Refracted Moments*. He also has a poetry-in-performance podcast launching spring 2025.

**Tanya Olson** lives in Silver Spring, Maryland. She is the author of *Boyishly*, *Stay*, and *Born Backwards*, all out from YesYes Books. She has received a Discovery/Boston Review prize and an American Book Award and has been named a Lambda Fellow by the Lambda Literary Foundation. Her poem "54 Prince" was chosen for inclusion in *Best American Poems*.

**Kathleen O'Toole** is the author of four poetry collections, most recently *THIS FAR* (2019). She is a resident of Gaithersburg, Maryland and the former Poet Laureate of Takoma Park, Maryland. Find her at www.kathleenotoolepoetry.com.

**Bethanne Patrick** is a writer, author, and critic whose memoir, *Life B*, is out (Counterpoint Press). She has served on the boards of the National Book Critics Circle and the PEN/Faulkner Literary Foundation. Her work has appeared in *The Virginia Quarterly Review*, the *Grace & Gravity* anthologies, and *The Rumpus*, among others.

**Richard Peabody** has spent most of his life in the DMV. He wears many literary hats—poet, author, literary editor, publisher, teacher, mentor. He co-founded *Gargoyle Magazine* in 1976. His most recent books are *Guinness on the Quay* (Salmon Poetry, 2019) and *The Richard Peabody Reader* (Alan Squire Publishing, 2015).

**Patric Pepper**, a retired engineer, holds a BA in philosophy. He's published two chapbooks, a collaboration with Mary Ann Larkin, and a full-length book, *Temporary Apprehensions*, winner of the WWPH Poetry Prize. His recent work has appeared in *Innisfree Poetry Journal, Mid-Atlantic Review, Full Bleed* and *Backbone Mountain Review*. He lives in Truro, Massachusetts.

**Martheaus Perkins** is the author of *The Grace of Black Mothers* (Trio House Press 2025). He loves milkshakes and long YouTube video essays. Currently, he teaches at George Mason University in Virginia. He can be found on Instagram and X @martheaus or martheausperkins.com.

**Kirsten Porter** is a teacher, dog rescuer, editor, and poet. Her poems have appeared in several journals and anthologies, including *Poet Lore, The Limberlost Review, This Is What America Looks Like,* and *Voices of the Grieving Heart.* Porter is the assistant to E. Ethelbert Miller and the editor of *The Collected Poems of E. Ethelbert Miller.*

**Erika Raskin** writes what she worries about. Her most recent novel, *Allegiance*, is about fascism coming here. Written well before the election, the book now tragically reads like a how-to, asking how far is too far when protecting family from authoritarianism. She's the fiction editor of *Streetlight Magazine*.

**Jamie Raskin** has served as the Representative of Maryland's 8th congressional district since 2017.

**Rachel Reh** is a writer and communications professional living in Washington, DC. She has been a featured reader for The Inner Loop and has been published in *Cool Beans Lit, BULLSHIT LIT, Bloomin' Onion,* and more. You may find her work at www.rachelreh.com.

**Mike Reis**'s poems have appeared in *Narrative Northeast, North of Oxford, Woven Tale, Crossways,* in the anthologies *Pandemic of Violence II: Poets Speak* and *Traitor/Patriot: A Reflection of January 6,* and elsewhere.

**Kim Roberts** is the author of *Q&A for the End of the World*, a collaboration with Michael Gushue (WordTech Editions), her seventh book of poems; and *Buried Stories: Walking Tours of Washington, DC-Area Cemeteries* (Rivanna Books), her second guidebook. She has edited two anthologies of poems by Washington, DC authors.

**Jessica Robinson** is the Executive Director of Better Said Than Done storytelling. She has performed at the National Storytelling Festival, on WGBH's "Stories from the Stage," and the Women's Storytelling Festival. Jessica is the author of the *Guide to Personal Storytelling* as well as *Stages: My Life in Stories*.

**Jennifer McKeen Rodrigues** lives in Fairfax, Virginia. She is trained as a certified yoga therapist and trauma informed yoga teacher, and is a queer, neurodivergent military spouse and mom. She has been featured in many lovely literary journals and anthologies, and has been nominated for Best of the Net with her photography.

**Diana Rojas** is the author of *Litany of Saints: A Triptych* (Arte Público Press, 2024). A one-time journalist, she grew up in Connecticut and New Jersey and graduated from NYU. Besides journalism, she's dabbled in fundraising, real estate, and child rearing. Rojas lives, taxed and unrepresented, in Washington, DC.

**Joseph Ross** is the author of five books of poetry, most recently, *Raising King* (2020) and *Crushed & Crowned*, (2023). He teaches English and Creative Writing in a DC high school and writes regularly at www.josephross.net.

**Tim Rowe** grew up in the DMV when Ballston was called Parkington and the Crystal City Underground opened to an astonished public. This is his first published story, and he's thrilled to have it appear in WWPH's anthology. He lives in Fairfax and works in Washington, DC.

**Heather Bruce Satrom** teaches English at Montgomery College. Her oral history project, "History in the Making: Documenting Stories of Immigrant and Refugee Students," won the American Association of Community Colleges' Faculty Innovation Award in 2024. A believer in the healing power of storytelling, Heather writes poetry and creative nonfiction. Her work has appeared in *WWPH Writes*, *Maryland Literary Review*, and *The Mid-Atlantic Review*.

**Jane Schapiro** is the author of three volumes of poetry, *Warbler* (Kelsay Books, 2020 Nautilus Award), *Let The Wind Push Us Across* (Antrim House 2017), *Tapping This Stone* (Washington Writers' Publishing House Award,

1995) and the nonfiction book *Inside a Class Action: The Holocaust and the Swiss Banks* (University of Wisconsin, 2003*). Mrs. Cave's House* won the 2012 Sow's Ear Poetry Chapbook competition. Her work has appeared in numerous journals. Schapiro lives in Fairfax, Virginia.

**Madeleine Schneider** is a data scientist excited about America's leadership role in Artificial Intelligence research. She is also concerned with the trend to put progress and profit ahead of policy, safety, and security. When she's not working on software development, Madeleine enjoys writing both short and long fiction. Her work has been published in *Artists from Maryland* and *As You Were*.

**Patricia Schultheis** is an award-winning author of over forty published short stories, and numerous essays and book reviews. Her history of Baltimore's Lexington Market was published in 2007; her short story collection, *St. Bart's Way*, was published in 2015; and her memoir, *A Balanced Life*, was published in 2018.

**Adam Schwartz**'s debut collection of stories, *The Rest of the World*, won the Washington Writers' Publishing House 2020 prize for fiction. His non-fiction has appeared in *Newsweek, Baltimore Sun, Baltimore Banner,* and elsewhere. He has taught high school in Baltimore for twenty-seven years.

**Ava Serra** (they/she) is a disabled, non-binary writer exploring light topics such as disordered menstruation, displaced Boricua culture, abusive survival confessionalism, domestic sapphic joy, and cautionary eco-horror. They are a poetry student in the University of Maryland's MFA program. For more about their work, visit avaserra.com.

**Leona Sevick**'s work appears in *Orion, Birmingham Poetry Review, Blackbird, The Southern Review, The Sun,* and *Poetry Northwest*. Leona serves on the advisory board of the Furious Flower Black Poetry Center and is provost and professor of English at Bridgewater College in Virginia, where she teaches Asian American literature. She is the 2017 Press 53 Poetry Award Winner for her first full-length book of poems, *Lion Brothers*. Her second collection of poems, *The Bamboo Wife*, is published by Trio House Press.

**Gregg Shapiro** is a poet, fiction writer, and entertainment journalist based in South Florida where he lives with his husband Rick and their dog Coco.

**Lisa Jan Sherman** is an improv teacher, cognitive skills coach, and has been a SAG-AFTRA member for over forty years. Lisa received a BA in Theatre and Speech from University of Maryland, and was a founding member of "'NOW THIS!' Improvised Musical Comedy Troupe." Currently, she's writing a musical *Fern Fiddlehead & Fronds*, portraying the empathic bond between humans and animals.

**Laura Shovan** is an award-winning children's author, an educator, and a Pushcart Prize-nominated poet. Her chapbook, *Mountain, Log, Salt, and Stone* won the inaugural Harriss Poetry Prize. Laura teaches MFA students at Vermont College of Fine Arts.

**Jessica Genia Simon** is a poet and author of *Built of All I Shape and Name* (Kelsay Books, 2023). Her poem "Even After" was nominated for a Pushcart Prize. She works at Brady: United Against Gun Violence, volunteers as a writer-in-residence with Day Eight, and lives with her family in Silver Spring, Maryland.

**Amber Bianca Smithers** is an actor, playwright, and teacher in the DMV area. She recently has been seen on stage in *Romeo and Juliet* as well as *Macbeth* at Chesapeake Shakespeare Company. Her other credits include Arts on the Horizon and Olney Theatre Center.

**Elnathan Starnes** has participated in various poetry readings in the DMV for decades. His first published poem, "Items in a Neighborhood," is featured in *The Great World of Days* (2021). Elnathan self-published his first children's book, *Put Your Seat Belt On*, and is currently working on his poetry comic book. Elnathan has his own children's entertainment and teaching artist business under the moniker Groovy Nate.

**Alice Stephens** is the author of the novel, *Famous Adopted People* (Unnamed Press, 2018). She is also a book reviewer, essayist, and short story writer. Her historical novel, *The Twain*, is forthcoming from Regal House Publishing in 2027.

**Danielle Stonehirsch** holds a BA in English Literature with a focus on creative writing. Her fiction, poetry, and essays have appeared in many online journals and print magazines as well as in anthologies *Reflections, This Is What America Looks Like, Roar: True Tales of Women Warriors,* and *Grace and Gravity: Grace in Love*. She was a 2021 Pushcart Prize nominee.

**Laura-Gray Street** is the author of *Just Labor, Shift Work*, and *Pigment and Fume*, and co-editor of three anthologies, most recently *Attached to the Living World: A New Ecopoetry Anthology*. Street is the Mary Frances Williams Professor of English and edits *Revolute* at Randolph College in Lynchburg, Virginia.

**Kristina Tabor** (she/her) is a writer of short fiction and nonfiction. Her work appears in *Best Microfiction 2023* and several literary journals. She is an MFA candidate at Randolph College and lives in the Washington, DC area.

**Julia Tagliere**'s work has appeared in *Gargoyle Magazine, The Writer Magazine*, and elsewhere. After earning her Master of Arts at Johns Hopkins, Julia joined The Writer's Center as their Undiscovered Voices fellow. She hosts the MoCo Underground Writers Showcase and serves as an editor for *Baltimore Review*; she's also a past Maryland State Arts Council grantee and a 2025 VCCA fellow. For more about Tagliere, visit justscribbling.com.

**Yermiyahu Ahron Taub** is a poet, writer, and translator of Yiddish literature into English. He is the author of two books of fiction and six volumes of poetry, including *A Mouse Among Tottering Skyscrapers: Selected Yiddish Poems* (2017). His recent translations include *Dineh: An Autobiographical Novel by Ida Maze* (2022) and *Blessed Hands: Stories by Frume Halpern* (2023). Visit his website at www.yataubdotnet.wordpress.com.

**David Taylor**'s collection, *Success: Stories*, received the WWPH fiction prize. His fiction has appeared in *Gargoyle, Jabberwock, Washington City Paper*, and elsewhere, and was nominated for a Pushcart Prize. He received his MFA from the Rainier Writing Workshop and is writer-producer for "The People's Recorder," nominated for Best Indie podcast in the 2025 Ambies.

**Lisa V. Terry** is a fourth generation native of Washington, DC and mother of two who spent thirty-four years practicing law in the District. She earned degrees from the University of Virginia and Vanderbilt Law School. Terry recently retired to devote more time to writing, including the completion of a memoir inspired by the loss of her beloved son.

**Naomi Thiers** is author of five poetry collections, including *Only the Raw Hands Are Heaven* (WWPH), *In Yolo Count*, and *She Was a Cathedral* (Finishing Line). Her poems and fiction have been published in *Virginia Quarterly Review, Poet Lore, Colorado Review*, and elsewhere. She works as an editor and lives on the banks of Four Mile Run.

**Hayley Igarashi Thomas** is a writer, content strategist, and unabashed idealist. Her work has been published by the *New York Times*, *McSweeney's Internet Tendency*, PBS, and others. She lives and writes in Maryland with her husband, two sons, and dog.

**Piérre Ramon Thomas** is a limp-wristed, white-mocha-latte drinking, Chocolate City native who writes whenever the queer spirits move him. Published works of his can be seen in *The Mid-Atlantic Review*, *WWPH Writes*, *BlueInk*, and *The Nomadic Poet*. Thomas holds a Bachelor of Arts in English and currently resides in Fairfax, Virginia.

**Martha Anne Toll** is a novelist and literary and cultural critic. Her second novel, *Duet for One*, was released in May 2025. Her debut novel, *Three Muses*, won the Petrichor Prize for Finely Crafted Fiction and was shortlisted for the Gotham Book Prize. Toll is a member of the National Book Critics Circle and serves on the Board of Directors of the PEN/Faulkner Foundation.

**Sally Toner** (she/her) is a Pushcart nominated writer and high school English teacher who has lived in the Washington, DC area for over twenty-five years. Her poetry, fiction, and non-fiction have appeared in *Northern Virginia Magazine*, *Gargoyle Magazine*, *Watershed Review*, and other publications. An empty nester with two grown daughters, she lives in Reston, Virginia with her husband.

**Erica Simone Turnipseed** authored *Bigger Than Me* (Atheneum/Caitlyn Dlouhy Books, 2023), *A Love Noire* (Amistad/HarperCollins, 2003), and *Hunger* (Amistad/HarperCollins, 2006). Turnipseed is also co-writer of an upcoming memoir, was anthologized in *Children of The Dream*, and is published in *Killens Review of Arts & Letters* and *The Vincent Brothers Review*. She holds anthropology degrees from Yale and Columbia universities.

**Joanna Urban** is an author and public relations strategist based in Washington, DC. Her short stories have appeared in numerous literary magazines and anthologies, and her writing has won awards and funding from the DC Commission on Arts & Humanities and the Leopardi Writing Conference. Read more of her work at penandprose.substack.com.

**Dan Vera** is a Borderlands-born, Queer-Tejano, DC-based writer and editor. Recipient of the Oscar Wilde Award for Poetry and the Letras

Latinas/Red Hen Poetry Prize, he's the co-editor of *Imaniman: Poets Writing In The Anzaldúan Borderlands* (Aunt Lute) and author of two books of poetry, *Speaking Wiri Wiri* (Red Hen) and *The Space Between Our Danger and Delight* (Beothuk Books).

**Cindy G. Wagner** joined the staff of *The Futurist* magazine as an editorial assistant in 1981 and became its editor-in-chief in 2011 until it ceased publication in 2014. She has continued to write, edit, and produce an email newsletter, *Foresight Signals*, until she fully retired in 2022. She's now attempting to learn to play piano.

**Claudia Wair** is an African American writer living in Virginia. Her fiction has been nominated for the Pushcart Prize, Best Microfiction, Best of the Net, and Best Small Fictions. Her work has appeared in *Pithead Chapel*, *Astrolabe*, *Writers Resist*, and elsewhere. She can be found at www.claudiawair.com.

**Jackie Walker** received her MFA in fiction from George Mason University. She has studied writing at Hurston-Wright Writer's Week and at the Jenny McKean Moore Community Writer's Workshop. Her work has been published in *Del Sol Review* and *Coming Off the Line: The Car in American Culture*.

**Laurie Ward** is currently pursuing an MFA in the low-residency program at Hood College, where she is also the vice president for marketing and communications. She lives in Frederick with her rescue dog, Tino.

**Raffi Joe Wartanian** is a writer, musician, and educator who teaches writing at UCLA and serves as the inaugural Poet Laureate in the City of Glendale, California. His writing has appeared in *The New York Times*, *University of Texas Press*, *No Dear Magazine*, and elsewhere.

**Bernardine (Dine) Watson** is a nonfiction writer and poet who lives in Washington, DC. Dine's book *Transplant: A Memoir*, won the 2023 Washington Writers' Publishing House prize for nonfiction. *Transplant* was also chosen by National Public Radio as one of the 2023 "books we love" and featured in *Poets and Writers Magazine* as one of its *5 over 50 debuts*. Her poetry has also appeared in numerous journals.

**Christina M. Wells** has published in the *Northern Virginia Review, bioStories, Big Muddy*, among other magazines. Her work also appears in collections, including *Real Women Write: Seeing Through Their Eyes*. She has been nominated for the Pushcart Prize twice. Find her at www.bychristinamwells.net.

**Bernard Welt**'s poetry and essays have appeared in many journals, art catalogs, and anthologies, including *The Best American Poetry*. He has an MA in Writing from The Johns Hopkins University and has a PhD in Literary Studies from The American University. He has also been nominated for National Endowment for the Arts Creative Writers Fellowship and the Lambda Literary Awards.

**Kathleen Wheaton** lived in Bethesda, Maryland for twenty-five years working as a journalist and as a Spanish and Portuguese interpreter. Her collection, *Aliens and Other Stories*, received the 2013 WWPH Fiction Prize; she was president of the press for eight years. She is a 2024-2026 Stegner Fellow at Stanford University.

**Marceline White** is a Baltimore-based writer, activist, and two-time Pushcart Prize and Best of the Net nominee. Her writing has appeared in *trampset, Prime Number Magazine, SoFloJo, Feral*, and elsewhere. Conferences and residencies include Aspen Words and Event Horizon. When she isn't working, she takes pictures of her cat and reminds her son to text her when he gets to the party. Read more at www.marcelinewhitewrites.com.

**DeBorah Gilbert White** is a social psychologist, housing justice and homelessness advocate, and a triple-certified coach. She is lead practitioner at S.P.A.R.K Coaching LLC, host of the "Empowered For Change" YouTube channel, and author of *Beyond Charity: A Sojourner's Reflections on Homelessness, Advocacy, Empowerment and Hope.*

**Patience Williams** works as a full-time Lecturer at Howard University. As an Interdisciplinary Fellow from Rutgers University, she completed an MFA in fiction writing and taught at Rijksuniversiteit Groningen in the Netherlands. Her creative nonfiction has been published in Amsterdam, Berlin, and the American Midwest, and her fiction has been published in Washington, DC.

**Robert J. Williams** is the author of *Strivers and Other Stories*, winner of the 2016 Washington Writers' Publishing House (WWPH) Fiction Prize. His work has also appeared in the *Callaloo* literary journal. A 2024 Kimbilio Fiction Fellow, he is the recipient of four Larry Neal Writers' Awards.

**Cherrie Woods** (aka Cherrie Amour) is an award-winning Baltimore-based poet known for her candid, narrative style. She is the author of *Free to Be Me: Poems on Love, Life and Relationship* and creator of the Words, Wine & Wings Poetry and Open Mic Show. Her work has been featured in *Paterson Literary Review, Understorey Magazine, Poet's Ink*, and more. Cherrie is currently working on her second poetry manuscript, *Sit Comfortably Elsewhere.*

**Katherine E. Young** is the author of two poetry collections, *Day of the Border Guards and Woman Drinking Absinthe*, and editor of *Written* in Arlington. Her translations of Azerbaijani, Kazakh, Russian, and Ukrainian writers have received international recognition. From 2016–2018, she served as the inaugural Poet Laureate of Arlington, Virginia.

**Vonetta Young** is a writer and strategy consultant based in Washington, DC. Her essays and fiction have appeared in *Indiana Review, Barrelhouse, Lunch Ticket, Catapult,* and elsewhere. She serves as Executive Editor and Nonfiction Editor at *The Offing.* Follow her on Instagram at @VonettaWrites.

**Mary Kay Zuravleff** is the award-winning author of *American Ending*, chosen for Oprah's Spring Reading List. Earlier novels include *Man Alive!*, a *Washington Post* Notable Book, and *The Frequency of Souls*, winner of the American Academy's Rosenthal Award and the James Jones First Novel Award. She lives in Washington, DC.

# NOTES ON AMERICA'S FUTURE ORIGINAL ARTWORK

**Cover art:** CAPITAL CROW
**Artist:** Dana Ellyn

Dana Ellyn is a Washington, DC-based painter whose work often draws on literature, current events, and personal experience to tell complex visual stories. A DC resident since 1989, she's been painting full-time from her downtown studio since 2001. Her paintings have been featured in galleries, museums, and private collections across the US and abroad. Known for her bold and layered imagery, Ellyn's art invites viewers to read between the lines—much like a good book.

Why we chose it: We sought a continuity from *This is What America Looks Like*, our anthology published in 2021, which featured an owl, also from Dana Ellyn's studio. The crow, a highly intelligent bird, is often a symbol in mythology of a messenger and a future-teller.

**Interior art:** THE STUPID WORDS PEOPLE SAY WHEN YOU HAVE CANCER
**Artist:** Deborah Tomlin

Deborah Tomlin, a Maryland native, is drawn to domestic life in her drawings and paintings. Common themes in her work include aging, loss, femininity, identity, independence/dependence. In 2022, Tomlin was diagnosed with breast cancer. Treatment led her to incorporate text, often from her journal entries. Dress patterns, yarn, and embroidery thread figure prominently, referencing mending and darning. Tomlin uses these materials to transform her visceral scars into something beautiful.

Why we chose it: The text-based artwork, which we revealed over multiple pages, reflected the emotional tumult captured in so many of the literary works.

Special thank you to the **DC Commission on the Arts and Humanities,** the **Maryland State Arts Council,** cover designer **Andrew S. Klein**, interior designer **Barbara Shaw**, and these **artists** for helping us bring our literary arts vision to fruition.

# ACKNOWLEDGEMENTS

We completed *AMERICA'S FUTURE: poetry & prose in response to tomorrow* with the support of generous grants, individual donations, and volunteer hours from so many. Thank you all:

## DC COMMISSION ON THE ARTS & HUMANITIES
## MARYLAND STATE ARTS COUNCIL
## AMAZON LITERARY PARTNERSHIP
## JEAN AND JOHN FELDMAN

| | |
|---|---|
| Fran Abrams | James Kronzer |
| Sandra Beasley | Jean Nordhaus |
| Mark Blech | Sharon North |
| Malve S. Burns | Kathleen O'Toole |
| Jay Cannon | Richard Peabody |
| Grace Cavalieri | Patric L. Pepper |
| Myna Chang | James and Connie Qualey |
| Bonnie Chernikoff | Thomas Qualey |
| Jack Curry | Jane Schapiro & Scott Brown |
| Marcy Dilworth | Leona Sevick |
| Amy Freeman | Barbara Shaw |
| Theresa Galvin | Laura Sturza |
| Janice and Robert Fries | Nicholas Talbot |
| Eric Goldstein | Bernardine "Dine" Watson |
| Mary Brigid Haragan | Sally Zakariya |
| Gail A. Kenna | Anonymous |

**Our press-mates, who reviewed submissions:**

| Poetry: | Prose: |
|---|---|
| K. Avvirin Berlin | Suzanne Feldman |
| Robert Herschbach | Len Kruger |
| Holly Karapetkova | Bernardine "Dine" Watson |

**Our WWPH Fellows:**

| | |
|---|---|
| Demitra Moutoudis | Kate d'Arcy |
| Eric Baker | Lindsey Leary |

**Special thank you to:**
Barbara Shaw, who has undertaken the heroic task of typesetting/interior design on almost every book from the Washington Writers' Publishing House in the last 50 years.

**Lastly, thank you:**
To all the readers, book buyers, independent bookstores, writers, and our own talented, generous press-mates. The Washington Writers' Publishing House will continue to thrive because of you.

**Washington Writers' Publishing House** is the longest, continuously operating cooperative nonprofit literary press in the United States. WWPH has published over 100 volumes of poetry, fiction, creative nonfiction, and works in translation since 1975. The press sponsors three annual competitions for writers living in DC, Maryland, and Virginia, and the winners of each category comprise the annual slate. In 2021, WWPH launched the online literary journal, *WWPH Writes*, to expand our mission to further the creative work of writers in our region. In 2024, WWPH launched our biennial works in translation series and the WWPH Literary Salons, bringing writers and the literary arts into communities. The Washington Writers' Publishing House is dedicated to fostering our region's diverse literary talents. More about the Washington Writers' Publishing House at www.washingtonwriters.org.

www.ingramcontent.com/pod-product-compliance
Lightning Source LLC
Chambersburg PA
CBHW020605040726
47498CB00003B/650